Unlovable

Book One in The Port Fare Series

SHERRY GAMMON

Cover Design:
Sherry Gammon
Girl: Gemma Wright Photography
Background: Inadesign

DEDICATION:

This book is dedicated to:

My beta readers; for all your help and wonderful suggestions.

My family; you make my Life a beautiful place to be.

And most importantly; to my Father in Heaven.

Preface

Before I could reach his lifeless form, Alan grabbed my face and lifted me onto my tiptoes; my battered lungs begged for air. Dragging his slimy mouth along my neck he muttered, "I've waited so long to have you I'm afraid I'm not going to be able to control myself as long as I'd hoped."

He stopped and pinched his eyes shut before dropping me back to the ground. "No, Alan, you can wait a bit longer for your revenge," he counseled himself while stroking my hair. "But maybe a little taste wouldn't hurt." He jerked my face to his, dropping his foul lips to mine.

Something inside me snapped. If I was going to die, I'd go out fighting, so fight I did. I raked my fingers over his face, digging up flesh, and while forcing my thumbs into his eyes, I brought my leg up between his, hard, crushing his groin.

He stumbled and fell on top of me, pinning my battered body to the ground. His weight added unwanted pressure to my already tender ribs, and I screamed out.

However, Alan's screams overshadowed mine; he was in serious pain. I scratched, bit, and punch every inch of him I could make purchase with, holding nothing back. Still reeling from my well-placed knee, he spewed out a list of profanities a mile long as I tore free and forced my broken body across the kitchen floor toward the gun. I was almost to the drawer, when, from his prostate position, he hooked my foot, dragging me back several feet.

I looked back at his sweaty face, now scarred and bleeding thanks to my fingernails. He leered at me. "You. Will. Pay. For. That."

1
SETH

"*A*bsolutely pathetic!" You'd think I really was an awkward high school senior instead of a *top of my class,* MET agent. Yet, here I sat at my ridiculously oversized desk, spinning a cheap Bic pen in tight little circles, lamenting my lack of courage.

"Get a grip, Seth, and talk to her already." I shoved the pen back into the desk drawer and slammed it shut. Only my self-imposed chastisement didn't help. I couldn't do it. I couldn't get up the nerve to ask Maggie Brown out on a date to save my life.

I crossed over to the window, frowning down at my scarred cowboy boots clapping against the linoleum floor. Not exactly my first choice in footwear, but they did provide me with a convenient place to hide my sidearm. It's not as if I could meander around the high school with a gun strapped to my chest.

Okay, focus. Maybe I should try making small talk with her; that's assuming I don't choke to death on my tongue first.

While considering a few other lame scenarios, my eyes wandered over my dreary surroundings. It was your vintage government-issued office. Aside from the obese desk that lay sprawled across the center of the room, cold and lifeless, a rusted gray filing cabinet sat stuffed in the corner, with a gray pleather chair leaning cock-eyed against it. A seriously out-of-date laptop, which was, believe it or not, gray, hummed loudly in the top right corner of the desk. The only bright spot of color in the room was the half-empty, blue and red Diet Pepsi can parked in the center of my desk.

Fortunately, I seldom had to be in my office. I worked throughout Upstate New York with the Mobile Enforcement Team, or MET. Being a specialized unit of the DEA, our job is to work specifically with local authorities, helping dismantle drug trafficking in urban areas. For the past five months, I'd been working undercover at Port Fare High pretending to be a student. Heroin use was on the rise in Port Fare, with three reported deaths from overdose last summer alone. The dealers made it stronger, therefore more addictive, and cheaper.

My assignment was to *buddy up* to the popular kids, figure out who used it, and from whom they bought the stuff. That meant I had to spend most of my days with the school's cheer captain and her groupies. Thanks to my wealth, she and her clique readily accepted me into their circle. She was the quintessential social climber and one shallow girl. I learned right away she didn't use heroin, but I wasn't too sure about some of her friends.

Three other agents worked undercover at the school besides myself. One of them worked with the different sports teams, another covered the known drug users at the school, and the last was a *floater*. His job was to blend quietly into the background.

I hated deceiving the students, but the dealers had to be stopped before more people lost their lives. I appeased my guilty conscience by telling myself we weren't after the kids who used the stuff; we wanted their supplier.

The case actually began last winter. I was on an assignment near Syracuse with my team captain, Booker Gatto. We were tracking a particularly unscrupulous drug dealer, trying to learn who his supplier was. The scum dealer's MO, Method of Operation, was to hang out around the local elementary schools. He'd lace candy and other goodies with drugs before offering it to them in hopes of getting them addicted. Nine children lost their lives before he was killed in a shootout at a local pool hall. We lost one agent that day. He left a wife and two small children behind.

The dead dealer's fingerprints and dental records turned up a big fat zero. His identity went to the grave with him, and we buried him simply as John Doe. Booker found the situation suspicious and had the case file sealed to the public to protect the team from retaliation.

We never learned who his supplier was, but we did stop the flow of heroin into the area, temporarily anyway. Unfortunately somewhere close by another piece of trash lurked in the wings to fill the void.

Word on the street was Rochester was the new hot spot for our elusive supplier, more specifically, the community of Port Fare. My town. Since volunteering for the assignment at the high school, I'd grown to know these kids. Mostly good kids, some a little lost, but overall they formed a good group. I made it my personal mission to catch the low-life if it was the last thing I did.

My thoughts of the high school brought me back around to my other problem. Maggie. She didn't fit into my assignment at the school, and I seldom—actually *never* got up the nerve to talk to her. The few times I ran into her in the hallway, my tongue had swollen to the size of a small whale, essentially blocking off the oxygen supply to my brain. Last week she celebrated her eighteenth birthday, and could I spit out the words *Happy Birthday* when I saw her in the library studying? Nope.

Before I could tear myself up again, my office door flew open. In sauntered my team leader and best friend, Booker. No, he was more than a friend; he was like a brother to me.

I laughed at him in his black, full dress uniform, including the standard issue Glock pistol tucked into a leather holster at his waist. I hated our wool uniforms, too itchy. Luckily for me, jeans and tee shirts fitted the required uniform of my current assignment, along with the boots, of course.

"What's up, Book?" I went back to my desk and sat down, my pleather chair squawking out in protest.

"We got a new lead on the heroin ring. It's the most promising one yet." Booker shoved the door closed behind him, causing the window to rattle. Flipping open a thin manila folder he took three photos out, tossing the top one onto my desk.

"This is Felix Hoffman," Booker said, tapping the photo of a seedy-looking man with stringy red hair and a pockmarked face. "He's a small-time thug with a record a mile long, mostly for dealing marijuana, but it seems he has new aspirations. He was seen in Applegate Park talking to a couple of new guys last week."

"I'm guessing we don't know who these *new guys* are?" The man in the photo had *creep* written all over him. Definitely not someone I'd want to run into in a dark alley, not without my Glock, anyway.

"Nope. However, word on the street is they have a powerful contact." He dropped onto the corner of my gray desk. "Do you remember that stabbing last week in Applegate Park?" I nodded, and he continued, "Cole's the doctor assigned to her case. He called me this morning when she came out of the coma, and I went over to interview her."

He set the file down and pulled out a small blue notepad from his breast pocket, flipping over a few pages. "Her name is Michelle Stringer, eighteen years of age—she's only a few years younger than you, kid." Booker shook his head. "She went into the park looking to score some grass, and came across our new friends instead. They intro'd themselves to her simply as Bill and Alan and tried to convince her to buy some heroin from them. She said she wasn't interested, but this guy Alan insisted that she try it. He said he only offered the good stuff, and she wouldn't regret it.

"He began bullying her around." Booker's eyes darkened as he spoke. He held zero tolerance for men who abused women. Understandable on all accounts, but especially after what he'd been through. "But it seems our Ms. Stringer is a second degree black belt," Booker said. "She got a few good kicks in until this Alan character drew out a pearl-handled knife from his pants. He proceeded to shove her into their car."

"What kind of car?" I sat up and reached for the pen I'd been spinning earlier, along with a slip of yellow paper from my desk drawer.

"Beige," Booker said, rolling his eyes.

"That narrows it down." I sat back, tossing the pen onto my desk.

"She did say it had several rust spots," he offered, jotting something down in his notebook. "Ms. Stringer stated Alan had fastened her wrists together with cable ties, and that he really got off on cutting her up with his knife, telling her he could make her scream for hours before she died if he wanted."

"Guy sounds like a real...charmer," I said, forcing back a coarse remark.

"After he finished with her, she was kicked to the curb, literally, and left for dead. An older man out walking his dog found her shortly after and called 9-1-1. It's probably the only reason she's alive, and the fact that Cole was the doctor on duty when she was brought in. I don't believe she would have made it otherwise. The guy's a miracle worker."

"What about the other guy? Bill, right?"

"Alan and his knife demanded most of her attention. She did say Bill wasn't too happy about Alan using a knife on her. The two men had an intense argument, but Alan was determined to punish her for kicking him. When Alan threatened to carve Bill up if he didn't shut his mouth, the argument pretty much ended."

"Was she able to give us a description?"

"She guesses Alan to be about six feet tall and Bill to be a couple inches shorter. Both men were dressed in black polyester shirt and pants, and Alan had on shiny black ankle boots with silver zippers."

"They're definitely not fashion icons," I said. "How about hair and eye color?"

"Slicked-back, dirty blond hair for both men. As for their eyes, is bloodshot considered a color?" he frowned.

"So they were high." That wasn't unusual; selling was how most dealers supported their own habit. "Anything else?"

"Only that Alan wore a one inch silver plug in his right earlobe." Booker flipped the notebook shut and tucked it back into his pocket.

"Is she willing to work with a police sketch artist as soon as she's feeling stronger?" Hopefully, this was the break we'd been looking for.

"Yes, I'll run the drawing through the files, and maybe we'll find a match." He slid the next photo onto my desk.

"Meet Barbara Brown. This old driver's license photo is the only picture we have of her. I'm still trying to find something more recent," Booker said, before swiping a drink of my now warm soda. He winced and set it back down.

"Haven't you ever heard of ice, kid?" Ignoring him, I looked over the photo. The woman's blue eyes looked familiar.

"It seems she's somewhat of a recluse," Booker said. "We're not even sure how she's involved yet. We do know that Hoffman's been over to her house almost daily for the past few weeks, and he doesn't come empty-handed."

"Drugs?" I asked, scanning the info beneath the photo. It stated she was only twenty-five years old when the picture was taken, yet she looked much older. I didn't pay much heed since it was a DMV photo, and when have they ever been flattering?

"Again, not sure. Some days he brings over a few grocery bags full of something and leaves an hour later empty-handed. Other days he comes with nothing more than a bottle of vodka, but when he leaves he has the weighted-down grocery bags from before. We thought about bringing him in for questioning until he was spotted with the guys in the park. Now we're hoping he'll lead us to them. Something tells me they're the big time players we've been after."

"What makes you so sure there's a drug connection between him and Barbara Brown? Hoffman could be her boyfriend." I didn't doubt Booker, I just felt bad for the poor woman.

"Because of her." He dropped the last photo from his file onto my desk. "Ma—"

"Maggie." I sat up sharply, picking up the photo. "I know her. She's a senior at Port Fare High. What does she have to do with this? Is she this woman's daughter?" I knew the answer before I asked the question. The eyes, they held the same pained expression.

"Yup. Physically she's a textbook case, kid. She's gaunt, with jutting bones, and she has dark rings around the eyes. She could be the poster child for Heroin Chic."

"You're wrong about Maggie. She's brilliant. She has a four-point-oh GPA, and she spends her lunch hour in the library most days. No one's mentioned that her mother does drugs, but I've heard she drinks a bit." That was a mild exaggeration. I'd overheard Maggie's ex-boyfriend Zack Finkle telling some of the guys in the locker room that her mom was an all-out drunk.

"Maybe I'm wrong, but look at the photo, kid. Something's going on with her."

I absentmindedly ran my thumb across Maggie's cheek in the glossy eight by ten before realizing Booker watched me. I grabbed my warm soda and took a swig. Yuck! His face split wide in a grin.

"So, you're sweet on her?"

"No . . . I . . . well, she's nice. The other students genuinely like her. In fact, she was dating this obnoxious kid until last week, and he'd been whining about her being a goody-goody because she wouldn't smoke grass with him. Supposedly, that's why they broke up. I sincerely doubt she's doing heroin. Or cocaine," I added before he could.

"Does she seem out of sorts when you talk to her?"

I cleared my throat. "I haven't actually talked to her." I dropped my gaze, wanting to hide my anxious expression.

"She makes you nervous, huh? Must be love. Puppy love, anyway."

"Shut up, Booker."

"Kid, you're in the presence of a master. Here's what you have to do, my callow friend. You joke around with her, tease her a little, you know, get her to laugh. Make it so *she's* the nervous one. That, my friend, is how you'll win the lady's heart."

"This coming from a guy who hasn't had a date in years."

"Because I *choose* not to date."

"Yeah, right." I laughed. "Look, she seems nice, that's all. I'd hate to think she's involved in this mess." I began casually spinning the pen on my desktop again, hoping my lie wasn't too obvious.

"I guess you'd better put on your game face. I'm adding her to your assignment. Pull back a little on the kids you're currently working with and refocus most of your energy on Ms. Brown. Make her your new best friend. Something's going on at her house, and only time will tell whether she's involved or not."

I dropped my head back against my chair and groaned. Booker laughed. "I have every bit of confidence in you." He slipped the photos back into the file and set it on the desk. "She sure is skinny. Anorexic, you think?"

"I don't know, maybe."

"Ask her out. The girl looks as if she could use a good meal . . . or three. Check her arms for tracks while you're at it."

"And how exactly do you suggest I do that? 'Hey, Maggie, you want a burger? Oh, by the way, do you mind if I check you for needle marks?'"

"You'll think of something." He got up and headed for the door. "One more thing, kid. Be *very* careful," he warned soberly. "She's only seventeen, which means she's still considered jailbait."

I chucked my pen at him, missing his head by no more than an inch. "She's eighteen as of a week ago." He chuckled and darted out the door.

Slumping back in my chair, a sickening feeling crept into my gut. *Maggie couldn't be on drugs, could she?* Scrubbing my face in frustration, I looked down at the photo of the pretty girl with the sad blue eyes and prayed that my partner and lifelong friend had it wrong.

However, he seldom did.

2

Maggie

"*A*bsolutely pathetic!" Sadly, pulling the comb through my hair once more did nothing to improve it. The dull brown strands fell lifelessly down the center of my back. Of course, technically, hair was already dead, yet somehow mine seemed deader than most. I carefully set the skinny comb on the edge of our avocado green sink. The bathroom was much too small for a countertop so the retro sink had to pull double duty.

"I wonder if Hillary ever has a bad hair day," I asked my reflection in the chipped mirror above the sink. "Probably not." Hillary was the cheer captain at my school, Port Fare High, and every boy's fantasy girl. Whatever.

I wasn't an ugly girl. I had nice eyes, sort of. Their blue color was somewhat pretty, despite the dark circles underneath them thanks to too many late-night study sessions. I had a good nose. It was straight and short, even if it did turn up a little too much at the end, but my skin was clear, this week anyway.

I jabbed my fingers through my hair again in hopes of infusing some life into it.

Nope.

I dropped my hands onto the sink's edge, forgetting about the precariously placed comb and sent it plunging into our pink toilet. Yet another great day in my boring life. I fished the comb out, poured bleach on it, and left it in the sink to soak. I wrapped a rubber band around my dead hair and went to my room.

The back seam of my one and only winter coat had ripped out right before Christmas, and I now had to dress in layers to keep warm. I pulled on a tank top and two tee shirts before grabbing my beige sweater off the bed and heading into the kitchen to pack some lunch.

Scooping up the mail off the wobbly kitchen table, I thumbed through it while standing next to our trash bin. "Hmm, junk mail." One was addressed to me: *Maggie Brown, You may already be a $1,000,000 winner!*

"Goodie, my troubles are over." I tossed the envelope into the dilapidated orange bin and gathered the peanut butter and the last of the bread from the cupboard before continuing.

The next letter was addressed to my mother. *Barbara Brown, you are invited to join the Wine of the Month club. Call 1-800—*"Oh, yeah, exactly what my mother needs." I ripped the invitation into several small pieces and filed it alongside the $1,000,000 advertisement. The only other piece of mail was the overdue electric bill. "Shoot." I set it beside the tattered dish drainer to remind myself to write out a check after school.

With only one slice of bread left, I made up half a sandwich for my mother. If anyone needed food, she did. I packed up my book bag and walked over to where her skeletal frame laid sprawled across the couch sleeping off last night's dinner: a bottle of vodka. I swept back a matted strand of gray hair from her prematurely-lined face—no one would have guessed her to be only thirty-four years-old—and kissed her cheek, something I'd have never done if she were coherent.

"I lo...bye, Mom." I wanted to tell her I loved her, but she'd never made our home a safe place for expressing emotions, and even though she was asleep, I still couldn't do it. I learned from an early age to keep my feelings buried deep inside, training myself never to cry in front of her. Having to endure her ridiculing if I showed her my true emotions would have killed me.

I thought back to when I was just seven years old. I'd fallen out of an apple tree and hurt my arm. Lying on a rotting heap of wormy apples, I screamed out in pain and within seconds, my mother was at my side.

"Shut up! You're embarrassing me." She had jerked me up by my injured arm and dragged me into the house. "Stop crying and go to bed!"

I remembered rubbing the tears dry from my cheeks, and forcing myself to stop crying. "My arm hurts, bad."

"Good. Maybe that will teach you to be more careful, cry-baby."

Two days later the school nurse had noticed my swollen, misshapen arm during recess and tried calling my mom for over two hours, but she never answered so the neighbor listed on my emergency contact card drove me to the hospital instead. It turned out my arm was broken in two places. And the reason my mother never picked up the phone? She was passed out from her liquid lunch.

Social Services showed up at our home the next day. My mother was sober by then and lied her way out of trouble, but she went ballistic on me after they left.

"If you ever pull a stunt like that again, I'll stick you in a foster home so fast your head will spin, then you'll no longer be a burden to me!" From then on I saved all my tears for my pillow.

Shrugging those memories away I turned and gave the room a quick once-over to make sure nothing lay around that she might stumble over and hurt herself on. Quietly closing the door of our dilapidated blue trailer, I tightened my antiquated sweater as the bitter cold wind sliced through it. "Oooh!" Spring couldn't come soon enough for me, and despite the beauty of Upstate New York, the winters were brutal.

The school was close, only twelve minutes away if I jogged, something I usually did during the winter months. It was the first day of school since Christmas break, and I looked forward to getting back into a routine.

When I reached the park near my home, a sporty red Lexus IS F pulled up alongside me. My heart skipped a beat. I knew the car and could easily pick it out in a crowd, along with its hot owner. Seth Prescott: beautiful car, beautiful hair, beautiful . . . seriously, what *wasn't* beautiful about him? He even had a way of making the scruffy brown cowboy boots he always wore look hot. He'd transferred to Port Fare High from some fancy private school last summer, and I'd developed a serious crush on him, along with every other girl in school. I knew he was out of my league, but it didn't stop me from indulging in a daydream or two. I heard he lived alone since his parents died a while back. Rather impressive for a guy who was only eighteen.

"Want a ride?" He flashed a to-die-for smile as a gust of wind caught his shoulder length brown hair, tossing the silky locks onto his face. His green eyes sparkled as he brushed the hair behind his ears and laughed.

Yep, he was freakin' hot.

I thought of the look on Hillary's face if she were to see me in Seth's car. *Priceless.* I quickly doused the daydream. "No, thanks." The idea of trying to make conversation with Mr. Tall and Yummy, even if only for five minutes, was more than I could handle this early in the morning. I'd rather walk. He let out a rush of air as if he had been holding his breath and drove away.

Crossing the school parking lot a short time later, my *ex*-boyfriend Zack Finkle cruised by in his rusted-out Chevy something or other. I quickly diverted my gaze to the ground. He honked, or rather *play*ed his horn in his search for a parking spot, all the while primping his spiky blond hair. Some goofy tune bellowed out of the car, and he gave his engine a punch of gas as he shifted gears. For some unknown reason I waved, though I had to wrestle back a sneer. He smiled and winked one of his dull gray eyes. Sick. We broke up after dating for two months. He insisted we sleep together. I insisted we didn't.

I won.

Weaving my way through the last row of cars, I was nearly plowed down by a bright yellow Mini Cooper driven by none other than Hillary Jeffers: cheerleader, beautiful, perfect in every way. Perfect hair, perfect skin, perfect clothes, and perfect pom-poms. She barely glanced in my direction. No surprise, she rarely acknowledged my existence. It worked for me.

Naturally, Zack had a thing for her, but Hillary only had eyes for Seth—and who could blame her? Even still, I had no doubt Zack would have her one day, the devious little worm. His family had considerable power in the community, which meant they hung out in all the *right* circles. Regardless of her lust for Seth, Hillary lusted after power and money even more. Zack was just her golden ticket.

I entered the main building via the gym door and went straight to my locker, running into Karen Mayes on the way. She was yet another tall, gorgeous cheerleader, but Karen was Hillary's opposite—she was nice. She looked toasty warm in her long, red sweater and black leggings.

"Hi, Maggie, did you have a good Christmas?" Her smile sparkled against her clear ebony skin, as did the shiny white headband in her hair.

"Yes, how about you?"

"Great. My family and I went skiing in Utah for a week. It was awesome. Have you ever been there?"

"No." Nor had I ever been skiing. After fighting with my locker combination a few times, I opened the door and shoved my extra books inside.

Karen carefully slipped her pom-poms in behind my books and gently shut the door. Her locker was jammed full of cheer paraphernalia, leaving little room for the blue and gold streamers. I let her keep them in mine.

"I appreciate you letting me use your locker. I guess it's silly to be this fussy over pom-poms, it's just that some of the other girls get rather nasty if they don't look perfect." Undoubtedly, she meant Hillary. "Did you get anything fun for Christmas?"

"Oh, you know, the same old boring things." Nothing.

"Yes, but those boring Christmases make the big Christmases even better, don't you think?" She lowered her voice. "Guess what? I got an email from Mrs. Connor over break. I'm getting a B!"

I'd helped her study for her English Lit class during the lunch hour. She got a D, and would've been suspended from the cheer team if she couldn't bring it up to a C.

"That's great."

"Thanks for the help. I lost track of how many lunches you skipped to help me."

Not many really. It wasn't as if I brought lunch very often.

"Hey, I have an extra donut. Do you want it?" She wiggled a tan sack at me. "It won't make up for all the lunches you missed, but it's a start."

"Are you sure?" I tried to sound casual despite the fact I was starved.

"Positive." She handed me a glazed doughnut from a small sack. "See ya later."

"Thanks." I eagerly stuffed the doughnut into my mouth. It tasted wonderful. Of course, hungry as I was, cardboard would have tasted wonderful. After licking the last of the icing off my fingers, I made my way over to my first class of the day, Modern Mythology.

Port Fare High divided the classes up into ninety-minute blocks. Each class was taught every other day, a plus for me since I hated math.

On the other hand, it could be extremely painful if you had a dull teacher. Case in point, the Modern Mythology teacher, Dr. Bore. Or as he was known amongst the student body: Bore the Snore. Not only was he a complete bore, but he was also a bit bizarre.

The self-proclaimed nonconformist was a thin, scrawny man with a feeble gray beard. It matched the straggly gray hair he kept tied back in a ponytail via a thin leather strap. He wore collarless shirts and, because the school policy stated male teachers had to wear a tie, he kept one draped about his neck, untied. He wore sandals every day. Nothing, neither rain, nor sleet, not even snow could keep him from wearing his silly Birkenstocks. If that wasn't bad enough, a weird odor hung on him all the time. I did my best to avoid standing too close to him.

His five or six minions sat in the front desks soaking up every word he had to say, while the rest of the class battled sleep. My favorite spot was the far right corner of the room where I sat unnoticed. Before class started, I dropped into my usual desk and doodled in my notebook, immediately becoming lost in my thoughts. So lost, I didn't notice who sat down next to me.

"Hello, again." I immediately recognized the deep warm voice and turned to look into Seth's delicious eyes. He wore a long-sleeved, yellow striped polo and a pair of well-worn Levis. I glanced around to see who he was talking to, only to discover there wasn't anyone else around.

"Hi?" Not meaning for it to sound like a question, I blushed.

"Maggie Brown, right?" I nodded cautiously at him. "Where do you live?"

Why did he want to know that? "Why?" I sounded rude, which wasn't my intent. Maybe I should have stuck to nodding. My hand sprung to a strand of limp hair that escaped from my rubber band, and I was about to begin twirling the hairs back and forth between my first two fingers, an anxious habit of mine. Thankfully, I caught myself and quickly dropped my hand back down.

"I noticed you were walking to school today, and it's pretty cold out. Would you like a ride in the mornings? My house is over on Ivy Circle. Do you live near there?"

Where else would this beautiful being live except for on the rich side of town? "Sorry, I live off Main Street, by Applegate Park. Thanks anyway."

He reached over and tucked the limp strand of hair behind my ear. His fingers felt warm as they brushed against my still cold jaw, and it forced another shiver down my back.

"It's not that far out of my way. If you'd like, I can pick you up," he said with a smile.

My first instinct was to wonder why he was acting so kind. What did he want? True, I had seen him around school, but we never hung out, let alone had a conversation.

"I'm trying to get in shape for track team tryouts in the spring." Okay, that was a shameless lie. "Thanks anyway."

He looked as if he was about to insist, when Hillary appeared out of nowhere, wrapping her arms about his neck. She wore a pink mini skirt and white shirt. How she stayed warm was a mystery to me.

"Good morning, beautiful." Hillary smiled as he turned and stood. I briefly wondered if I looked as mesmerized as she did when looking at him. "Will you help me with the mythology homework? You never called back last night, naughty boy. Trying to avoid me?" She stuck out her bottom lip in a pout and slid her arm around his waist.

"Sorry, Hillary. I was busy and forgot."

"I'll forgive you if you come over and help me before class starts." She flashed him another impish pout and turned to leave. He followed like a whipped puppy, but not before he glanced back at me and mouthed, "We'll talk later."

Okay, weird. I had no idea he even knew my name. Apparently, Hillary had her hooks into him deep. She whistled. He jumped. I wondered if a guy would ever care for me like that. "Maybe if I was built like Hillary," I mumbled under my breath.

I actually enjoyed the single life since breaking up with Zack. No one tried to force me into compromising on things I wanted, or didn't want.

While dating, Zack constantly tried pressuring me into trying alcohol. No thanks. Living with an alcoholic all my life gave me ample cause to avoid the stuff. He also tried getting me to smoke pot, which in my book was the same as alcohol except more destructive.

However, his all-time favorite thing was to try pressuring me into sex . . . with him, naturally. Ha! As if. A ripple of disgust washed over me as I remembered his wet, sloppy kisses. Since breaking up, I'd tried to figure out why I ever dated him in the first place. Loneliness, I suppose. But now that I was free, loneliness wasn't so bad. I loved my independence immensely. I vowed never again to have a boyfriend hanging around me like a noose. I was a liberated woman who didn't need a boy to be happy.

Dr. Bore droned on and on. It felt as if class would never end. To break up the agony, I pulled out my new class schedule and verified the changes. Everything was pretty much the same as last semester, except I added a fourth period culinary class and had to switch my Community at Large class to second period.

Community at Large, or CaL, was my favorite class. Students from the high school drove over to Hunter Hills, the local elementary school, and assisted the teacher in the classroom for an hour with various activities. I worked with the emotionally needy children. Over half the class was in foster care, having been through unspeakable horrors already in their young lives. CaL was the highlight of my day. Truthfully, it was more like the highlight of my life. I felt more alive there than I did anywhere else. I willingly gave those kids the real me I didn't trust to anyone else. It felt liberating, and truthfully, they did more for me than I could possibly have done for them.

The bell rang, rousing me out of my daydream. Since carpooling to the elementary school was mandatory, I hurried toward the CaL classroom to find out who I drove with.

"Hey, Maggie, how was your Christmas break?"

Melody Winkmyer. We'd known each other since the third grade though we rarely hung out. She was short, maybe five-foot-two, and had tons of short, curly brown hair. Her face was always a bright red, as if she'd just run a marathon. She was also a wizard on the lacrosse team. "Have you heard the latest?" Gossip. Melody should have a PhD in it by now. To be sure, the girl knew something about everyone. "Mark and Debbie broke up.

That was news. They had been a couple since tenth grade, and everyone assumed they'd get married after high school. "Debbie and her family went on a cruise over Christmas break, and she met some guy from Mexico. They're engaged."

"Not."

"Debbie told me herself. Her parents are livid." Melody's cheeks glowed with excitement over the news. It made me uncomfortable.

"How's Mark doing?" I liked Mark, he was a decent guy. This had to be difficult for him.

"Well, he's not in school today." She smiled broadly. I was about to change the subject when Hillary rushed past me. Seth walked directly ahead of us. No doubt she tried to catch up to him.

Melody frowned. "Are those two still an item?" Hillary reached Seth and looped her arm through his. She proceeded to flip her long strawberry-blond hair, drawing attention from every male within a hundred yards. I had to pull my head back to avoid being smacked in the face with it.

Her frown deepened and she whispered loudly, "Never mind. Does he ever date regular people like me?"

"There are plenty of other guys out there. Zack and I broke up."

"No thanks, he's too *handsy*." So true. He had little respect for anyone's personal space, especially if that someone were female.

"I heard Seth keeps a comb in his back pocket in case his precious hair dares to mess up," she again whispered loudly. I hoped he was too busy drooling over Hillary to overhear her, though he'd have to be deaf not to. "I also heard he ducks into the bathroom between classes to check up on it. Girls only like him because he's hot. I'll bet his personality totally sucks. *And* did you know Hillary changed her schedule around so they would be in all the same classes?"

"I don't know him very well, but he seems nice." She rolled her eyes and accused me of having a crush on him before running off after another friend. I hurried on ahead, wanting to get there before the crowd.

The CaL classroom was full. I worked my way to the back, waiting for my carpool assignment. The teacher, Miss Coy, came in and tried to call the class to order. She was a small soft-spoken woman and it took her several tries to quiet the room down. Eventually, a techno-geek helped her hook up a microphone. It only made it worse. Her petite voice kept breaking up over the speakers. I leaned toward her as if it would help me to understand better.

"Most of you had this c—ss last s—ester and wo-ld like you to conti—e driving with the same p—ple. H—ever some of you are new, or h—ve switched perio—. Who does not —ave a ride this seme—er?" My hand and four others shot up. Before Miss Coy could ask for volunteers, Seth Prescott turned to her and said something.

Seth? I had no idea he had signed up for CaL. He didn't seem the type: a good looking, seemingly self-absorbed guy, working with children? I quickly chastised myself for judging him unfairly. I'd become too judgmental lately and decided my New Year's resolution this year would be to rein it in. Might as well start now. *I will not judge*, I repeated over in my mind.

Miss Coy said something in reply to Seth before calling the class to order again. "Who can t—ke —?" She rattled off the other four student's names, nine kids volunteered, and she made the assignments. "Maggie Br—, you'—be riding wi-h—" Her voice broke up again making it impossible for me to understand her. She continued. "These assi—ments are for the e—ire semest—, no exceptio—," she added sternly. I raised my hand to ask of my fate, when Seth appeared next to me out of nowhere.

"Ready, Maggie?" Seth rattled his keys in front of me. I gawked at him as if he had lost his mind. Surely Miss Coy hadn't assigned me to ride with him? "I'm afraid you're stuck with me for the entire semester. You heard what she said about switching rides."

Why did he volunteer to take me? The expression on my face must have been obvious because he added, "I believe we're both in Mrs. Mathew's class at Hunter Hills, correct?"

I groaned silently and nodded. There was my answer. What in the world would we possibly have to talk about on the drive over? Hair gel? He could probably give me some pointers. His hair always looked great even after the wind had tossed it onto his face. I heaved my book bag up onto my shoulder, smiled politely, and followed him out to the parking lot.

An arctic blast cut through my thin sweater as he opened the car door for me and I let out a gasp. He was around and in the car in record time, cranking up the heat and twisting the vents in my direction. "You really should wear a warmer coat," he said. "You could get pneumonia wearing only that." His car had black leather interior. It was beautiful and cold. I was glad the heater worked well.

"I love this sweater," I mumbled through my chattering teeth. Besides, it's not as if I had another choice. Rich people like him didn't have a clue what . . . *You're judging him, Maggie.* I smiled, tightened my sweater around me, and blocked out the negative thoughts.

Before long, we lapsed into an uncomfortable silence. Neither he nor I seemed to know what to say. I wrenched myself closer to the door while stealing a quick glance at him. I was surprised to see his hands wrapped tightly around the steering wheel, so tight his knuckles turned white. I looked out at the road to see if maybe we drove on ice. It looked clear to me.

Finally, Seth broke the silence. "Why do I make you nervous?" He had a slight smile on his face now. "By the way, you should slide to the center of the seat, it's much more comfortable."

"I'm comfortable, thanks." In actuality, the armrest dug into my hip, causing me significant pain. I shifted a bit, making it worse.

"Isn't Hillary taking this class with you?" I desperately wanted to change the subject.

"No, cheerleading practice was switched to second period. She had to drop CaL." He chuckled softly, leading me to believe he'd heard Melody in the hall earlier. How embarrassing.

Only when we pulled up to the school did I realize my fingers were tangled up around my hair. Seth looked over at me and smiled. My face went pink as I untwisted them. He jumped out and came around to open my door before I could get out.

"Thanks for the ride."

He nodded. "This is my second semester here. It's my favorite class."

"Mine, too," I said, astonished.

"Why is it yours?" His face looked sincere, as if he was truly interested in what I had to say.

"The kids love you, and they don't care what you wear." I thought of my thin worn out sweater. "And they don't care what your hair looks like." That was aimed at his vanity. For a split second, he smiled. "They love you and want you to love them, no strings attached. It's . . ." I trailed off in search of the right word.

"Pure love."

"Yes, pure love." I couldn't have said it any better. This was the one place I ever felt loved or wanted. My mother certainly didn't love me. At least she never expressed it in any way. As a child, I longed for her to gather me onto her lap and read me a story, or brush my hair and tell me I was pretty. She never did. She never hugged or tucked me in at night, and she never made me dinner or any other meal for that matter. She had a wicked mean streak, and when she was upset, her harsh words nipped at my heart. She was a cold, distant woman who drank too much.

A year and a half ago things changed—for the worst. She was rarely sober anymore and seldom left the house. Her words took on a new cruelty. They cut clear to my soul, some days shredding it into pieces. Words like: *get out of my sight, you lazy girl*, or *can't you do anything right, you unlovable nothing*? And my favorite, *I should've given you up when I had the chance.*

As we approached the school door, a passage from my favorite Victor Hugo novel *Les Misérables* crossed my mind. *For Jean Valjean there was no sun, no beautiful summer days, no radiant sky, no fresh April dawn.* Completely lost in my pain, I didn't feel the tears brimming up in my eyes until one spilled over the edge.

Seth gently turned me around to face him. "What's wrong?" He peered into my eyes, I felt as if he burrowed down into the dark recesses of my soul. His fingers ran softly across my cheek, brushing away the tear. There was an undeniable tenderness about him, making my heart flutter. His reaction caught me so off guard I stammered for a moment not knowing what to say. Should I tell him about my pathetic life, explain to him how unloved I was or how I could totally relate to these children and what they felt?

I opted for the safe answer, like always. Show no emotion, keep it locked inside, they can't hurt you if they don't know anything about you.

"It's the cold air, it's burning my eyes."

Clearly, he didn't buy my lame excuse, but to his credit, he said nothing. He held the school door open for me and led us down the hall.

Crying? What the heck was wrong with me? It must be PMS! I stayed a few steps behind him, secretly drying my face and running through a calendar in my mind.

Approaching the classroom, I peered around his shoulder and saw twenty-two little smiles eagerly awaiting us, with their little cherub faces pressed up against the glass before the door promptly flew open. Out they came, jumping on Seth and me, knocking us both to the floor. Their reaction to him stunned me. Apparently, they loved him as much as they did me.

Zane, a tenderhearted blond boy, was now perched on my knees. "Why are you here early, Miss Maggie?"

"I had to change my school schedule to this hour."

"Wow, our two most favoritist teachers at the same time," swooned Noah, a sweet little guy with big brown eyes. "I'm the luckiest boy ever!" He smiled as Seth helped me up off the floor.

"You know what this means," Elise said, a stunning, curly-haired blond girl.

"What?" Seth asked.

"It means you two have to get married." She smothered her giggle into her hands, along with several other little girls, while some began chanting, "Kiss her! Kiss her!" Seth laughed loudly, scooped me into his arms, and before I could protest, planted a big noisy kiss on my cheek. *Wow, his cologne smelled heavenly*. I laughed as the girls cheered and the boys made gagging sounds. He released me when their teacher, Mrs. Mathews, a tall, middle-aged Korean woman with long, silky black hair, came out into the hall and shooed them back inside.

"Alright, children, settle down." As always, her voice was gentle. "We now have Mr. Seth, along with Miss Maggie as our visiting teachers for this hour. Since we haven't had our guest teachers read to us for several weeks, we're going to separate into two groups for story time." She quickly divided the kids up and sent the groups to opposing ends of the room. Harrison, a precious redheaded boy, chose several books for me to read as the rest of my group settled into beanbag chairs or on small carpet squares. Noah curled up in my lap and began stroking my cheek.

The time flew. Occasionally, I'd hear Seth read a line with exaggerated drama and the children would laugh. I tried not to look over at him, yet my eyes were drawn there as if by some unseen force. He glowed. He seemed at home with the little first graders, three of whom sat on his lap. I was taken aback by this side of him.

Halfway through the hour, Mrs. Mathews had us switch places so the children could spend equal time with both of us, though Noah insisted he stay with me. I looked at Seth as we crossed the room. He smiled and winked. I dropped my head as my face turned at least four shades of red, and my mind flooded with suspicion. Why did he act this way? Did he think I was going to be another notch in his belt?

Elise tugged at my arm. "What's wrong, Miss Maggie?" I didn't realize my expression had deteriorated into a scowl. Nudging the negative thoughts out, I began reading to my new group.

By the end of class, my ill feelings toward Seth had almost vanished, that was until he slipped his arm around my shoulders while we walked down the hall toward his car. I pulled away and gave him an icy glare.

"Sorry," he said, wrestling with a smile. "My car is out this way." I glanced around and realized I had turned down the wrong hall. I nodded curtly and walked toward the correct door, completely humiliated by my childish overreaction.

I settled quietly into his car, and we drove back to the high school, again in tortured silence. If I didn't know better, I'd swear he was as nervous as I was.

Clearing my throat, I attempted to make conversation as we approached the school. "The kids really like you," I said.

"Yeah, probably because I'm so hot," he teased. I think . . . I hoped.

Augh, Melody.

"You know, I'm surprised the three of us can fit in your car."

"Three? I do believe there are only two."

"Me, you, and your oversized ego. I believe that makes three." I jumped out before the car came to a complete stop, slamming the door shut behind me. I tried placating some of my guilt, though why I should feel guilty I had no idea. It was Melody who criticized him, not me.

"You're welcome," he shouted to my backside.

Just because he did something kind didn't mean he wasn't an egomaniac, I reasoned, still trying to salve my wounded pride.

Later at lunch, I cut through the cafeteria on my way to the library. The placed reeked of rotten food and gym socks, not the most enticing smells for a lunchroom. Forty long gray plastic tables with attached benches divided the room into rows. Spaced evenly across the ceiling were a dozen humming fluorescent lights, and down the center of the room sat three black garbage cans spaced between the tables, adding to the ambiance.

Seth and Hillary snuggled together at their usual table near the front of the room, all giggles and jokes. Never once did he look my way, which was just fine with me. Who needed an arrogant snob in their life? I had enough to deal with without adding him to the list, including the nagging voice in the back of my head telling me it was wrong to judge him. It really needed to shut up.

I arrived home from school to find my slimy neighbor, Mr. Hoffman from across the road, walking back toward his haggard gray trailer. My guess was that he had spent the afternoon with my mother and a bottle of vodka, something he seemed to do all too regularly over the past three weeks. I opened the door and found my mother passed out on the couch and surmised I was right.

My mom used to have lots of *friends* coming by to visit until I realized they all used her for what little money we had. After I'd gone to the bank and set up a checking account *with* direct deposit, *and* kept the checkbook hidden, the supposed friends evaporated. Except for Hoffman. He moved in a few months ago and they became fast friends. He gave me the creeps.

I began cleaning the house so I didn't have to think about the aching hunger in the pit of my stomach. Our pocket-sized trailer consisted of an extremely small living room-dining room-kitchen combination. The sparse mismatched furnishings were tattered beyond repair.

A brown couch sagged horribly in the middle, a blue armchair—minus an arm—and a rickety kitchen table with two wobbly folding chairs outranked by far Goodwill's worse donation. Toward the back of the trailer was our micro-chip sized bathroom, and opposite the bathroom, were two nine by seven foot bedrooms. My mother rarely used hers, preferring to spend most of her days and nights passed out on the couch.

Throughout the house was linoleum—cold brown linoleum covering the floors, invariably littered with an empty booze bottle or two and a few stray tissues. The walls were painted a blanched white, bare and tedious, mostly because we didn't have the money to decorate them. I'd used thumbtacks to hang some old beige pillowcases over the tall narrow windows to afford us privacy.

My frantic cleaning efforts were rewarded. I found eighty-three cents under the chair's flattened cushion. I finished my housework and ran to the store to buy some day-old bread.

***

Most of my lunch hours were spent in the library studying. That way I didn't have to watch others eat, but not today. I had a peanut butter sandwich, and I ate in the cafeteria sitting alongside Melody who asked me to sit with her before anyone else did. On any given day, I battled hunger headaches. This afternoon, however, it was a tension headache from listening to Melody's insipid gossiping. I made several attempts to change the subject and finally gave up. The girl was like a dog with a bone. I tried to chew loudly on my dry bread and crunchy peanut butter. Nevertheless, her voice still hacked through the white noise.

"Hillary said you're riding with Seth to CaL class now." Melody adjusted her black polka dot shirt as she spoke. "How many times did pretty boy fix his hair on the ride over?" I shrugged, dropping my head back down to my lunch. "You're trying to be nice by not saying anything, but you know I'm right. Look at them. They're the perfect couple."

They sat a few tables away from us, and I hoped they couldn't hear her this time. I didn't dare look, and instead nodded silently and continued staring down at my dehydrated bread.

"They sit there never speaking to anyone who isn't in their little clique. They think they're better than any of us because they're rich and good-looking." She snorted loudly. "They're totally self-absorbed. It's as if the rest of us don't exist."

I wiggled around uncomfortably in my seat, debating whether to say something about Seth and the way he loved the CaL kids, or that I had indeed seen him hanging out with lots of different kids around school, not just the popular ones. But I didn't. Instead, I swallowed the last of my sandwich and gathered up my things.

"I have to go, Melody. Thanks for sitting with me today." Some of what she said was probably true, yet I couldn't stop thinking about him yesterday with the children. I rushed to culinary class, relieved to be away from her.

The advantage of a cooking class was you got to eat what you created, and hungry as I was most of the time, I'd even eat *my* cooking. The classroom was close to the cafeteria, and with my hasty departure, I arrived ten minutes early. I chose a desk in the far back corner and hoped the teacher wasn't one of those control freaks with a seating chart.

The classroom was huge. Twelve two-person desks occupied one side while the opposite end of the room housed twelve white stoves with small counters to the left of each, along with four stainless steel refrigerators spaced out across the back.

Soon the class filled up. Several of my friends stopped at my desk to ask how my Christmas was. Since everyone had already partnered up before coming in, I sat alone at my desk when the teacher arrived. I hoped that she'd pair me up with someone who cooked better than I did.

"Alright everyone, take your seat." The teacher, Mrs. Gianchi, was a feisty Italian woman with dark hair she wrapped tightly in a bun and anchored to the top of her head with several clips. Her smile was warm and generous, and her cheeks glowed bright pink, presumably from the heat of the ovens in the room. I'd seen her walking around in the halls before with her flowered aprons, and they usually looked nice, but today she had on a striped dress and the combination of the two made my eyes hurt.

"Good afternoon." She stepped her petite frame up onto a small stool so everyone could see her better. "We're going to jump right into cooking today with an easy lesson on candy making." She explained how we needed to mix up the ingredients and record the effect the various temperatures had on the candy mixture as it heated up. She directed us toward the stoves, dividing everyone up into pairs. When she came to me, I still didn't have a partner.

"How can this be?" She pulled out her roll book. "There's an even number of students enrolled in class." Before she found the list, Seth appeared out of nowhere, startling me.

"Sorry I'm late," he said with a grin.

This couldn't be. We now had *three* classes together.

"There you are," Mrs. Gianchi said to him, closing her book.

"I was held up. It won't happen again." He looked over at me and quietly added, "I had to fix my hair." Heat overtook my face and I looked away.

"I need you to partner with Maggie."

He smiled broadly at Mrs. Gianchi's request. I turned my back on him as he slid up behind me, standing much too close. I moved a few inches away, hoping he wouldn't realize it. He did and scooted even closer. I got the distinct impression he was teasing. I folded my arms across my stomach and glued my feet to the floor. He'd have to walk over me if he thought I'd give him another inch. My eyes stayed fixed on the teacher, and yet I *felt* his smile burrowing into the back of my head. She handed me the instructions, and moving toward the small counter, I accidentally bumped into him. Still ignoring him, I began measuring and pouring items into the pan.

"Would you like my help, or am I supposed to stand here and look pretty?" he asked. I passed the recipe over and signaled for him to continue. He poured and measured so quickly I had a hard time keeping up with what he did.

Neither of us spoke as the temperature of our candy mixture slowly rose. Bore the Snore's class was more thrilling than this . . . well, maybe it wasn't quite *that* bad. Thankfully, Mrs. Gianchi interrupted our rampant excitement. "Class, remember to drop a small amount of your mixture in cold water at each temperature gauge, and record the reaction on your worksheet."

An eternity later, the stupid mixture finally reached 230 degrees, our first test temperature. I reached into the pot, scooped up a spoonful of the sugary substance and was about to drop it into the glass of cold water, when an all-too-familiar voice startled me, causing me to spill the liquid candy.

"Seth, what did you do in a previous life that doomed you to be stuck with her for a partner?" Hillary. She was dressed in jeans and a cute black shearing jacket with a white fleece collar that made her alabaster skin glow. I never felt uglier. She gave me a supercilious look as she folded her arms across her chest. Her perfect chest. I quickly folded my arms cross my not so perfect chest, as if it was a big secret God had forgotten to give me breasts. "Nice sweater, by the way," she added. "It just screams trailer trash."

"That's enough, Hillary." Seth frowned and glanced over at me. It surprised me he actually shut her down. Impressive, though it didn't seem to bother her at all since she just flipped her hair and twisted his face back to hers.

"My notebook is still in your car from last night." She actually purred as she walked her fingers up his arm. "I need it for my history class. May I have your keys?"

"I put the notebook in my bag this morning. Wait here, I'll go get it."

Hillary and I both watched him walk over to the desk and rifle through his book bag.

Abruptly, she coiled back to me. "You're so out of his league, girlfriend." Her voice was low and her face tight. "But even if he did ask you out, it'd be for one reason and one reason only. Your kind are merely toys for boys like him."

Racking my brain for a witty comeback, I came up flat and turned back to the thermometer. It read 315 degrees. Sure, now the dumb mixture heated up fast. We'd missed every reading in-between. I pulled the pan off the burner as Seth returned with the red notebook. Hillary tucked it under her arm and blew him a kiss as she left.

"It's ruined." I slammed the pot onto the back of the stove, causing the contents to splash everywhere. "If your airheaded girlfriend hadn't come in and interrupted us, we wouldn't have failed this cooking lab. Now we're going to get an F on the assignment." For the life of me I couldn't figure out why I let those two upset me like this.

His jaw tightened. "Hillary's on the honor roll, so I guess that blows your airhead theory, and she's not my girlfriend. Please let Melody know, won't you?"

He snagged the candy worksheet, wrote down the answers, and tossed it back at me, muttering that something came up and he needed to make a phone call. He turned and stormed out the door without saying another word. Mrs. Gianchi rushed over.

"What is the matter with Seth?" I shrugged, trying not to look guilty. She picked up the worksheet and smiled. "He's such a nice boy and what wonderful penmanship."

Geez, even the adults were bedazzled by him.

"This worksheet looks correct. Once you've cleaned up this mess, you may leave," she said, pointing at the candy splattered on the stove. She walked away, leaving me to wallow in my misery. It took me the rest of the class period to clean up the hardened mess.

My mind replayed Seth's angry words in culinary class on my walk home, and I took offense to his comment. Melody was the bad guy here. I'd never said anything about him.

On the other hand, I didn't stop her from maligning him or Hillary either, and I did laugh at a few of her comments. As hard as I tried to appease my guilty conscience, I still felt terrible. I had been a victim of false rumors before and even though they were lies, it still hurt. I swore to myself that the next time Melody started ranting about Seth, I'd speak up. My decision helped ease the guilt somewhat, and I picked up the pace. It was cold.

I got home and took a long hot shower to warm up my frigid body. My mom had already ingested her daily allotment of booze and was passed out on the couch. I thought about helping her into bed, only the last two times I'd tried, I was rewarded with some pretty nasty bruises. She was an ornery drunk. Sometimes it was best to let sleeping dogs lie.

3

With a ten-page research paper for my mythology class looming over my head, Sunday morning I got up early and went to the library while my mom slept. I could have chosen to do ten hours of community service, the alternative Bore offered those who didn't want to do a paper, but without a car I didn't have that option. He insisted we become mindful of our community. To quote Bore, "The needs of our community are not a myth." A pretty good idea, only for me it meant spending more time away from home since we didn't have a computer.

In my rush to leave, I accidentally pushed my big toe out the end of my worn blue sneaker. "Great." I hurriedly tied the ruined shoe and said goodbye to my mother, mostly out of habit. She still slept off yesterday's vodka and was resting up for today's onslaught. She didn't stir. Even though I knew she wouldn't acknowledge me, a slight twinge still tugged at my heart. I ignored it and left.

The frigid morning welcomed me with a bone chilling blast of icy cold as I stepped off the porch and right into a slush puddle. "Yuck!" I shook the mess out of my shoe and trudged off, making record time thanks to subzero motivation.

While tracking down information on local children's charities, my eye caught the calendar hanging on the wall above the reference desk. January ninth. Thirteen years ago today my world changed forever.

I remembered my grandmother and I being in the kitchen. She tied a yellow ribbon in my hair to match the dress she'd made me: blue with white and yellow daisies. I sat on a stool, fidgeting. The room smelled of fresh-baked cookies, and I desperately wanted one.

"Hold still, sweetheart," she said, fishing the silky ribbon through my ponytail and tying it into a bow. "There, perfect." I jumped off the stool and spun around in circles. The dress had a full skirt, and when I swirled around, it floated out in a huge circle.

"I love it, grandma. Thank you very much. It's delightful." I ran over and gave her a big hug.

"Delightful? What a big word for such a little girl."

I looked up into her blue eyes and watched her smile fade. She cupped my chin and kissed my forehead. "I guess it's a good thing you're mature far beyond your four and a half years."

She took a tissue from her pocket and wiped her eyes. "Alright, Princess Maggie. Scoot along and find your grandfather. Let him know your mom will be here any minute." I spun around one last time and skipped off to find him. "And no cookies. You'll spoil your appetite," she added.

I found my grandpa in the bathroom as he finished shaving. "Oh, my, aren't you the sweetest little princess in all the land."

"Thanks, Grandpa. Mom's on her way. Why is she coming over?" I sank down onto the edge of the tub and studied him as he put on his tie.

"It was her twenty-first birthday a few days ago, remember? We're going out to dinner to celebrate tonight." He looked over at me. "What's the matter, Magpie?"

"Do I have to go and stay with mommy again?" I seldom saw her when I was very young, and the few times she did come to visit, the three of them would usually end up arguing. My grandfather would demand she act more responsibly, and I'd have to go stay with her for a day or two. My grandmother would prepare a backpack for me to take, putting cereal, peanut butter, jam, and some bread in it. She'd taught me how to make sandwiches and had me practice pouring cereal into a bowl and adding milk. Of course, at my mom's place I usually had to add water since she never had milk.

My mom would hate it when I played with my toys in her living room and often banished me to the bedroom. "Get out of my hair," she'd demand. I spent most of the time alone playing with my dolls.

After a couple of days my grandparents would check on us, they'd have another huge fight, and I'd go back with them until my mother came around again, and the cycle would repeat itself.

"Not today, princess." Sorrow touched his face as he spoke of my mother, and I felt bad for having said anything. "Hey, how about a butter-rum Lifesaver?" He held out a tattered roll of the candy, inviting me to take one.

"Grandma will be angry if I have one before dinner." He always tempted me with butter-rum Lifesavers, and I always fell for the temptation.

"I won't tell if you won't," he whispered.

"I heard that, Harry," my grandmother chided from the other room. "You'll spoil her dinner."

"Yes, dear," he said, handing me one with a wink. I popped the candy into my mouth and sucked on it until it dissolved into nothing.

My mother arrived a few minutes later reeking of alcohol. At the time I didn't know what the smell was, only that she smelled funny. We all climbed into their car with my grandparents up front. I sat in a booster chair next to my mom in the back.

On our way to the restaurant, an uninsured drunk driver ran into us, killing my grandparents instantly. I wasn't hurt, thanks to my car seat; however, my mom hadn't worn her seatbelt, and she was thrown from the car. She hurt her right leg and her back and never fully recovered from the injuries. With what little insurance money my grandparents had, she bought the singlewide trailer we currently called home. I didn't know how we'd have survived otherwise. It wasn't much, but it was paid for. I often wondered how different things would have been if not for the accident.

I gathered a few books and went back to working on my research paper. It was stupid to dwell on the past, it only depressed me. Around noon, the librarians began setting up tables in a conference room off to the side for a luncheon. I did fine until they brought the food out. The smell drove me crazy. I used the last of the bread to make my mom a sandwich before I left and hadn't eaten anything since lunch yesterday. Unable to stomach the enticing smells of food any longer, I shoved my belongings into my bag and left.

The wind pounded me mercilessly, making it difficult to keep from being blown over. Reaching the corner, I collapsed onto a bus stop bench and dropped my head to my knees, exhausted and dizzy. Somehow, I had to find a way of getting more food into the house without my mother knowing about it. If I spent too much of her money on food, she'd berate me for my selfishness, but the hunger headaches which plagued me and now this dizziness was plain ridiculous.

I heard a car pull up next to the bus stop. Too weak to look up, I kept my head down. "Are you alright?" It was Seth. Unbelievable.

"I'm fine. Just waiting for the bus." I kept my head down, still not bothering to look at him. I was surprised he even stopped. We'd hardly spoken since the candy disaster in culinary class earlier in the week.

"You'll have a long wait. This bus doesn't run on weekends." I glanced up at the bus sign. Sure enough, it was a 'weekday only' bus. I closed my eyes and dropped my increasingly dizzy head back into my hands.

"Come on." Silently, he appeared at my side with an arm around my waist before I could argue. "You look terrible. Let me take you home."

"Did I ask your opinion on my outfit?" I tried sounding fierce with my retort, but thanks to the dizziness, it sounded silly more than anything.

"That's not what I meant. It's your face. It looks awful."

I snapped my head up to his. I'd known of Seth's high cheekbones, having drooled over them many a time. Today, however, they were slightly pink, probably from the cold. It gave his face a warm friendly glow. It was then I noted his mouth for the first time. It was definitely kissable, with its full round lower lip and the Cupid's bow on the upper. There was a strong temptation to reach up and . . . I jumped back a few inches and shook my head to clear it. I desperately needed some food.

He laughed. "That didn't come out right. I meant you look pale. Please let me take you home," he said, sliding the arm of my sweater up above my elbow.

"What are you doing?" I pulled my arm away from his warm hands.

"Just checking your pulse to make sure you're still alive," he chortled.

"I believe a person's pulse is in their wrist."

"Oh, yeah. Sorry. I didn't do so well in Human Physiology." He began guiding me toward his car.

I pulled back. "I don't need a ride, thanks. Really, I'm fine," I said as a gust of wind came by, blowing me back into his arms.

"I can see that."

Too weak and dizzy to fight anymore, I allowed him to lead me over to the car. He opened it, and I stood there for a moment, debating.

"Please get in, Maggie."

Impressive, he actually looked concerned. I decided that pride was easier on a warm day and settled into the car. He turned the heater vents toward me as he had before and set the temperature on high. Our trailer never felt this warm.

"Thanks." I wasn't sure he understood me through my half frozen lips. Holding my hands in front of the heater vents, the warm air blew up my sleeves and down my thin sweater, thawing my frozen body. It felt wonderful. He didn't make a single comment about my sweater, or the hole in my sneaker, though the fact that I kept the shoe tucked strategically under the seat might have been why.

Or maybe he was a really nice guy, and I should cut him some slack.

"Warm enough?" Short of starting a small fire, I had no idea what he planned to do to make it any warmer.

As I thanked him, I noticed the undeniable smell in his car. "Why do I smell food?"

"I'm delivering lunches to some of the local senior citizens."

My first thought was to question why, until I remembered our mythology class assignment. He must have opted to do the community service.

"Are you sure you're okay? What did you have for breakfast?" He felt my forehead, causing goose bumps to dance up my back.

"I was in a hurry this morning and forgot to eat." And the lies kept piling up. Besides, he didn't need to know about our family struggles.

"If I give you a lunch, will you eat it?" He looked at me skeptically.

Great, he thinks I'm anorexic. Oh, well, may as well feed the anorexic rumors. My clothes hung on me anymore, and I'd heard the whispers as I'd walked down the hall at school. "No thanks, I'll eat something later."

"You know these lunches don't have a home, and if you don't eat them they'll go to waste." How sweet, he tried to encourage the anorexic to eat. I muffled my laugh.

"Why don't you eat it?" I dared him.

"I've already had my lunch," he said. "Here." He grabbed two Styrofoam boxes from the back seat and held them in front of me. "You have your choice of a chicken or roast beef sandwich." He recited the menu as if from a brochure. "There's also a choice of steamed mixed vegetables or broccoli smothered in cheese, and a brownie." He tempted me once more with the small white boxes, and my stomach let out a huge growl. Ugh! I thanked him and took one, forcing myself to pick casually at the food instead of inhaling it. I was unbearably hungry.

"I have two more stops, if that's alright with you. They're on the way. I believe you said you live over by the park, right?" he asked, right as I took a huge bite of the chicken sandwich, blowing my *casually picking* plan. I could only nod.

"The first delivery is to a man named Frank McSheehy. He was injured in World War II and struggles with getting around these days. He fell and broke his hip three months ago, and now he's temporarily confined to a wheelchair. Oh, one more thing, he likes to talk. You've been warned." He winked, causing my heart to skip a beat. *For crying out loud, Maggie, get a grip on yourself.*

We pulled up in front of a tiny run down cottage on Front Street. A frail-looking man, Mr. McSheehy I assumed, sat by the front window waiting for us. He pushed open the door when we reached the porch. The petite man all but disappeared in his oversized wheelchair. A few wisps of white hair danced around on the top of his head with the wind, and his thick black-rimmed glasses made his eyes bug-like in appearance.

"Good afternoon, my guardian angel." He held out his hand and shook Seth's warmly. "Who is this beauty by your side, an angel in training?" He took my hand, squeezing it softly.

"Maggie's a friend of mine, although an assistant would be helpful," he said. "Maggie, this is Mr. McSheehy, also a friend of mine."

"Come, sit down for a minute." He led us inside and pointed to a coffee table in the living room. "I was looking through some photos of my days in the war." He had several photo albums spread out on the small table. "I promise to keep you for no more than ten minutes. You still have to deliver lunch to Miss Ethel, correct?" Seth nodded.

Seth and I sat on a small tattered couch while Mr. McSheehy went through several pages of his album with us. He had received the Purple Heart during World War II, of which he was very proud. He shared some photos he had taken on the day the Americans liberated the concentration camp, Gusen.

"This was taken in May, 1945. That's me," he said, pointing to a handsome young soldier. "My troop went into the Gusen camp in Austria. The day we arrived thousands of bodies had to be buried in a mass grave, and about three hundred people a day died thereafter. Not only were they starving to death, there was also a horrible typhus epidemic throughout the camps."

He slid a photo across the table toward me of several dead bodies piled on a cart. The people looked like skeletons with skin on them. It broke my heart. "There was no food in the kitchen. We were able to find some potatoes in storage and made a thin soup to feed them. We were also able to make up some unleavened bread out of oats.

"The enemy was barbaric. Tens of thousands of Jews died in Gusen, and we as people have become complacent." He shook a finger in the air dramatically, stretching up tall in his rickety wheelchair. "We seem to have forgotten that some things are worth dying for, number one being our fellow man. Fighting to free God's children from wickedness like this," he held up the picture of the dead bodies in the wheelbarrow, "that price will never be too high for this soldier to pay."

His story touched my soul, and for the first time ever I felt a connection to the past. I swore never to forget what Frank McSheehy and his fellow soldiers did that day in Austria.

After a few more stories, Seth stood. "Mr. McSheehy, we need to get over to Miss Ethel's." Seth took my elbow, guiding me toward the door. "How about next Saturday we deliver your lunch last, and you can share more of your experiences with us?"

"Oh, no. You, a handsome young man, here with a beautiful young woman," he nodded his head toward me. "You don't need to listen to an old man ramble on about days long gone."

"I'd love to hear more." Something in my eyes must have told him of my sincerity because he cheerfully agreed to let us return next week for another mini history lesson. After a hastily offered goodbye, we headed over to Miss Ethel's.

"It's sad that so many of our senior citizens are ignored or shoved into rest homes unnecessarily. Many still have a lot to offer," I said as we drove down a crooked narrow street.

"I feel exactly the same way," Seth said. The guilt I felt for judging him choked me. I had been slowly turning into my mother and didn't even realize it until that very moment. I had an ache in my gut, which for once wasn't from hunger.

Our next stop was at a shabby green house on Ridgemont. A woman with a deeply lined face and short, choppy gray hair—Miss Ethel, Seth informed me—stood at her window waiting. However, unlike Mr. McSheehy, she looked angry.

"Her bark is worse than her bite, most days." I looked at him warily, and he chuckled. "Don't worry, I'll protect you."

"Yer late! Talkin' to old jabber jaws McSheehy again, I 'spose." She planted her hands firmly on her wide hips. She glared hard at Seth as we entered her humble home. He smiled and her pursed lips gave way to a grin, though she tried to stop it. She dropped her hands into the front pockets of her faded orange housedress and forced her mouth back into a grim line.

"I'm sorry, Miss Ethel. Tell you what. Next Saturday we deliver your lunch first."

"That'd be good," she said, looking over at me. "My, who's this pretty little thing with big blue eyes?"

"This is Maggie." Seth put his arm around my waist as he answered. It startled me. It also felt kind of nice. "Maggie, Miss Ethel."

Before I uttered a word, Miss Ethel's eyes narrowed on me. "You sure are a skinny little gal. Bet ya I cou'd snap one of them scrawny collarbones of yours in half without even tryin'. Are you one of them anorexians?"

"No, I'm not anorexic, just petite." *So much for feeding the anorexic rumors.* I walked back over toward the door and stood there waiting to leave.

"Ya know, boys don't like huggin' and kissin' skinny gals, missy. My husband, Jack, God rest his soul," she touched her forehead, chest, and each shoulder with her heavily creased right hand before continuing. "He always said men don't like kissin' and huggin' sticks. He said gals with a little meat on their bones is more comfortable to have your arms 'round, and a lot more fun." She laughed mischievously. "They isn't as ornery cuz they ain't hungry all the time, like them scrawny gals."

Horrified, my face flushed a deep scarlet. To Seth's credit, so did his. Undaunted, she continued.

"You like kissing her all bony like that, Seth?"

"I haven't kissed her yet, Miss Ethel." His red face now carried a grin from ear to ear.

Will the earth please open up and swallow me whole? Did he say yet?

"Why not, boy?" She looked genuinely surprised. "Is you one of them gay fellers?" She didn't ask the question with any repugnance, merely curiosity.

"No, I'm not, Miss Ethel." The stupid grin never left his face. "I'm very much a heterosexual." Evidently, she didn't know what the word meant because her brows knit in confusion. "I like girls," he said reassuringly.

"So what ya waitin' fer?" She didn't let him answer. "She's too skinny for you, ain't she? I'm telling ya, boy, a few home-cooked meals will fill her out in all the right places, if ya know what I mean," she said with a crooked grin.

"I agree wholeheartedly. Thank you for the advice."

I desperately wanted to leave.

"Get going, and don't forget next Saturday yer comin' here before McSheehy's." He nodded, giving her a peck on the cheek. "You bringin' Bones with ya?" I wondered if the verbal abuse was ever going to stop.

"She can come if she wants. Maybe I should take her to Burger Palace instead, see if I can fatten her up a bit before I kiss her."

"Bye." I opened the door and ran for the car. I'd have run home if I knew where we were. Instead, I plopped down into the seat, slammed the seatbelt into position, and crossed my arms over my chest. Seth slipped casually into his seat.

"I warned you that she's a spitfire."

"What about the protection you promised before we went in?"

"She wasn't so bad. She's worried about how skinny you are. You do look as if someone could snap you in half without much effort." He softly took my arm as I reached for the door. I looked back to demand he let me out of the car, and somehow my face ended up only a few inches from his. The closeness stunned me into

44

silence. That and the overwhelming desire I had to kiss him. I was crazy, no doubt about it. Why in the world would I want to kiss a guy who drove me insane?

"Maggie, I'm sorry." His eyes burrowed into me, rendering me speechless. I nodded, shoved my hands between my legs and pinned them there to keep from reaching out and pulling his mouth down to mine. "I'll take you home."

I sat silently, forcing my breathing to slow. We arrived at the park a few minutes later. "Alright, where to from here?"

"Let me out here, thanks. I need the exercise."

"Maggie, please tell me where you live? It's cold. Let me take you home."

"I told you. I'm thinking about trying out for the track team in the spring. I have to be in shape." For a moment I wondered why I cared what he thought of me. Nevertheless, at the stoplight I took my book bag and darted out.

"Here." He handed me the last lunch from the back seat. "You may as well have this," he said, frowning. I hesitated, but hunger won out. I took it, thanking him, and walked to the middle of the park and began doing stretches I'd seen the kids who were actually on the track team do as he drove away. I waited five minutes before walking home.

"Where you been?" My mother's speech was slurred in an all-too-familiar cadence. She rolled over and looked up at me through her bloodshot eyes, blinking to clear her vision. She rolled back over, passing out completely. I grabbed a blanket from my bedroom and covered her up. Contrary to popular belief, alcohol depletes body heat. I put the lunch in the fridge, retrieved my AP Calculus book from my bag, and began the long, tedious journey down the road of confusion. *I hate math.*

The rest of the day and half of the evening I spent struggling through my assignment. More than once I had to untangle a knot I'd made in my hair with my fingers. I really needed to stop twisting my hair. After a particularly grueling problem, I slammed the book shut and slid it across the table in surrender, near tears. "I'll bet Seth understands this garbage."

"Who you talking to?" To my surprise, my mother sat upright on the couch. Wondering if she had eaten yet today, I took the lunch out of the refrigerator and placed it on a plate before handing it to her.

"What's this?"

"Food." Still annoyed over my Calculus homework, the answer came out harsh, not a good thing. "What have you eaten today?" I softened my tone, fearing she'd become angry. Then she'd drink instead of eat; again not a good thing.

"None of your b'isness." Her speech was still slurred. "Who's the mother here? Me!"

"Mom, please eat." She shoved the food back at me, spilling half on the floor. Ugh. "You drink too much." Frustrated, I gathered up the mess, now covered in dirt from the floor, and reluctantly tossing it in the garbage. I'd learned from sad experience that it was pointless to argue with a drunk.

"Get o'er here, young lady." As she started to stand up, her eyes appeared to move in opposite directions, and she fell back down onto the couch. "What I do with my life is none a' your b'isness."

"You don't do anything with your life except drink, that's my point. You wake up, and you immediately get drunk. The moment you start to sober up, you start drinking again. It's not much of a life, Mother." I ignored my "don't argue with a drunk" counsel, but first Seth, then math, now this. How much could a girl take in one day?

"You ungrateful li'l brat. I paid for this house, and I pay for the food. You're nothin' but a leech, you unlovable nothing. Get out of my house." I thought to mention that she didn't pay for the food but the government did, only to what point? I grabbed my sweater and house key and left, chastising myself for fighting with her.

The clouds hung low in the night sky helping to keep the temperature above freezing. It had to be forty-five degrees out, not too bad for 10:45 p.m. in the middle of winter. I slipped on my sweater and walked down to the park knowing it would be well lit there. The city didn't bother with streetlights in my rundown neighborhood.

After an hour of roaming around the park, I'd calmed down and managed to shove away the bitter words my mom spewed at me. She was sick and her words shouldn't upset me. She didn't mean them. At least that's what I told myself.

Applegate Park had become my favorite refuge over the years. In the summer, the shade from the tall leafy trees kept me cool, and in the winter, they blocked some of the wind as it howled through their naked branches. Sadly, over the past two years it had become known as *the place* to buy drugs, making it a somewhat scary place to be at night.

It was also a mecca for couples who came here to make out, even in the dead of winter. Walking through the trees, I had to step around more than one couple tangled up in each other's arms. I wondered if Seth had Hillary in a lip lock somewhere. Clearly, no one could accuse her of being an unlovable nothing. Dropping onto a bench, my mind wandered back to Seth's soft, full lips smiling at me this afternoon, his piercing green eyes . . .

Eyes!

I shot straight up. A man dressed all in black stared at me through the trees. His hair was slicked back from his face, and the lamplight reflected in the silver plug in his right ear lobe. He looked to be about my mother's age, though the expression on his face was anything but paternal. He was on his cell phone, except whoever he spoke with didn't have his full attention. *I* did. His eyes swept my body, while his tongue lapped repeatedly over his lips, as if he were imagining what I would taste like.

I was the only one in the park who was alone, completely alone. No one would notice if I disappeared. It'd take days before my mother would be sober enough to figure out that I hadn't come home. My heart beat so furiously, I feared it would explode out of sheer terror.

I thought to start screaming, except the strangely dressed man only *looked* at me, so that was probably overreacting. I needed to leave. I jumped up and walked quickly toward the nearest park exit in the opposite direction. He followed. I was about to take off running when someone seized my arm from behind. My voice froze in my throat, making it impossible to scream. To my surprise, the creepy guy hadn't grabbed me. Seth Prescott had.

"Sorry I'm late, love, thanks for waiting." He pulled me into his arms and whispered softly, "There's a man dressed all in black following you. Pretend we're here together."

"What?" I tried nudging him away, except I shook too hard.

He pulled me closer, dropping his mouth back to my ear. "If you'll notice he's not watching the couples here, just you. He thinks you're alone and therefore an easy target. Maybe if he believes we're here together, he'll leave."

How did he know what the greasy haired creep thought? What if he was wrong? Did he have a plan B? I was all for running away. He dropped his lips to my neck and started nuzzling against it softly. I stood perfectly still.

"That's a pitiable effort, Maggie. Put your arms around me and at least pretend this is enjoyable," he hissed in my ear. I slowly slid my arms around his waist between his shirt and jacket and was surprised at how sinewy his body was. My hands felt the bulge of muscles in his back as they made their way up to his shoulders. I felt the warmth of his skin through his shirt and all the while, his lips caressed my neck and jaw. My eyes slowly shut, to help with the illusion.

"Can you see him? What's he doing?" His voice sounded rich and low in my ear. I forced my eyes open, bringing me back to reality.

"He's dropped back into the trees, but he's still staring at us." Seth asked me another question, however the sound muffled against my skin, and I couldn't understand him. I turned my face toward his to ask him to repeat it, and realized our mouths almost touched. We had to kiss. There was no way out of it. Anything else would've looked awkward. I pressed my mouth onto his.

His lips were soft and warm on mine, though somewhat hesitant. And I felt incredibly stupid. He obviously did not intend to really kiss me. Why in the world would this gorgeous guy want to kiss me anyway? I started to pull away when his hands began winding their way through my hair. He held my face gently to his as his mouth moved carefully against mine. It felt wonderful. My head swam as I drew myself tighter against him, again, to help keep the illusion going.

After several moments, he pulled away. I didn't open my eyes, instead drawing my bottom lip into my mouth to get one last taste of him. Suddenly realizing how long my eyes had been shut, I popped them open to see him smiling down at me. I was mortified.

"Did he leave?" His thumb stroked my cheek.

Refocusing my thoughts on the man in black, I glanced around. "No, he's still watching us, but he moved over by the northwest exit gate now."

"Then I guess we better keep up the act." Before I could answer, his mouth dropped back onto mine, and this time there was an undeniable eagerness to his kiss. I struggled to stay calm. If only he hadn't tasted so incredibly good and felt so incredibly warm. Zack's kisses never made me feel like this. Seth slowly spun us around until he faced the northwest gate. His lips never left mine while his eyes searched the park. Finally, he pulled away.

"I think he's gone. Come on, I'll take you home, just in case," he said, sliding his hand in mine. "Which way is your house?"

"No, I'm fine." I pulled my hand free, taking several deep breaths trying to regain my composure. "He went the opposite way of my house. Anyway, I only live a few minutes from here. Bye."

"Maggie, we can do this two ways. Either you let me take you home, or I'll follow you without your consent. Simply put, you're not going alone."

"I live east of the park, and he went toward the northwest. I'll be fine."

"What if he decides to double back? You did hear about the girl who was stabbed and left for dead in front of those buildings a few days ago, correct?" He pointed to a row of abandoned buildings adjacent to the park.

Grrr! He was right. Her story was *the* topic at school lately. Moreover, it was almost midnight, definitely not safe to be out alone. "Fine." I stuffed my hands into my jeans pockets and stomped off speedily toward my house.

My five-foot-six stature proved no challenge for Mr. Six-Foot-Two. He easily matched my stride.

"Where's the fire?" he asked. I slowed a bit, not wanting to look as foolish as I felt. When we reached my corner, I spun around to face him.

"Why were you in the park? Did you have a date?" Like, perhaps with Hillary?

"No, just out with a friend." A nice, safe generic reply. He must be trying to keep his options open.

"Here's my street, thanks for walking me home. See you at school tomorrow." I said it fast and without taking a breath. It would've been a miracle if he'd understood. I started walking again, and he continued to follow. "Really," I called over my shoulder. "Thanks again for your help at the park, you're a lifesaver."

"Anytime. Well, not *any*time. Hopefully, you're smart enough not to take midnight strolls through the park anymore." I twisted around and glared at him. He flashed an impish grin before taking my arm. "Maggie, please allow me to see you home—all the way home."

Evidently he wasn't giving up.

"Alright. Thanks." I had no choice. I stuffed my hands back into my pockets and walked on.

He didn't say anything until we approached my trailer. "Truth is, I was hoping for a goodnight kiss, you know, after the park and everything."

I ignored him and increased my pace again. After a few more steps, I had a small brainstorm and sallied around with a smug expression. "Sorry, it's not cold enough to kiss you."

He looked puzzled. "Okay, you've lost me. What does the cold have to do with you kissing me?"

"Simple, the river Phlegethon will have to freeze over before I'll ever kiss you again." Dr. Bore would be proud of my mythology reference. Seth just threw his head back and laughed. "I'm glad you think that's funny."

He gently, but firmly, took my chin in his hand. "Methinks the lady doth protest too much."

He did not *just misquote Shakespeare to me.* "I watched you taste my kiss back at the park, Maggie. You enjoyed it as much as I did. You know it and I know it." His voice rumbled soft, low, and yummy. I yanked my head free and walked up the small path to my porch.

"Sooner or later, Maggie, our lips will meet again. Personally, I'm voting for sooner."

I wheeled around, almost losing my balance. "Why do guys like you think every girl wants to make out with them? I don't get it."

The playful grin vanished from his face. "I didn't ask you to make out, Maggie. Goodnight." A twist of guilt clutched at my belly as he walked away.

Safely inside my house, I slithered down the closed door, burying my face in my hands. There was no need to be cruel. My mother was right. I was an unlovable nothing.

"You're back?" It shocked me to find my mother still awake. Her voice carried a strange tone. Probably disappointment that I returned.

"Yes." Thankfully, the lights were still off. I didn't want to explain to her why my face was flushed.

"Go to bed. You have school tomorrow."

Geez, my mother picked the strangest times to go parental on me.

I forced my weary body up and headed toward the bathroom, fully intending to wash off Seth's kisses and forget the whole night ever happened. I marched down the hall, *past* the bathroom, and instead went straight into my room, dropping onto my bed. My mind wouldn't stop thinking about him. I ran my fingertips over my lips, remembering.

"Stop." I rolled over, forcing myself to sleep. Sorry to say, my thoughts of Seth didn't end. He stayed front and center in my dreams. I gladly welcomed the hideous sound of the alarm clock the next morning.

4
Seth

*"H*ere's the artist rendering of the man who attacked Michelle Stringer." Booker placed the drawing on my desk as I ate my breakfast, a bowl of Honey-Nut Cheerios. "Hmm, looks tasty, kid," he said dryly.

"It's not as if I have all the time in the world to make a hot breakfast. I have to get to school and do my job, unlike some of us." I frowned at the soggy O's. Man. I'd be glad when this assignment was over.

"Someday you'll be in charge of your own team, and you can call the shots." Booker set a mug down next to my bowl. "To show you my heart's in the right place, I made you some of my famous hot chocolate."

I inhaled the sweet, chocolaty steam escaping from the cup. "Formula number seven?"

"Would I bring you anything less?" He sat and propped his black, hard-soled shoes on the corner of my desk, beaming as I savored the warm liquid.

"Are you ready to share the secret ingredient with me?" I asked between sips.

"Nope." His grin broadened. "So does the drawing look like the guy from the park last night?" he asked, pointing to the picture.

I studied the man's face. "It's hard to tell. It was pretty dark, and he was alone. Didn't Ms. Stringer state there were two of them?"

"Yes, but that doesn't mean they can't do a little business alone." He had a point. The drug community had no problem stabbing each other in the back.

"You watched this guy walking throughout the park, but didn't witness any drug deals going down?"

"None." I laughed. "However, most of the people in the park last night weren't exactly looking to score. Well, not drugs anyway. There was a whole lot of making-out going on. Once he spotted Maggie, his demeanor changed. He stayed hidden in the trees, as if he was tracking a defenseless animal, and he kept licking his lips." Repulsed, I shoved my breakfast away.

"I worked my way over toward him just as he got a phone call. He was angry and kept telling whoever it was *'no'*, and that he was in charge, all the while watching Maggie."

I got up and walked over to the window, resting my arm on the sill. "He said there was this hot girl who was all alone and that he was a man with needs." My jaw tightened. "He kept smiling and scratching himself."

Booker walked over and patted my shoulders. "She's okay, Seth. You saw to that."

"I should've arrested him."

"On what charges? Gawking at a cute girl?" Booker laughed. "I'd have had to charge you, too. I'm sure you were doing some pretty heavy gawking yourself at Ms. Brown."

"I can guarantee you my thoughts weren't lascivious. All I wanted was to talk to her. He, on the other hand . . . "

"I have no doubt your thoughts were pure, *Son of a Preacher Man*," Booker said, walking back over to my desk. My dad served in the Air force as a Chaplin, among other things, and Booker was forever singing the old Dusty Springfield song to me as we grew up. "This guy was probably some loser guy hoping to score. No need getting uptight over nothing."

I knew Booker tried to downplay the incident. Until we had any evidence proving otherwise, he saw no need for me to tie myself up in knots. Vintage Booker. Out to save the world.

"Which reminds me," I narrowed my eyes at him, "it's not working."

"What's not working?"

"The scheme you had to, how did you put it? 'Win the lady's heart.' Cheesy, Booker, even for you."

"What's not working? You must be doing it wrong," he said playfully.

"You said to make her laugh, make *her* the nervous one. Well, she doesn't laugh at my jokes. Instead they seem to put her on edge.

Although, I do believe she's nervous. She has this cute habit of twisting her hair around her fin—" I looked over at Booker. His chest bounced with laughter. I smiled. "I did kiss her last night," I admitted. "Twice, actually."

"See. I hate to say I told you so," he glowed proudly.

"But she got mad after I did."

"You must be a pretty rotten kisser. Did she kiss you back, or was she cringing the whole time?"

"I kiss just fine, thank you very much. And yes, she kissed me back. Actually, she kissed me first," I bragged. "But I don't think she's interested in having a boyfriend. Maybe I should try being her friend."

"No, no, no. You're making real progress, kid. You need to—"

Thankfully, a knock on my office door brought Booker's love advice to a premature end. In walked a lanky, blond woman in an MET uniform.

"Hey, Connie. What's up?"

"Captain, you said you wanted to be notified if another stabbing occurred with the same MO as Michelle Stringer." Booker nodded slowly as Connie handed him a sheet of paper. "A twenty-four-year-old female identified as Tammy Byrne was found shortly after two a.m. behind some empty buildings near Applegate Park. She had several knife wounds almost identical to those of Ms. Stringer. She didn't survive, Captain."

"Was she raped?"

"It's hard to tell. The body's a mess, but the forensic team doesn't believe so. Sir, the woman who discovered the body is a reporter for *The Democrat and Chronicle*. She and a staff photographer were there doing an exposé on the growing drug scene at Applegate Park. It's already hit the morning papers."

She handed the report over to Booker along with a small plastic bag. "This was found under the body. We couldn't get any fingerprints off it. We're not even sure it's part of the crime scene, but I thought you might want to see it."

"Thanks, Connie." Booker closed the door as he read over the paper.

"What's in the bag?"

Booker twisted the baggy, quickly pulling the small notebook from his left breast pocket. "I believe the guy who attacked Michelle

Stringer had a silver plug in his right ear lobe," he said, thumbing through his notes.

"A silver plug?" I took the evidence bag from Booker. "The guy in the park last night wore a silver plug." I shoved it back into Booker's hands and stumbled over to my pleather chair, all but falling into the cold seat. Dropping my elbows on the desk, I buried my face in my hands.

"Book! If I hadn't hung around the park after the stakeout . . ."

"I know, kid, I know. Look, you better get to the school. I'll talk with the team and head over to the crime scene, and see if I can find anything."

"I'm going with you," I said, burning my throat as I downed the last of my hot chocolate.

"Seth, you'll be late for sc—"

"I'm not going. This murder is part of the assignment too."

"Maybe. This could be some random killer. We don't know for sure if he's part of the drug investigation."

"So why are you following up on it? Why aren't you letting the local cops handle this?" I had him there, and he knew it.

"Okay, fine," he said, slipping the plug into his pocket. "Once this murder hits the school, there's going to be lots of talk. I want you and the team all ears for the rest of the day."

"*If* we finish this before school ends, I'll go. The other three agents can keep their ears open."

"Seth, don't you think Maggie is going to need someone to lean on when she hears about this?"

I hadn't thought about how she'd react. She'd probably take it hard. "Let's get going so I can make it back in time for class." I jumped, snagged my jacket from the top of the filing cabinet, and rushed for the door.

"I suppose when we're done I'll have to write a note for the principal explaining why little Sethy was late for school today," Booker said, to which I gave him an elbow to the ribs.

"Oof!" He laughed, rubbing the spot.

I was the first one out of the car. The size of the crime scene sickened me. Tammy Byrne must have put up a good fight. Booker checked in with the lead detective on the case.

"Detective Michaels," he said, greeting him with a handshake. My palms were sweaty so I nodded to him instead. "I read your preliminary report. Have you learned anything new?"

"Only that the victim wasn't raped," Michaels said, showing Booker the preliminary autopsy. "Her face wasn't touched, but her body was a mess. They weren't random cuttings either, Captain. This guy knows his way around anatomy."

"Like a doctor, maybe?" I asked, though I couldn't imagine someone who'd spent years in medical school throwing it all away to be a murderer.

"Not necessarily. My old man was a farmer, and we butchered our own cows, chickens too, for that matter. These cuttings were precise, but crude, not skillful like a surgeon's. Maybe the perpetrator's a farmer or a butcher."

"Good call. I'll run a check and see if there are any local farmers or butchers with a violent record," Booker said. "Let me know if any new leads turn up. We're going to look around."

We passed under the yellow police tape and searched the area, but found nothing new. I couldn't believe the amount of blood everywhere, and I prayed the slime ball had cut the poor victim up postmortem. Otherwise, Ms. Byrne suffered tremendously.

I tried to keep Maggie out of my thoughts, but it was tough. It could very easily have been her blood we sifted through. She could have been the one—

"Hey, sit down before you pass out." Booker took my arm, steering me over to a couple of dented trashcans. "I know you want to be here, Seth, but I think you should head over to the school. I don't need you fainting onto potential evidence."

I nodded weakly. Wiping my damp hands off onto my jeans, Booker arranged for a patrol car to take me back to the station for my car. He was right. I was useless here. I needed to be at the school. I needed to see Maggie.

11

Maggie

Stepping out of the shower, I gasped at my naked reflection in the glass door. The bathroom scale confirmed my fears: my body had whittled down to ninety pounds. My shape resembled a boy's far more than it resembled a girl's. The bones between my breasts protruded so effortlessly you could easily count each rib. It was no wonder everyone kept commenting on my baggy clothes. Repulsive. Kicking the shower door shut, I tucked a towel around me and went to dress.

I decided to wear my one decent blouse and the jeans I saved for special occasions, not that there were many of those in my life. Though probably a bit fancy for school, no one would mistake me for a boy today, despite my lack of curves. I laid the outfit out carefully on my bed and went to the closet for the pair of tan closed-toed pumps given to me by a neighbor. She'd fallen and broken her arm while wearing them, and afraid of meeting the same fate, I hadn't worn them yet. Today, I decided I'd be brave. I could be as pretty as Hillary. Possibly.

After fifteen minutes of working on my hair, I gave up. I mean seriously, how do you fix flat and dull? I gathered it up into my usual ponytail, letting it fall lifelessly down the center of my back and hurried into my room. While slipping the cream-colored blouse on over a white tee shirt, I noticed a missing button so I weaved a safety pin into place on the underside. Next, I pulled on my jeans; they hung loose on me. I'd lost so much weight since last wearing them, they fell dangerously low on my hips. I dug out an old frayed belt my mother used to wear when I was a kid and slipped it through the belt loops, hoping my shirt was long enough to cover it.

The mirror verified my thoughts; if Hillary were trailer trash, you couldn't tell us apart. How completely depressing. With no time left to change, I strapped on the pumps. At least they looked nice. I tugged on my sweater and ran out the door.

"Well, hello, little guy." On my doorstep sat a small, furry dog who was nothing more than a tan and brown fur-ball with the sweetest brown eyes I'd ever seen. He jumped around, wagging his tail feverishly. I bent down to let him sniff my hand, which he licked, a good sign, and I picked him up. He lapped away at my face as I searched his tattered collar for a dog tag. I remembered seeing him once before running free around the park.

"Okay, little guy, calm down." I couldn't help but giggle as he continued to bounce in my arms. "Where do you live?" He answered with the cutest little soprano bark I'd ever heard. "Sorry, cutie, I have to go to school." I gave him a hug and put him back down. He promptly began following me to the corner.

"No." I stomped my foot hoping to deter him. He perked up his ears and tilted his head sideways at me as if to ask why he couldn't follow.

"The street is too busy. You might get run over." He barked and trotted back toward my trailer. I chortled and hurried off to school, making sure to take a different route, not wanting to take the chance of running into Seth. The embarrassing park-kissing incident was still foremost in my mind.

I was able to avoid him all morning, and at lunchtime, my luck still held out. No Seth sightings yet. I debated whether to go and eat in the library, but if the librarian caught me, it would mean a six-week ban from the place. Quietly entering the cafeteria, I took a seat in the back corner and pulled out my half-sandwich, groaning silently as Melody made a beeline toward me.

"Don't you live over by the Applegate Park?" I nodded slowly as she smiled and dropped the local newspaper, *The Democrat and Chronicle*, onto the table in front of me.

Local woman found dead near Applegate Park
Local resident and college student Tammy Byrne was found brutally stabbed to death behind an abandoned building near Applegate Park shortly after two a.m. Friends last saw Ms. Byrne as she made her way home taking her usual route through the park

around midnight. A witness reported seeing a man dressed in black wandering throughout the area all evening, but said the man disappeared around the same time as Byrne.

The family has issued the following statement: ""Tammy was a beautiful, bright young woman who dedicated her life to helping others. We are asking anyone with information that could assist the police in capturing the evil person or persons responsible for stealing our daughter's life away to please come forward."

People in the area are being advised to use caution when going into the park after dark.

"Can you believe it? Someone was killed within a few blocks of your house last night. Freaky, huh?" Melody reread the words aloud over my shoulder. Waves of nausea rolled through me as my hands fisted around the newspaper. It felt like the breath had been stolen from my chest. It should have been me. If Seth hadn't shown up when he did, it would have been.

"Sorry, Melody. I have to . . . go . . . do something." My brain was a mass of incoherent thoughts.

"You look like you're going to be sick. What's wrong?"

I ignored her, running out to the hall. I had no idea where to go, I just needed to be out of the crowded cafeteria. I ran down the hall and right into Seth.

"Are you alright?" He held tight to my shoulders, a good thing, too, since it was the only thing keeping me from hitting the floor. "I'm guessing you've heard about the Tammy Byrne murder?" I stared at him wide-eyed, unable to speak. "Maggie, you're okay. Take a slow deep breath. Maggie, take a deep . . ." I heard nothing else. It was as though I sunk through mud when suddenly, something strong and warm pulled me out. Seth. I laid my forehead on his chest, his wonderfully muscular chest.

"Deep, steady breaths, Maggie." Nodding against his chest, I inhaled deeply and held it for a few seconds before letting it out slowly. I repeated the process until eventually my head started to clear. I pulled back, but Seth held tight to my shoulders.

"If you hadn't come to the park, it would have been me."

"Maggie, you're safe." He slipped a hand around my neck, resting his thumb along my jaw.

I looked up into his eyes as tears spilled down my face. "But Tammy Byrne's dead. Her family will never see her again, never hold her again." I dropped back onto his chest crying even harder. He stroked my hair and continued to hold me, uttering soft words of comfort. After several minutes, I forced myself to regain my composure. Seth gently wiped the tears from my face.

"Sorry, I shouldn't cry like a babbling idiot." I felt humiliated by my childish outburst.

"Showing sorrow for someone you've never met is hardly foolish, Maggie," he said. "It shows compassion."

"Thank you for helping me last night. I didn't tell you that, not really."

"Don't mention it." He brushed a stray piece of hair from my face, sending a shiver racing down my spine as my eyes dropped to his lips. I took another deep breath to clear my head again.

"We should let the police know we saw that man in the park."

He agreed, dropping his hand from my face. I immediately missed the comfort of his touch. "I'll call them after school."

I stepped back to make some room between us. I was too caught up in the emotion of everything and needed space. Not realizing we were next to the stairwell, my foot slipped back and down a step. Seth caught me around the waist before I fell. He also caught me just as Hillary came around the corner. Her eyes narrowed when she saw me in Seth's arms. I quickly righted myself and pulled away. Regrettably, I didn't notice that the heel of my shoe had broken off, and I stumbled again. Seth caught me . . . again.

"Am I interrupting anything?" Hillary stepped closer, her grip tightening on her book bag. She probably imagined it was my neck.

"No." I pulled free of Seth and removed my ruined shoe, thanking him once more. I used the opportunity to get away and raced to the bathroom. Once inside, I ran into the first open stall and plopped down, still wrestling with the nauseous feelings inside me.

Poor Tammy. I should've been the one killed last night. No one would have mourned my death. The tears began flowing again. It took more than half an hour before I was able get myself under control. I fiddled with my broken shoe, finally giving up and limping out of the stall. To my surprise, I wasn't alone. Leaning against the sink, with her arms folded across her perfect chest, stood Hillary. I hobbled past her and went to the far sink to wash my face.

She pounced. "Keep your hands off Seth."

If looks could kill. I ignored her.

"What makes you think you can steal him away from me?" She ran a condescending glare up and down my length. I felt stupid. She was right, but it still hurt to hear.

"Of course, if you're giving him what he wants, he may stay with you until boredom sets in, which in your case," she eyeballed me again, "shouldn't take too awfully long."

I took a paper towel, ran it under the cold water, and wrung it out before pressing it to my sore puffy eyes. "I'm not after him. Maybe he's after me. Did you ever think of that?" I hoped to get under her skin a little with my comment. Okay, maybe a lot.

Bingo. She had thought of it and it bothered her, a great deal I'd guess by her shrill laugh. She moved closer.

"Like I said, if you're giving him what he wants, he may stick around for a while. Maggie, guys like him only play with girls like you, if you catch my meaning." I did. "But they fall in love with the good girls, like me."

"Let me get this straight. You're saying popular guys prefer egocentric, stuck up, snotty girls, correct?" I wanted to sound as if I were simply gathering information, like a poor misguided soul, and she was teaching me one of life's great mysteries.

"No, stupid. They play with the trampy girls until they tire of them, or use them up. They marry the good girls."

"I guess that would explain why he's dating you at the moment and not me. He's obviously not ready for marriage. I mean, seriously, he is only eighteen." Good one, Maggie. I attempted to fix my pathetic hair and gave up and settled on adjusting my pathetic sweater instead before turning to leave.

Hillary had other plans. She drew up in my face, so close I smelled her sour breath. What did she have for lunch anyway?

"He's mine, and a simple piece of trailer trash like you doesn't stand a chance against someone like me. *Capice*?"

"Why are you so worried then?" Her eyes flared at my question. She looked intimidating, if not downright evil. I decided to try to smooth things over, sort of. "I'm not interested in him. He's shallow and stuck up, a perfect match for you." Despite the smug grin on my face, I knew he was none of those things. "We're just friends, not even friends really, more like acquaintances. He means nothing to me." A twinge of guilt pricked at my heart with the comment. It bothered me more than having her in my personal space at the moment.

"Maybe punching you in your ugly face will help you to remember he's off limits." Her threat took me by surprise. I had no idea cheerleaders punched people. She pulled her fist back and threw it toward my face. Luckily, I'd spent years dodging empty booze bottles lobbed at me by my mother and promptly ducked out of the way. Her fist slammed into the mirror and it cracked.

"You're crazy." I started for the door, but she caught my sweater, and jerked me around. She took another swing. My arm shot up to block it. The blow made contact with my forearm, causing a bitter sting. Before she could hit me again, the bathroom door popped opened and in walked the Vice Principal, Mrs. Volkel. Hillary immediately released my sweater.

"May I inquire as to why two of my best students are in *this* bathroom during the lunch break? You are both aware that only the restrooms next to the cafeteria are to be used during this hour, correct?" She had her hands on her hips and an annoyed frown on her mouth.

"Hi, Mrs. Volkel." Hillary was all saccharine smiles and lucent charm. The evil glint in her eyes had completely vanished. Astounding. "Love your shoes. Are they new?" Hillary sounded genuinely charming, in a sick, twisted kid of way.

"Yes, they are." Mrs. Volkel relaxed, dropping her hands to her side. "I purchased them at *Carmichaels* during their after-Christmas sale."

"That place is expensive. I'm envious." She flashed a fake smile. Mrs. Volkel bought it, hook, line, and sinker. She was actually impressed by the fact that a popular cheerleader thought her shoes were cute. Pitiable really.

Watching her spin her evil web, I thought back to our tenth grade year. She and some of her friends set up an internet site entitled *GeeksWeBe.com*. She posted mean-spirited photos, along with acerbic commentary on fellow students who had committed, in her words, *a fashion faux pas.* The unforgivable trespasses included such things as puffy bangs, tee shirts tucked into slacks, and the dreaded fanny pack. If she hadn't been forced to shut down the site after posting a photo of the science teacher wearing socks with sandals, my sweater would have surely made the list. She also charmed her way out of a suspension by claiming her goal was to help the fashion misfits. Yeah, right.

"Shoe trouble is why Maggie and I are in here, Mrs. Volkel," Hillary said. I looked at her wondering what instant lie Little Miss Webmaster had come up with this time. "She broke her shoe, and I brought her here to see if it could be fixed somehow. I didn't want the other students to see her like this. They might make fun of her. More than they already do, I mean." *Ouch!*

"Hillary, you are a real role model for other students." Mrs. Volkel looked as if she were about to cry. Me, I wanted to throw up. "Were you able to fix her shoe?" She dabbed the corner of her left eye.

"No, it's not a very good quality shoe," *aka cheap*, "it can't be fixed. The good news is they're easily replaced. I saw a pair almost exactly like them in the window of a discount store on Saturday. I'll drive her over there after school," she said, flashing another fake smile. "I'd hate for her to ride the bus with a broken shoe."

"Thank you for your kindness." Mrs. Volkel patted Hillary on the arm.

I'd had enough and limped toward the door.

"Wait a minute. Do either of you know how this mirror got broken?" I looked at Hillary, anxious to see her next performance.

"Not a clue. It was already broken when we came in here." Another perfect lie. Not a muscle on Hillary's face twitched, not a hint *anywhere* on her face she lied. The girl should be charging for this show.

"It was probably one of those kids from the bad side of town." I winked before adding, "You know how they are."

Mrs. Volkel gave me an uncomfortable look. "Yes, um, well, we'll never know. I'll put in a work order to have it fixed before someone gets hurt on the broken pieces. Off to class, ladies. The bell is about to ring."

I rushed out, wanting to get to culinary class before the halls filled and everyone saw me hobbling along. I sat in my usual back corner trying to understand how my simple boring life had suddenly gone crazy.

"How are you doing?" Seth asked, taking me by surprise. Stealth technology had nothing on this guy. It was as if he appeared out of thin air. "Sorry, I didn't mean to startle you," Seth said, putting his hand on mine. The warmth of it reminded me of how warm his mouth was, and I slowly pulled my hand away pretending to look for something in my book bag.

"I'm better, thanks." I threw him a quick smile and returned to my bag to keep up my pretense.

"Is this a new outfit? I like it." My face flushed at his compliment, and I buried it deeper inside my bag.

"Thank you. No."

"How's your shoe? Were you able to fix it?"

"No, it's hopeless."

"Let me take a look at it."

"Don't worry about it. They're cheap shoes," I said, as if it were no big deal that I now had only one pair of shoes to my name—one pair with the toe ripped out.

"Maggie, the shop teacher's a genius. He can fix anything. Let me run it over and see what he can do."

Figuring there was nothing to lose, I handed him the shoe. Maybe now I wouldn't be mysteriously partnered to cook with him if he weren't here, something I hadn't been able to avoid yet. I watched him saunter out the door before turning my attention to Mrs. Gianchi.

"Class, today we're going to have a contest." She was perched atop her stool once more with a sunflower print apron on. "By the stoves I've placed several different ingredients, and if you'd like to use it, a cookbook. Your assignment is to come up with something spectacular to eat. Your creations will be judged on taste, presentation, and creativity."

I'm dead. My cooking skills were poor at best. My only hope was a talented partner. I looked around trying to remember who always did well in class.

"Your creation has to be completely finished, including cooking time, within one hour. To make this fair we'll draw names to determine who you'll be partnered with. If your last name starts with the letters A through L you'll pull a name out of the bowl."

Finally some good news. The odds of choosing Seth's name were pretty slim. Just in case, I stood back refusing to take a turn until someone else drew his out first.

I waited and waited, but no one drew Seth's name. *This cannot be happening.* It came down to my boy-crazy friend Julie and me;

still I waited. "Julie, your partner is Erin Steel," Mrs. Gianchi said, reading the slip of paper. "Which means, Maggie, you'll be working with . . ." she pulled out the last piece of paper, "Seth." I mouthed as she read it aloud.

"Mrs. Gianchi, Seth isn't here, should—"

"I'm back." His voice made my stomach quiver, in a good way. "Look, your shoe's as good as new," he said, handing it to me.

It did look as good as new. Better actually, you couldn't tell it had been broken. I put the shoe back on, twisting it around to see if it would hold. Solid, of course, would it dare be anything less?

"Thanks."

"What's the assignment? By the way, how'd you rig it so we'd be partners again? You didn't bribe Mrs. Gianchi did you?" His eyes narrowed playfully.

I ignored his last two questions and explained the assignment. You'd have thought he'd won a million dollars. "This is great. We can create whatever we want." I'm glad he found it exciting because my perception was entirely different. He looked over the ingredients and thumbed through the cookbook before tossing it aside.

"Are you up for an adventure?"

"Sure, why not?" What else could possibly go wrong today? He started dividing the ingredients into different sized portions. I leaned up against the stove and looked around the room at what the others did.

"Maggie, we're a team, remember?"

"I'm a lousy cook, Besides, I have no idea what you're doing."

"I'm going to show you. When we're done, not only will we win the contest, you'll also know everything there is to know about garlic," he said, presenting me with a large white clove of the stinky stuff.

"I hate garlic, I think," I said, grimacing. He grinned widely at my pinched expression.

"Well, you won't after today." He explained what herbs worked best with what foods, and he was passionate about properly cooking the meat. I learned how to *pan sear* it to preserve the moisture and how to use a meat thermometer. "It tastes better if you don't cook the life out of it," he said.

We chopped carrots and onions, mixed together flour and some of the herbs, combining it all together before pouring it over the *cheap*–according to Seth–steak we'd browned earlier. By the time we were done, my head was so stuffed full of information, it was a miracle it didn't spill out my ears. I found him enjoyable to be around when he didn't flirt. He had me laughing more than once with tears streaming down my face. We finished with ten minutes sparing.

"Try it." I shook my head at his request. No garlic. "Here, Maggie, smell it." I took a small whiff of the creation as he finished arranging the meal perfectly on a plate, down to a small sprig of parsley. "For color and your breath," he informed me. It smelled wonderful.

"Okay, okay, I'll try it." He spooned up a small bite and fed it to me. It tasted wonderful.

"Mmmm! What are you going to call it?" I grabbed a spoon and shoveled another scoop into my mouth.

"I can't decide. How about 'Bit of Heaven.' What do you think? Too over the top, isn't it?"

"It certainly fits. This is amazing." I took another bite. "Any other ideas?"

"Seth and Maggie, you're next," Mrs. Gianchi said, interrupting him. "Let's see what you've created. Presentation: lovely, Maggie. Full marks. Did you use all the ingredients?" She looked over at our counter. "Good. However, the real test will be in the taste." Seth handed her a fork. "It certainly smells delicious." She took a small bite. "Marvelous. The meat is incredibly moist. Have you decided on a name for the dish?"

"I've decided to call it *Maggie's Kiss*," Seth proclaimed proudly. All the color drained from my face as Mrs. Gianchi glanced at me and smiled.

"My, my, dear, you must be quite the little kisser. This dish is wonderful. Full marks for both of you." Moving toward the front of the room, she again shook her head in amazement.

"I can't believe you. Do you have any idea how embarrassing that was?"

"I wasn't trying to embarrass you, Maggie." He was actually puzzled by my reaction. Boys were so dense.

"It's okay, forget it." It was pointless to argue. "Let's clean up this mess before the bell rings." I had to admit the name was kind of sweet. At least no one else heard him.

Mrs. Gianchi called the class together from her stool as we finished. "You've done well today. I'm proud of your creativity. Some of you should consider cooking as a career, and some of you should continue working hard at your other studies." She smiled. "The winners in today's contest are Seth and Maggie for their creation entitled—"

No, please don't say it aloud, please, oh please!

"Maggie's Kiss."

Ugh! Several of the guys belted out catcalls as Seth grinned. A few even slapped him on the back as if to congratulate him.

Will this day ever end?

"I've set out some plastic forks and paper plates on the counter. On your way out the door, please take a small sample of Maggie's Kiss—Steve, I heard that. If you even try you'll have detention for a week." His freckle covered face went bright pink.

Most of the guys crowded around the dish for a taste. When Steve walked over, Seth positioned himself between us, but it didn't stop Steve from playfully winking at me.

Seth put the last of it onto a plate and handed it to me as the bell rang. "Sorry if I embarrassed you, Maggie. I didn't think she'd announce it to the entire class." His devilish smile didn't look very repentant to me. My thoughts went to Hillary as I took the plate and left. If she heard about this, I'd be dead.

I used my alternate route home again to avoid Seth. If he did try to find me, I never saw him.

Since we could no longer afford a phone, I went straight to our weird neighbor's trailer, Mr. Hoffman, to use his. It took him forever to answer the door, and I was about to give up when it flew open.

"Can I use your phone?"

He stood in the doorway wiping his nose on his dirty green shirtsleeve and raking his eyes over me.

"Sure thing, hot stuff." He scratched himself before reaching into his pocket for his cell phone. He laid it in my hand, keeping contact with my skin much longer than necessary. "Who ya calling? Maybe I can help?" He winked a watery yellow eye.

Repulsive. "I need to call the police," I said, *after* punching in 9-1-1. He backed off and went into the kitchen. I guess the last thing Hoffman wanted was the police nosing around our neighborhood. More than once, I'd seen him selling weed in Applegate Park. He was probably afraid they'd raid his trailer.

After a brief conversation, the operator informed me an officer was on the way. Setting the phone down on the porch railing, I quickly thanked Hoffman and left.

I changed into my sweats and began pacing nervously up and down the living room, waiting. The thought to move my inebriated mom into her room was interrupted by a light tap on the door. I opened it to the sight of a handsome police officer with the letters MET embroidered across his black jacket.

"Hello, I'm here to speak with Maggie Brown."

"That's me," I dribbled out stupidly, still ogling him. He was incredibly good looking with his dark wavy brown hair and deep brown eyes. His broad shoulders gave me the impression that this guy was serious about his workouts. Not quite as tall as Seth, though still quite tall. He was probably the only human on the planet who could give Seth some competition in the gorgeous department. Well, almost. He flashed me a heart-stealing grin, and I noted the dimples on either side of his smile that could only be described as *WOW*!

"May I come in?"

"Sorry, yes. Please do." *Snap out of it, Maggie.* "Have a seat," I said, pointing to the one free piece of furniture in the room. He glanced over at my mom snoring softly on the couch.

"No, please, I don't mind standing," he said, gesturing for me to sit down.

"I'll get a chair from the kitchen." I reined in my hormones and dashed the two feet into the kitchen to grab the least rickety chair we had.

With pen in hand, he started asking questions about the man from the park, which I answered to the best of my memory.

Then the questioning took a strange twist. "You were in the park with Mr. Prescott between eleven-thirty and midnight, correct?"

"How did you know that?"

"I came here directly from speaking with Mr. Prescott. He said the two of you were in the park when you saw the man in question." I nodded soberly. "Midnight is a bit late for you to be out, seeing it was a school night and all. You're how old? Seventeen?" He looked over at my mother disapprovingly. *Great, now the hottie cop thinks he's my father.* "What were you doing out so late?"

Not wanting to go into the whole argument with my mother, I simply said, "I turned eighteen last week." A mild threshold I celebrate with relief. Now I no longer had to worry about Social Services butting their noses in my life. It was why I didn't get free lunch at school, fearing if I filled out the forms, government people might come snooping around my house. Not a good idea. "I was with Seth also. He's eighteen."

"Seth does seem like a responsible young man. You have good taste in boyfriends, Miss Brown." He smiled and reached into his pocket for a small card.

"He's not my boyfriend," I said, a little too fiercely. "He's just a friend."

"Really? Huh." He handed me his business card and asked me to call him if I remembered anything else. He thanked me for my help as he slid his pen into a breast pocket and gave another sideways glance at my mother.

I quickly opened the door for him to leave and found the dog from earlier sitting on the porch. I knew I had to think fast. A stray dog without tags meant only one thing, the animal shelter.

"There you are. I've been searching for you everywhere, you naughty boy." I scooped up the dog, and he licked my face. The hottie cop chuckled.

"Friendly little guy, isn't he?" He reached over and rubbed the dog on the head. "What kind of a dog is he?"

I shrugged. "Probably just a mutt of some kind."

The dog snapped at the officer. "And that's exactly why I prefer cats," he added, laughing. "Does he have a license? It's a law in this county that all dogs must be licensed. Is he yours?" He continued to rub the dog's head, though clearly the fur ball didn't like it.

"No, but I'll let the owners know when I see them." That wasn't a lie. If I found out who owned him, I'd tell them.

"I could take him to the shelter if you'd like. We'll make sure his shots are up to date, and even have him neutered. It's a free service offered by the local shelter." The dog snapped once more at him as if he understood what he said.

Smart doggy. Now stop it, or he'll haul you away.

"That won't be necessary," I said. He nodded and left. I looked down at the business card in my hand and wondered why Officer

Hottie thought Seth and I dated. Correction. The hottie was a *captain*, Captain Booker Gatto, to be precise.

I shook my head. I didn't need to be thinking about boys or men right now. I had a ton of homework to do and dwelling on the male species, no matter how good looking, wasn't going to help me finish.

I went to the refrigerator, took out the leftover Maggie's Kiss, and divided it up between two plates for my mom and me. I put some of mine onto a paper plate for the dog. He stuck his nose up at the food, probably still full from all the garbage cans he'd raided earlier, and instead curled up by my feet for a nap. I scratched him behind his ears for a few minutes trying to think of a name for him. "How about Brutus?" The dog cocked his head. "No? Maybe Prince. What do you think, you little ball of fluff? You like the name Prince?" The dog dropped his fluffy head down onto his paws. "That's it. Fluffy. It's perfect. Do you like it?" He barked loudly. "Since I don't speak dog, I'm guessing you do. I have to do some homework, Fluffy. You'll have to entertain yourself for a while."

I steeled my brain for another battle with numbers, but only after making sure all the doors and windows in the house were locked.

6

"*W*hat is that noise?" I lifted my head up from off the table. As my mind cleared, I realized it was my alarm clock screaming at me from the bedroom. It was 7:13 a.m., and I'd spent the entire night sitting, or rather sleeping, at the kitchen table. The last thing I remembered was letting the dog out when he scratched on the door around eleven p.m.

I stood slowly, stretching the kinks out of my back and vigorously rubbed at the red mark on my forearm from where my head had been resting. I could hear my mother's snores as I passed her bedroom to switch off the alarm.

"Thanks for letting me sleep at the table all night, mother," I said to the door, wondering for the umpteenth time if she cared about me at all. I took a quick shower and dressed for school. Racing out the door twenty minutes later, I ran smack into Seth.

"Good morning, beautiful." Forcing my eyes from his heart-stopping green eyes, I straightened my sweater and headed down the street.

"Thank you. What are you doing here?" I asked, marching past his Lexus.

"I brought you some breakfast." He held out a *Bagel Heaven* sack, the contents of which caused the small brown bag to bulge.

"I've already eaten," *sort of.* "Thanks, anyway." It smelled delicious. *Bagel Heaven* was the hot spot for most of the student body, and even though I'd never eaten there before, I'd heard about it.

"You can eat it later," he said, stuffing the sack into my book bag. "It's freezing today. Wait here, I'll get my car." Before I could refuse, he was gone, pulling up alongside me with the passenger door ajar a few seconds later. I decided to accept the ride rather than freeze to death and climbed in.

"You should eat the bagel while it's still warm. The cream cheese practically melts in your mouth."

"I've already eaten, remember?" I stole a whiff of the warm bagel. Heaven itself couldn't possibly smell that good.

"Thin as you are, it won't hurt to eat a second breakfast. Hobbits eat second breakfasts." I bit my lip to keep from laughing at his analogy. "You know, Hobbits? J.R.R. Tolkien? Lord of the Rings?"

"Yes, I'm familiar with the story." Everyone on the planet was familiar with the story.

"Never mind." He grumbled something under his breath about a great joke and looked back over at me. "Why do I make you nervous?"

"You don't. Why do you keep asking me that?"

He leaned over and tugged softly on my fingers. I was twisting my hair again. "Because it seems every time I talk to you, you start doing this. Not that I mind. It's kind of cute."

"It's kind of cute I twist my hair, or it's kind of cute you make me nervous?

"Both."

"I twist my hair mostly out of boredom, sorry to disappoint you." I smoothed out the tangled mess and mentally slapped myself. *Get control, girl.*

I was relieved the foul tempered Hillary was nowhere to be seen as we pulled into the parking lot. I thanked him for the ride and the bagel, vowing silently to never again twirl my hair. I took off running for the bathroom to devour the bagel. I couldn't very well eat it during our class after making such a big stink about not being hungry. I chided myself again for my foolish pride, but not before stuffing a huge piece of the delicious bagel into my mouth.

"Slow it down, girl. You're chowin' on that as if you haven't eaten in a week." *Oh! Not Melody.* Within seconds I had the low-down on the two new transfer students while she dragged me down the hall to mythology. I nodded, shoveling pieces of the bagel into my mouth as she continued her babble. We stepped into the room as the bell rang. Melody ran to the front row and dropped into the desk next to Hillary. As *my* luck would have it, Seth sat next to the only empty spot left in the room. I dropped my books down on the desk and sank into my seat.

"Psst." I ignored him. "Psst," he said again. He motioned for me to lean toward him and I wondered what bit of torture he had in mind for me next. He reached for my face, and with his thumb slowly caressed my bottom lip, stealing my breath away. He popped his thumb into his mouth and licked it, sending the blood coursing through my veins at an inhuman speed. He mouthed the words, "Cream cheese," which, thankfully, helped me to regain my composure. I mouthed back, "Annoying," and turned away. Out of my peripheral vision, I saw him silently laughing.

"Good morning, my fellow humans." *Oh. My. Gosh. Mr. Bore is such a nerd.* "It has been brought to my attention by one of your classmates," Bore said, grinning at Melody, "that the syllabus for this course has a typo. It states you are to do either ten hours of community service, or a ten-page paper on community service. However, it should read *a twenty-five* page paper on community service, not ten." The class, myself included, let out a collective groan. Where would I find the time to do a twenty-five page paper? Leaving my mom alone for long periods was difficult. Too easy for her to get hurt. Even going to school some days proved a challenge. It was why I hadn't taken an afterschool job, though we certainly could use the money. I brought the idea up to her once, but she forbade it, saying I had responsibilities at home and she wouldn't pick up my slack, as if that had ever happened.

I still brooded over the news when class ended. Gathering up my belongings, I moped silently to Seth's car, hoping CaL would cheer me up.

"You're not upset over the whole cream cheese thing are you?"

"What?"

"You know, back in Snore's class. Are you still angry with me?"

"I was never angry, just annoyed." His comment jogged my memory back to yesterday and the whole Hillary incident. "Do you know your endless flirting almost got me killed yesterday?"

"Killed?"

"Okay, maybe that's an exaggeration. Hillary cornered me in the bathroom and told me to stay away from you. She said you were hers, and then she tried to punch me in the face, twice. If Mrs. Volkel hadn't walked in, who knows what she might have done."

"Cheerleaders don't punch people. Are you sure you didn't misunderstand her?"

I pulled up the sleeve of my sweater, showing him the huge bruise on my forearm where I had deflected one of her blows.

His eyes focused on the mark. "I made it clear to her we were just friends, and she agreed saying she didn't want to be tied down her last year in high school. Does it hurt?" He gently caressed the undamaged skin around the bruise.

"Maybe if you didn't flirt all the time, girls would actually believe it when you say you only want to be friends."

We pulled into the elementary school parking lot before he spoke again. "I don't flirt unless I mean it, Maggie, and despite what you think of me, I don't lead girls on."

"So the whole cream cheese incident back in Dr. Bore's class was a misunderstanding and not flirting?" I couldn't understand why I always overreacted to him. I was usually pretty easygoing. I hated confrontation and he made me nervous. I found myself snapping at every little thing he did.

He opened my door and stood there, close, making it difficult for me to get out. I slid halfway between him and the car and stopped, unable to move any further. He stood firm, looking me dead in the eyes. It felt a bit unnerving to say the least. His eyes dropped to my mouth, and I thought for a moment he might kiss me. Instead, he shook his head and went into the building leaving me to follow.

Mrs. Mathews suggested we play games with the kids, and they decided on hide-and-seek. Seth and I had a difficult time finding hiding places given that we were significantly taller than a bunch of first graders. After an exceptionally long seeking turn, I recommended we play something else.

"No, Miss Maggie," Elise said, bouncing up and down on her toes. "One more time, please." Her request took me by surprise since she and a few of the other children talked during the last two rounds of the game instead of participating. Soon all the kids joined her in chanting, "one more time," and jumping up and down. Seth, being Seth, joined them, looking silly in a cute kind of way as he bounced about. I had to laugh.

"Okay, as long as you three hide this time," I said, pointing to Elise and her little posse.

I was met with a resounding *yeah* from thirty first graders and one hot twelfth grader. Harrison started counting as Noah led Seth to the other side of the room. He sounded excited as he explained how he'd found the perfect hiding spot.

"Miss Maggie, you can hide in here." Elise dragged me to a closet I hadn't noticed before and stuffed me inside.

It held stacks of colored paper and various craft supplies, along with an oversized easel. "There's enough room for the two of us," I said, squishing over to the side. There wasn't much room, though certainly enough for a first grader.

She giggled. "I'm afraid of the dark." She giggled again and shut the door. A few moments later the door popped open, and Seth was forced into the closet next to me. The door slammed shut. Seth and I stood facing each other, neither of us able to move. He laughed softly.

"I'm glad you think this is funny. However, you're standing on my foot." I bumped against his incredibly muscular chest and immediately wished I hadn't touched him. I needed to get out, fast, and began searching for the doorknob.

"You're wasting your time. They've locked the door."

I found the brass knob and jerked it frantically. It wouldn't budge. I was about to demand that they unlock the door, when Seth's fingers fell softly across my lips. "Shhh, listen." His warm breath caressed my cheek. "Can you hear them? They're right outside the door."

I pulled my mouth away from his fingers. "I don't hear a thing." *And I really have to get out of here.*

"They want to know if we've kissed yet, especially Elise. She's quite the romantic." Seth was clearly amused by our predicament. "We shouldn't disappoint them. They are young." I felt his hands steel around my face, with his mouth so close to mine I could almost taste him.

"Kiss me, Maggie." He ran a thumb slowly across my lips, and repeated, "Kiss me." His lips were a fraction from mine, his voice a mere whisper. I held my breath, trying fruitlessly to control myself, only the desire was too strong. No matter how hard I fought it, I wanted to kiss him. The thought of feeling his warm mouth on mine again made me shiver in anticipation.

I give up. I started leaning into him—

"Children, where are Mr. Seth and Miss Maggie?" Mrs. Mathew's voice disrupted my incoherent thoughts. Seth immediately let go of my face as the kids ratted each other out on the other side of the door.

"Elise and Noah locked 'em in the closet 'cuz they wanted 'em to kiss," Zane tattled, with several others chiming in.

"Oh my goodness! Where's the key?" A few seconds later, the lock rattled and the door flew open. I was the first one out.

"Are you two alright?" We both nodded. "Are you sure? Maggie, your face is quite red." Seth's face lit up in a wide grin. *Not a flirt? Ha!*

"I'm fine, just a little warm, that's all," I said, smoothing my hair.

"Children, you need to apologize this minute, and if you ever do that again we won't have the visiting teachers come back here." The children quickly apologized, as did Mrs. Mathews once more.

"Will you read to us?" asked Zane.

"Our time is up. Sorry, we have to go," Seth said as disappointment filled their faces. "The next time we come we'll do some reading, okay?"

"If you hadn't locked them in the closet, we may have had time for a story." Mrs. Mathews gave Elise and her little group a stern look. Elise ran up to Seth, whispering something to him.

"No, I did try though," he said. Knowing precisely what she had asked him, I stormed off to wait at the car.

"That's exactly what I was talking about earlier," I said as he crossed the parking lot behind me.

"Sorry, you've lost me." We drove out of the lot before I could compose myself enough to speak without becoming angry.

"Before we went inside you said girls misunderstand what you say."

"True."

"Kiss me?" I quoted him, my voice dripping in sarcasm.

"Right this minute? I don't think it's a good idea since I'm driving. Would you like me to pull over, or can you wait till we're back at school?" His twisted grin was more than I could take.

"There, you did it again. That's flirting," I folded my arms in triumph. "That's why Hillary thinks you two are an item."

"Yes, that was flirting. However, I want to kiss you. I don't want to kiss her."

He wasn't serious, was he? No, I decided, just more of his flirting.

"How is Hillary supposed to know you're teasing when you talk to her like that?"

"I told you already, I don't flirt with her. I only flirt with you." He looked at me without a hint of a smile. Why would he say these things?

Because guys like him only play with girls like you. I could see Hillary in the bathroom glaring at me in her condescending way as she said those exact words yesterday.

"I know I'm not the type of girl you like to date, so you can save your games for Hillary. I won't be used." My voice shook with anger. He pulled the car into the school parking lot, slamming hard on the brakes.

"I don't like being accused of something I haven't done." His eyes changed into an eerie shade of green, though still completely hot. "Maybe the other guys in your life are after one thing, but I'm not."

"What other guys?" What exactly did he imply with that statement?

"Zack?"

I didn't bother correcting him. I climbed out of the car and slammed the door shut; so did he.

"You've cut every guy out of your life for the actions of one moron." He turned and practically vaporized across the parking lot. I followed, running to keep up.

"Why should I give up on my dreams for some guy? Just because I don't have money and live in a trailer doesn't mean guys can take whatever they want from me. Like I said, I won't be used."

"I'm not trying to use you, Maggie, and for your information I do understand how you feel."

"Yeah, I'll bet it's rough going through life good looking, rich, and popular. I'll bet you hate waking up in the morning knowing there'll be a ton of people who you know you can trust, and who are glad you exist. How do you manage?"

Softness permeated his eyes, and he reached out to brush some loose hair from my face. "It's not as great as you think, Maggie, never knowing if someone only likes you because you're popular, or if they're a real friend, especially after they learn you have money."

The bell rang in the distance. I turned and quietly walked to my next class, leaving Seth standing there as it began to snow. I felt ashamed. Except for his relentless flirting, he really was a nice guy. I should have calmly told him his flirting bothered me. Why did I have to be such a jerk?

Once at home, I hopped into the shower to warm up. The cold had permeated to my core and the hot water felt good as it slowly thawed my body. I leaned back against the shower wall, letting the drops bathe my face. The hot water also melted my cold heart.

I'm a mean, cruel person who doesn't deserve love.

7

"*My* head is killing me." I slammed my hand down onto the alarm clock, silencing the hideous ring as the memory of last night rolled over me.

I'd cried myself to sleep.

Dragging my pounding head gingerly out of bed, I took a couple of aspirin before pouring a bowl of Cheerio's and eating it dry.

Forty-five minutes later, I muttered a goodbye to my mother, which she ignored as she made her way into the bathroom, undoubtedly seeking aspirin for her hangover.

We had an ice storm sometime during the night and the snow shrouded the town in a good quarter-inch of ice. It looked as if God had coated the earth, including each and every tree branch, with a sparkly glaze. It was beautiful. More importantly, it meant the snow would be frozen solid, and my feet wouldn't get wet walking to school.

My morning jog was brisk as the ice crunched loudly under my feet. Instead of finding Mr. Googolo, my Calculus teacher, when I trotted into class fifteen minutes later, Vice Principal Volkel stood in the front of the room. She wore a bright plum dress and matching shoes.

"Students, please take your seats—Steve, if you want detention, do that one more time." He immediately dropped into his chair. "It seems Mr. Googolo's car door is frozen shut so he'll be a bit late. He has asked that I have you do the assignment on page 184. He'll be quizzing you, therefore I suggest you spend this time studying and not talking."

Great. I wanted some help with the last lesson, now I had to try to figure out a new assignment. I opened the book; it may as well have been written in Japanese. I leaned over to my left. "Steve, do you understand this stuff?" He shook his head.

Julie sat in front of me, fingering her curly-red hair. I reached over, tapping her on the shoulder. "Do you understand the lesson?"

"No. You should ask Seth for help," she said, turning to face me. "He's really good at Calculus." She laughed at my sour expression. "Don't you like him? I think he's really cute." Her eyes darted to Steve who scowled at her, and she immediately turned back around.

After several futile attempts to figure out the lesson, I gave up and resorted to my doodling.

Apparently, I wasn't the only one having trouble. A few minutes later Julie slyly slipped me a piece of lined notebook paper. Across the top she'd written *The Hottest Guys at Port Fare High.* I had to laugh. I'd never met anyone as boy crazy as Julie. She'd listed five guys, and beside each name she'd written a number she entitled *Hotness Factor.* Seth's name was first. She rated him a twelve on a one to ten scale. I thought that was a little low.

Steve was next on the list, rated at a ten. He'd probably be lower on the list next week when she'd moved on to another guy.

She had scribbled a small note across the bottom asking me to agree or disagree. Enjoying the diversion, I wrote my answers, agreeing with most of her choices and bumping Seth's number to twenty-three. It wasn't as if he'd ever see it. It also made me feel a little better after treating him so poorly yesterday. I added a few names to the list, giggling a little too loudly. Mrs. Volkel came walking over before I could pass it back. "Is there a problem, Miss Brown?"

"I don't understand the assignment," I said, slipping the note coyly into my book bag.

She took the book and thumbed through the pages, handing it back quickly. "Miss Brown, Seth Prescott's an excellent math student. I suggest you give him a call and ask him for help." She smiled, before adding, "And unless you'd like me to share the note you and Julie have been passing back and forth with the class, I had better not see it again."

"Yes, Mrs. Volkel." I resorted back to my doodling, trying not to think about Seth and his *hotness* score.

***

My eyes scanned the cafeteria in search of a friendly face to share my lunch hour with. Melody sat at the far table on my left. I immediately looked to the right hoping to find someone else. Sadly, that someone else was Zack. I cringed when he called my name. I didn't look in his direction, hoping I'd be able to sneak out before he reached me. I didn't. He slithered up next to me, snaking his arm around my waist.

"Come over here and play along," he said. I shot him a hard glare. "Please, I won't ask you for another favor if you do this for me."

"Do what?"

"Shut up, I'll explain later. Follow my lead, Maggot." I looked up and saw he led us straight to Seth. After my childish outburst yesterday, I had no desire to see him up-close and personal. To compound the matter, Miss Perfect Pom-Poms stood next to him.

"You think you have a chance with her? Look who she's with," I whispered, absentmindedly twisting the stray hairs next to my cheek.

"She didn't seem to remember him this morning during Spanish Three. In fact, I could hardly keep her off me." He puffed out his chest, and then scowled. "And stop twisting your hair. You look like a freak." I quietly dropped my hand. "Steve Boyer says she and Seth are just friends. Melody thinks they're doing the nasty."

"Why do you have to make it sound dirty?" I tried elbowing him in the ribs. He tightened his grip.

"Not everyone's a prude like you."

"Wanting to wait for sex doesn't make me a prude."

"Blah, blah, blah, save the sermon, Maggot. I've heard it enough from you to last me a lifetime."

It was pointless talking to him. Zack was a narcissist through and through. Considered the star of the baseball team, he always made a point to remind me about his *special skills* while we dated. Who could have believed anyone would want to keep track of hits, runs, and 'RBI's,' whatever that was? Surprisingly he asked me out. We didn't exactly run in the same crowd. I now regretted having ever dated him, and hated that I'd shared anything about my life with him. It was a mistake that wouldn't happen again.

"Hillary," Zack said as we approached them. "You know my girlfriend, Maggo-ah-Maggie, right?" This couldn't be good. I tried to pull away, only he tightened his grip further. "Please," he hissed in my ear. I folded my arms and kept quiet. Seriously, I needed to have my head examined.

"I heard you two had gotten back together. Strange, because Melody's been telling everyone you broke up before Christmas break." Hillary spoke directly to Zack, probably hoping I'd disappear.

"A little misunderstanding." He smiled and kissed my cheek. I shoved my hand into my pocket to keep from wiping off the slop. Disgusting. "We made up last night." He gave a tug on my waist, and I forced a smile. Seth's eyes narrowed, but he said nothing.

"Do you and Seth want to double date with us to the Winter Festival this weekend?" Zack asked.

My mouth dropped open before I could stop it. *This* was his plan?

"Sure, sounds fun," Seth said. My eyes and still gaping mouth turned back to him. He smiled widely and slipped his arm around Hillary's small shoulders. She beamed.

I had to think of a way out of this awkward scenario. "I can't. I've a huge paper due in mythology, and I have to get started. It's due soon."

"It's not due for six weeks. You've got plenty of time," Zack said, pinching my waist.

I felt defeated. My mind was now completely blank. "Fine."

"I hate to be rude, but we're going out for lunch. We'll see you two later," Hillary said, looping her arm around Seth's and gloating directly at me.

I really can't stand this girl.

"You two are welcome to come with us, my treat." The look on Hillary's face tempted me to accept Seth's offer, only the idea of having to watch her wrap herself around him for an hour stopped me.

Zack, on the other hand, had no problem accepting a free lunch. "Sounds great."

I jerked out of his grip. "No, sorry, I'm busy. Maybe next time." Before anyone pressed me about my plans, I raced out of the cafeteria.

"I'll give you a ride home today, babe," Zack belted out across the room as I rushed through the door. Groaning, I went straight to the library and secretly ate my peanut butter sandwich, safe and sound with Washington Irving and Ichabod Crane.

***

I immediately planted myself in the empty chair next to Julie when I got to culinary class. Seth entered the classroom seconds later. Julie practically drooled when he walked past our desk heading toward the back to sit with a large kid named Dwayne. It was lecture day, which meant I didn't have to worry about being teamed up with Seth to cook.

After school, I tried to take a new way home in hopes of avoiding Zack. Sadly, he discovered me jogging across the track field.

"Not so fast, girlfriend." He cinched his arm around me, dragging me to his car and practically shoving me inside. He started driving toward his house, not mine.

"Where are we going?"

"Relax." He shook his head as if I were some pathetic moron. "I want to let you know the game plan."

"Game plan?"

"For the Winter Festival, stupid."

"If you keep insulting me, I'm not going anywhere with you."

"Here's the deal: I want to go out with Hillary, and she only goes after guys who are involved with someone else. Well, except for Prescott." He tightened his grip on the steering wheel. "Anyway, she gets a thrill out of stealing guys away from their girlfriends. Wild, huh?"

He turned down his street, continuing with his sick fantasy. "I need you to pretend we're dating again. We don't have to *really* date, of course, we could make out if you want." He smiled wickedly.

"Disgusting."

"Still as frigid as ever."

"I'm—"

"Just come with me to the Winter Fest," he said, overriding me, another charming trait of his. "You'll have to hold my hand, that's it."

Yeah, right, as if he'd ever kept his word. "I see a few flaws with your plan. One, she likes Seth. Two, why would she even think about dating a creep like you when she has him? Three—"

"She told me she doesn't like Prescott, she's only using him. She said she could have anyone she wants on the side, as long as no one finds out. Those were the exact words out of her hot little mouth," he said with a wicked grin. I looked at him in disgust. "Maggot, do you realize how many guys are trying to steal her away from him? Imagine the reputation I'd have if I stole Prescott's girl. Anyhow, I'm not interested in a permanent relationship. Rumor has it she's a total make-out whore." The guy's expressions sounded crude at best. How he had made it on the honor roll was a mystery to me.

"You're sick. I'm not going to help you use her."

"She's giving it away, Maggot. How can you use someone who's giving it away? Besides, she really hates you for some reason." A dark expression filled his face. "If Hilly thinks she lured me away from you, who knows what could happen? What did you do to make her hate you anyway?"

"Nothing. She's delusional."

"You should have seen how excited she got when I told her we were dating again. She came on to me like crazy in the cafeteria until Prescott showed up. She has to keep up the pretense in front of him. She needs him."

"Needs him for what?" The more I got to know Zack and Hillary, the more I realized how perfect they were for each other.

"He's rich, popular and people are naturally drawn to him for some reason. Even the teachers treat him like an equal instead of a student. He has a lot of power at Port Fare High, Maggot, and Hillary loves power. She's an unbelievable manipulator." He wagged his brow.

Why did I ever go out with this guy?

"What do you think this little scheme of yours will do to Seth when he finds out his girlfriend's cheating on him?"

"The guy can have any girl he wants. He'll just find another one, *if* he finds out that is."

"And you think I'll help you because . . ."

"Because we're friends," he said, smiling sweetly. I stared back at him coldly. "Because if you don't, I'll tell everyone we slept together." His eyes were now as cold as mine. He meant what he said, and even if I denied it, the seed would be planted, and many would doubt my word. This was why I preferred to be alone. This was why I trusted *no one*.

"You're vulgar and disgusting. You two deserve each other." At the next stop sign, I jumped out of the car and started walking back toward my house.

He stuck his head out the window and yelled, "Is that a yes?"

I wheeled around, glaring at him for a moment. I felt trapped, just like with everything else in my life. "Fine, but this is last time I'll ever do anything for you."

I took off running before the tears started. I wasn't about to give Zack the satisfaction of seeing me cry. After several minutes, I slowed to a walk, chastising myself for crying again as I dried my face.

I was sick of Zack and sick of feeling trapped. I refused to let him manipulate me anymore. If he wanted to try and get Hillary away from Seth, he'd have to do it without me. I'd simply explain it all to Seth tomorrow on the way to CaL class. He seemed like a reasonable guy. He'd believe me. I hoped.

I'd tell him about the rumors Zack wanted to spread about me too, though the rest of the school would think I slept with Zack. That might be a problem, but as long as Seth knew the truth and believed it, I could live with that.

I also realized that I cared too much about what Seth thought. It was why I treated him so rudely. I'd been trying to drive him away before he could hurt me. How pathetic. I fell for the most popular boy at school, just like every other girl. Despite his flirting, he'd never really like me. Zack said it best. Seth could have any girl he wanted. He certainly didn't have to settle for trailer trash.

I started jogging again, partly to keep warm, mainly to forget what a silly fool I was. My house was another four miles away. It gave me plenty of time to clear my mind. I pulled the hood of my sweater up over most of my face in an effort to keep the wind from whipping against my skin. It also made it impossible to see the guy standing on the sidewalk until I almost ran him down. I twisted to the side to avoid a collision, and watched my book bag fly through the air.

"I'm sorry. Are you alright?" I picked myself up and looked around to see if my poor victim survived.

Seth? Was the entire universe conspiring against me?

I noticed he held a fistful of mail in his hand as he stepped toward me. "I'm fine. What are you doing here, stalking me?" He smiled slightly. I could tell he was still hurt by my bitter outburst yesterday. He helped me gather up the spilled contents of my bag.

"No. Ah—Zack and I had a fight, and I decided to walk home. You live here?"

He nodded. I looked over at the picturesque, two-story, red brick house. It took my breath away. A large, white porch wrapped around the front of the house, along with two bay windows; one on the main floor, and one coming off what I guessed to be an upstairs bedroom. A wooden swing, begging to be sat in, hung from the ceiling of the porch, with an antique watering can perched on one end. Connected to the wraparound porch was a vast wooden trellis with dozens of dormant vines weaved liberally through the slats, promising a plethora of flowers come spring.

Several tall old trees occupied the yard, each had to be eight feet around minimum, and were encircled by large dormant flowerbeds. Without a doubt, this yard would rival any for its beauty in the spring and summer months. His red Lexus was parked in the driveway near a well-worn basketball hoop.

I couldn't imagine Seth living in a more perfect house.

"So, you and Zack got back together?" His voice sounded cool. I pulled my eyes away from his house and back to his hard stare. My mind instantly wandered back to the kiss in the park and the almost kiss in the closet. I had to leave and rein in my over-active hormones.

"I can't talk right now, gotta go. See ya."

"Wait, I'll give you a ride." His features indicated the opposite.

"Track try outs, remember?" He didn't say another word despite the fact he still watched me as I rounded the corner. Before he said another word I took off like a bolt.

I should've apologized and debated whether to go back before thinking better of it. I'd look ridiculous after almost tackling him, or maybe I tried to find an excuse because I was a sniveling coward? Probably the latter.

My mother's government check came yesterday, and I stopped to buy some groceries. I found a small, ripped bag of dog food in the *scratch and dent* section for a dollar in case Fluffy came back.

With my arms loaded down with almost more than I could carry, I continued home. When I arrived, I found the trailer in complete shambles. Throwing up, my mom had vomited everywhere except for in the toilet, causing the house to reek of the vomit-alcohol mixture. I made up some chicken broth and took it in to her as she lay semi-conscious across her bed. "Mom, here. Drink this."

"Go away, you stupid girl. Do I look like I can eat right now?" she said, flinging her arms around. I dropped back to keep her from spilling the broth.

"Mom, when was the last time you ate? You're probably hungry."

"I can take care of myself, you arrogant, brat know-it-all. Get out of here!"

I set the broth on the nightstand and left. Something hit the door as it closed; most likely it was the broth.

After cleaning up the house, I sat at the kitchen table for several hours doing homework, finishing at midnight. Dressing for bed, I mulled over the options pressing me. First and foremost, I had to forget about my feelings for Seth. Falling in love with him was not an option. He also deserved to know about Hillary and Zack. I recalled my berating insults to him in the parking lot, remembering what he said about people using him because he was popular and rich. Zack and Hillary fitted the profile to a tee. So consumed with myself, I never once considered someone else might have problems, too.

"Tomorrow, I'll try and redeem myself and see just how unselfish I can be," I muttered, buttoning up my too small pajama top. "I'll also find out if this is nothing more than a guilty conscience, or if I truly want to change."

8
Bill and Alan

Bill bounced the basketball against the wall of their small dilapidated living room, laughing when it ricocheted wildly and collided with his brother's head.

"Knock it off, jerk, or I'll cut up your face." Alan shoved his brother into a steel column that supported the ceiling of the basement apartment. Bill reverberated, landing in a heap on the filthy green carpet.

"Hey, what's buggin' ya?" Bill jumped up, rubbing his newly bruised shoulder before smoothing his silky black shirt back into place.

"I'm bored, that's what's buggin' me, and I'm hungry." The police were out in force since Alan murdered the co-ed. He didn't dare wander around in public, worried someone from the park might ID him. "I wish I could disguise myself like the old man does. He's pure genius at it," Alan said with envy.

Bill knew the boredom got to his brother. He watched Alan pull out his knife and lovingly caress the blade before picking at his teeth with the tip. "Why don't we order some pizza?" Bill suggested, setting the basketball in the closet and grabbing the newspaper. He was anxious to see whether new information emerged on Alan's latest screw up.

"I'm tired of pizza," Alan groaned. "I'm the son of a big shot drug smuggler. Harry Dreser's boy shouldn't have to eat takeout. I should be swimming in money, eating fine food, and pawing beautiful young girls, not stuck in this rat-infested dump." Alan kicked an empty Gatorade bottle out of his way as he slumped onto the couch.

Sadly, their father's smuggling business had run into hard times. First, and in Alan's mind, most importantly, their accountant embezzled a large part of the family's fortune leaving them nearly broke. They had to sell three of the four family homes to pay off their business associates, or be killed.

His father's thriving business went from one-hundred-twenty-three employees down to seven, three of whom were family. To try to recoup their losses, Harry had sent their brother Jeffery to Upstate New York, specifically Syracuse, to work up some new clientele. Their hometown in Arizona overflowed with drug smugglers, and with the degrading embezzlement on everyone's mind, the dealers went elsewhere to buy their stuff, fearing the Dresers would abscond with their money.

Jeffery turned out to be a big mistake, spending most of his time targeting elementary school kids, claiming they'd be an easy mark. Oh, he built the business alright, but it also sparked an outcry from the community like no one had ever seen before. Someone ratted him out, probably a disgruntled junkie, and, subsequently, a couple scum MET agents murdered Jeffery. His death threw the old man's health into a tailspin from which he still hadn't recovered.

In the past, Bill and Alan had been the *muscle* for the business, making sure debts were paid and mouths kept shut. Harry didn't think they had the brains to do much else. Now with Jeffery gone, Harry had no choice but to send Bill to Rochester in hopes of getting the family finances back on track. Alan joined him in December after serving time in the local jail for an *accidental* stabbing involving a fifteen-year-old girl.

Alan loped over to the grimy basement window and peered out. "Do you think Hoffman's going to be able to run things when we're not here babysitting him?" he asked. Bill had been in charge of training someone to take over the daily grind once things ran smoothly, then they'd move on to a new area in New York.

Only he hadn't done it. In fact, he'd hardly done anything before Alan showed up. The old man was furious and cut off most of their allowance until the job he sent them to do was complete. If it weren't for Alan, they never would have found Hoffman. The guy was perfect for the job: eager, stupid, and easily intimidated. He had an impressive list of clients too. Mostly weed, but that was easily remedied. Getting a weed user to try something new was rarely a challenge.

"I don't know. Hoffman's dumber than a stick," replied Bill.

Up until Alan had arrived, Bill's idea of drumming up business meant slinking around in back alleyways, only those weren't places to find *new* customers. Schools were. Dance clubs were. Any place young people hung out. Starting in December, Alan had focused on the bedroom community of Port Fare and he'd increased things threefold. He ran the list of new customers over in his mind and smiled proudly. Apparently, the old man was wrong about Alan. *Who's the freakin' screw-up now, pops?*

Alan did all the work, and it wasn't easy, either. Upstate New York was cold, very cold. Moreover, they were cops patrolling everywhere, probably because of the three overdoses last summer. That too was Bill's fault. How many times had Alan told him to mix more filler in the dope? Dad's stuff was strong and had a good reputation, but Bill could never get the mixing ratios correct. *He* was the freakin' screw-up, not Alan.

That being said, Alan was a man of compulsions. Case in point, the other night at the park. He'd become obsessed with the skinny young girl he saw wandering around alone the moment he laid eyes on her. No surprise, he always had a soft spot for *young and pretty.* He knew instinctively she'd put up a fight. He loved it when they did. When he closed his eyes, he could almost hear her pleading. It made his neck hairs bristle in excitement.

If her stupid boyfriend hadn't shown up, he'd have had her. Because of that he had to settle for a college girl. He hated college girls. *Way too old*, Alan thought, skimming his fingers along the knife's blade. It needed sharpening again. The little adventure with the coed dulled it.

"Hey, check it out," Bill said, holding up the newspaper. "Saturday the town is having some kind of festival. There'll be lots of people around, and we'll be able to go out and mingle easier. Crowds are great for getting lost in," he said, hoping to distract his brother.

Bill was relieved to find no new information about the murder. He'd grown tired of cleaning up Alan's messes. All his life he had to clean up after him. His brother acted rashly, never thinking things through. Seldom did a plan work if Alan had conceived it.

As children, Bill had to come up with all kinds of schemes to get Alan out of trouble. Bill forged Alan's report cards so the old man didn't know he'd failed English and PE in eleventh grade. He came up with the idea to plant the $50,000 in their sister's room so she'd be blamed for stealing it when in fact it was Alan. She got beat pretty good for that one, the little brat.

When they grew older, Alan's troubles only grew in severity. Things like grand theft auto, assault and battery, and armed robbery, to name a few. Always there to save the day, Bill took care of everything.

But what Bill couldn't control was his brother's fixation with knives, which was why Alan ended up spending time in jail for hurting a fifteen-year-old girl with one. Bill got a beating that day. Remembering the pain, his stomach tightened.

Alan used to chop up small animals as a teenager, making their father so angry he sent Alan to work in a slaughterhouse when only fourteen years old. Harry had hoped Alan would work out his obsession with the blade. Instead, it exacerbated the problem. Alan left there having refined his skills instead of relinquishing them. Granted, the skill came in handy when they had to teach a shifty dealer a lesson, Bill reasoned, but when he used it to torture, and sometimes kill young girls, it was just plain disgusting. Alan never raped them though; he just butchered them up.

Like he did Tammy Byrne.

Bill begged him not to go out. He'd seen the restless look in Alan's eyes and braced himself for the upcoming trouble.

Upon his return, blood covered Alan's clothes and he refused to change out of them. He wanted to relax and relive the *event*. Sicko. Bill had to get him drunk before removing his clothes to burn them in the sink. He also had to bleach the knife, again.

Saving Alan had become a full time, tiring, frustrating job.

"I'll go insane by Saturday." Alan stomped over to the refrigerator and yanked the door open. Empty. He slammed it shut. "You know what I really want."

Bill shook his head. "We can't take any more chances. The old man will have our hides if we blow this."

"Don't you think I know that?" Alan sneered at his brother. "I need to get out and see something besides your ugly face. Maybe a soft female face. One with huge—"

"Alan," Bill said, interrupting his brother's concupiscent thoughts. "If we wait until the festival, we'll be able to score big. The place will be crawling with potential clients." *He hoped.* "Maybe you can find a sweet young thing there that'll need your help using for the first time. You love it when it's their first time."

"I want the girl from the park." Alan flung his knife across the apartment, embedding it three inches into the wall.

Bill slammed the newspaper down in frustration and broke a small glass end table that sat next to the couch. He was tired of this. It had to end. Enough was enough. He was done taking Alan's lumps, and he was done cleaning up after him. Only their father could control Alan. He dug out his cell phone from his pocket. "I'm calling dad."

"I'll make you a deal." Alan had to think fast. He realized he'd pushed his brother too far, and the last thing he needed was for Bill to get the old man involved.

"We go back by the park and watch for the girl to show up. You'll only have to drive around, I swear, I won't even get out of the car unless I see her. If she's not there, I won't bring it up again, *and* I'll go to the festival with you on Saturday." Alan wasn't too keen on the whole festival idea. Too risky. Nevertheless, he hoped it would pacify his stupid brother.

It did. He smiled as Bill sighed and shoved his phone back into the pocket of his slacks.

"Deal." Alan knew he'd win the argument. Once he set his mind to something, no could change it. He did wonder if any girl would be stupid enough to go to the park alone again after the last *incident.* But come Saturday, they'd do some serious business.

9
Seth

"Honey, I'm home."

"Hey, Booker, I'm in the kitchen." I preoccupied myself with cooking—my way of unwinding, or in this case, *forgetting* the last couple days, for a few hours, anyway. I could still see Maggie standing in the parking lot accusing me of using her, mistrust written all over her face. The face with the amazing blue eyes.

So much for forgetting.

"Hello, is anyone in there?"

"Huh?" I snapped out of my mini-daydream to find Booker standing next to me, waving a hand in front of my face. He was dressed in a pair of worn 501's, and a long-sleeved, deep purple Henley with a gold tee shirt underneath.

"I asked *what are you making for dinner*, three times." He shook his head at me, an exaggerated look of pity on his face. "This wouldn't have anything to do with your new assignment, would it?"

"Maggie?" I asked casually, stirring the cream sauce before it burnt.

"Please tell me this is what I think it is." Booker took a spoon and dipped it into the sauce. Raising it to his nose, he inhaled before slipping the spoon into his mouth and moaning. "It is. Beef Burgundy. I love your Beef Burgundy." His dark brown eyes immediately scanned the counter. I knew what he looked for.

"Forget it, Book. I already added *it*, and put *it* away." He forever hounded me to reveal the secret ingredient. *Nutmeg.* I was surprised he hadn't figured it out yet, he usually did. "Of course, you know what you have to do to get it."

A remarkable connoisseur of hot chocolate he took great pleasure in creating new formulas. His number seven was my personal favorite, but he wouldn't share the recipe. Old family secret, he'd say, but we both knew that wasn't the case.

"Deal?"

He debated for a moment before shaking his head. "No deal, kid. You're a better cook than me. I have to have one recipe I can outdo you with."

I shrugged casually and added the steak to the sauce. Frustration pinched his brow as the steam rose from the pan, trailing up to his nostrils.

"Oh man, I'm starving. How much longer before Cole gets here?" He took another spoonful of the sauce, moaning once more as, no doubt, my master piece bathed his taste buds and meandered down his throat.

"Twenty minutes. Add some salt to the wild rice, will ya?"

"So, how *is* your new assignment coming along?" Booker walked over to the bar and planted himself on one of the stools he'd built. He was a master carpenter. When I bought my home two years ago, it was a disaster, and we'd spent the next year and a half remodeling it. Actually, Booker did the lion's share of the work, I was more or less his apprentice and gopher, but I learned a lot.

He scooped up my latest copy of *Bon Appétit* from the towering pile of mail I hadn't gone through yet and began skimming the pages.

"It's not going very well. I'm alienating her more than anything. I think she hates me." Truthfully, I was still upset with her. How could she lump me in with a moron like Zack? It also seemed odd to me they'd gotten back together. I'd watched the way he treated her the last time they dated, and listened to the crude things he said about her in gym class. Why would a girl with major trust issues, and clearly trust wasn't something Maggie did easily, date a lying weasel like Zack?

I stirred in the mushrooms and onions, covering the pan to let everything simmer a bit. "Maybe you should reassign her to Garrett Woolley." He was the floater agent at the high school. "He's a likeable guy."

"Possibly in a few weeks. I'm not ready to give up on you yet. You're my best agent, Seth. I have complete confidence in—" Laughing, he set the magazine down and picked up a crumpled piece of paper from the pile of mail.

"You think my bills are funny? By all means, laugh away. You can pay them while you're at it." I walked over to see what caught his attention.

"Like you need me to pay your bills," he said. I didn't, thanks in large part to him. After my parents died, he helped me invest the insurance money into some profitable investments. The guy had the Midas touch, no doubt about it. If I never worked again, I could still live comfortably.

He began reading aloud. "'*The Hottest Guys at Port Fare High.*' Looks like you're number one, my friend." I tried snatching the paper out of his hand, but he held it out of my reach. "Look. There's a rating system of one to ten. Someone wrote down twelve, crossed it off, and changed it to twenty-three. Not bad, kid."

I lunged forward, this time getting hold of it. I read the list as Booker studied it over my shoulder.

"Correct me if I'm wrong, but I do believe this list was made up by at least two different girls . . . well, I'm assuming they were girls," he teased. "Look at the different handwriting." He pointed to the first five names at the top and the names added near the bottom. I immediately recognized some of the handwriting.

"This here looks like Maggie's handwriting," I said, pointing to a few names at the bottom.

"It seems she's the one who upgraded you to a twenty-three," he said, thumping me on the back. "And you claimed she hated you. Wrong."

"I don't understand. Maggie's never set foot in here. How did this get on my counter?" I sat down on a stool, trying to make sense of it all. "Wait a minute. This afternoon when I was getting the mail, she came jogging down my street and practically plowed me over. Her book bag spilled out, and I helped her pick everything up. This must have gotten mixed up with my mail," I said, looking over the list again.

"Knock, knock." Cole walked in the back door carrying the round baguette I'd asked him to pick up from the Little Bakery in town. He was dressed like he always was; blue scrubs and scuffed up leather clogs. "Here's the bread," he said, handing me the still warm brown sack.

I did a quick scan for a bandage. It was a rare occasion when he didn't have one stuck to some part of his body. It'd become a game between Booker and me. There it was; left hand, little finger. I knew well enough not to question him about it. He was self-conscious about his clumsiness. Besides, once Booker discovered it, he'd tease him enough for the both of us.

"Dinner will be ready in about twenty minutes. Just waiting on the rice. How's work going?"

"Yes, by all means, Doc, tell the *Hottest Guy at Port Fare High* and myself about your day." Booker laughed and swiped another sample of dinner.

"I guess I missed the joke," Cole said. Booker offered him a spoonful of the sauce, along with the list. Cole eagerly accepted both, groaning with pleasure as he swallowed the sauce.

It was probably the first meal of the day for him. If you looked up the word *workaholic* in the dictionary, it would say, "See Cole." He was the kindest, gentlest man I'd ever met. He definitely had strong ideas about life and the world in general, only he had a way of professing them without coming across overbearingly.

He was the opposite of Booker in that way. Cole was the calm to Booker's passion. While both men had exceptional work ethics, Booker knew how to play, where Cole seldom did. I couldn't remember the last time I'd seen him wearing something other than his hospital garb.

Differences aside, Cole, like Booker, was a good man. Compassion poured out of both, and their integrity was unquestionable. It was that quality I admired the most. They reminded me of my dad. Honorable. Cole was a med student at the University of Rochester when we met. I had a Biology lab that was way over my head, and he helped me out. I introduced him to Booker, and the three of us became fast friends.

"I'd say you have a few admirers at the high school. It doesn't appear as if you'll be overlooked for the prom," Cole said with a chortle.

"Good one, Doc. Hey, are those new scrubs?" Booker bantered.

Cole ignored him. "Do you know who wrote this?"

"N–"

"Yes," Booker interrupted me. "Maggie, the girl he's sweet on. I'm afraid our little boy is growing up." Booker wiped away a faux tear. To his credit, Cole *tried* not to smile.

"He doesn't know that for sure." I took their spoons away. Between the two of them, a fourth of the sauce was already gone.

"Tell me about her," Cole said while Booker set the table. He must have been hungrier than I thought.

I took a glass bowl out of the cabinet above the stove, then chopped up some roma tomatoes for a salad. "She's cute, smart, kind. You should see her with the kids at the elementary school. She lights up whenever we're there. They adore her. She gives up her lunch hour to help other students. She . . . What?" I frowned at their goofy expressions.

"I wish you could see your face. You're partially glowing. It pains me to say this, but you're right, Booker. Our little boy is growing up," Cole sighed.

"Keep it up and you two will have to fend for yourselves tonight," I said, placing the finished salad down onto the table.

"I'll be fine." Booker smiled. "I have some leftover lasagna I can warm up. Cole, on the other hand, will starve."

"I can take care of myself, thank you very much." Cole pulled a tomato slice out of the salad and stuffed it into his mouth.

"That's right. I heard you and Ron were good friends," Booker said innocently, the first clue a joke was coming. Booker was many things, but innocent wasn't one of them.

Cole studied him for a moment. "Okay, I know I'm going to hate myself for asking, but who is Ron?" Cole leaned against the counter and folded his arms across his chest, looking every bit the six-foot-three-and-three-quarters inches that he was.

"You know, Ron, as in Ronald McDonald."

I groaned. That was bad.

"I can cook," Cole said indecisively.

"Doc, you're the only person I know that can burn water."

"I have never burn—okay, once. Are you ever going to forgive me?"

"You ruined my favorite pan."

As they continued the horseplay, I arranged the rest of dinner on the table, grateful the harassment of me had ended, temporarily anyway.

While we ate, Cole shared with us the details of a particularly gruesome bowel operation he'd observed that day. He removed a pen from his pocket and drew a diagram of the bowel on the back of his hand, something he habitually did whenever a piece of paper wasn't readily available. Booker turned three shades of green before asking if we could talk about something else.

"Fine, someone broke into my house last night. Is that better, ol' weak stomached one?" He added a few more details to the drawing as he spoke.

"How do you know? Did they *leave* something?"

"Ha-ha. There's a broken window and a set of footprints leading out the back door." Cole set the pen down and scooped the last of the meat onto his plate. Booker frowned at the now empty serving platter.

"The last time I was at your place you had a twin bed, a dresser, and an eleven-inch TV—black and white, if I'm not mistaken, and that's it." Booker put his plate in the sink before scrounging up a bag of sour cream and onion potato chips from the pantry.

"I don't spend much time there. The only reason I bought the dumb house was because you insisted I needed a tax write-off."

Cole purchased the yellow Cape Cod on Chestnut Lane after he completed his residency two years ago. He got a great deal on it because the builder had only finished the first floor before running out of money. Cole, with Booker's help, picked it up for a song. I'd be willing to bet he hadn't slept there more than a handful of times. Growing up with six brothers, Cole hated being alone, something that never happened at Port Fare hospital.

"And it's a color TV, for your information," Cole said, snatching the chips from Booker.

"We had better install one of my security systems. They have never been hacked into, as you well know," Booker said, swiping the chips back.

Booker's systems were top of the line. I'd never seen so many backup alarms. It made them a real pain to install.

"If I had something worth protecting I would. Whoever broke in didn't take anything. They probably just needed a warm place to sleep. It's been a brutal winter," Cole said, walking over to the refrigerator. "You got any dessert, Seth?"

"No, sorry, ran out of time. I have a huge English Lit test tomorrow, and I've been studying most of the afternoon. I think there's an ice cream sandwich on the top shelf of the freezer."

Cole looked at me strangely before removing the ice cream. "Sounds as if you're taking this whole school assignment pretty seriously. Studying?"

"It's a good class," I answered defensively.

He laughed.

"Cole, leave our hottie valedictorian alone and let's go outside and have a game of Horse. We need to work off dinner," Booker said. He walked over to the coat closet and retrieved the orange basketball from the back corner and one of my fleeces.

Cole actually groaned. "Not basketball. I suck at it, and you know it." He wadded up the ice cream wrapper, tossed it toward the garbage can, and missed.

Booker laughed. I cringed. No matter the sport, Cole somehow managed to injure himself and usually someone else during the game.

"Fine, hottie here and I will play Horse, you can play pig, and we'll even spot you the P and the I." Booker dribbled the ball a couple of times and pretended to shoot a hoop, then stopped. "On second thought, let's head over to Applegate Park and take a few laps around their jogging trail."

"Good idea. I'll get my sneakers from the car." Cole darted out the door before we could change our minds. So far, jogging was the one activity Cole could do without endangering anyone.

"It amazes me that a man so gifted at saving lives can't manage to play a sport without killing someone," I said while Booker put the ball away. I rubbed an aging bruise on my ribs where Cole had accidentally elbowed me the last time we'd shot hoops.

"Sports? Heck, the guy can barely walk without having to get stitches." We both laughed. "Did you see it? Left hand, little finger." I nodded, Booker shook his head.

"So, why Applegate Park? Why not the high school?" I asked, changing out of my boots. "The track there is lit up ten times brighter than the narrow jogging trail at the park."

"I don't know," he said, a little too easily. "I just got a feeling."

10
Maggie

*I*t was the first time I'd ever seen Bore the Snore genuinely excited, in a dull tedious kind of way. He spent the first ten minutes of class blabbering on about the facts and myths surrounding werewolves, speaking with such intensity I would have thought he truly believed in them. When Dwayne from culinary class tried contradicting him on something he'd said, Bore gave him a week of detention for disrupting the class with nonsense. Funny, I thought mythology was all nonsense.

After berating Dwayne, he settled back into his dull mode delivering a dry lecture on the evils of SUV's, *again*. What SUV's had to do with mythology was beyond me. Sometimes one had to wonder about the man's thought processes. I blocked out the rest of his droning and instead rehearsed my little speech for Seth.

When the bell rang, I jumped out of my seat and ran toward the parking lot in an attempt to beat Seth there, my stomach churning the entire way.

I wasn't fast enough. There he stood, looking beautiful, waiting for me with the car door open, only his usual smile was nowhere to be seen.

"Thanks." My courage deserted me, and we slipped quietly into the car.

"You're welcome," he said, flipping the radio on and maxing out the volume. We rode to the elementary school listening to loud, mind-numbing music. Once at the school, he bolted inside, leaving me standing in the parking lot.

On Thursday, he wasn't in school, and Friday was simply a repeat of Wednesday. When we arrived at the school, I didn't bother hurrying. I knew he would be inside before I was out of the car.

"Children, take your seats. There's an assembly later today and class will be ending a little early," Mrs. Mathews said. "I thought we could draw some pictures for Mr. Seth and Miss Maggie, thanking them for the fun activities they've done with us so far this year."

They began wiggling around with excitement while I gathered the art supplies from the cupboard. Seth positioned the chairs around a big table in the middle of the room. While the children worked on their projects, we circled the table, carefully staying opposite of each other as we observed them. Many drew pictures of themselves smiling or playing with a toy, while some made pictures of the different activities we had done throughout year. Zane drew a picture of Seth and me reading books to him.

"I like to pretend you're my mom and Seth's my dad when you read to us. Is that bad?" My stomach twisted painfully as Zane explained the drawing. He'd been in three foster homes already in hopes of finding a permanent family, but so far nothing had worked out.

"No, Zane, that's wonderful." How my heart ached for these kids, these innocent victims who never asked to be born. I gave him a big hug and continued looking over the children's artwork.

Mrs. Mathews and I started gathering up the art supplies when they'd finished. I hadn't seen Elise's artwork yet and listened quietly in the background as she explained her drawing to Seth.

"This is Miss Maggie," she assured him, pointing to a stick figure with a large head and mismatched eyes. "I didn't know which Miss Maggie to drawed so I drawed a sad Miss Maggie."

"What do you mean?" Seth's curiosity seemed as peaked as mine. I inched closer, looking over his shoulder as best I could from a few feet away.

With her cherub face deep in thought, she began twirling a strand of her curly hair around her finger. "Before you and Miss Maggie camed here together, she looked different. Her eyes looked sad at first, but then she looked happy when she left." Seth sat down, and she climbed onto his lap before continuing. "But when you camed *with* her to class, her eyes looked happy all the time. She peeks at you and smiles sometimes."

Embarrassing. I wanted to stop her, but didn't want to look as if I'd been eavesdropping either.

"That's how I knowed she loves you and that's why I locked you guys in the closet so you could kiss her."

"So this picture is of Maggie before we started coming here together."

"No, this is her today. She has been sad for two times now and she never gets happy. I don't like it. You should try to kiss her again. Do you want me to lock you in the closet?" She looked hopefully up at Seth. "But you have to promise not to tell Mrs. Mathews. She said if we do it again we have to wash the desks instead of going to recess."

Seth laughed. "No thanks, Elise. Miss Maggie doesn't want me to kiss her."

"Yes, she does." She looked genuinely shocked he'd say such a thing. I quickly peered around for the teacher, hoping she'd break up their little chat. Elise took her small hands, wrapped them around Seth's grown up face, and looked into his eyes with all the earnestness of a six-year-old. "She's just scared."

"Alright, Elise, we need to go. Our visiting teachers can leave early today." Mrs. Mathews took her by the hand as she thanked Seth and me for coming.

Did I really look that bad? I shut the classroom door and walked silently to the car, leaving Seth inside to hang the last two pictures on the bulletin board. I had to tell him about Hillary and Zack. I wasn't sad. What Elise saw on my face was nervousness, that's all. She misunderstood.

Seth settled into the car several minutes later. When he turned the key over in the ignition, a loud crackling noise, followed by a popping sound made me jumped. "What was that?"

"I just blew my speakers."

I tried hard to stifle my laugh, though I could've sworn I saw the tiniest grin on his face. I took a deep breath. I had to do this. I had to let him know about Zack and Hillary.

"I acted like a big jerk on Monday, and I'm sorry for hurting your feelings." Wait. I hadn't planned to say this. What was wrong with me? Apparently, I had more to say because the apology continued to gush out of my mouth. "I'm uncomfortable with the flirting, and I should have told you instead of verbally attacking you. You've been very kind to me, and I do want to be friends. I hope I haven't blown that. I shouldn't have judged you like I did either, and again, I'm sorry."

He sat there in stunned silence looking at me. It felt like an eternity. Finally, he spoke. "I'm sorry, too. I shouldn't have said anything about Zack. If I'd known you two were dating again I wouldn't have."

"Zack and I aren't together." His eyes narrowed slightly as I made every effort to tell him as gently as possible about Zack's plan and about what Hillary had said.

"I told you, Hillary and I are just friends, although I don't know if I want to continue with the relationship anymore. Zack can have her, and he doesn't need to go to the Winter Fest to get her either."

"Zack said if I didn't go along with the plan he'd tell everyone I slept with him, which is a lie." My two fingers tangled up around my hair again. I hadn't notice it until Seth's eyes followed my hand.

"I wouldn't have believed him. You have too much going for you to throw your life away on a loser like Zack, though I'd like to know why you ever dated him in the first place." He reached over and tucked the stray hair behind my ear.

I asked myself that exact question many times. "I don't know. Besides, he kisses like a wet fish. Come to think of it, his breath smells like wet fish." He laughed at my wrinkled up nose.

I smiled. "So, can we be friends?"

"Yes, and if I slip up and start flirting just pop me upside my head," he said with a goofy grin.

"No lecture?"

"What?"

"You know, about the way I spoke to you the other day. No lecture? No, 'Maggie, you should learn how to express yourself without acting like a fourth grader,' or something along those lines?"

"I'm sure you've lectured yourself far more harshly than I ever would. You shouldn't be so hard on yourself."

I felt embarrassed by his kind words knowing I didn't deserve them. "What about the Winter Fest?"

"I guess we'd better go, though popping *fish boy* in the mouth would be ten times more enjoyable," he muttered. I couldn't agree with him more.

"Maggie." My heart skipped as he said my name. "You don't really think this double date will stop him from spreading lies about you, do you?" I shrugged, not wanting to think about it at the moment. It felt too good having the tension between us resolved.

"Hey, are you hungry?"

"I could probably eat something." *Okay, starving as usual.*

"Since we got done early, I was thinking of making a quick stop at the Burger Palace, my treat. What do you say?"

"Do you think we have time for a second breakfast, Frodo Baggins?"

He threw his head back and laughed. "Very funny, Samwise Gamgee." I also couldn't help noticing how green his eyes shone when he asked what I wanted at the drive up window. *Just friends, Maggie.*

Sadly, my happiness was short lived. Walking to my biology class half an hour later, I ran into Melody and Hillary giggling away in the hallway. Melody looked over at me and giggled again. Hillary sneered and left.

"Maggie, come here." Melody's eyes were all aglow. She must have gotten a juicy bit of gossip from Hillary and needed to share it before she exploded.

"Hey, Melody, how's it going?" I searched the far corners of my mind trying to come up with an excuse why I needed to be to class early.

"You're not going to believe what Hillary just told me."

"I'm not interested in what Hillary told you." I turned to leave, when she clutched my arm, digging her bright pink fingernails into my bicep.

"She and Seth did it." *No way.* "She said he has a huge mahogany four poster bed, and his—"

"Stop. I don't believe it, and I don't want to hear about it, either."

"I heard it right from the horse's mouth," she said indignantly.

"Why did she tell you, Melody? It's not as if you're best friends. It doesn't make any sense."

"We may not be best friends, but we *are* friends." She was more than a little miffed by my comment. "She knows I keep confidences." I laughed out loud at her. "There're lots of things I don't share with other people, Maggie. You'd be surprised at what Zack told me." She shot me an ignorant grin and left.

I didn't want to believe what she said about Seth, or maybe I hoped that in the end he'd have chosen me. A stupid idea, really. Why would he, especially if Hillary gave him what I wouldn't? Recommitting myself to a life of celibacy, I wondered how comfortable nun's habits were as I continued toward my class.

By noon, the cafeteria buzzed with the Seth-Hillary rumor. Zack sat at a table by himself, appearing deep in thought—a first for him. He wore a pair of expensive baggy jeans, which hung halfway down his butt, and a gray tee shirt with the name *Hollister* sprawled across the front. Mr. Original.

I searched around for Seth and found him sitting next to Hillary and her little clique, but he glared hard at Melody. He turned to me and smiled weakly. I smiled and waved. I debated whether to go and talk to him, as a friend, but decided instead to try to weasel out of Zack what he'd said to the gossipmonger concerning me.

"What lies have you been telling Melody about me?" I dropped my book bag down hard onto the table. He jumped.

"I don't know what you are talking about." He wadded up his uneaten pizza into a napkin and tossed it on his tray.

"If you're not going to eat that, can I have it?"

"You're absolutely pathetic, Maggot. Begging people for their garbage is a new low, even for you." He tossed it into the garbage can close by.

"It wasn't for me. There's a stray dog running around my neighborhood, I wanted it for him." Why I bothered explaining myself to a heartless jerk was beyond me.

"Like I said, you're pathetic." He wiped his hands off onto his jeans and leaned back in his chair. "I suppose you heard about Hillary and Seth?"

"Yes, but don't believe everything you hear." He only grunted. "Does this mean our double date is off for tomorrow, and I don't have to worry about you spreading any more lies about me?"

He sat staring at Hillary for a few moments before he answered. "Actually, this whole rumor thing is good news. It means the *other* rumors about her are true."

"What other rumors?" There were too many flying around for me to keep up.

"That she's a make-out whore. Obviously, she's willing to make-out if she's sleeping with that idiot. At the very least I'll be getting some lip action Saturday." His excitement made me ill. "If we happen to disappear at the festival Saturday, Seth'll have to take you home."

"You're revolting." I started to stand up when he grabbed my sweater.

"Don't worry, frigid one. He won't try anything with you. Why should he? He has a million girls to choose from, why would he pick a girl he'd have to beg to get what he needs?"

I stormed out of the cafeteria only to hear him yell after me, "Pick you up at 6:30 tomorrow, Frosty."

11

Saturday morning I made my mom a light breakfast. Her stomach still bothered her. I allowed myself only a single slice of bread in hopes of getting food at the festival. I worked on my homework, trying in vain to forget that I'd have to spend the entire evening with Zack.

He played his horn in front of my house at exactly 6:30, and I dragged myself outside. The sun had long gone, and the night sky was gloomy, which ironically mirrored my mood. I zipped my sweater up briskly and sulked to his car.

"Hurry up, will ya? We have to meet 'em at the entrance in fifteen minutes." He groaned as I sat down. "You're seriously wearing that vile sweater?" I folded my arms across my stomach and said nothing.

Seth and Hillary waited for us by the gate when we arrived. Seth had on his signature cowboy boots and a dark blue hoodie with the words *Port Fare* embroidered across the back in gold. The school colors never looked so good. He smiled at me and shoved his hands into the front pockets of his well-worn jeans.

Hillary had on a cropped white fur coat with an adorable pair of khaki pants. Her hair hung like spun silk around her beautiful face.

The perfect couple.

She threaded both of her arms tightly around Seth's right elbow, gloating. I dropped my eyes and forced myself next to Zack, strictly for the body heat. He took my hand, and with significant effort, I didn't flinch. Well, almost. Out of the corner of my eye, I saw Seth's shoulders bounce in laughter, and I smiled at the ground.

I'd never been to the Winter Fest before. It was magical. Small, twinkling white lights laced throughout trees. A light breeze caught the branches, and it appeared as if tiny fairies danced about the limbs. Ten yellow brick buildings filled the area, several of which had huge fabric banners flying across them.

A giant Corvette-shaped banner swayed on the building that held the car show. I pulled a face at the thought of having to go in there. A macabre clown-shaped banner graced the building that held the Funhouse. Another banner shaped like a giant bottle of Pepsi hung over the food court.

Green, pink, and blue paper lanterns strung along the sidewalks on a thin wire. They appeared to float in midair. There were carnival rides outside too, although anyone crazy enough to ride one would probably get a severe case of frostbite.

Both Zack and Seth wanted to go into the car show first. Zack quickly became enthralled with the shiny automobiles, not to mention the scantily dressed girls who modeled alongside them. I couldn't figure out what the girls had to do with the cars, but they made Zack happy. And because the area was jam-packed with people, I didn't have to hold his hand, which made me happy.

After what seemed like years, we moved on to the Midway packed already with carnival games and boisterous game operators. The operators attempted to draw customers into their cubicles with a challenge to "try your luck" at winning a myriad of prizes hanging from the walls of each booth.

Regrettably, the Midway was more accommodating for handholding. Zack grabbed my hand, squeezing it. I attempted to break free, but he held tight, dragging me to the Water Gun Shoot.

"Alright, young man," the operator said, handing Zack a water gun. "The object of the game is to shoot this water pistol at that red cup. The more water you get into the cup, the bigger the prize."

Smugly, Zack aimed the green plastic gun at the cup. "Watch this. I've been voted 'Most Valuable Player' on the baseball team for two years running now. This will be a cinch." *If only I had a nickel for every time I'd heard him say that.*

Despite his athletic prowess, he only managed to win a three-inch pink pig. Hillary squealed with delight. "Pink is my favorite color, Zack." *Oh, there was a shock!* He gave it to her without a second thought, blushing as she kissed his cheek.

Armed with a malicious grin, he handed me the gun, knowing full well I'd fail miserably. Numerous times while we dated, he forced me onto the ball diamond at the high school, insisting I help him with batting practice, and numerous times I beaned him with the ball, most of the time accidentally.

I snatched the gun roughly out of his hand and pointed at the target. True to form, I missed each and every time. Not a single drop landed in the stupid cup.

Zack took great pleasure in mocking me, and naturally Hillary laughed at his ill-mannered display. She took a turn next. "I don't know, Zacky, I've never done this before," she said, ripping the pistol from my hand.

Zacky? I rolled my eyes, as did Seth.

Even she managed to do better than I did, winning a poster of some antiquated rock star. Seth stood vexed with his arms across his chest, saying nothing the entire time, at least not with his lips. I half expected him to smack Zack on the head. He didn't. Too bad.

After Zack finished humiliating me with the water guns, he led us to another game. It consisted of three wooden bottles stacked on each other, and the object was to knock them over with a baseball. The game operator handed Zack three baseballs.

"Watch this." He winked at Hillary. She smiled and fluttered her eyelashes. Zack, clearly flustered by her flirty eyes, missed the bottles on all three tries.

"How about you, big guy?" The operator held out the baseballs to Seth, tempting him while pointing at me. "Want to win a prize for the pretty little gal?"

"As a matter of fact, I would." Seth picked up a ball, handed the guy a dollar, and took aim. Bam! The three bottles practically exploded into the air.

"Nice arm. Want to try again for a bigger prize?"

"Why not?" Seth again handed him a dollar, threw the ball, and blew away another three wooden bottles. He repeated his conquest three more times and was rewarded with any prize he wanted. He grabbed the huge stuffed fish hanging above his head and handed it to me. Hillary giggled.

Seth leaned over and whispered in my ear, "Remind you of anyone? And it's big enough you'll have to use two hands to carry it, if you do it right."

Hillary slithered her way between the two of us. "Seth, why did you give it to her? You're *my* date." She gave him her famed pouty little frown.

"You have a pink pig, Hillary," he said dryly. She went to take his hand and missed as he shoved them into his pockets. She settled for his arm. "Come on, let's get something to eat."

I arranged the fish across my stomach, wrapping my arms over the top of it and snuggling it close against me for warmth. Zack scowled. I looked at him innocently. He turned and stormed off ahead.

The food court was crowed. Zack, trying to impress Hillary, let me choose whatever I wanted to eat for dinner. I got the pepperoni pizza because I got two huge slices. The only open seating was outdoors. I swallowed a groan as we walked out into the bitter night air. "I bet you wished you'd worn a real coat now," Zack scoffed in my ear.

Seth set the food down on our table and slipped off his fleece, exposing a long-sleeved green shirt with a white tee shirt underneath. Not saying a word, he draped the hoodie around me. I tried to give it back, only he assured me he wasn't the least bit cold. I slipped in my arms and zipped it up tight. It smelled just like him, definitely a good thing.

"She gets your coat, too?" Hillary looked at him indignantly.

"Are you cold?" Seth asked, his tone blunt. She picked up her hamburger and took a small bite without answering.

When I finished, Seth offered to buy me another piece. I politely refused, though I was tempted to accept it and take it home for my mom.

Zack had parked himself next to Hillary, and judging from the expression on his face, felt the timing was right to make his move. We sat quietly as Hillary and Zack giggled and picked at their food. My hand went mindlessly to my hair, and I began twisting a strand.

"Will you stop doing that, Maggot?" Zack said, sneering over at me.

Setting his Diet Pepsi can down hard, Seth cleared his throat. "Her name is Maggie." Zack shrugged and went back to drooling over Hillary.

"Which car was your favorite?" I decided to try small talk to ease the tension.

"They didn't have my favorite car. I'm an SLR Roadster fan," Seth said after swallowing the last of his hot dog.

"A what?"

"An SLR McLaren Roadster. It's an incredible car." He practically cooed the words.

"Have you ever seen one in person before?" Zack asked. The talk of cars pulled him away from his prize, and she was none too happy about it.

"I've driven one." The smile on Seth's face made me laugh. How could anyone be that excited over a hunk of metal?

Hillary started fidgeting as the guys droned on about cars, not that I blamed her. I certainly hadn't meant to ignite the whole car-lust thing again. She slipped her arm around Zack's shoulders and began toying with his hair. "Let's go over to the Funhouse," she purred in his ear. She got up and tossed her barely touched hamburger in the trash. I couldn't believe she'd waste all her food, and my thoughts returned to my poor mother at home, eating nothing more than a dry cheese sandwich tonight. She and Zack walked off toward the building with the clown banner.

"Do you want me to take you home?" Seth ran his hand over my hair. It felt nice, really nice. Too nice. "I somehow have the feeling they wouldn't notice if we left."

"I've never been inside a Funhouse before, and since we're already here we may as well have some *fun*." I tucked the stuffed fish under my arm, and we walked toward the Funhouse. Once inside, Seth took my hand to lead me through the crowd.

"Seth, here's your fleece back. Thanks for letting me borrow it." I noticed a tight expression on his face when I handed it to him.

"What's wrong?"

"I'm not sure. All evening I've had this strange feeling we're being watched." He reeled around, searching the crowd.

"There are a lot of people here. I'm sure someone is looking at us." Well, looking at him anyway.

"True. My mistake." He smiled, putting his hand on the small of my back and aiming us toward the Mirror Maze.

"Are you sure you don't want to wear this?" Seth asked, holding out the fleece. "You look pretty in blue." Seth winked at me and a shiver plummeted down my spine.

"That's dangerously close to a flirt," I said, my voice a little wobbly.

He held up his hands, silently proclaiming his innocence with a shake of his head. Then, without warning, he grabbed my arm and pulled me behind him as if to protect me from something.

"I'm starting to feel a little paranoid," I said, looking around to see if there was anything abnormal going on around us.

"Sorry." He laughed. "Guess I had one too many Diet Pepsi's today. The caffeine's gotten me a little jittery. Come on."

If this were him a little jittery, I'd hate to see what he'd be like if he were to ever drink a cup of coffee. He'd probably have a nervous breakdown.

A metal pole with a green flag marked the entrance to the Mirror Maze, along with a worker dressed like the grim reaper. Zack and Hillary entered before us.

"You'll know when . . . if . . . you've found the right exit," the reaper explained in a macabre voice. "There'll be a pole just like this one, except the flag will be red. If you become confused and can't find your way out, don't worry. I'll find you . . . eventually. You can't hide from me." He laughed diabolically.

The mirrors were deceptive. More than once I ran into one or missed openings I thought were mirrors. I had new sympathy for all those poor mice running through mazes in search of cheese. Seth had little trouble maneuvering the mirrors, though he did run into one when he looked back over his shoulder.

Before long, the overhead lights flickered and an announcement blared over the speakers. "The Winter Festival will be closing in ten minutes. Please exit the park in an orderly fashion, and thank you for coming to this year's festival."

Somehow, I turned and Seth didn't. I couldn't see him anywhere. A sense of foreboding clutched at me and panic took control.

"Don't be ridiculous. You're not a child." After chastising myself for acting stupidly, I took several more turns, becoming even more tangled up in the maze. To make matters worse, no one else was around, and the bizarre silence felt eerie.

I came around another corner and stopped dead. The man from the park stood directly in front of me, this time with a purple plug in his right earlobe. He also wasn't alone. Next to him stood a slightly smaller, yet nonetheless menacing man. Dressed almost identically in black polyester pants and shirts they looked alike, only the smaller one wore white sneakers instead of black ankle boots. Their heavily blood-shot eyes lit up, and they each flashed a sickening smile at the exact same moment. I planted the stupid fish in front of me as it would offer some form of protection. My thoughts flashed to Tammy Byrne, and my knees went soft. I couldn't scream. I couldn't run. The larger of the two stepped toward me and ran into a mirror.

They *weren't* in front of me. It was only an illusion of the mirrors. I found my strength and took off running.

"Seth!"

"Maggie, where are you? Is everything okay?" Nearby, his voice sounded desperate.

I stopped and looked around. "The creep from the park is in the maze, and he brought a friend. Please, help me."

I saw someone out of the corner of my eye and spun around. It was them, except this time no glass stood between us. I screamed and took off. I looked back over my shoulder to see them only a few feet behind me now. I darted around a couple more corners and ran into Seth, collapsing into his arms.

"Are you alright?"

"Yes. Let's get out of here, hurry."

"Grab my hand and hold on tight," he said as we practically flew through the maze to the exit.

"How did you get through so easily?" I said, flustered.

"A little trick I picked up years ago. Don't look at the mirrors, look at the ground. It's real easy to find the openings that way," he said, catching his breath.

"You couldn't share that with me when we went in?"

He bent down and pulled up the pant leg of his jeans, then stopped and walked over to the exit, ripping the metal pole with the red flag out of its stand. "Wait here." With that, he headed back into the maze.

"Seth, No." But he was gone. I paced back and forth calling out his name. He didn't answer. It felt as if hours passed, when in reality it was probably only seconds. Then I heard it. Several loud crashing sounds as if the mirrors were being destroyed. He reappeared with his cell phone and several small cuts on his hands.

"Are you alright?"

"I'm fine. They got away." He actually looked disappointed.

Oh, yeah, way too much caffeine today.

"I called the police. They'll be here soon," he added, placing his phone back in his pocket.

"You're bleeding." I took his hands in mine and wiped off the small droplets of blood from his knuckles.

"Superficial wounds, that's all. I don't even need a bandage," he said, brushing off my near hysterical tone. "Maggie." Seth cupped my face in his hands. "I'm fine. You, however, look as if you're about to faint." He stroked my cheeks with his thumbs, scanning my face.

I wanted to kiss him. The thought hit me with undeniable force. Why did I think about kissing him at a time like this? I needed serious help.

"Maggie?"

"I'm fine," I said, snapping myself back into reality. I glanced over his shoulder and saw the two men dart out a side door. "There they are," I pointed, "leaving through that door." He turned to follow them.

"No! Please don't leave me."

His jaw tightened as he reluctantly turned back and led me over to a bench to sit down. Zack and Hillary stood off to the side. She flirted with a muscular college boy with the words *University of Buffalo* tattooed across his left bicep just below the sleeve of his blue tee shirt. Zack's eyes narrowed as she gave the guy a flirty grin. Man, the girl was a piece of work.

I sat down on a bench as people ran toward the debris. "How many mirrors did you break?"

"Let's just say they won't be using the House of Mirrors anytime soon," Seth said with a sheepish grin. He paced back and forth, never wandering far from my side. Twenty minutes later, Captain Gatto arrived, along with a young female cop.

Seth greeted Captain Gatto warmly, shaking his hand. "How are you doing?"

"Good thanks. This is Officer Whelks." They nodded to each other. "Can you tell us precisely what went on here?" Captain Gatto asked.

Seth explained everything, though he was somewhat sketchy about how many mirrors he'd broken. When Officer Whelks pressed for more details, Captain Gatto cut her off.

"How many mirrors he broke is beside the point, Officer Whelks." Captain Gatto turned his attention to me. "Are you sure he was the same guy from the park?" I nodded. "It's a good thing you had your boyfriend with you. I'd hate to think what might have happened if you were here alone."

I started to deny that Seth was my boyfriend, but decided it wasn't important in light of everything else.

"There was another murder day before last over by the park. Of course, this one was drug related," Officer Whelks said. "You weren't trying to buy drugs, were you? If I'm not mistaken, this is the second time you've had a run in with these guys." Her eyes fastened on me.

"I don't do drugs." I couldn't believe she tried to turn this around onto me.

"Maggie wasn't trying to buy drugs. We were walking through the Mirror Maze and got separated when those two guys appeared," Seth snapped at her.

"Whelks, why don't you talk to some of the witnesses? I'll finish up with these two," said Captain Gatto. She nodded and left. I watched her walk over toward Hillary who still flirted up a storm with the UB college boy.

"Sorry, sweetheart, she's a rookie. She gets a little excited. No harm intended."

He asked us a few more questions before leading Seth away to the broken mirrors. When they'd finished, Seth came back over to me.

"We should try and find Zack and Hillary," I said. They were no longer in the Funhouse, and Officer Whelks now flirted with the UB boy.

"Let's look outside. Do you feel alright?" Seth asked.

"Yes, I'm fine." He held my arm as we walked outside. I started to suggest we split up and look for them, but he shot the idea down before I finished my sentence.

"No, we stay together." He put his hand gently on the small of my back, and I shivered. I seriously needed to get my reactions to him in control. He took off his fleece and slipped it around me once again.

"No, Seth, I'm fine."

He frowned, daring me with his eyes to remove it. I quietly zipped it up. We walked through several buildings with no luck, eventually discovering them next to a small building near the entrance with their lips glued to each other and their hands all over the place.

"Yuck," Seth said. They never saw us. Seth bent down and whispered so as not to disturb them. "I'll take you home." His warm breath sent *another* shiver down my back. He pulled the coat around me tighter.

"Thanks." I tossed the fish down, kicking it toward the garbage can. I looked up at Seth hoping he wasn't angry at the way I treated his prize. He wasn't. He kicked it, too.

As soon as we got in his car, he cranked up the heat again, steering the vents in my direction as before. He also pressed a small button on the dashboard I hadn't noticed before, and heat began radiating throughout my seat. He laughed at my surprised expression.

"I had them change it out for one with a built in seat warmer when they replaced my speakers. Does it work well?"

"Yes, isn't yours working?"

"I only had the passenger seat replaced," he said casually, as if he had picked up a loaf of bread from the store.

For a moment I wondered if he replaced the seat just for me, then decided I needed to get over myself. After scolding my narcissistic thought, I snuggled down into the deliciously warm seat.

He stopped along the way and bought us a couple of large shakes, mine chocolate and his vanilla. I found him easy to talk to, and we sat outside my trailer, with the car's heater on, for over two hours doing just that. With caring for my mother consuming most of my energy, I'd never taken the time to cultivate any close friendships. I hadn't realized how much I'd missed out on until that moment. I finished off my shake embarrassingly fast, and he gave me his, claiming he wasn't as hungry as he thought.

I opened the car door, removing his jacket as I got out.

"Thanks for the coat."

"Why don't you keep it? I have several, and besides this one looks good with your blue eyes." I started to protest when he interrupted me. "Maggie, please keep the coat. I can't stand watching you walk around in this flimsy . . ." he quickly added, "although cute, sweater every day, knowing how cold you are. I have four others in my closet collecting dust anyway." Not knowing how to argue that without sounding ungrateful, I slipped it back on. "If it will make you feel better, you can earn the coat. I could use your help delivering lunches to the seniors on the weekends. It's only two hours each day, and you can count it for your mythology project instead of writing the paper."

"That's a great idea."

"Don't look so surprised. I do come up with good ideas every now and again." He tugged the jacket's hood down over my eyes and laughed.

"I didn't mean it like that," I said, sliding it back. "The assignment's been like a noose around my neck, and I had no idea how I was going to finish it. Helping with the lunches is the perfect solution."

"Can you start next weekend?"

"Yes, and thanks, Seth, for everything. You're a real lifesaver. Good night." I turned toward my door. He followed. I looked back at him, puzzled.

"What's the matter?"

"I'm not letting you go into the house alone. It's pitch black in there. The attackers could be hiding inside, Maggie. You seem to be a magnet for them, in case you hadn't noticed." I had noticed actually. "I'll go in and look around first."

Panic set in. I knew exactly what he'd find and it wouldn't be the two goons; it would be my mother passed out on our ratty brown couch and an empty vodka bottle lying on the floor next to her.

"Seth, we've been sitting here for two hours. We would've spotted anything suspicious by now. Besides, my mom's here. I'm sure everything's fine. She's probably asleep, and if we wake her, she can be really cranky without her eight hours of beauty sleep," I said, laughing nervously.

"If you think I'm letting you go inside alone after all that's happened, think again." He gently pressed past me, took the key from my hand, and slowly opened the door.

"Where's the light switch?" I reached around him, flipping it on. I cringed as my mom flung her hands up to block the light from her eyes. None of my friends had ever seen my mother before, not even Zack.

"Turn that thing off. Can't you see I'm trying to sleep, you selfish little brat." She slowly sat up on the edge of the couch.

"Hello, Mrs. Brown. How are you?" Seth was the perfect gentleman. I wished I were dead. "My name is Seth Prescott. I'm a friend of Maggie's from school."

She tried to stand up, but collapsed. Seth caught her and set her gently back down onto the couch. The sleeves to her faded pink blouse slid up as he did. She jerked her arms away and tugged them back down.

"You're a friend of Maggie's, ah? She never brings her friends here." Her eyes closed in an effort to regain her balance. She forced them open and looked up at Seth. For a few seconds they twitched strangely.

"Wow, you're a handsome kid. What does a boy like you want with Maggie?" Suspicion etched her brow. "Just what kind of friend are you?"

My cheeks flushed. "We have a few classes together, Mom."

"Unless I'm mistaken there are no classes at midnight."

"We were on a double date. I was with another guy, and Seth offered to bring me home." The rest of the details weren't necessary.

Much to my horror, she spoke again. "Yes, I'll just bet he did. I know exactly what you want with her, young man, and you're not fooling me with your refined manners either." She drew herself up off the couch and limped toward her bedroom. She stopped and turned back to Seth. "I'm warning you now. If she gets pregnant I'm not taking care of another baby."

Burying my face into my hands, I sank to the floor in horror.

"I'd never disrespect your daughter, Mrs. Brown. She's a great girl, and you're lucky to have her." His tone left little doubt of his anger.

She snorted. "That's what they all say until they get what they want, then you're stuck with a screaming little brat on your hands," she pointed her chin to me and grimaced, "and he's nowhere to be found." She stammered into the bathroom and shut the door.

How completely and utterly humiliating.

Seth walked over to me and pulled me up to my feet. I couldn't look at him. I fought with everything inside me not to cry. He slipped his thumbs under my chin and lifted my face to his.

"I'm really sorry," I said, trying to pull away, only he wouldn't release me.

"Maggie, she didn't mean what she said. She's had a bit too much to drink tonight. It's the alcohol talking."

I was about to tell him this was how she always was and that she wished I'd never been born, but I couldn't get the words out. Instead, I put on my best fake smile and nodded.

"You're right. Alcohol does cloud your mind."

"I'd better get going," he said, still holding my face. "Thank you for a lovely evening. Despite the whole mirror incident, *and* Zack and Hillary," he said wryly. "I had a nice time tonight." He looked at my mouth as his thumb softly traced the outline of my lower lip. I was about to lean into him when he pulled his hands away. "That would definitely be considered flirting. Sorry. See you Monday."

I wanted to be angry with my mom for her embarrassing display. I wanted to be angry that Seth knew more about me than I had ever allowed anyone to know. I wanted to be angry with both Zack and Hillary for what they had done to us tonight, yet I couldn't.

I laid Seth's fleece on the rickety chair in my room, and changed into my PJ's, pulling the fleece back on after brushing my teeth. Mmmm, it still smelled like his aftershave. "Oh my gosh, what is wrong with you, you stupid, stupid girl?" I ripped off the coat, tossing it across the chair again. I didn't want a boyfriend, and I didn't want to be used by some guy either.

Yet inside I knew Seth wouldn't do that. He'd never use a girl. He was like no one I'd ever met. He was the kind of person I wanted to be, and I was falling more and more in love with him every day. However, his being a guy I knew he'd have expectations, and I wasn't going to meet them. I had my own dreams and expectations.

But having a secret crush on him wouldn't hurt anyone. I reached over and grabbed the jacket. "Yup," I giggled. "I'm a stupid girl."

12
Seth

"*Good* morning, Barry Bonds. How's the arm doing today, slugger?"

I did my best to ignore Booker's teasing and continued thumbing through mug shots.

Undaunted, Booker persevered. "Twenty-three mirrors. Twenty-three. That has to be a record. Do you have any idea what the chief's going to say when she gets the bill for twenty-three mirrors? I'd hate to be in your shoes." He grinned and took a sip of the hot chocolate he held.

"Next time I'll draw out my service revolver and explain to the crowd that there is no need to fear, I'm really an undercover MET agent trying to bust up the local heroin ring," I said dryly. "I knew they were there, Book. Everywhere we went I could feel someone watching us. I should have trusted my instincts and left before we went inside the Funhouse."

"Any luck with the pictures?"

Rubbing my strained eyes, I shook my head and slammed the last book shut. "Nothing, nada, zilch. I can't believe these guys have no criminal history."

"In *this* area, they're most likely from out of town. We'll put out an APB across the state. Someone's going to recognize them."

Booker picked up the artist's sketching of Alan and winced. "A face only a mother could love. The guy has zero fashion sense. I mean, seriously, black polyester?" He set his cup down and started thumbing through mug shots. "Maybe they're not the big time dealers we thought they were. Maybe they're wannabees like Hoffman."

"Speaking of Hoffman, I met Maggie's mother last night. Before you ask, I checked for track marks. Her arms were clean."

"As you well know, the arm isn't the only place for needle marks. There's the feet, and—"

"I couldn't very well strip her down, Book. And in answer to your next question, I didn't smell it in the air either. If she's smoking the stuff, it's been quite a while. No sticky black residue on the walls or light switches, or *anywhere* as far as I could see, and I saw no drug paraphernalia lying around."

"When I spoke with Maggie after the Byrne murder, I didn't see any either," Booker said, taking a sip from his cup.

"I did notice the place smelled like a brewery. Maggie was pretty embarrassed. I felt bad. How could a mother embarrass her own daughter like that with no remorse?" I shook my head in disgust.

"How's the unrequited love coming along?" Booker offered me a drink from his mug. It was good.

"I like it. New recipe?"

"Avoiding the question?"

"We're friends, and growing closer," was all I would comment to. She needed time. I could wait until she learned to trust me.

"She should be eating out of your hands by now if you're doing what I told you to do."

"It wasn't working. We're friends, and that's good enough for now. I'm taking it slow. She . . ."

Booker yawned dramatically.

"When you start dating . . . *if* you ever have a date again, we'll compare notes. We're friends. We'll get there. She's worth the wait, Book."

Booker's face softened. "You really have it bad for her, don't you? I don't believe I've ever seen you this *gone* about anyone before." He took his mug back. "Okay, enough of this love drivel. Let's find these two scumbags before anyone else gets hurt."

Booker pulled me out of my chair and parked himself down in front of my antique laptop. Booker frowned while waiting an eternity for it to boot up. "Geez, kid, cave men had faster computers than this."

"Tell me about it. Try filing a police report on that dinosaur."

Several minutes later, he began typing a memo for the police stations across the state. These two polyester men had to have been in trouble before. People don't just turn evil overnight. Unless I missed my guess, these two had a long, lengthy criminal past, and Booker and I intended on finding it.

13
Maggie

It'd been three weeks since the Winter Fest. Every morning without fail Seth picked me up for school and brought me home again afterwards. When I tried protesting, telling him I'd lose all my muscles for the track team tryouts, he volunteered to take me to his gym.

"I work out with the weights there," which explained his gorgeous body, "but they also have a running track that's free to the public. We can go together. I've wanted to incorporate some cardio in my workouts anyway."

I didn't protest the rides again. I wasn't too upset really, with all the murders lately and the whole Funhouse fiasco. Besides, it was comforting not to have to walk to and from school alone.

I also enjoyed my time delivering lunches to the shut-ins. Since I was now part of the Lunch Swap team, I had to wear a uniform. It consisted of jeans and a white tee shirt with the Lunch Swap insignia, a ham sandwich embroidered on the left breast pocket. Seth said it was okay to wear the jeans to school if I wanted. I questioned whether the owner would be angry if I did, but he reassured me the guy was a cuddly old teddy bear, and I didn't have a thing to worry about.

"Mr. McSheehy's hip is almost healed," Seth said as we pulled up in front of the small house on Front Street. I was relieved to hear he was doing better. I'd been adding some of the chicken from my lunches into his, hoping the extra protein would help expedite his healing. "Did you notice he used a cane last week?" I nodded as he handed me McSheehy's lunch. "And have you also noticed he has a crush on you?"

"Seth, Mr. McSheehy is eighty-seven. I doubt he has a crush on me. He's too old."

"Once you reach eighty-seven you no longer have feelings?" He cocked a quizzical brow at me. "Watch how he acts while we're here. It's as if I don't exist." I shook my head and walked up to his door. "I'll leave you two alone if you want," he said. I playfully smacked him on the chest as the door flew open before we could knock. There stood Mr. McSheehy with a huge grin on his face.

"Hello, Maggie, you look lovely." He hugged me gently. I could hear Seth's quiet laughter as he closed the door behind us.

"Hello, Seth, how are you?" Mr. McSheehy shook Seth's hand, not nearly as warm a greeting as I received. "Tell me, son, what took you so long to bring this lovely lady with you?" He directed us over to some chairs and we sat. "She's easier on the eyes than old Sam." He patted my hand as Seth coughed to cover his laugh.

"My dear, please don't be offended, but I've noticed the sad state of your shoes. I'd like to help."

Shoot. I'd forgotten to tuck them under my chair. He drew a small worn leather coin purse out of his pocket and began digging out some money. "Son, please take her shopping for new shoes after you leave here."

"No." I softly pressed Mr. McSheehy's hand and coin purse back. "Thank you anyway. I planned on getting some new shoes, and just haven't had time to go to the mall yet." I felt terrible for lying, but I'd rather die than take money from a sweet old man who barely had enough to live on as it was.

"Mr. McSheehy, I'll take her shopping as soon as we're done here. Next week you won't recognize her feet."

"You two had better get going. It's supposed to snow six to ten inches tonight and those shoes will never do. I'd miss you if you became ill and didn't come," he said, patting my hand gently. "You remind me of my daughter. She was lovely also, and kind, like you. She died of influenza when she was only sixteen," he said though teary eyes. "Be off with you now. Scoot."

"I guess this disproves your crush theory," I said, climbing back into his car.

"That was really sweet." Seth made a U-turn, heading in the opposite direction of my house.

"I thought he was our last delivery, where are we going?" I double-checked the list to make sure.

"To buy you some shoes." He looked at me as if it was obvious.

"I didn't bring any money." I didn't have any money.

"You can pay me back later."

"Seth," I swallowed hard. "I can't . . ."

He pulled over to the side of the road. "Maggie, you know I can easily afford this, right?" He cupped my chin in his hand. "Please let me help, as a friend."

I thought for a moment. "Okay, but," I said, holding up a finger, "only if you'll let me work them off, like I am with the jacket. I'll continue helping you deliver lunches until you feel like I've paid you back, fair and square."

"Deal." He smiled and slowly pulled my face close to his, kissing my cheek. My poor heart went crazy. "Still friends, right?" I could only nod my reply, mostly because I couldn't speak. "Good, let's go shopping." He held my face a moment longer before letting go.

Seth took me into several shoe stores in the mall, each one more expensive than the other, and I refused to try on the shoes. Finally giving up, he asked which store I wanted to try. I dragged him to a discount shoe store where I'd once gotten shoes as a child. *The Shoe Horse*.

A huge sign hung above the door of a black stallion rearing up on his haunches wearing white high-top sneakers. Several years ago, a neighbor had brought me here while shopping for her little girl. The store offered a 'Buy one, get one free' sale, and she let me have the free pair, even allowing me to choose the pair I wanted; shiny pink shoes with black bows. I wore them until the soles clapped when I walked and my toes bled from being pinched at the end.

"Maggie, these are not very good shoes. They'll hardly last a year." Shaking his head, he flipped the shoes over and looked at the soles.

"But look." I pointed to an aged sign in the store window. It looked like the same sign that hung there all those years ago. I got the impression this 'Buy one, get one free' sale happened often.

"A deal isn't always a deal."

"I think you want me to buy expensive shoes so I'll have to keep helping you deliver the lunches," I teased.

"Hmm, I hadn't thought of that. We're going back to the expensive store for sure."

"I'll help you until college starts, I promise. Are you sure the people who run the charity don't mind?"

"I can do whatever I want." He smiled angelically. With that face, I didn't doubt it.

I tried on a pair of heavy-duty brown shoes. They weren't exactly attractive, but they'd keep my feet warm and dry. Neither rain nor snow could possibly get through these marked down, ugly bad boys and they were marked down, a bonus. Seth made a face when I showed him. He picked out a cute pair of slick black snow boots from the window display. He gave the thumbs up after I tried them on.

He wandered off toward a display of socks as I placed the ugly shoes back in the box. My eyes landed on a pair of black, strappy pumps on display next to me. Unable to resist, I quickly slipped them on. They look so pretty. I walked over to a mirror and pulled up the hem of my jeans a few inches to get a better view.

"They look good on you, Maggie," Seth said from behind. I spun around quickly and lost my balance. "Sorry, I didn't mean to startle you." He held my arm to steady me.

"I'm fine." I hurried over to a stool and slid them off, putting my holey shoes back on. "They're not practical. I doubt I'd ever wear them."

"Sometimes you need to step outside your comfort zone. It's okay to let your hair down and take a few risks. It's not as scary as you think and it's certainly more fun." I got the feeling we were no longer talking about shoes.

"I'll just take these two pair, thanks."

I gathered both pair and took them to the register. Outside the store, he led me to a bench in the mall, and removing the ugly brown shoes from the box, he handed them to me with a contorted frown. I laughed and gave him my holey shoes.

"May I?" he asked, holding them over a trash can.

"No, I've had them for a long time. They've served me well."

"Why do you still need them?"

"They'll make good slippers. If I come home from school and my shoes are wet, I can slip those on." I beamed proudly at my prudent thinking. "And thank you, Seth. You really didn't have to do this."

"You're welcome, though I could've gotten you slippers too."

He gave me the leftover lunches when we arrived at my house. Tucking the shoeboxes under his arm, he walked me to the door.

"Thanks for your help today."

"You're welcome. Why do you need my help delivering the lunches anyway?"

"I like the company." He ran his hand through my hair, playfully ruffling it up. "A friend of mine named Sam used to help deliver the lunches. He's ninety-two and had a stroke a few months back, and it became too much for him. You met his grandson Booker the other night at the festival. He's the detective who interviewed us."

Cute Detective Booker Gatto was a friend of Seth's? Small world.

"Thanks again, for everything."

I rested my back against the doorframe and watched him drive away, wishing I didn't care for him as much as I did. I didn't want to get involved with anyone. Just friends, that's all I wanted, no matter how much my heart screamed at my head for more. I tossed my silly heart's ranting out and went inside.

There was blood everywhere.

14

"Mom!" I followed the blood trail to the bathroom and found her in a heap next to the toilet, moaning. "Mom, what's wrong?" I dropped to the floor and pulled her frail body into my arms, searching for wounds.

"What do you think is wrong?" she hissed. "I'm sick, you stupid child." A fountain of blood abruptly gushed from her mouth, spattering my clothes.

**

We arrived at the hospital via ambulance. They immediately rushed my mom away while an aide abandoned me in a dreary waiting area off to the side. I was left alone to pick at some loose threads on the sea foam green couch under the annoying flickering of fluorescent lights for nearly three hours. If someone didn't talk to me soon, I'd go mad.

"Hello, I'm Dr. Colter. Are you here with Barbara Brown?" I jumped at the deep rich voice of the long-legged doctor as he stepped toward me. I had to tilt my head back to see his face. He wore brown leather clogs and blue scrubs that intensified the color of his deep blue eyes. His golden blond hair softly framed his gentle face, and when he stepped closer, I noticed a few freckles peppered across the bridge of his straight nose, giving his handsomely chiseled face a youthful appearance. He also had a small round bandage on the underside of his jaw.

"I'm assuming you're her daughter, Maggie, correct?" I nodded again and shook his hand. "I need to ask you some questions, if that's alright." He proceeded with a few routine questions about her health history, making notes on her chart as I answered. He then went straight to the root of the problem. "Does your mother have a drinking problem?" I whispered a yes and lowered my eyes to the ground. "For how long?"

When has my mother not had a drinking problem? "She's been drinking all my life."

He led me over to the couch, and I sat down. "Maggie, your mom has developed several ulcers along the lining of her stomach and the alcohol is exacerbating them, which was why she was throwing up blood. I'm afraid she'll need to stay here for a few days. We'll have to give her a blood transfusion, and I'd like to admit her to our detox program, though she's insisting she doesn't have a drinking problem."

In my dreams I shifted uncomfortably on the couch.

"She is also refusing to let us do any further tests on her. I'd want to check her liver and pancreatic functions," he said, sitting down next to me. "Her coloring is somewhat poor, and I'm afraid she has other health issues, apart from the ulcers, that should be addressed. Without running the tests, we can't treat her properly. Will you speak with her over the next couple of days and encourage her to let us do the tests?"

"Sure, I'll try." But I knew she wouldn't listen to me either. He led me to her room, and before leaving he told me she'd been sedated and probably wouldn't be awake until tomorrow. A nurse brought me a pillow and blanket, along with some clean hospital scrubs to change into. In my rush to get to the hospital, I'd forgotten about the blood all over my clothes.

I slept very little in the lounge chair next to my mother's bed and rose with the sun the next morning. I spent the rest of the day wandering around the hospital, thinking about the homework I couldn't do and watching my mother sleep. Whenever she woke, she'd yell at me to *"get me out of this stinking place."* Dr. Colter came in to see her shortly before dinner.

"Hi. I haven't been able to speak to my mom about the tests yet. She's slept most of the day."

"The medication she's on tends to cause drowsiness. I'm hoping to take her off it tomorrow." He put his hand on my shoulder and gave it a gentle squeeze. "You should go home and get some rest, you're exhausted. Is there a phone number we can reach you at?" I gave him the phone number of my neighbor, Mr. Hoffman, and left, taking the bag of soiled clothes with me.

The sun had all but disappeared over the horizon, and the heavens shone in ribbons of orange and deep red. It felt peaceful, and

I walked slowly to drink it in. All too quickly, the sky began fading to an inky black, the peaceful feeling vanished, and I now felt unsafe. I tightened my grip on the bag and continued for home, exhausted, mentally and physically.

"Hi, what are you doing out here alone?" It was Booker Gatto in his police cruiser. He smiled at me as if we were old friends while his eyes combed down my scrubs. "Nice outfit. Do you work at the hospital?"

"Hello." I gave him the short version of a long story. "I was visiting someone, and I'm on my way home now."

"How are you getting there?"

"I was going to take the bus, but I forgot my money." I wondered how much trouble you could get into for lying to a police officer. "I guess I'm walking."

"Miss Brown, I'll take you home. I can't in good conscience let you walk home alone." Since I was dead on my feet, I was glad he offered. I slumped down into his car and tried not to fall asleep with the car's gentle rocking.

"How's our mutual friend doing?" he asked. I looked at him, bewildered. "Seth Prescott," he reminded me. I nodded, my mind still back at the hospital.

"Yes, he mentioned he knows your grandfather. They volunteer at the same charity, the Lunch Swap."

Booker laughed. "Lunch Swap *is* Seth's charity."

"*His* charity?"

"Yes. His father started it and after he died, Seth took over." You could have knocked me over with a feather. Seth Prescott, a senior in high school, owns the Lunch Swap.

Oh, no. I had completely forgotten about helping Seth today. I couldn't call him and apologize since we didn't have a phone, and even if we did, I didn't have his number. Just when I thought it was impossible to feel any worse.

Captain Gatto and I exchanged a few pleasantries, he insisted I call him Booker from here on out, and he dropped me off at my house. I hesitated on the porch, not looking forward to the mess ahead of me, but I had homework inside waiting to be tackled and standing on the porch wouldn't get it done.

I opened the door wanting to shut it again straightaway. It smelled worse than I'd remembered. Dragging out the cleaning supplies, I began scrubbing. Thankfully, we didn't have carpeting otherwise it would have taken a lot longer than two hours to finish. After several more hours of grueling math homework, I finally crawled into bed at 2:20 in the morning.

When the alarm went off at 6:45 a few short hours later, it took every ounce of my self-control not to chuck it across the room. While showering, thoughts of not only my mother, but also of Seth were front and foremost on my mind. I had misjudged him terribly. He was a pretty terrific guy. He owned the Lunch Swap. How many eighteen-year-olds *did* charity work, let alone owned a charity?

After dressing, I started toward Mr. Hoffman's house to use his phone, meeting up with Gertie, my elderly neighbor from across the street instead. She let her demon cat inside and asked me in for a freshly baked cookie. I explained my need to call the hospital, and she insisted I use her new cell phone, a recent gift from her grandchildren. I followed her as she waddled slowly inside. Her stupid cat I'd nicknamed Lucifer hissed and spit at me the entire time.

Her home was smaller than ours, but it had a welcoming ambience to it. The mouth-watering smell of hot chocolate chip cookies permeated my nostrils, along with the stench of litter box. My eyes turned to the cat and it hissed at me once more.

Small, hand-crocheted doilies decorated the backs of all the chairs, and a large one covered the middle of the couch. She had several worn area rugs throughout the living room and kitchen, and two antique lamps that flooded the room with rosy lighting. I couldn't make out the fridge's door with so many photographs of her children, grandchildren, and three recent additions. "My great-grandchildren," she pointed out proudly.

I made the call and thanked her for the use of her phone. "Here, my dear," she said, handing me a bag of cookies as I headed out. "Have a good day at school, and dress warmly." Homemade cookies, the last time I had them was when my grandmother and I baked some the morning of our car accident.

I rushed back over to my drab house to finish getting ready. I just finished brushing my teeth when someone knocked at the door. Fearing the worst, my heart immediately began pounding.

Stay calm, Maggie. You talked to the hospital, and she's fine. Despite my calming words, I ripped the door open so fast I was surprised it didn't fly off the hinges.

"Seth." I took a step back. I hadn't expected him at all.

"Aren't you going to school today?"

"Yes, I'll get my stuff." I scooped up my book bag and followed him out to his car. "About Lunch Swap on Sunday, I'm sorry, something came up, and I completely forgot about it. I owe you double time now."

"Don't be silly. I understand."

"I feel awful. We don't have a phone, so I couldn't call you, not to mention I don't have your number."

"Don't worry, Maggie, things come up. Is everything okay?"

"Ah, yeah, everything is fine, really." I debated for a moment about whether to tell him, finally deciding against it. Too humiliating. Instead, I changed the subject. "Did Mr. McSheehy ask about the shoes?"

"Yes. I thought he was going to start dancing when he found out you bought two pairs." We both laughed as Seth did a dead-on imitation of Mr. McSheehy. It felt nice to be distracted, even if it was for only a brief moment.

"Well," Seth said, getting out of the car, "I'll see you at lunch." He started to leave, then turned back. "Are you sure everything's okay? You look upset, and I won't even mention the dark circles around your eyes." He ran his index finger softly under my eyes.

"Thanks for pointing out how bad I look." I playfully pushed his hands away.

"Sure, what are friends for?"

"I had a ton of Calculus homework last night, and I think I have the wrong book. Mine's written entirely in Japanese."

"I love Calculus. I'll help you with it."

"Nobody loves Calculus, at least nobody normal does."

He chuckled. "You'll love it by the time I'm done helping you, you'll see. If not, I'll kiss you so long and hard, you won't care about Calculus anymore."

"I don't care about Calculus now. And for the record, that was definitely flirting."

He grinned innocently and left for his class.

Between my lack of sleep and worrying about my mother, I had a difficult time concentrating on school. By lunchtime, my nerves were frazzled. Usually loud shouts and laughter filled the cafeteria. Today, however, the room gave way to low whispers and murmurings. I nervously sat and waited for Seth.

"Hello, Maggot." I cringed. Apparently, the silent treatment Zack had been giving me was over. He dropped into the seat across the table from me.

"Hi." I swallowed a less civil reply. He had a stupid grin smeared across his face, looking as if he were dying to say something.

"What?" I spit out impatiently. I may as well let him say whatever he wanted to say. Maybe then he'd go away.

"I hear your drunkard mother's in detox at the hospital, Maggot."

Before I could react, Zack flew out of his chair with the assistance of Seth, who had lifted him up into the air. He dropped him forcibly onto his feet, causing Zack to stumble and fall back a few steps. Seth followed. He arched his arm back before throwing his fist straight into Zack's jaw, sending him flying across a table before he landed on his rear. To my surprise, several people in the immediate vicinity cheered.

"Her name is Maggie," Seth said before spinning back to me. "We need to talk—outside." I slipped on my coat as he placed his hand on the small of my back, guiding me out into the parking lot.

"I thought we were friends." His eyes froze me in place.

"We are."

"You have a pretty warped idea of what friendship is, Maggie. I walked into my first period and was cornered by Melody, who blabbered on and on about how *my friend* spent the past day and a half in the hospital with her sick mother. You couldn't let me know?" He stood only inches from me, his breath beating against my face as he lectured. "You could have mentioned it this morning when I picked you up, Maggie, but no, you sat there in silence, not saying a word." He turned away and ran his fingers through his hair before circling back around and continuing. "This isn't my idea of friendship. I don't know what you call it. A convenience for you, maybe, but friendship, *no*. Whatever it is, it certainly isn't what I want it to be. Maybe we shouldn't *be* at all."

I couldn't take it, not on top of everything else. My eyes filled with tears and I snapped, "Wait here. I'll go get a knife and you can plunge it into my chest and finish me off." Not expecting my reaction, his eyes widened. "Sorry I'm not one of your little cheerleader friends who can pour their guts out to anyone who'll listen." My tears ran wildly while my entire body shook with anger. I needed to leave and turned to do so when Seth stopped me, cradling me into the warmth of his chest. It caused me to cry harder.

"I'm sorry." His voice mellowed as his hands stroked my hair. "I didn't mean to add to your problems. If you want to talk, I'm here. I'm done acting like the village idiot."

It felt nice to be in his arms, as if someone actually cared about me. He listened, never judging or criticizing, just listening as I told him what had happened with my mom.

"Do you want me to take you over to the hospital after school to see her?"

"That'd be great, thanks." The bell rang as he wiped a few stray tears off my face.

"Did you know Hillary and Zack broke up?" he said, taking my hand. "They dated for a total of one week. It seems she wouldn't sleep with him so he dumped her. She's so upset she's telling all the girls he's gay." He chuckled. "He can't get a date, not with a girl anyway. I did hear Rick Thompson from his science class wants to ask him out."

"Ugh, I thought Rick had better taste than that," I said.

"We'd better hurry to culinary class. Hopefully we're cooking something delicious. I didn't have time to eat lunch, you know. I decided acting like a fool and harassing a friend was more important." He pulled my hand to his lips and kissed it softly. I faked an exaggerated shudder. He laughed and kissed my hand again.

"You know this could be considered flirting."

My warning fell on deaf ears as he answered, "It sure could."

Rounding the corner, an ominous welcoming committee greeted us. "Mr. Prescott." Next to Vice Principal Volkel stood Zack nursing a large red mark on his chin. "Zack Finkle has accused you of punching him, but it seems no one in the entire cafeteria saw what happened. Is this true?" She looked at Seth in disbelief, only before he could answer, Hillary appeared out of nowhere.

"I saw the whole thing, Mrs. Volkel." Uh-oh, I remembered how much Mrs. Volkel worshipped Hillary. Seth was toast. "Zack began clowning around in the cafeteria, flirting with his girlfriend Maggo—ie here," she pointed at me with a brutal look in her eyes. "He tripped over his own two feet, and Seth tried to catch him, accidentally hitting him in the face. Zack made this whole thing up because he was embarrassed."

Mrs. Volkel turned to Zack. "Mr. Finkle, that will be a week's worth of detention for lying." He began to protest, as did Seth, except she ignored them both and escorted Zack to her office by the scruff of his shirt. Hillary didn't say a word to us as she turned and walked away. I had little doubt she tried to score points with Seth.

"Weird," Seth said. We walked down the hall, joking about the expression on Zack's face as he flew across the table. I laughed so hard my side ached. Once inside the classroom we had a pop quiz, but no food. I slipped my lunch out of my book bag and split the sandwich with him, along with half the cookies. He tried refusing until I gave him a hard glare. He drew a panic-stricken expression on his face and took the sandwich, his hand shaking in mocked terror. What a goofball.

***

My lack of sleep caught up with me on the drive over to the hospital after school, and I fell asleep in Seth's car.

"Maggie." Something warm brushed against my cheek. I awoke to see his face only inches from mine. I looked into his eyes, down at his mouth and back to his eyes. One more time my stupid eyes dipped to his mouth.

"Sorry." I shifted away from him. "I haven't slept much the past few nights." I scooted out of the car and sucked in a lung full of cold, crisp air to clear my head.

Walking into my mom's room a few minutes later, I recognized the expression on her face instantly; she wanted a drink.

"Hi, Mom, how're you doing?" I leaned in awkwardly to hug her, and true to form, she shoved me away.

"How does it look like I'm doing, stupid?" Her insults were commonplace to me, but I felt embarrassed having Seth hear them. I'd hoped she'd play nice if she knew we had company.

"Mom, do you remember Seth?"

She stared at him for a moment before nodding. "Yes, yes, the handsome boy. What are you doing here?"

"I brought Maggie to see you. She's been worried."

"I wonder what this random act of kindness is going to cost her. Wait, let me guess, you brought her here purely out of the goodness of your heart." She was beyond sarcastic now, she was behaving downright rude.

"Mother," I said, shame washing over me.

"I have homework to do, Maggie. I'll be in the waiting area studying until you're ready to go. No rush," he said, walking out the door. My mother didn't wait for it to close before she started up again.

"Maggie, he's much too handsome. Mark my words, he's only after one thing."

Thanks, Mom. You sure know how to build me up. I walked over to the window and leaned against the sill. "When are they going to let you leave?"

"Tomorrow. Why? Are you planning on letting him into my house while I'm gone?" She narrowed her eyes. "You stupid—" Dr. Colter came in cutting off her insult. I noticed he walked with a slight limp.

"Good afternoon, Maggie, how are you doing?" He smiled warmly and limped over to my mom.

"Hello, Dr. Colter. I'm fine, thanks. Did you hurt your leg?"

"Oh, well, yes. It's nothing. I twisted my ankle getting out of bed this morning," he said, his ears now bright red. "Just one of those freak accidents." He turned to my mother. "Mrs. Brown, how are you feeling?"

"I want a drink, that's how I'm feeling." The agitation in her voice was tangible.

"We've talked about this. The drinking has to stop, Mrs. Brown, your body can't take much more. Think about Maggie."

"Why do you think I drink?" she said, folding her arms tightly across her body.

The warm smile abruptly left Dr. Colter's handsome face. "Your blood count is increasing." His tone had turned cold and formal. "If you continue to improve we may send you home as early as tomorrow."

"I want to go now."

"Not a wise choice, Mrs. Brown. You may need another transfusion, and if you go home now you'll be back in here by the end of the week." She grumbled something under her breath I couldn't quite hear. Judging from the way Dr. Colter's jaw clinched, he heard it just fine. "You should reconsider going into our rehab program. We have an excellent unit here at—"

"I already told you I'm not going into rehab. There's nothing wrong with me. Get out."

He didn't fight her. What would be the point? If she wouldn't help herself, there was no rehab program in the world that could help her. "Good afternoon, ladies." As soon as he left, my mom started on me again.

"This doesn't mean you and that boy can go into my hou—"

"Time for your medicine, Mrs. Brown." A perky young nurse came in with a syringe full of something and injected it into the IV tubing. "Hello, I'm Natalie DeLyzer, and I'll be taking care of your mother tonight. I'm afraid this medication is going to make her sleepy. You may want to say your goodbyes quickly." My mom's eyelids already drooped as I brushed the hair off her forehead.

She shoved me back without opening her eyes. "Go away, brat."

"It's the medication, honey. She doesn't mean what she's saying." Not having the heart to disagree with her, I left.

I was tired of loving a woman who didn't love me back.

I made my way over to Seth. He and Dr. Colter talked in the lounge area. "Hey, that didn't take long. No need to rush on my account." Kindness filled Seth's eyes even now after the terrible way my mom had acted.

"They gave her something to help her sleep."

"This is who you're waiting for?" Dr. Colter smiled widely at Seth.

"This is the girl I was telling you about, Maggie Brown. Maggie, this is Cole."

"Yes, her mother's a patient of mine. You should take this pretty young lady home. She needs some sleep. She's hardly left her mother's side."

"I will. See you later, Cole."

"Do you know everyone in town?" I asked, walking to the car.

"I know one doctor and suddenly I know everyone?"

"Booker Gatto?"

"That still hardly constitutes everyone, Maggie."

"Speaking of Booker, he gave me a ride home from the hospital last night. Why didn't you tell me Lunch Swap is your charity?"

He shrugged modestly. "I don't know."

"Are you going to tell me about it?"

"Fine, while I make us some dinner." We drove to the local Wegman's grocery store. He filled the small cart with an assortment of foods, including, red, green, and yellow peppers, scallions, boneless chicken breast, Jasmine rice, and stewed tomatoes, to name a few.

"All this for one meal?" I tried not scowling at the huge bulb of garlic he sat on the checkout counter.

"A lot of this is for the Spanish rice, it's my favorite. And remember, you like this now," he said, pointing to the garlic.

Back at my house, he had me mix up some honey and butter for the brown bread he bought while he worked feverishly over the rice dish.

"Where is your garlic press?" I handed him a knife, and he rolled his eyes. A few minutes later he asked for our cheese grater. I again handed him a knife. He shook his head. "We should have done this at my house."

I set the table as he added sautéed chicken breast to the rice. It sizzled deliciously in the pan, and my stomach quivered in anticipation.

"Okay, enough stalling, Mr. Double Standard. Spill it," I said, sitting down to the feast.

"Double Standard? How do you figure?" He sprinkled a minuscule amount of salt on his rice after taking a small bite.

"You want me to tell you about everything going on in my life, yet you neglect to mention we've been delivering lunches for *your* charity."

"Maggie, holding everything inside because you don't trust anyone and not bragging about a charity you run are two totally different things."

"Possibly." Amazing how well he knew me already.

"Don't let the left hand know what the right hand is doing. Sounds familiar?"

"Fine, the left hand just found out about the right hand, so tell me."

"My dad started the Lunch Swap, wanting to give back to the community, and I think he wanted me to be aware of the needs of others around me." Seth sliced each of us a piece of bread before continuing.

"He believed there were those who didn't want a handout and if offered a free lunch they wouldn't accept it, which is why the Lunch Swap isn't free. For example, Mr. McSheehy lectures at local schools and organizations a couple of times a year about his experiences in World War II. Instead of paying him, the groups who schedule him donate the money to Lunch Swap, which helps defray the cost of the lunches. Miss Ethel crochets baby blankets. I take them to a local thrift store, and whatever money they make on the blankets, they donate to the Lunch Swap. Some of our clients do services for each other," he said, spreading honey butter on his bread. "Others help out by coming into the shop and preparing the lunches. To be part of the Lunch Swap family you have to donate time or a service to someone within the community. It's unimportant how small the act is, it's the act itself that matters. We're helping each other. No one has ever been turned away because there's always something a person can do to qualify."

"It's a great idea," I said, slathering a large chunk of honey butter on my bread. It tasted delicious.

"The senior citizens love it because they feel useful again, and they don't feel guilty for taking a handout because it's not. I learned a lot while working with my dad, and after he died, the best way I could show my appreciation for all he'd taught me was to continue with the Lunch Swap."

I looked at him in awe. He was an amazing guy.

"What's the matter?"

"Nothing," I said with a smile.

He reached across the table, touching my hand. "I thought we were past the whole blocking me out thing."

"A leopard doesn't change its spots overnight."

"As far as I know you're not a leopard." He raised his brow at me.

"I was thinking you're an amazing person. There, happy now?"

"Yes," he said, grinning smugly. "Did that hurt?"

"Horribly." I grimaced in mock pain.

"Do you want me to kiss it better?"

"Amazing, yet still a hopeless flirt."

"Only with you, Mags," he said. "Only with you.

After dinner, he took my hand while we walked out to his car, and my heart skipped a beat, or maybe three, I hardly noticed anymore. I'd grown accustomed to my body's overreaction to him.

"Dinner was wonderful, thank you. Are you sure you don't want to take some home? There's enough left to feed a small army," I said, pulling my hand away to help steady my heart. Okay, maybe I still noticed.

"Positive, you keep it." I slid my hands into my pockets, cold nesting in every pore of my body. Seth reached over, zipped my jacket, and tugged the hood up.

"Maggie, I don't like the idea of you sleeping here alone, not with these killings going on."

"Seth, I'll be fine. I stay here every night and nothing has ever happened."

"Why don't you spend the night at my hou—"

"No!" My heart leapt into my throat. I knew it. We hadn't even dated and it already started.

"Maggie, I didn't mean anything by it. Don't overreact. If it makes you feel better, you can stay at my house, and I'll come back here and sleep."

"That'd be silly. I'd be alone there, too. Why does it matter whose house I'm alone at?"

"The murders have been on this side of town, Maggie. I wasn't suggesting anything else."

I guess that could have been what he meant. "Sorry. I'll be fine."

"Be careful. Lock the doors and check all the windows." He pulled out a cell phone, punched several buttons, and placed it in my hand. "Here, take this." His hand immediately sprung up to my mouth. "If you don't take it, I'll throw you over my shoulder, drag you off to my house, and tie you up in the basement. Your choice," he said sweetly. "If you need me, if you get scared, if some strange feeling invades your body and you feel like you want someone to talk to," he said, arching an eyebrow, "call me. I programmed the speed dial, button number one, to call my cell directly."

"If I have your phone, how can I call you?"

"This is a pay-as-you-go phone. I picked it up for you at the hospital gift shop," he said nonchalantly.

I felt ashamed for jumping to conclusions. "I don't deserve a friend like you."

He took my face in his hands and looked into my eyes for several moments. Sliding his hands around to the back of my neck, he pulled me slowly toward him and caressed my cheek with a kiss no more than half an inch from my lips. "I'll see you in the morning," he whispered against my skin.

Oh, man, I'm in so much trouble.

15

*E*arly the next morning, I called and checked on my mom. The nurse informed me that she'd had a rough night, and Dr. Colter had changed her medications around to see if that would help ease her through the withdrawals. He wanted to bump back her release date to Friday. She'd throw a fit.

Seth called as I finished my shower. "Are you still alive?"

"Sort of." I patted the water off my face. "The undead came in the middle of the night, and, well, I hope you don't mind having a friend who's a vampire."

"I hear they're not so bad once you get past the whole blood sucking thing."

"Good, hurry over, I'm thirsty. Maybe I'll nibble on you a little before school." I realized I flirted as soon as I sputtered out the words. Me, flirting, definitely a first.

"Hmm, is that a promise?"

Realizing I had no comeback, I abruptly ended the conversation and finished getting dressed. Seth knocked on the door as I tied my sensible brown shoes. "Come in."

"There're crazed killers running around, and you yell 'come in' without knowing who's at the door?" He shut the door behind him and checked to make sure the living room window was locked.

"I heard your car."

"Unless you can see through the door, you couldn't be sure."

"Ah, that's part of my new vampire skills, x-ray vision." I smiled slyly.

"Impossible."

"How do you know? Are you some kind of vampire aficionado?"

"I meant *you* are impossible."

I laughed. "Let me grab my book bag, and we can go."

"Wait." He caught me around the waist, pulling me next to him. "You said if I hurried over you'd give me a little nibble."

"I thought we were just friends, Mr. Flirt, remember?"

"What if I want to be more than just friends? What if being just friends isn't working for me anymore?" Without a hint of a smile, he leaned forward to kiss me.

But I didn't want him to, did I? Fortunately, or unfortunately, I wasn't sure which, someone began pounding on the door, saving me from having to decide.

"Come in," I said automatically. Seth threw me an exasperated look. I cringed. "Sorry."

My neighbor, Mr. Hoffman, entered with the customary sneer on his face. "Is the hospital going to be calling me all day?" Certainly not the first time he'd complained about having to take a message for us.

"I have a cell phone now so they won't bother you," I assured him.

"When does your Mom get home?"

"Probably not until Friday."

"She owes me money." His voice was a low grumble.

"Money? What for?" As if I didn't know already. Booze. Since our phone service got canceled the day before Christmas for lack of payment, she'd been asking Hoffman to pick it up for her. I'd always leave a check for him in the exact amount, but she must have increased her order again. I had no idea how I'd pay for it.

"See, your mom's been running a little low on her vodka lately, and I've been buying some for her. She said when her check came she'd skim a little off the food budget to pay me back," he said, looking at Seth, then back to me. He stepped closer, and I drew my head back. He reeked of alcohol and cigarettes, a gross combination.

"A pretty young thing like you, maybe we can work out a deal so your mom doesn't have to pay so much in cash," he murmured low in my ear, running a finger up my arm.

Seth crossed the room and had Mr. Hoffman up against the wall in less than a second. "Get. Out. Don't *ever* touch her again. Don't even *look* at her. Do I make myself clear?" Mr. Hoffman's eyes popped open wide. He nodded, saying nothing as he lost his balance and slid to the floor. He scrambled to his feet, and Seth handed him a wad of folded up bills from his wallet. "Does this square up what her mother owes?" He nodded at Seth, still too frightened to speak. "Get out."

I felt stupid. "Thanks." I headed to his car, and stood quietly, waiting for him to open the door.

"Your mother . . ." His eyes turned a brilliant green and his face burned bright with anger. Clearly fighting for control, he didn't finish his sentence. He ran his fingers through his hair and opened the car door without another word.

We drove to the school in deafening silence. As always, he was around to my side of the car before I could get out. "How do you do that?" I smiled, hoping to lighten the mood. "You move stealth-like. One minute you're over there, and then suddenly you're next to me. It's very impressive. In fact, I don't even hear you approaching. It's like *poof,* suddenly you're there."

"I do not *poof,*" he protested drily. With a whole lot of effort, I held back a giggle. I jumped in front of him and began walking backwards to see his face.

"Do you have a magic wand up your sleeve?" I pressed. He shoved the arms of his shirt up, proving there was nothing up his sleeves, so to speak, although I did get a look at some really great forearms. He took hold of my shoulders, guiding me through a group of kids who passed us. "Seth, please don't let Mr. Hoffman upset you." I halted my walk, not wanting to chance a collision. "I've had to deal with creeps like him my whole life. You learn to ignore them."

He looked at me as if I was insane. "You're okay with what happened?"

"No, it's disgusting, it makes my skin crawl, but that's life. There's nothing I can do except deal with it."

"Maggie, it's not how life is. Your neighbor's a creep. Most people don't live like that, and you shouldn't have to either. You do realize the reason you go hungry all the time is because your *mother,*" he said the word with choler, "drinks your food money away."

"She's sick."

Gently shaking me, he let out a rush of air, his mood noticeably calmer now. "And you say I'm the amazing one. I think not." Wrapping his arm around my shoulders, he softly kissed my forehead as we walked to mythology together. I felt somewhat nervous having his arm around me, yet a part of me enjoyed it too much to say anything.

After school, he took me to the hospital. I stayed for only a few minutes. Mom was unbelievably rude, not to mention angry at having to stay longer. "I may actually prefer her drunk," I said as we left.

By Friday, she wanted out badly. Due to a paperwork glitch, we weren't able to leave the hospital until almost ten p.m... Seth drove us home and helped me get her inside and into bed. She was still heavily medicated, but not heavy enough to stop her from harassing Seth. To his credit, he said nothing.

"Thanks, *again*. I owe you more than I can ever repay," I said, walking him to the door.

"I'm keeping track, you know. So far, you owe me quite the kiss. Don't worry. I'm not ready to collect . . . yet."

"When did we rescind the no flirting thing?" He answered with a shrug as he turned to go. "Wait, here's the phone back. I won't need it anymore, thanks." I dug down into my pocket to retrieve it.

"Maggie, I'd feel much better if you kept it at least until w— they catch the killers. Remember, all the murders have been on this side of town," he pointed out.

As soon as he left, I went straight to bed. Lack of sleep was my biggest enemy. I became downright loopy, if not totally unreasonable when I didn't get enough. Thankfully, tomorrow was Saturday. It meant two things: sleeping in and delivering lunches with Seth. I smiled, tucked the threadbare purple blanket under my chin, and drifted off.

I didn't sleep well at all, waking up several times during the night in a panic and running to check on my mom. At 6 a.m., I finally gave up on sleep altogether and got dressed.

I was excited to see it had snowed. I could wear my new boots. After weeks of false promises from the weatherman, we finally received some decent snow. I slipped them on and shoveled our sidewalk. When I finished, I began clearing off Gertie's and discovered Fluffy fast asleep on her porch. "Hey, dog, are you two timing me?" He came bounding across the snow, barking for me to pick him up. I quickly finished and took him back to my house.

Seth suggested we take him along on our lunch deliveries, which turned out to be a big mistake. It took us twice as long to finish, having to fight to keep the dog from getting into the food. Normally spending extra time with Seth wouldn't have bothered me, only with my mom being fresh from the hospital I worried about her being home alone.

By the time he dropped us off, it was nearly three o'clock. Fluffy darted out of the car door as soon I opened it and took off after Gertie's cat. Aside from the free food, it was apparent he didn't like the car ride. I rushed into the house, setting the extra lunches Seth always gave us on the table.

"Mom, I have some food, are you hungry?" I tossed my fleece on the couch and ran to my room to change out of my boots. The house was too chilly for bare feet so I pulled on my makeshift slippers and my old sweater before heading back to the kitchen for some food. I found my mom standing by the table, glaring down at the lunches.

"Hey, Mom. How are you feeling?" I zipped up the sweater against the cold.

"What did you do to Mr. Hoffman?" Her voice was as cold as ice. It stopped me dead. "He told me to leave and never come back again." I surmised she must have gone over there first thing to get some vodka.

"Mom, we don't need him anymore. You're getting better. It's been almost a week since you've had a drink. You can do this, Mom. The doctor sai—"

"I. Don't. Care. What. The. Doctor. Said. *I* decide what's best for me." Her erratic breathing and red face worried me.

"Where did you get that coat?" She pointed to the fleece Seth had given me. "Did you take what little money we have and spend it on yourself, you self-centered brat?"

"No, Seth . . . gave it to me." As the words left my mouth, I knew she would twist his gift into something salacious.

Her eyes narrowed. "And what exactly did you give Seth for the coat?"

"Nothing, Mom, he's not like that."

"They are all like that, so don't kid yourself." She turned back to the lunches and continued with her inquiries. "What about this food? Did he give you these also, or did you buy these because you're too lazy to cook? These are expensive."

I had never served her one of Seth's lunches in the Styrofoam container before, having always set it on a plate for her. "No, they didn't cost us anything, I—"

"*Liar!*" She took the lunches and flung them across the living room, the contents spewing everywhere.

"Mom, I worked for those." As I explained Seth's charity to her, she stomped across the room and stood less than six inches from me.

"You stupid idiot." She slapped me hard across the face. "Don't you see what he's doing? He's using you. I won't raise another child if you get pregnant, do you understand?" Not having her full strength back, she stumbled against the table.

"I'm not sleeping with him," I said, rubbing at the sting on my cheek.

"Hah! I've seen the way you look at him. You've been warned, young lady. You will not bring a child into this house, is that clear? I'll drag you down to the clinic, and you'll get an abortion, like I should have done with you." She dropped heavily onto a kitchen chair.

I felt sickened by her words, and told myself the alcohol withdrawals caused her hideous mood, but my heart still broke to pieces. She was my mother, for crying out loud, did she feel nothing for me?

"I met your father while at a party with one of my girlfriends. I was only sixteen years old. He was incredibly handsome, just like your precious Seth." She dropped her head against the back of the chair and shut her eyes. She never spoke of my father. Whenever I had asked about him, she'd say he was a loser and drop the subject.

"He plied me full of gin and tonics all night. I can't remember how many exactly, but too many. The next morning I found a note on the pillow. *'Hey, Betty, thanks for a great time.'* Not only did he get my name wrong, he didn't even sign the note." She snorted. "I never did learn his name. When I figured out I was pregnant, it was unsafe for me to have an abortion. I was so angry. I didn't want a stupid baby to take care of. I didn't even want you back then." She rose off the hard kitchen chair, limped slowly over to the couch.

I was too stunned to move.

"After my parents found out I was knocked up, they practically locked me away. I couldn't drink again until after you were born.

They railed on me daily, lecturing me on the dangers of drinking while pregnant. For some unknown reason they cared about you." She grumbled something under her breath, shaking her head in disbelief. "I decided to give you up for adoption. My parents arranged for me to meet with a social worker named Debbie Watcher. She wasn't much older than me, maybe five years, and we became fast friends." She smiled while reminiscing about her old friend. I couldn't ever remember seeing her smile before. It looked strange. "We'd sit in her office telling drinking stories for hours. We even planned a huge celebration party for after you were born. Not to celebrate you, but to celebrate my freedom."

Nausea invaded my every pore. I thought deep down inside she cared about me and just had trouble showing her emotions, like me. I was wrong. Never before had I felt so completely alone; I mattered to no one. I was a zero, a cipher, an unlovable nothing as she had always claimed. No longer capable of standing, I dropped to my knees.

Oh, God, please just let me die, now.

"Do you know why I didn't give you up when you were born?" Apparently, my mother wasn't done destroying me. She continued, even though I didn't answer her. "One day Debbie came to visit me at the house. She was one of the few allowed in to see me. My parents trusted her." She laughed. "She'd been drinking and let it slip that if I kept you, I could get government aid to help raise you. All I had to do was fill out some forms. I had no idea it was that easy.

"After you were born, I used the money to move out on my own, finally free of my meddlesome parents. About six months later, they found out I was drinking again, and we had a huge fight. I agreed to let them have you if they didn't tell social services, so that I could still get my money. Everything was working nicely until they got killed in that stupid accident. I got burdened with you and a permanent limp." She glared at me. I felt the tears stinging my eyes, but there was no way in the world I'd give her the satisfaction of seeing me cry. Numb, I silently cleaned up the tossed lunches.

"Two more months, Maggie, then you're out of here, and out of my life. I'll no longer have to take care of you. You've been nothing but a drain on me from the moment I found out I was pregnant, but soon I'll be free."

I lost it. Withdrawals or no withdrawals I'd reached my limit. "Take care of me? When have you *ever* taken care of me?" I peeled myself off the floor and continued in my rage. "You care more for your booze than you do for me. *You traded me away* for that stupid bottle of vodka you lovingly nurse all day long!" I saw something flash in her eyes. Tears, maybe? No, not from my mother.

"I cook. I clean. I put you to bed at night. Please enlighten me, when have you ever taken care of me, or loved me for that matter?"

"Get out of my house," she yelled at the top of her lungs. "I regret ever giving birth to you, you unlovable nothing!" She picked up a glass from off the coffee table and shied it at me. I turned and left as it hit my shoulder.

The cold winter air propelled me back against the door. I wanted to go and get Seth's fleece, only there was no way I'd go back inside. I started running, not caring where I ran to, simply running. I wanted to run away, away from everything and everyone and never come back, leaving my miserable life behind.

It started snowing, a heavy wet snow, and soon shivers overtook me. I'd gotten used to riding in Seth's warm car, and my body rejected the cold I inflicted on it now. I kept forcing myself to run to try and increase my body heat. My legs began to feel numb, and still, I pushed harder. The tears flew, and no matter how hard I tried to stop them, they kept coming. More than once, I collapsed on the ground, sucking in air to nourish my oxygen-deprived lungs. When the pain from my mother's words started to engulf me again, I forced myself back up onto my feet and took off running once more.

Only after coming around the corner on Ivy Circle did I realize where I was. Sprinting onto Seth's porch, I didn't knock. Instead, I stood there, panting hard. Why had I come here? Seth didn't love me.

But I did love him, and not only did I love him, I needed him. And I never needed anyone before. I needed him to help me somehow mend the shredded soul my mother had taken such delight in destroying. I needed to feel his arms around me. I needed—

The door flew open and Seth's eyes met mine in complete surprise. "Maggie, what are—" He grabbed me, pulling me inside.

I threw myself into his arms. "Kiss me," I said, shocked by my own bluntness. He held me back, staring into my eyes for several moments.

"Maggie, what's wrong? Did something happen to your mom?" His brows were knit tight with concern, but not desire.

"No! Please, kiss me." I couldn't help but beg him. How utterly pathetic. I tried to reach for his face, but he held my hands firmly down at my sides.

"Are those men after you?"

"No." Defeated, I dropped my head onto his chest. I *was* totally alone. All his flirting was just that, flirting. I had allowed myself to fall in love with someone who didn't return my feelings, who would never return my feelings. My mother was right. *I am unlovable. I am nothing.*

"Maggie, please," he said, stroking my wet hair. "Tell me what's wrong."

For some reason he began shaking me.

"Stop it, why are you shaking me?" My teeth chattered as I spoke.

"I'm not shaking you, you're trembling." My entire body trembled. Seth scooped me up in his arms and carried me to a bench by the door. Pulling a blanket from off the edge of the bench, he wrapped it around my body and set me down on his lap. His hand vigorously rubbed my back in an effort to warm me up.

"What happened? Please, Maggie, you must know you can trust me by now." I couldn't stop shaking, and I felt as if I were in a dream. Everything began spinning, and I lowered my head onto his shoulder.

"Maggie!" He sounded frustrated. Could I trust him? I did feel safe here with him. Even if he didn't love me, he was still my friend, if nothing else. My heart was about to explode with sorrow, and I began to cry again. He pulled me in closer. "Please," he pleaded softly in my ear, "you can trust me."

I couldn't hold it in any longer, the hurt was too big. The bitter ugliness poured out of my mouth. I told him every horrible thing my mother said, every horrible name she called me, including that I was unlovable. Crying harder now, my breath jerked painfully in my chest.

"It's not true, Maggie." The anger in his voice was unmistakable. He gently wiped the tears from my face, caressing my cheek in the act.

"Mmmm, your hand… hah… is … hah… really warm." While pressing my face into his hand, I tried to steady my breathing.

"No, Maggie, you're really cold."

He leapt up and carried me up the stairs, rushing me through a bedroom and into a huge bathroom. He set me down in a chair next to the biggest bathtub I had ever seen. He started filling it with hot water as billowy white steam clouds danced through the air.

"What are you . . . hah. . . doing?" I felt disoriented and closed my eyes.

"You're going to take a hot bath. Your body temperature is dropping, and we have to get it back up. Do you like bubble baths?"

"I don't know, I've . . . hah . . . never had a bath, at least not that . . . hah . . . I can remember. We have a shower . . . hah . . . in the trailer." My teeth chattered, and my breath still rippled. Seth's brows pulled together in a frown once more.

"Bubbles. Girls like bubble baths."

I wanted to ask how he knew that, and maybe suggest it was a sexist thing to say, but my energy level rapidly dropped. I was also curious to know why he had bubble bath in the house, except the image of Hillary in this tub was more than I could handle at the moment. I shoved it out of my head.

He knelt in front of me, unwrapping the blanket, and removing my ragged sweater. He tossed both next to the door. "Where are the coat and new shoes we bought for you?"

We bought? "I left in a . . . hah. . . hurry." His jaw tightened as he removed my shoes. Still dizzy, I leaned back against the counter for balance. He unbuttoned my shirt and pulled me next to him to slide it down and off, setting me back against the counter again.

"I'm going to go outside the door. Take off your jeans and tank top and hand them out to me. Can you get into the tub by yourself?"

"Yes," I said, standing up and immediately falling over. He caught me around the waist.

"Are you sure?"

"I don't really have many . . . hah . . . options, do I?" I steadied myself with the counter. Seth picked up the wet things already taken off me, closing the door behind him as he went out.

I started peeling off my wet jeans. Since I was shivering, and the jeans were drenched from the heavy snow, the task wasn't easy. Seth's knocking on the door every ten seconds to ask if I was all right didn't help much either. I finally managed to remove the rest of my clothing, handed them discreetly out the door, and climbed into the bubble bath. I cringed aloud as I sank down into the mountain of bubbles. The hot water stung skin. Before too long pleasure replaced the pain. I couldn't remember ever experiencing anything so enjoyable. Seth had to be right about girls liking bubble baths. This girl certainly did.

Slowly, very slowly, the shivering stopped as my body warmed, though my toes and fingers stung painfully in the process.

"Maggie, how are you doing?"

"Better, thanks." My breathing had returned to normal.

"I have some warm broth I want to bring in. Are there enough bubbles to keep you covered?"

"Yes." I sank down deep into the tub until only my face peaked through. He entered with his eyes closed and walked over, never once peeking, and handed me the cup of broth.

"Thanks, for everything," I said, taking the broth from him.

"You're welcome." He started to leave, and without looking back added, "Your mother is wrong, Maggie, you know that, right?"

I didn't say anything. I couldn't out of fear I'd start crying again.

"I'll be downstairs when you're done. If the bath gets cold, just add more hot water, and don't fall asleep in the tub. I don't think you'd like it much if I had to drag your naked body out of there and give you mouth-to-mouth resuscitation." There was a definite twist of humor in his voice as he shut the door.

I added hot water twice and caught myself falling asleep twice. I decided to get out before Seth did indeed have to come in and rescue me.

Even though the bathroom was well heated, the air was much colder than the hot water, and I immediately started shivering again. Having no clothes, I wrapped myself up in a huge towel. I also couldn't stop yawning. I timidly opened the door that led into the bedroom he had carried me through earlier.

The room was lovely. Along one wall was a magnificent antique armoire with beveled-mirrored doors. The far wall had a huge bay window with a built in bench-seat beneath it. A long slit of daylight peaked through the oatmeal colored, lace curtains hanging in the window. A huge antique brass bed sat centered along the inside wall. It was quite tall and had a small wooden step next to it, presumably for help getting up into it. A silky, deep green quilt laid spread across the length. I gave way to another yawn just looking at it.

"I'll lie down for a few minutes until Seth comes back with my clothes. I doubt he'll mind." I climbed up onto the big bed, dropping the towel onto a chair next to the bed so as not to get the bedding wet, and crawled beneath the soft quilt. The bed felt every bit as soft as it looked, and I sank into it, tugging the quilt around me, cocoon like. It felt wonderful. Suddenly remembering why I was in this big wonderful bed, I curled up on my side, shut my eyes tight, and refused to let my mother's voice enter my head.

***

"Maggie. Maggie." I felt someone rubbing my arm and calling my name, only the voice didn't sound like my mom's voice. I forced my eyes open.

"Seth!" I sat up quickly, and the quilt slid down my shoulder, my bare shoulder. I quickly tugged it back up.

"I'm naked!"

"Yes, you are." Seth smiled mischievously. He sat on the edge of the bed.

"Why, how—" Confused, I looked around the room and it came back to me, all of it. I sank back down onto the bed, pulling the quilt over my head.

"How are you feeling?" He pulled the quilt away from my face, exposing my eyes.

"Naked." I pulled the quilt around me tighter. "Is this is your bed?"

"Yup. I know it's not a four poster mahogany bed, but I like it." He smiled softly. The rumors about him and Hillary were a lie. "When was the last time you ate something?"

"Yesterday. I finished the last of the leftover rice dish for lunch." I watched as his face clouded in anger.

"Can I ask why? What about the two lunches I gave you earlier?"

"My mom was upset. She thought I used her money to buy them, and she tossed them across the room."

He silently rose off the bed, pulled out a sweatshirt and some sweatpants from the armoire, laying them on the foot of the bed. "Your clothes are almost dry. Put these on, they should keep you warm. You can change into your things after dinner."

"If those sweats fit, I'm never eating again." I smiled, hoping the grave expression would leave his face.

He tossed a thick pair of white socks onto the bed next to the sweats. "The pants have a draw string waist, so you should be able to tighten them enough to stay up." His face softened. "Do you want chicken, chicken, or chicken to eat?"

"Darn, I was hoping for chicken." I slumped down on the bed, feigning disappointed.

"You must be feeling better."

16
Seth

Walking down the stairs to prepare dinner, I thought about Maggie standing at my door just over three hours ago. It took all I had not to pull her into my arms and kiss her. There she stood with her wet, snow-packed clothes plastered to her malnourished frame and those hapless blues eyes driving tears down her waxy hollowed cheeks, begging me to kiss her. Everything inside me screamed, 'Hurry, before she changes her mind.' Nevertheless, I didn't.

"Yup, I deserve a medal."

But the last thing she needed was to have me slobbering all over her, not that I was a bad kisser. Well, I didn't think I was. I mean, I'd never had any complaints. Anyway, it wasn't what she needed. She needed a refuge from the storm, a place to feel secure, and someone to reassure her she wasn't an *unlovable nothing*.

Those brutal words rode roughshod over me. How could a mother be so heartless? Coming from a loving home, I struggled to understand that kind of cruelty from a parent. My mom and dad would have done anything for me. We certainly weren't the perfect family, but I knew I was loved. Always. No matter what.

I gathered Maggie's clothes from the dryer and started to take them up to her before deciding against it. My gut told me she regretted her decision to come here, and even more so she lamented having shared what her mother had said. If I took her clothes up to her now, she'd make up some lame excuse about why she had to leave, and I wasn't about to let her leave until she had some food. Until she had a lot of food.

I set the clothes down on the end of the counter, picking up the phone as it rang.

"Hey, Seth, how's she doing?"

"Hello, Cole." I called him after getting Maggie situated in the tub. When she started shivering, I knew I had to act fast before hypothermia kicked in. "Better. My nerves wouldn't settle down until I went in and found her sound asleep. I'm happy to report her ashy colored cheeks are now a soft rosy pink."

"Good, she'll probably sleep for a while."

"She's up now. I'm going to feed her some dinner." I debated whether to wake her, and if it not for the purple shadows under her eyes, I wouldn't have. She was half-starved. I had no idea how she'd managed to keep going on what little she ate. I'd spent hours trying to figure out a way to get more food into her, but couldn't come up with anything short of embarrassing her. She was the most guarded person I ever met.

"Great. Make it something high in protein and fattening. The poor kid's nothing but skin and bones," Cole said, echoing my thoughts.

"I'm making my chicken stir fry. It was what we ate on New Year's Eve. Sound good?" I decided to make it because of the sauce. Not only did it call for an entire cube of butter, it also had a cup each of cream and coconut milk and some sesame oil. It was undeniably high in calories. Booker and Cole complained every time I'd made it. They'd gorge themselves, then blame me because they'd have to up their workout routine for the next week.

"It certainly should put some meat on her," he laughed. "And remember, the next time someone has hypothermia, you shouldn't dump them in a tub of hot water. Warm them up slowly, preferably with your own body heat."

"I don't know, Cole. I can't imagine she'd've liked it if I were to try and strip her naked so we could crawl under a blanket together."

He laughed. "Point taken, though you could've used heating pads and hot water bottles." I hadn't thought of that. "Hate to cut you off, but I'm being paged. If you need me, call my cell."

"Alright. Thanks."

"Oh, one more thing. If you have any leftovers, save some for me."

I removed the chicken breasts from the marinade they'd been basting in and arranged the strips neatly on a plate. Placing some fresh ginger on the cutting board, I began shaving off a few thin slices of the yellow root.

"Her mother doesn't deserve her," I muttered angrily, shaving a much too large chunk off and nearly gashing my finger open.

Anger. It happened every time I thought of Barbara Brown. She was one very nasty woman. I kept telling myself she was sick and not in her right mind, but remembering Maggie standing in my doorway, brokenhearted and shivering, made it tough to remain objective.

I wondered if she knew Maggie had gotten a full ride scholarship to Stanford, or that she had turned it down to attend the local community college here in the area instead. I wasn't the least bit surprised when Maggie told me about it. "How could I take care of my mother if I were clear across the country," she'd said.

Maggie was the antithesis of her mother.

I snagged a slice of red pepper and slipped it into my mouth as Maggie descended the stairs dressed in my over-sized clothes, looking very self-conscious. The sleeves were rolled up on the gray sweatshirt and the waistband hit her mid-thigh.

The sweatpants hung on her, and judging from the large bulge that was under the sweatshirt, I guessed that she'd cinched them up quite a bit. Despite the fact that she'd rolled up the legs, they still pooled around her ankles. She looked wonderful. I watched as she timidly came down the stairs, checking out her surroundings.

This part of the house was where Booker and I had done the most renovating. The dark cherry railing and intricate hand-carved spindles along the staircase turned out a real pain to install, but it was worth it. The staircase curved around, opening on each side.

To the right lay the family room. One of Booker's old girlfriends helped me decorate it. In the center of the room was an overstuffed deep green couch with several plush burgundy pillows and a gold microfiber throw angled across one corner. At first I wasn't too keen on having the blanket and a bunch of pillows lying around, but after she'd arranged everything, it looked pretty good.

A small round cherry table holding a phone and a brass reading lamp was positioned on the right side of the couch and a matching oversized man-chair, as I liked to call it, was angled inward on the other end.

A large, flat-screen TV clung to the wall above a glass-enclosed fireplace. I wanted a bigger TV except there wasn't enough room. On the other side of the fireplace stood a cherry cabinet with ornate glass doors, filled with DVD's. Gathered burgundy drapes hung in the bay window on the far wall. The family room joined a huge kitchen at the bottom of the grand staircase.

The kitchen was my favorite room with black slate countertops and tall cherry cabinets Booker had built. I had numerous copper and silver pans, along with a large cast iron frying pan hanging from a baker's rack suspended from the ceiling. It looked as if the area was set up for a chef, not a high school senior.

In the middle of the kitchen stood a huge island cabinet and four wooden bar stools with padded dark leather seats. Several inset lights spread liberally across the ceiling lit up the kitchen, as did the accent lights running across the cupboard tops.

"This is so beautiful," she said quietly.

"Thanks." I washed off the Portobello mushrooms and placed them on the cutting board. "I decided on chicken, I hope that's okay with you."

"Goofball."

"I heard that, Mags." I ran my eyes over her again. "Don't you look like a sexy beast in those clothes?"

"Yeah, I've had at least ten proposals of marriage just walking down your stairs."

"I hope you turned them all down. You're mine." I smiled and wagged my eyebrows, testing the waters. I was curious to see if she'd thrown the walls back up around her, something she excelled at.

"Give it a rest, Seth." *Yup, they were back up.* "Sorry, I didn't mean to snap. I'm just not in the mood for flirting."

"Here." I handed her a piece of French bread I'd bought earlier. She sat on a stool and devoured it with a look of euphoria on her face. Anger once more licked at my insides as I watched her. I quickly handed her another piece when she'd finished, which she ate with the same zeal.

She walked over next to me and picked up a water chestnut. "What can I do to help?"

"Nothing, have a seat. Would you like more bread?"

She rolled her eyes. "Seth, I'm fine." She curled her arms up into a flexing pose, showing off her muscles, or rather the pretend muscles, in her arms. "I'm a tough cookie."

"Yes, you are." I stroked her cheek softly. "Do you like stir-fry?"

"Never had it. We're real big on cereal and sandwiches at my house." She laughed. I didn't.

She looked over the ingredients spread out on the counter. "What are these?" She held up the white bulb in her hand.

"Water chestnuts."

"They look yummy, and please stop staring at me as if I'm going to melt," she said, gently. "Here, I'll help you cut up the vegetables."

I pulled a knife out from a large butcher block set on the counter, reluctantly handing it to her.

"I'm not going to slice my wrists open if that's what you're thinking."

"I wasn't, except now that you've said . . ." I narrowed my eyes playfully.

"Ridiculous." She began chopping up some carrots, helter-skelter like.

"Hey, what did they ever do to you?"

"What? They are only carrots."

I put my hand over hers and placed another carrot in front of her, guiding her hand and the knife over the carrots, chopping them patiently. "Don't these look more appetizing?" I asked, cleaning off the knife.

"They're beautiful," she teased. "Do you think they feel better about being chopped up nicely?"

"You can be quite sarcastic sometimes."

"You just noticed?"

"Cooking is an art, Maggie. The presentation is almost as important as the taste. Have you been sleeping through culinary class?" I asked, rinsing off the knife before proceeding.

We continued chopping, slicing, and making small talk about vegetables. She asked me about my parents and how they'd died.

"My dad was a Chaplin in the Air Force, and we traveled a lot so I've lived all over the world." I left out the part about him and Booker's dad being on the same undercover operations team.

"My mom and dad made what was supposed to be a quick trip to Guatemala to say good bye to his troops since he was retiring, only they never returned home. The plane suffered mechanical failure and crashed into the Sierra Madre mountain range. There were no survivors.

"My family and Booker's were pretty tight. I moved in with him for a while until I was back on my feet. He was a real lifesaver. He helped me buy this house and taught me about woodworking. We renovated it together. It was good therapy."

"How long did it take you?"

"A couple years," I said. When she asked when exactly my parents had died, I began fidgeting around, opening and closing drawers loudly in an effort to stall her until I could think up a good cover story.

I was saved from answering when she began rubbing her temples. I helped her back onto the bar stool, and she let the subject drop. "We're pretty much done. I'll finish."

I poured several different seasoned oils into a wok. When the oils began popping in the heat, I added the chicken strips, browning them before adding the veggies, each hissing loudly as they hit the oil. Steam and smoke spirited out of the pan making the kitchen come alive with the aroma. I poured the ingredients for the sauce in a separate pan as the stir-fry cooked.

"Where did you learn to cook like this?"

"When we were stationed in France, I took a class. After moving back to the States, I took a few more classes with my mom." Tired of me playing spy with my dad all the time, she wanted me to have other interests so we enrolled in the cooking class together, and my love for cooking was born.

While I finished the meal, Maggie insisted on setting the table. I held out her chair as she sat down, stealing a whiff of her hair in the process. *Thanks for all the etiquette lessons, Mom.*

Maggie ate two helpings of dinner, spooning up the extra sauce off her plate when she'd finished. We were both too full for desert: a high calorie, carb laden, chocolate creation chilling in the refrigerator. We'd have it later, or maybe I'd send it home with her, along with the leftovers from dinner. Sorry, Cole.

I suggested we sit by the fire when we finished. She curled up on the couch while I went over to the fireplace and flipped a brass switch on the wall. The fire roared to life.

She laughed. "I'm guessing you were never a boy scout?"

"You've got to love the ease of a gas fireplace," I said, settling down next to her. We sat quietly for a few minutes watching the flames dance around behind the glass. I doubt she had any idea of the battle raging inside me as I debated whether to put my arm around her. Nervously, I bit the bullet and slipped my arm around her tiny shoulders, nudging her close.

Big mistake.

Her fingers sprang to her hair, and she began twisting the thin brown strand around frantically. I didn't mind the twisting, I thought it was cute, but I knew what it meant; she was nervous, and probably not in an "Oh, goodie, he's going to try and kiss me" way. More likely it was an "Oh, no, he's going to try and kiss me" way. Girls truly should come with a manual.

The stupid phone rang before I could make my big move. It rang several times, but I made no effort to answer it.

"Aren't you going to get it?"

"No, I'll let the machine. I'm too comfortable to move."

The machine picked up the call. "Hello, Seth here. Please leave a message."

"Hey, Seth." Maggie flinched at the voice. "It's Hilly. I've missed you. Sorry about deserting you at the festival and leaving with Zack. He lied and said you and Trailer Girl were . . . I know, disgusting thought." She giggled.

Hillary was the bane of my assignment. I'd asked Booker if we could reassign her and her friends to another agent, but he said no, saying we had a good relationship going, clearly his opinion. Although she didn't do drugs, she had friends who were, one being Zack. He only admitted to smoking weed, but the rumors going around the school recently were that he did more, a lot more. Hopefully, he'd be the ticket to our dealers.

"Anyway, um, I've come to my senses. I realized you would never, well, not with her anyway." The longer 'Hilly' continued to babble, the faster Maggie's fingers twisted her hair.

"I know we're just friends and all, but my parents are out of town for the weekend, and I'm all alone. I'd love it if you'd come over, and you know, keep me company. I'm sure we could think of—" I'd had enough and reached around the wooden end table, unplugging the phone line.

"She's delusional." I settled back down and bravely put my arm around Maggie again.

She ripped her fingers out of her hair, *ouch, that had to hurt,* and pulled away.

"You know, Seth, you and Hillary make sense." She stood and walked over to the fire, holding her hands to the flames for warmth. "You two come from the same circles. You should—"

"I don't believe it. Please tell me you're not doing this." I tried, unsuccessfully, to remain calm. I felt as if weeks of patience and hard work were about to blow up in my face. Instead of us becoming closer, she now pushed me further away. Was she actually going to suggest I hook up with Hillary?

"Doing what?" she asked, stunned by my reaction. She was clueless as to how I felt. Had I not spent weeks dropping hints? Had she not noticed any of them? Did she feel nothing for me other than friendship?

Impossible. I'd seen the way she looked at me, not to mention what happened earlier at my front door. This was beyond maddening.

"Now that you've calmed down, you're trying to distance yourself from me. You're back behind the wall you've built."

"What are you talking about? I don't have walls around me."

I rubbed my face in frustration. She couldn't possibly believe that, could she? Okay, fine. She wanted proof, I'd give it to her. "Who's your best friend, Maggie?" I walked toward her. "Who do you call at three in the morning when you just want to talk? Who do you confide in when your heart is breaking?"

She said nothing. She knew I was right, and there was no denying it.

"You have this wall around you," my words flew out fast and furious now, "and the second someone gets a peek inside, you add another row of bricks, like today. When you first got here . . " My face warped into a tortured expression, and I couldn't finish my sentence.

"I was upset and exaggerated the situation. I'm embarrassed actually. It really wasn't a big deal." She tried sounding nonchalant only I knew she lied. Self-preservation, Maggie was an expert at it.

She didn't want me close to her. She lived a hard life, filled with pain, and no doubt she saw me as just another person to hurt her. She probably felt it was better to break it off before she got hurt. I could hardly believe she really thought she was unlovable.

She continued. "I was mostly upset with my mom for throwing the lunches across the room. I was pretty hungry, and if I allow myself to become really tired like I did, I'm completely unreasonable."

"Stop." I held onto her shoulders, fearing she'd run if I didn't. "I can't go on pretending any more. I don't want to be just your friend. I'm in love with you." That wasn't how I'd imagined telling her the first time. I had envisioned something much more romantic. My bulldozer approach probably would push her over the edge, but since I couldn't take it back, I forged on.

"I want to be the one you need and the one you call. I know you'll deny it, Maggie, but I think you feel the same way. I swear I can see it in your eyes every time you look at me."

My confession seemed to floor her completely. She stood there with her mouth hanging open saying nothing for several seconds. They were the longest seconds of my life.

17
Maggie

"Come on, Maggie, admit it."

Yet I couldn't. My mouth wouldn't form the words I'd never uttered aloud to another living soul. I had to do something quickly because with every fiber of my being, I knew what came next. I did what I do best when backed into a corner; I lashed out.

"Hillary's not the only one around here who's delusional."

Seth's face went hard. He dropped his hands from my shoulders, and I felt sick for hurting him. I snatched up my clothes from the counter and ran up the stairs to change, not realizing he followed me. I no sooner shut the bedroom door when it flew open again. He grabbed the clothes from my hands, tossing them onto the bed. He wrapped his warm hands around my face and pulled me next to him.

"Are you saying I don't matter to you?"

"No. We're friends, good friends." I swallowed hard at my words.

"So if I were to kiss you, it wouldn't mean a thing to you?"

"It'd be like kissing my brother," I whispered.

"Is that right?" He ran his thumbs along my jaw, sending a shiver up my back. He smiled. "Let me show you who the delusional one is, Maggie. Oh, and if I'm boring you, feel free to stop me at any time." He leaned forward and in one swift motion captured my mouth with his before I could utter a word.

My head screamed out in protest. My body, on the other hand, rebelled against me. While the battle raged in my mind, my arms wrapped themselves around his waist holding him tight. He pressed his mouth firmly onto mine as he tunneled his hands through my hair, holding my face to his. His lips felt incredibly soft and warm as they moved hungrily against mine.

No. This is not what you want. He'll be like every other boy, my head yelled. *He'll make demands. Don't trust him.* My mother's cruel words played repeatedly in my head, and I knew I should push him away.

But I didn't. With my poor heart pounding wildly, his kiss spilled through to my soul, and I was lost. His lips never left mine, yet he was all over my mouth. Never before had I felt anything this wonderful. I knew I'd pay dearly for my surrender, but I'd gladly pay it. I hoped the kiss would never end. A throaty sigh escaped my lips, and he drew me even closer.

As each of my bones melted, one by one, somehow I had the strength to remain standing. It felt as if the entire world ceased to exist. There was only he and I left, alone and together. My heart and soul swam in a sea of pure joy.

He started to pull away, except I wasn't ready yet and didn't loosen my hold on him. He pulled me back tight and whispered my name against my lips, which caused a fire to explode inside my heart. My soul was so tangled up in him I had no idea how I'd survive after he left me.

When he pulled back the second time, I didn't stop him. I dropped my head onto his warm chest, trying to catch my breath. He held me against him, his breath as erratic as mine.

"I can feel your heart beating against my chest," he whispered. I could feel his, too.

After my breathing slowed somewhat, I lifted my head and looked up into his eyes. I could feel the fear rising up now that I could think clearly again. "Please don't hurt me. When you're tired of me, just let me know. I promise not to be a clinging vine." I sounded vulnerable and completely pathetic, and I never hated myself more. I was a fighter, not a weak hapless wimp. I didn't need anyone, certainly not a guy, to make me happy.

Only I wasn't happy. I was alone. And I was sick and tired of being alone. I was also very much in love with him. It frightened me beyond words.

"Maggie," he said, stroking my hair. "I'm not going to get tired of you, and I certainly don't plan on hurting you, not on purpose, anyway. But I don't want to be just here." He kissed me softly on the lips. "I want to be in here, too." He brushed my head with his lips. "And in your heart. I've never loved anyone like this before." With that declaration, he kissed me again with a kiss every bit as enjoyable as the last one. When he stopped, I was breathless again. "And I have no intention of letting you go." He rolled his eyes as if I were crazy to think such a thing.

We'll see.

"Do you still want to go home?" I shook my head at his question. "Good. Let's go back down by the fire." He took my hand and led me downstairs. We sat watching the flames fluttering around, neither one speaking. It felt right to be in his arms. I looked up at him and smiled.

"What are you thinking?" He softly stroked along my chin with the back of his hand.

"I was thinking about how beautiful you are."

He frowned. "Women are beautiful, not men. They're . . . I don't know, handsome or something. Certainly not beautiful."

"If you say so." After all, who was I to argue with this beautiful creature?

"I love you, Maggie." His eyes were soft and warm. I wanted to say it back. I certainly felt it. I loved him and had loved him for some time, yet the fear of saying it aloud overwhelmed me. I nodded as guilt ripped at my heart. How could I not tell this guy I loved him after all he'd done for me? He'd proven repeatedly he was trustworthy. Yet even with my self-inflicted guilt trip, I couldn't say it.

"Let's start knocking down those walls of yours. Tell me something about yourself no one else knows."

"What do you want to know?" Nervous, I picked up his hand in mine, weaving my fingers through his.

"Tell me your life story."

I took a deep breath, ordered myself to remain calm, and began the boring vignette that was my life. I told him about the fights my mother would have with my grandparents and about how my grandma had taught me to feed and take care of myself.

"I don't remember my grandparents very well, being so young when they died, though I do remember feeling safe with them. It was something I've never felt living with my mom."

I shared with him the details of the car accident and about my mother's non-stop drinking. He drew our intertwined fingers to his lips as I spoke.

"Thanks to my grandmother's preparations, I was able to survive life with my mother. Over the past two years, her drinking seems to have gotten worse. I think I prefer her drunk. She's pretty nasty when she's sober." It felt good to share my history with someone, like a huge burden lifted off me. "I've never told anyone about my life before, it's liberating and scary at the same time. Quick, tell me some deep dark secret about yourself to even this whole thing out. I mean seriously, all I know about you is you're a saint who runs around doing good deeds and rescuing damsels in distress."

"I'm not a saint, Maggie. I have my skeletons."

"Let me guess, you slept in one Sunday and missed church?"

"Very funny, let me show you how funny." He reached for my waist and started tickling me. I squealed and wiggled free, jumping off the couch as he chased me into the kitchen. I ran around the center island and did my best to keep it between us, except with his uncanny speed I was no match. He caught me, pulling me to his lips again. This time I didn't try wiggling free.

"What were we talking about?" I asked a few moments later.

"Who cares?" He started to kiss me again when a vibrating sound interrupted us. He picked up his cell phone off the kitchen counter. "It's Hillary. She's a persistent little pain."

"Wait. Let me answer it."

"I've never seen this sadistic streak in you before. I like it."

I put it on speakerphone and set it back down on the counter. "Hello."

"Who's this?" demanded the snotty voice on the other end of the line.

"Maggie Brown. Who's this?" I remained calm while Hillary's voice grew more anxious.

"This is Hillary. Why are you answering Seth's phone?"

"I had dinner at his house, now we're . . . busy." Seth mouthed, *you're asking for trouble*, as I continued to torment Hillary. "What do you want anyway?"

"I want to talk to Seth, Trailer Girl." Seth came up from behind, wrapping his arms around me.

"Mmmm, that feels nice." I shut my eyes and cuddled into the warmth of his chest.

"What did you say?" It was official. Hillary'd gone ballistic. I half expected her to reach through the phone and smack me.

Seth snatched up the phone. "We're busy, Hilly, got to go, bye." He set it back down. "Delusional." He took my hand and led me back to the couch. "Do you like old movies?"

"Sure."

He walked over to the cherry cabinet and started rummaging through the DVD's.

"I haven't seen the original Star Wars movies."

"I'm talking *old* movies, Maggie. Classics, like *Singin' in the Rain*, *The Philadelphia Story*, or how about *Oklahoma*?"

I'd never heard of any of them. "You pick one. I trust your judgment."

I pulled the blanket from off the back of the couch and wrapped it around me while he put the DVD's in the player. He rolled his eyes and mumbled, "Star Wars," under his breath before pulling my feet onto his lap and massaging them. I could definitely get used to this.

I fell asleep somewhere during *Singing in the Rain*, and didn't wake up until I heard a man singing about *A Surrey with the Fringe on Top*, whatever that was. My head lay on a pillow next to him, his head leaning back against the couch as he snored softly. I sat up and his eyes sprung open.

"Hey." He looked at me and smiled. "I guess we fell asleep."

"Guess so." I laughed, adjusting the oversized sweatshirt. "What time is it?"

"3:30."

"In the morning?"

He nodded. "Do you want me to take you home? Will your mom be worried?" He ran his hand through my hair.

"I doubt it. She probably locked me out, and I didn't bring my key, either." If she had passed out, she'd never hear me knocking on the door.

"You're welcome to stay here. I'll sleep in one of the spare bedrooms. It's almost morning anyway," he said.

I stiffened slightly.

"I'll even put a dead bolt on the bedroom door if you'd like so you won't have to worry about me sneaking in during the night to steal kisses."

"I'll take my chances." I leaned up to kiss him and yawned instead.

"Are you bored with me already?"

"Sorry."

He picked me up and carried me up the stairs.

"I'm capable of walking, Seth, I'm not that tired."

"I know. It's just easier to kiss you if I'm carrying you." He gave my nose a quick peck.

"I can't believe you can carry me up a full flight of stairs and not get winded." I gave his arm a squeeze; the muscles bulged under my grip.

"And yet a few kisses from you can knock the breath right out of me. Go figure."

"We had better not kiss anymore. I wouldn't want to wind you." Thankfully, he didn't listen. He set me down next to his bed and dipped his mouth to mine, kissing me softly.

"Good night," I said, my voice barely above a whisper. I snuggled down into the comfortable mattress and shut my eyes, a smile planted firmly on my face. Someone loved me. Me, the unlovable nothing was lovable after all.

18
Bill and Alan

"What's the address again?" Alan asked. His nerves were raw since receiving the phone call from their father earlier. It had taken several long agonizing months to find out who had killed their brother Jeffery, but now they knew. Finally, justice would be served.

Because the murder was part of some ongoing investigation by undercover MET trash, the killer's identities were kept secret from the public. Even so, Harry Dreser had a way of making things happen. Money talked after all. Alan wondered how loud it had to talk this time and hoped it wasn't financed by his trust fund, if there was any of it left.

The report their father had emailed them stated three bullets had entered Jeffery's body. One had entered his right calf causing little damage—the cop who fired that shot would live, for now. The other two hit his heart simultaneously, causing it to explode. The guilty swine, Captain Booker Gatto and Detective Seth Prescott would *have* to pay. Dearly. Painfully.

Currently, their father Harry had very little info on Prescott, but assuredly he'd find out all he could. In the meantime, Gatto would be the first to atone, and Alan had formulated their retribution perfectly. Desiring to maximize the pain and grief for as long as possible, he and his brother had decided to kill the cop's loved ones first, one by one.

Alan not only wanted to cause pain for the cops, but also fear, along with a healthy dose of paranoia. Soon, everywhere they went, Gatto and Prescott would be looking over their shoulders wondering when it would be their turn. The brothers didn't intend to let them have a moment's peace until justice was administered slowly and painfully. Heroin sales could wait. Nothing would stop the Dreser family's revenge.

"This is it. Ninety-six Country Cottage Lane." Alan pointed to a small ranch style home with a white picket fence running around it. "Cut the engine. I don't want him to hear us coming. Like I always say, we gotta blend in."

Blend in? Bill had to laugh as the rusted-out Gremlin sputtered twice before rumbling to a stop. The car stuck out like two Mormon missionaries at a rap concert, as did the stupid clothes Alan had forced him to wear. Black polyester blending in? Right. *And I suppose the stupid purple plug in your earlobe blends in too, dimwit?* No one would ever accuse Alan of being the sharpest knife in the drawer.

"There's a light on inside. Let's go see if we can—" Bill and Alan slunk back against the house as the back door swung open. An old man stood on the threshold slipping on a tan coat.

"Garbage man comes tomorrow. I'll be right back," he said in a gravelly voice.

"Take your cane," replied an elderly woman's voice from inside the house.

"And tell me, Martha, how do you suppose I use my cane and carry a garbage bin?" The man mumbled while buttoning his coat.

"I heard that, you stubborn old man. Take your cane."

"Go back to your crossword puzzle, woman." The elderly man lowered his voice this time. He snatched up the near-full bin, leaving the cane hanging on a hook by the back door.

Alan leaned over to his brother. "You got to love a man that doesn't let a stupid broad tell him what to do. Too bad we have to kill him."

"I thought Pop said the old guy was a widower." Bill stretched around, trying to see inside the house.

"It looks like Gramps got himself a little sugar. Just one more person to add to the list, I guess." Alan smiled at Bill, who nodded in agreement.

The night sky was crystal clear, allowing the full moon to flood the narrow pathway from the house to the street with light, something neither Bill nor Alan liked. They weaseled around to the side of the house, staying out of sight.

The old man situated the trash bin on the curbside and speedily turned back toward the house, waddling as quickly as his two feet could carry him.

"Hello, Samuel," Alan said with an oily voice. He stepped out from the shadows of the house, and the old man jumped back.

"My name's George, not Samuel." He cringed slightly, eyeballing the matching shirts the men wore. "You two in some kind of bowling league?"

Bill laughed. "I told you these were stupid clothes." Their father was the expert at disguises, so much so that he'd been able to avoid being arrested on numerous occasions while incognito. It was a talent he tried, and failed, to pass on to his sons.

"Shut up," was the only defense Alan offered.

Brilliant comeback, Bro, Bill thought. However, now wasn't the time for an argument, now was the time for a little revenge.

"Who are you?" asked George, squinting at Alan. "Is that a bingo chip stuck to your earlobe?" He shook his head and muttered, "The full moon does bring out the weirdos." George turned back toward his house. Alan stepped in his pathway.

"I'm Alan Dreser, and this is my brother Bill." George stared blankly at the two. "Surely your grandson's been gloating over how he murdered our brother, Jeffery," Alan sneered.

"My grandson? I don't have a grandson. I have four granddaughters, and *six* great-granddaughters." The old man shook his head, remembering how little bathroom time he'd had the last time the girls came to visit. How much make-up did nine and ten year-old girls need to wear anyway? "Okay, boys, enough is enough. What do you want? You guys on drugs? I don't have any money, if that's what you're after."

Bill had to admire the old man's feistiness. It was almost a pity to have to kill him. "Funny you should mention drugs. We were here building up the family business when we got a phone call this morning from dear old dad," Bill said. "He's been trying to figure out who exactly killed our brother, and it turns out that slime ball grandson of yours and his buddy are the guilty party. We're here to get a little revenge."

"You guys are nuts. Get off my property before I call the cops."

Bill's anger boiled over, and he gave George a shove. The old man stumbled back and fell against the house, wishing now he had brought his cane.

For once it was Alan who remained calm. He patted his brother on the shoulder and pulled him back. "Police? Tsk, tsk, Samuel. Don't you mean you'll call your grandson?" He raised his brow quizzically.

Police? Grandson? It was then when George remembered that his old friend Sam Gatto lived at *sixty-nine* Country Cottage Lane, and his grandson was indeed some kind of undercover cop. These two bozos must have mixed up the addresses. It wouldn't be the first time. He constantly received mail for Sam. If the US Postal Service couldn't get it right, these two lackeys didn't stand a chance.

"Okay, let's cut to the chase. Gatto and Prescott have to pay for what they did, and everyone they love is going to pay, too. We're not stopping until you're all dead." A hint of bitterness crept into Alan's voice now.

"I'm telling you, boys, you've made a mistake." George carefully righted himself, weary of where the conversation moved.

"Nice try, old man, but you have to get up pretty early in the morning to fool a Dreser," Bill said. "Our family has been successfully trafficking heroin for almost thirty years, and not a one of us has served jail time for it." Bill puffed his chest out as he spoke.

Heroin? George swallowed hard. "Listen, fellows, my name is George, and it has been since the day of my birth. Would you like to see my driver's license?" He took another step toward the house. Alan didn't budge.

"I've had enough of the lies, Samuel. I'm afraid it's time for you to die." Alan whipped out his pearl-handled knife and seized the old man by the coat collar, heartlessly tossing him to the ground. George howled out in pain, cradling his already tender hip.

"Hurry, Alan, before someone hears the old fool."

"My dear brother, you know I never hurry my work. It gives me indigestion." Alan laughed wickedly.

Bill shook his head.

"Oh, alright, keep your shorts on, but next time we're not going to rush," Alan said, squatting and running the silver blade slowly across the old man's neck. George twisted violently and screamed out in agony. Bill crouched and slapped a hand across the man's mouth, cutting off the sound.

"Let him scream. It makes it all the more enjoyable." Alan grinned and thrust the knife into George's soft stomach, basking in the cries now pouring out of George.

"This is better than any drug. You gotta try it." He gave the knife one more gratifying twist before wiping the saturated blade off onto his black pants and handing it over to his brother.

Bill didn't care for knifes, preferring to do his work with his fists and a two-by-four. Tonight, however, the need to avenge his brother's death coursed strong through his veins. Bill took the knife and shoved it roughly into George's side. "Nobody kills a Dreser and gets away with it," Bill said, lunging deeper.

"I'm not Samuel," he whispered, already weakened by the blood loss.

"George. George, where are you?" A gray-haired woman in a fuzzy yellow bathrobe and matching slippers came waddling around the corner of the house. Two rotund brown and white bulldogs accompanied her, their bellies dusting the ground as they padded along on their leashes. "George!" she screamed, spying the two men surrounding her fallen husband. The dogs began howling savagely and, pulling free of the woman's grip, bolted toward their downed master.

"Oops, it seems we *do* have the wrong man." Alan laughed cruelly.

Bill drew the knife from the quivering body and handed it to his brother. "No hard feelings, ah, George?"

They left him there, wailing in agony, running far too speedily for a pair of fleshed-out bulldogs to catch them.

19
Maggie

It was hard to believe how much my life had changed for the better since falling in love. Most notably I ate like a king. Every morning Seth greeted me with a kiss and a bag from Bagel Heaven, in that order. He also made us delicious homemade lunches, flat out refusing to buy 'cafeteria fodder', as he called it.

Regrettably, my afternoons were still dull. I spent them cleaning the house and looking after my mother while he took care of Lunch Swap business. Then around seven, he'd show up with dinner in hand for everyone, though my mother seldom ate with us.

After dinner, we'd sit and do homework until her reproofing became unbearable, then we'd head out to his car and talk. Well, mostly talk. We still hadn't discussed personal boundaries. There hadn't been a need to, all he ever did was hold and kiss me. Though I was relieved, I was sure the time would come when he wouldn't like it. I dreaded that discussion.

Whenever I was with Seth, I left my cell phone with my mom in case she needed me. But she never called. Her drinking had increased significantly since being released from the hospital almost four weeks ago. So had her visits from Hoffman, much to my dismay. I wondered if there was something romantic between them, but the thought was so repulsive I wouldn't let my mind go there. She grew thinner at an alarming rate and it scared me. She also slept more and more every day. When I suggested she go to the doctor, she went off on an hour-long tirade, reminding me once again that she was the mother, then she grounded me from seeing Seth for two days. I didn't bring it up again.

Sunday Seth came late to pick me up for our lunch deliveries. When we pulled up to Miss Ethel's, she stood on her porch wearing a bright green jumper with a *fit to be tied* expression plastered on her face. She glared directly at Seth, impatiently tapping her foot against the railing. Her shoes were hard to miss with their bright orange color.

"I apologize, Miss Ethel. We had to switch the delivery schedule arou—"

"Excuses are like armpits, mister. Everybody's got'em, and they all stink."

I bit my lip to keep from laughing. She had finished crocheting a few blankets for the thrift store and invited us in as she gathered them up. "Here ya go, done ahead of sched'ul."

"They're lovely, Miss Ethel." I smiled, hoping to smooth things over as I took them from her.

"Speakin' of lovely, you look good, Blue Eyes." It was the name she often called me. "You gainin' weight, ain't ya? And yur face is all rosy too. I told ya, boy, give her some home cookin' and she'd fattin' up nicely. I'll bet she's more fun kissin' now, too," she said with a wink.

"Much more fun, Miss Ethel. Thank you for the suggestion."

She was right. I had gained weight, twelve pounds to be exact. My clothes, which usually hung on me, now fit better. I even had a few curves, though nothing compared to Hillary's. Miss Ethel wasn't the first person to mention the color in my face either, and I noticed how much healthier my hair looked. Actually it shone. No doubt, some of the changes had to do with being loved, but it certainly didn't hurt that I ate three square meals a day.

Outside, Seth scooped me into his arms, leaving my feet to dangle several inches off the ground. "Come here my fattin' up girlfriend and give me some kissin'." After some yummy kissin', he set me back down.

"Do you think I'm getting fat? Look at how tight my jeans are." I pulled at the waistband. There was less than an inch give.

"I'm not answering that silly question," he scowled as we got into the car.

"It's just that my jeans have never been this tight before, it feels weird." He continued to ignore me. "Would you still love me if I weighed three-hundred pounds?" I pulled down the sun visor and looked at my face in the mirror. Puffing out my cheeks, I tried to imagine myself chubby. He reached over and caught my puffed up face, turning it toward his.

"I'm in love with you, not this fleshy exterior. Granted, it's a lovely exterior, even though it could use another twenty pounds or more, it's simply a shell of who you are. I love your soul, that's who you really are, and this lovely body is simply a beautiful bonus."

As he kissed my forehead, his angelic-like expression turned impish. "You know, mathematically speaking," *ugh, him and math,* "if we were to figure how many square inches of you there are, and then if I were to give you one kiss for every square inch, at your present weight I'd be done in about ten minutes. However," he continued with his goofy delusion, "if you weighed three hundred pounds it would take about a month to get them all in. If you weighed six-hundred pounds, I'd probably be busy for a couple of years, but if you weighed eight-hundred pounds, and frankly, the mind boggles at the thought, I'd probably have to kiss you your entire lifetime to get through. So no matter how big you become, clearly, I win."

I let the subject drop.

"Do you have any homework?" he asked, rounding the corner near my home.

"No, I'm done. Do you?"

"Yes, Spanish, but only an hour's worth. Do you want me to drop you off at your house until I'm done?"

"No, I have a book that Julie's been bugging me to read. Let me grab it, and I'll read while you're studying." It was a romance novel, not my usual genre. I was more of a historical fiction person, but the novel was quite popular at school, and I was curious about all the hoopla.

"Sounds good. What's the name of it?"

I told him and he groaned. "Mags, vampires don't sparkle," he said dryly.

"Seth, vampires don't really exist, and your only concern is that these ones sparkle?" He shook his head. "And I suppose you think people really walk down the street and break into song and dance spontaneously?" I teased, making fun of the musicals that were near and dear to his heart.

"Those movies are classics." I mouthed the words as he said them.

When we got to my house, I ran in and found Hoffman sitting alongside my mother, each with a drink in their hand. She hurled a couple of insults in my direction while Hoffman's eyes grazed over me. Yuck. I grabbed the novel and left.

At Seth's, we found Booker parked in the driveway, leaning against the hood of his car. "Hey, Booker, good to see you." The two men greeted each other with a warm handshake.

"Hello, Maggie." He smiled as Seth wrapped his arm around my waist. "How is your mom doing?"

"About the same, thanks for asking." Seth led us into the house, and I sat down on the bar stool while they stood in the kitchen talking.

"How's Sam?" Seth asked, pouring Booker a glass of homemade lemonade.

"That's why I'm here. There was another murder last night. This one was on the east side of town near my place." Seth's eyes narrowed as Booker described what happened.

"One of my father's friends, George Keifer, was taking out his garbage around eleven p.m. When he didn't return, his wife went looking for him with their two portly bulldogs in tow. She found him on the side of the house with two men hovering over him as he lay on the ground. They took off running when the dogs broke free." Seth led him into the living room and they sat down on the couch.

"He'd been stabbed several times and died within seconds after she reached him." Booker adjusted the huge gun that sat on his hip as they talked. I got the feeling they wanted privacy so I excused myself and started preparing lunch, clanging bowls and doing my best not to listen. Try as I may, a few words still broke through, words like "revenge," and "drug trafficking," words I didn't want to hear. I hoped Booker's grandfather was safe because it sure didn't sound good. When they finished, I asked Booker if he wanted to stay for lunch.

"No, thanks," he smiled. "You are a lucky man, Seth. Better not let her go."

"Not a chance," he said firmly. I blushed, they laughed.

After lunch, we sat on the couch eating homemade chocolate cookies we'd baked last night. Seth hadn't mentioned Booker's visit, but I could tell it bothered him. Sam was his friend and he was probably concerned for his safety. "I got the impression Booker's worried about his grandfather. Is everything alright?"

"He's a little anxious because the murder was so close to his home. Now," he said, abruptly changing the subject, "how about we watch a movie? Maybe something scary. I'm thinking Alfred Hitchcock's *Psycho*?"

I shuddered. "A scary movie? Is that some kind of subliminal plot to trick me into snuggling with you?"

"I was hoping to steal a few of those incredible kisses of yours during the movie."

"Like you have to steal those from me. For you, they're free for the taking." I wrapped my arms around his shoulders. They were tense. I thought to press the whole Booker issue except it seemed a little hypocritical of me to pry. I pressed my mouth to his instead. The tension slowly eased from his body the longer we kissed.

"Okay, lets watch *Psycho*," he said, breathless.

"Why don't we snuggle and *you* can scare a few kisses out of me instead of watching a creepy movie?"

"No way. It's a great movie. You'll love it." He rubbed his hands together sinisterly.

"I doubt it."

And I was right. By the time the movie finished I was a nervous wreck. Half the time my face was hidden behind a pillow, the other half was spent *wishing* my face was behind a pillow, and never once did I kiss him.

"I'll never watch another movie like that again," I vowed. He began mimicking the music from the horrid shower scene, laughing at my tightly pinched expression. "You are sick."

"Mags, *Psycho* is a classic. It's one of the all-time greats."

I shivered. "Speaking of *Psycho*," I got up from the couch, "I'd better go home and check on my mom." I couldn't help but smile as he tried not to laugh.

20
Seth

"Game's over, kid," Booker said when we got back into the car. We'd spent the morning at George Kiefer's funeral, and Booker was a mess. He hated funerals. They only served to remind him of everyone he'd lost. We hoped the services would draw out the killers. It didn't, just sorrow-laden family members and friends.

"Game? What game?" I flipped on the radio and searched for something to calm his nerves.

"I've gotten the okay for you to tell Maggie about us," he said heavily.

"Why?" I'd been waiting for this, dreading it beyond measure. I wasn't ready to tell her, not yet.

"She needs to know before it all blows up in your face. Things are getting dangerous, Seth. These guys want us dead."

Before he died, Mr. Kiefer told his wife the men were heroin dealers and they wanted revenge on us, but he didn't live long enough to tell his wife their names, so we still couldn't ID them. Disgruntled drug dealers commonly mouthed off about getting even with the cops who arrested them and it was usually just talk. Evidently, these two were serious.

"Booker, she's under constant surveillance. I spoke with the city sheriff and requested a local detective be assigned to watch over her whenever I was unavailable." The captain readily agreed. He'd lost his son to a heroin overdose last summer and was more than sympathetic to our cause. He wanted the two men brought to justice, and he committed to do whatever it took to make it happen.

"You're wearing yourself ragged, Seth. The longer you wait, the harder it's going to be."

"What exactly do I tell her? 'Hey, Maggie, I've been lying to you all this time. I'm really a cop, MET to be exact. Oh, and one more thing, we believe your mother is somehow involved in a heroin ring, so despite the fact that you have major trust issues, don't let this mess with your head.'" I wasn't being fair, this wasn't Booker's fault.

Booker's tone softened. "Listen, kid. She's going to find out one day. Besides, if you tell her now we can search her place and clear her mother's name."

"Her mom's not involved. I told you that already. She's a drunk—a mean, heartless drunk, not a junkie."

"You know that, and I know that, but the chief isn't going to take our word on it. We need to search the house." Booker still had doubts about Maggie's mom, and out of respect for me, he'd held off on questioning her. He desperately wanted to search their trailer, but purposefully hadn't gotten a search warrant. For that, I was grateful.

Booker changed the subject. "We have a stake-out scheduled Thursday night, and it's your turn to ride shotgun."

"I rode shotgun last time, and I also did the food run, twice. Why don't you ever ride shotgun?" He playfully tapped his captain bars in answer to my question.

I was more than happy to let the argument about Maggie drop, even though I knew he was right. She had to be told, but if we could just wait a little longer, maybe she'd be so crazy in love with me that she'd take it all in stride.

Yeah, right, who was I kidding? She'd flip out.

"Someone broke into Cole's house again, and I'm putting a security system in for him this afternoon. He still hasn't finished the upstairs, so it will go quickly," Booker said. "I could use your help."

"I thought he didn't want a system. What happened to protecting the indigents from the brutal winter?"

"They swiped his TV."

21
Maggie

Thanks to Parent-Teacher conferences tonight, there was no school tomorrow, which meant a three-day weekend. I could hardly wait. I had it up to my eyeballs with my insuperable Calculus class. If I never saw another derivative again, it'd be too soon. To celebrate the long weekend, I refused to study for Monday's test until Sunday night, late. Seth quieted the radio as we pulled up in front of my house.

"I have some bad news. I'm going out of town tonight and won't be back until noon tomorrow."

"Do you have to go?"

"Sorry, I've got some things to take care of, although I won't be having fun if that helps." It was the third time since we started dating that he had to go out of town to take care of *things,* yet he'd never say exactly what for.

"While I'm gone, think of something fun you want to do when I get back." He leaned over and kissed me good-bye.

"You're leaving now?" I asked. He nodded weakly. "Fine, I'll see you tomorrow." I got out, slamming the car door a little too hard.

"Don't be angry, Maggie," he said, lowering the window and leaning across the leather seat.

"I'm not angry, I'm disappointed. I was looking forward to being with you."

"That's a good thing, right?"

I turned to see his grin smoldering in my direction and melted. "Yes, Pollyanna, it's a good thing."

"I thought you slept through that movie." I shook my head. "I'll try and call, love ya."

I moped into the house, tripping over several empty alcohol bottles strewn across the floor. "Hoffman must have been here again, not even she can drink this much by herself." I cleared the discarded bottles to a chorus of soft snores before searching the fridge to see if she had eaten anything and found several more unopened bottles inside. I was tempted to toss them except I didn't want to suffer her wrath when she discovered them missing. Besides, she'd only buy more. I covered her up, went into my room, and sunk my teeth into my vampire romance novel till I fell asleep.

Early the next morning, I woke to an icy cold house. I turned the thermostat up, but the heater didn't turn on. "I know I paid the electric bill." I tried a light switch, still no response.

I opened the front door, and my eyes landed on the problem: a bright yellow *Termination of Services* notice tacked to the doorframe. I called the power company and was informed that they never received my check, but they'd be happy to reinstate my service as soon as the balance was paid.

My mother must have forgotten to mail it. It wasn't the first time. Thankful that we had a gas stove, I turned the burners and oven on. At least we'd have some heat. Next in my effort to warm up, I pulled on Seth's fleece, drawing in a deep breath. "Mmmm." It still smelled like him, although the scent had faded somewhat.

After a bowl of Honey-Nut Cheerios, my new favorite cereal, I grudgingly took out my Calculus book. My new plan was to study while Seth was gone, then I could spend all my time with him when he got back.

Before long, the sky outside went gray, and subsequently, so did our trailer making it impossible to get through my work. It also grew colder. I piled all of our blankets on my mom to keep her warm and did some jumping jacks to get my blood pumping. The phone rang, saving me from having to jog in place.

"Hello, beautiful," said the delectable voice on the other end of the line. "I'm about thirty minutes away. I'll stop by and pick you up."

"No, my mom didn't mail the electric bill, and we have no power here, I'll meet you at your house. I need to keep moving to stay warm."

"Maggie, I don't want you outside by yourself. The killers are still out there somewhere."

Oh, brother, he was too protective. "All the attacks have been at night. It's only noon," I reminded him.

"Maggie, please."

"Seth, I'm freezing."

"I'll b—"

"Seth?" My phone battery died and without power, there was no way to charge it. I checked on my mom once more, her skin toasty warm. I shut off the stove to prevent any accidents and left.

Seth's overreaction made me a bit jumpy. More than once, I felt as though someone followed me and increased my stride. He came tearing into the driveway ten minutes after I'd arrived, skidding to a stop.

"You don't listen very well, do you?" Agitation ruled his face as he flew across the lawn.

"Would you prefer me frozen?" I snapped back at his Neanderthal attitude.

"I prefer you alive." He grabbed me and planted a searing kiss on my mouth. Instantly, my heart began its familiar dance in my chest. I wondered if all our disagreements would end up like this. *I sure hope so.* He set me free all too quickly, his mood considerably lighter. "Sorry, I've been worried about you."

"I locked my windows and doors like you told me. In any case, the murderers have never broken into a home to kill someone." Silly boy. "You look tired. Have you been out necking all night with another girl?" My subtle attempt to evoke a confession fell flat.

"I was with Booker," he said. I cocked an eyebrow at him suggestively to which he rolled his eyes. I took his hand, leading him toward the house. We could finish this conversation inside before I froze to death.

"Maggie, we need to talk. There's something I have to discuss with you."

I dragged him straight to the kitchen, forcing him to sit down on a stool. I stood facing him. "Did you really miss me?" I didn't give him time to answer before stretching up to his neck, kissing its length.

"I missed you," I whispered against his skin. He smelled wonderful, which reminded me. "You know the jacket you gave me?" He muttered what sounded like a yes in reply. "I can barely smell you on it. You need to wear it around for a few hours and make it smell good again." He nodded and pulled me to his mouth.

Yep, he missed me.

Dragging myself out of his arms, I said, "I really wish you weren't such a great kisser." He looked at me as if I had lost my mind. "Hear me out. If you kissed like Zack, you know, all wet and sloppy," I involuntarily shuddered, "I wouldn't want to kiss you all the time. And if I didn't kiss you all the time, I wouldn't have to force myself to stop kissing you all the time either."

"I think your brain's frozen. Have you eaten today?"

"Yes." Evidently, he didn't appreciate my logic.

"Well, not enough."

He led me around to the counter where we made up some chicken salad with nuts and cranberries. While we ate, Seth wore the fleece to 'stink it up', as he said. He offered to sprinkle some of his aftershave on it, but I protested, insisting the smell came from off his skin.

I drained the last of my milk and set the cup in the sink. "We should probably check on my mom, she may have sobered up."

"I'll make up a sandwich for her." He gathered the chicken salad and whole wheat bread from the fridge.

"What did I ever do to deserve you?" I worked my arms around his waist from behind, resting my cheek on the back of his yellow shirt while he made the sandwich.

"I was thinking the same thing."

"You were wondering what I did to deserve you, too?"

"Now you'll have to kiss me for that remark." He twisted around to face me, licking his lips repeatedly until they glistened with spit.

"What are you doing?" I held his face at arm's length.

"I'm making my kisses wet and sloppy so you won't have to force yourself to stop," he said innocently.

"Don't you dare." I quickly wiped off his mouth before he could kiss me.

"Spoil all my fun." He turned back to the sandwich.

On the way to my house it began to sprinkle. I unrolled my window a crack to smell the damp air. Since it was still a little chilly out, I turned on the seat warmer instead of rolling up the window. Seth laughed.

I shrugged. "I love the smell of rain."

"Do you think your mom's awake?" He handed me the now *Seth stinky* fleece. Mmmm.

"I don't know. If she is she's probably upset I'm not there to insult." I said it jokingly, though we both knew it was the truth.

"Maggie, she's hidden behind the alcohol for so long, she doesn't know how to show her feelings anymore." He pressed my hand to his lips.

"Hmm," I said noncommittally, and unrolled the window a bit more before snuggling further into the seat.

We slid to a stop as Seth pulled up in front of my trailer. "What's wrong?"

"Did you leave your bedroom window open?" He pointed to my open window on the side of the trailer.

"No, there's no heat, why would I leave . . ." Someone must have broken in. I shoved the door open, but before I could get out Seth was at my door blocking me.

"Stay here." His fierce tone left little doubt he wasn't making a suggestion. He crouched low and went around the side of the trailer, looking through the open window. Coming back to the front, he pulled out his cell phone.

"I'm not waiting for you, I'm going in. Hurry." He stuffed the phone into his pocket, cutting off what sounded like protests from whoever was on the other end.

He walked over to the car. "Don't follow me. Do you understand?" He flipped the passenger seat down horizontal. "Get down low."

"Please don't go in alone." Ignoring my plea, he locked the door and hurried off. He ran around to the back of the house, hopping a rickety six-foot fence in the process.

I panicked and cautiously climbed out of the car. Unable to climb the tall fence, I ran straight to the front door and opened it just a crack. To my surprise, the two creeps from the park greeted me. Why couldn't I get away from these pathetically dressed goons?

"Well, well, well. Lookie who we got here," the larger of the two said as he tugged the door open widely. He grinned, or maybe it was a sneer. It was hard to tell.

"What did you do to my mother?" I demanded, wiping the droplets of rain from my face.

"This old drunk's your mama?" he laughed. "Small world, ain't it, girlie?" He ran a hand over my cheek and clicked his tongue, his grin widening. "I've wanted to meet you something bad."

"Wh-what are you doing here?"

Before he could answer me, Seth flew through the window on the back of our trailer, holding a gun.

"MET. Freeze!" he shouted, running toward me.

My new *friend* grabbed a clump of my hair and spun me around with my back pressed against his chest. The guy's body odor was enough to stop a truck. It didn't help my queasy stomach.

"Your boyfriend's MET?" he hissed banefully in my ear.

"No, he's a senior at Port Fare High," I said, doubting my own words. Seth was a cop? No, he couldn't be.

"What's your name, pig?" he asked Seth.

He answered slowly. "Detective Seth Prescott."

"Detective? What?" I was sickened clear through my soul. The hand in my hair tightened, and I let out a sob of pain.

Seth started toward me. "Come one step closer, she dies." As the man spoke, I felt something cold and hard glide across my neck. A knife, an incredibly sharp knife. He barely applied any pressure, yet its keen edge nipped at my skin.

Seth threw his hands up in the air, his gun now pointing at the ceiling. "You hurt her, it will be the last thing you ever do," Seth vowed.

"Do you have any idea who I am?" The creep's voice had gone from playful to rancorous. Seth answered him with a shake of his head. "I'm Alan, and this is my brother, Bill."

Seth looked bemused. Clearly, the names meant nothing to him.

"No? How about Dreser? Does that name ring any bells?" he asked, spit flying from his mouth.

Seth's eyes widened. "Yeah, thought so," said Bill smugly. "And I'm willing to bet you remember killing our brother, Jeffery?" Again, Seth shook his head. Bill groaned loudly. "You killed him over in Syracuse, at Chuckey's Billiards. Does that—" Bill paused and smiled as Seth's face now registered fear. "Oh, yeah. You *do* remember, all too well."

Stay calm, Maggie, I instructed myself. It felt as if I were in a dream, a very bad dream, and any minute now I'd wake up alone in my bed. Seth was a high school senior, like me, not an MET . . . cop . . . agent . . . whatever you called them.

I ripped my eyes from Seth, looking over to my mother. Her breathing was shallow and irregular, and I desperately wanted to see if she was hurt.

"Let her go, then we'll talk," Seth said. I turned my attention back to the three men. Seth's gun was now pointed at Bill's head, but he watched Alan's every move.

"I don't think so, scum." Alan let go of my hair and aligned my body more fully in front of his. There was no way Seth could take a shot and not hit me, assuming he even knew how to shoot the dumb thing.

"Your brother was dealing heroin to eleven- and twelve-year-olds," Seth said, his jaw clamped tight.

"It's a free country," Alan flipped. Seth's face tightened. "So you on some undercover assignment at the high school?" Alan pressed.

Murder? Drugs? Undercover? Seth looked at me, saying nothing, just looking.

"Answer me, scum!" Alan pressed the knife tighter against my throat. A warm trickle of blood ran down my neck.

"*Yes,*" Seth bit out.

No! He's just Seth, hottest guy at Port Fare High. He runs a charity. He's an amazing cook. He's kind and giving, and he . . . loves . . . me . . . ?

"Let me guess, you were assigned to keep an eye on little girlie here and her complete waste of a mother." Alan rubbed his cheek against mine and laughed. "And I bet she thinks you're really in love with her." Both the creeps laughed, and Alan hissed in my ear, "My bet is you've been duped, girlie."

My bet is the creep is right.

I began trembling. I was an assignment? That was it? Yet it made sense. Of course I was an assignment. To think I meant anything more to him was ridiculous. He could have any girl he wanted, wasn't that what Zack said? So why would he pick me . . . unless he had to. Trailer Girl was purely an assignment. I'd fallen in love with an undercover cop who only did his job. I meant nothing to him.

"Maggie, don't listen to them. They are playing with your head. They're drug dealers, and their dad is a notorious smuggler," Seth pleaded. But it was too late. I knew the truth and was disgusted with myself. *What a stupid, stupid girl I truly am.*

My knees gave out, and I started to drop. Alan cinched his arm around my stomach tighter, so tight I had to fight to breathe.

"Let her go, and we can work out a deal," Seth bargained.

"Put the gun down, kick it away," Alan said, his hot breath licking at my ear. It was clear he didn't want to deal. Seth slowly set the gun down and kicked it down the hall, *away* from the men.

"Not a smart move, cop." Bill, whose brow trickled with sweat, now had a small silver gun pointed directly at Seth. "You and your scumbag friend—" His rebuke was cut off by the sound of sirens, several sirens. "Leave her, and let's get out of here," he said to Alan.

"Not without the girl. I've waited—"

"We leave now, *without* the girl, Alan. We won't be able to escape if we have her weighing us down."

"What about him? Are we just going to let him live? No way."

"Yes, he hasn't paid for what he's done yet. We stick with the plan."

"Do you honestly think I'm going to let you leave with her?" Seth interrupted. "There'll be ten cop cars here within seconds. You have no choice. Let her go."

"If we let her go, he'll only follow us. We should bring her with us as a hostage," Alan said. He lowered his head again, running his cold nose along my neck and inhaling. My stomach heaved.

"I have a better idea. We need a diversion, and I got the perfect one," Bill said. It was the last thing I heard. Regrettably, it wasn't the last thing I felt as my head slammed into the doorframe. My world spun away.

***

"Maggie, wake up, please." Seth's voice reached into the deep dark hole I lay in and pulled me out. I felt his lips pressing against my forehead before realizing I was on the floor. What in the world was I doing on the floor? I forced my eyes open as I sat up. "Maggie, are you okay?"

It all came back to me in one wave, a tsunami. Seth was a cop or MET or something. "You lied to me," was all I could think to say.

"Can we talk about this later? You need to be examined. There's a lump on your head." I reached up, cautiously touching my sore head. Not only was the lump big, it was also very tender.

"Where are those men?"

"They took off." Sensing my agitation, he moved away from me. "They won't get far. Half the force is after them as we speak."

Half the . . . No more. No. More. I stumbled over to my mom. Her breathing came out in short puffs.

"I didn't find any injuries on her. She may have gotten some bad stuff."

"Stuff?"

"Ah . . . drugs. Heroin, I'm guessing." He kicked at a loose piece of linoleum as he spoke, never looking my way. "It could be alcohol, Maggie, but like I said before, those two are drug dealers."

So that was why a scrawny girl and an alcoholic mother merited their own personal cop. They thought my mom did drugs. Seth posed as my friend so he could . . . What? Arrest her? No. That wasn't it. He'd have done that by now. Why *hadn't* he questioned her, or even tried to search my house for drugs?

Then it hit me. *Because my mom was simply the bait. He used her.*

"And where exactly do you think she's getting the money for drugs?" I jumped up too quickly, becoming dizzy. Seth reached out to steady me.

"Don't touch me! You lied. Tell me the truth. Who are you, and what do you want with us?"

"I'm undercover MET. It stands for Mobile Enforcement Team. Booker and I are on the drug task force. I've been assigned to Port Fare High to try and find out where the influx of heroin is coming from."

It poured off his tongue so fluidly it had to be the truth. It made sense why he and Booker seemed like such good friends. They were cops together.

"Over the past eight to ten months, heroin use has skyrocketed in Port Fare." Seth's eyes searched my face, trying to judge my reaction. I held myself still, not giving in to my desire to fly into a rage.

"You think my mother is what, a dealer? A user?" My incredulous tone caused him to wince. Good.

"We feel she is somehow involved, though we don't know how yet. But we're not after small time dealers at the moment, Maggie, what we really want is the supplier."

What in that statement was supposed to comfort me? This was *not* happening. The police used my mother for bait, but why was I befriended?

The next thought hit me like an eighty-pound anvil to my chest. "You think I'm involved somehow, don't you?"

His silence was deafening. Finally, he spoke. "At first, maybe a little, but I don't anymore."

"Oh, well, thanks. It's nice to know my *boyfriend's* pretty sure I'm not a druggie." I sat down next to my mom, burying my face in my hands.

"Maggie, my feelings for you have nothing to do with the case."

I shook my head, wondering if what he said was just another lie. "You know how important trust is to me, yet you've done nothing but deceive me."

"I couldn't tell you, Maggie. I was undercover. You're involved, albeit indirectly. I had to keep you in the dark. You were part of my . . . assignment."

At that very moment my heart broke completely. I should've known something was up the moment he started talking to me. Of course this beautiful man could never really love the *unlovable nothing*. He used me to get to my mother. I was merely a pawn.

"Go away." My voice sounded strange even to me, as if someone else spoke. "Get out and go away. Leave me, leave us, alone."

"Maggie. You're overreacting. Calm down. After your mother's settled at the hospital, and you're checked out, we'll go back to my place. You need some time to let your mind catch up with all of this. I'll answer all your questions—well, the ones I'm allowed—"

"Get out. *Now*." I sounded pretty brave for a small girl up against a guy with a big black gun. The arrival of the EMT's cut off my rant. They rushed in, rattling off questions as they started an IV on my mom. Seth told them he believed she might be under the influence of some kind of illegal drug. I didn't argue. I was in way over my head.

"Miss Brown, would you like to ride along with us?" the EMT driver asked, after loading her in the ambulance.

"Maggie, I'll take you," Seth said quietly.

I turned to the medic, "Please get me out of here." I peered out the back window of the ambulance at Seth's face as we drove away. He looked devastated, and why shouldn't he be? His cover had blown up in his face and he'd have to start all over again with some other stupid unsuspecting girl. Booker pulled up and got out of his car as we pulled away.

I was beyond distraught and couldn't hold back the tears any longer.

22
Seth

While Maggie lay unconscious in my arms, I'd called in the ID on the two men and the manhunt had begun straightaway, although I didn't hold my breath. If they were anything like their father, they'd be hard to catch. The man was a chameleon.

Booker arrived first and immediately left again to coordinate the search. He now returned, probably to check on Maggie and to find out exactly what had happened.

"Are you positive they were the Dreser boys?"

I nodded soberly as I watched the ambulance drive away. Never in my life would I forget the look of betrayal in Maggie's eyes. Never.

"I heard they'd run into some money troubles in Arizona, I just never imagined they'd come this far north. Of course, Harry Dreser's known for doing the unexpected. This is big, bigger than I originally thought." Booker was like a walking encyclopedia when it came to drug smugglers. He knew of each one, and he knew their territories.

"So Jeffery was the dealer killed in Syracuse." He shook his head in disgust. "The whole family's trouble. That would explain why nothing came up when we tried to ID the body. Daddy Dearest probably paid someone to erase Jeffery's file, not even his dental records were a match. Big time smugglers like Dreser have an endless supply of money, and more than enough stooges to help cover their tracks." He looked at me. "Are you okay? They didn't hurt you, did they?"

"She knows," I said, shoving my hands through my hair. "The Dreser's were in the house when we arrived. I pulled out my gun." In my mind I could still see the knife at her throat, with a thin trickle of ruby-red blood racing down it. The cut was superficial, but it still made me sick.

"I'm guessing she didn't take it so well," Booker said quietly.

"She freaked. She thinks I used her, just like Zack, only I wasn't trying to sleep with her, I just wanted to toss her and her mother into jail, that's all."

"Seth, that's not what we're doing here and you know it. Everything will be okay. Give her some time."

"Everything will be okay? Like it was with Lisa or Heather? Or how about Nikkolynn?" To bring up Booker's past was a low blow. I felt horrible as soon as the words left my mouth. "I'm sorry, man. I shouldn't have said that."

"Come on. Mags is nothing like Lisa or Heather, and she's definitely not like Nikkolynn," he said casually, as if those women hadn't torn his heart into a million pieces. "You don't think she'll blow your cover at the high school, do you? Never mind, stupid question, of course she won't."

"Nope, she won't. I should've come clean sooner. You were right. I—" Booker's police radio interrupted us.

"Captain Gatto, Officer Whelks here." Her voice crackled with static. "I'm sorry, sir, they got away."

I don't know who yelled at poor Whelks more, Booker or me. By the time we finished, she was in tears. Great, something more to feel guilty about.

"If you two are done abusing my officer," interrupted the chief over the radio, "I'd like to send her home. She's been on duty for fifteen hours straight." The chief wasn't a woman to mess with. She protected her officers like a mother bear protected her cubs.

Booker walked me over to my car after we apologized. He'd ordered a search warrant for Maggie's place and knew I didn't want to be here when it came through.

"I'll call and have Jeffery's body exhumed tomorrow. I want it checked out, just to be sure."

I barely listened now. My mind was wrapped up in Maggie. If I'd blown it with her . . .

"Go home. I'll call you if anything turns up." He gave my left shoulder a squeeze. "She needs time, Seth. This is a lot to take in. It's going to be alright, trust me."

No, it wouldn't be alright. Not this time.

23
Maggie

*O*nce at the hospital, an aide escorted me to a private waiting area where I fought to compose myself. When I didn't wonder what happened with my mother, I could still see Seth in my mind, standing in my living room, with his gun. He was a liar, and he used me. He was no better than Zack. At least with Zack I knew from the get-go his true nature.

Dr. Colter came into the waiting room, saving me from another meltdown. "Hello, Maggie. Please, sit down." I took a seat on the edge of a green chair. "Can you explain what happened exactly?"

I gave him a quick rundown of what went on in the trailer, leaving out the whole undercover cop thing. I wouldn't expose Seth, even if he did use me. When I got to the part about having my head used as a battering ram, my hands shook. I stuffed them between my knees to steady them.

"How long were you unconscious?" Before I could answer, he pulled a small pen light out of the breast pocket of his scrubs and checked my eyes. "I want you to have a CAT scan. Are you experiencing any dizziness or nausea?"

"No, I'm fine," *aside from a killer headache*, "I don't need a CAT scan."

"Maggie, I'm afraid I'm going to have to insist," he said, lifting my chin and examining the cut on my neck. "This wound's superficial. I'll have the nurse clean it and put some ointment on it. When was your last tetanus shot?" I shrugged. Had I ever had one? "We'd better give you one just to be safe," he said, making notes on the palm of his hand.

"Now, back to your mom. There doesn't seem to be any blunt trauma to her body. When was the last time you saw her awake and coherent?"

I had to think for a minute. "She wasn't awake when I left for school yesterday. However, there were three empty bottles of alcohol lying on the floor when I arrived home. She must have been awake sometime during the day."

"Three empty bottles? Can she drink that much?"

I shrugged. "I've never known her to. She may have had the neighbor, Mr. Hoffman, over."

"Maggie, your mother is in a coma, which I believe was brought on by her alcohol abuse. With her unstable health, it wouldn't take much. Her blood count is still good, and I'm running some tests on her liver and pancreas to check a few things, as well as a brain scan."

Brain scan?

"I'd also like to do a drug screen to make sure we're not dealing with any other substances."

"My mom's not on any medications. I told the nurse that when I filled out all the paper work."

"Maggie, it is not uncommon for those with addictions to have more than one. I just want to rule everything else out. That way we can give her the best possible care," he explained gently.

Why all of the sudden did everyone think my mom was a drug addict? This was getting ridiculous.

"I'm afraid she is going to be here for a while. You should go home and try to get some sleep. We still have your cell phone number, correct?"

"Yes," I said weakly.

"Is Seth coming to pick you up?"

"No." His eyes opened wide at my overreaction to his question. Then I remembered he was a friend of Seth's.

"Is there a problem? I mean, nothing happened when Seth chased off those men, did it?" He nervously fidgeted with the chart in his hands.

Did he know about Seth? They were pretty chummy whenever I'd seen them together. *Play it cool, Maggie.*

"He has a hard test tomorrow. I'll call one of my girlfriends," I sputtered out.

He raised his eyes to mine. They were filled with trepidation. "I'm guessing something more happened with Seth and the two men that you're not telling me," he said calmly.

He knew. Did everyone in this stinking town know about Seth except me? "You know about him and Booker." It was a statement, pure and simple.

"Occasionally, I help out with some of their cases."

"You're in on the lie, too."

"I wouldn't exactly call it lying. We were under—"

"A lie by any other name still stinks, Dr. Colter." I said sharply.

"Yes, I suppose it does."

"I'd like a full drug screen done on my mother and myself." Might as well clear this all up and get these men out of our lives, once and for all.

"No one believes you are involved, Maggie."

"Even so, I want it done. I want all doubt removed from everyone's mind."

He nodded. "I'm terribly sorry about all of this, but my hands were tied. This is an undercover operation."

I'd had enough for one day, and didn't want to discuss this whole mess anymore. "Can I see my mother?"

"Certainly." He escorted me to a private room off the emergency department. My mom looked small and frail in the middle of the hospital bed. She had all kinds of wires and tubes hooked up to her and an oxygen mask strapped to her peaked face. I softly stroked her brow, and carefully laying across her body, I cried.

When I composed myself, I followed Dr. Colter to the x-ray department. He gave me a clean bill of health, along with a painful tetanus shot, after the results from the CAT scan and drug screen came back negative. I thanked him, hustled down the nearly empty hallway, and went to the maternity floor waiting area. It was two a.m., and I wasn't about to walk home in the dark after my run-in with the men at my house.

There were a couple of families anxiously awaiting the arrival of a new member. Despite the shouts of glee, I was grateful for the extra bodies. I found a plush maroon chair in the corner, curled up into it, and fell asleep almost instantly. It had been a long miserable day, and I refused to think about it for another minute.

I spent the next morning reading to my mother from some ancient magazines I confiscated from the waiting room. My mind saturated with information about the vast uses of Styrofoam, and how to cook an entire Thanksgiving meal that fed six for under twenty-five dollars.

Staying with her occupied my mind, leaving little room to think about Seth. Walking home later that day was another story. I barely made it inside before losing control and falling hard onto the floor. "Fool! You stupid fool! Why did I let my guard down? Why?" I twisted onto my side and clenched my stomach. I felt so totally and utterly deceived my body physically hurt.

Then the anger hit again.

I drew myself up off the floor and pushed everything out of my heart, except my mom. I wouldn't waste another minute pining over Seth. I was a means-to-an-end for him, period, and it wouldn't happen again. Lesson learned.

Walking into the kitchen, I found an abandoned search warrant on the counter. The police had searched my trailer. I felt angry and violated all over again. I crumpled it up, tossed it into the garbage can, and began straightening up while I made a mental list of what needed to be done to keep us safe, finally deciding on a dead bolt for the front door and some window locks.

Now I needed money. That was a major problem. I searched the kitchen and bathroom, but they were a total bust, as was my room. Under the couch cushions, I found a total of eleven cents. I shoved the paltry coins into my pocket and plopped down on the couch in complete frustration.

The only place I hadn't checked was my mother's room. She'd always forbidden me from going in there unless I had to help her into bed after a long day of drinking. Did she have money she didn't want me to know about? No matter how little food we had in the house, she always seemed to have enough for her booze.

On the other hand, maybe she'd forbidden me from going in there because she *was* doing drugs and didn't want me finding out.

The thought chilled me to the bone. There had to be a reason Seth thought she was involved in this mess. Sucking in a deep breath, I decided to check.

I walked slowly into my mom's sanctuary. The long narrow room was an absolute mess. Housekeeping was most certainly not her forte. Arranged long-ways on the wall and extending to the doorway of her closet, the unmade bed occupied most of the room. The only possible way for her to get into bed was to crawl in from the top, which was probably why she opted to sleep on the couch most nights.

Some tattered sneakers and a clean bed sheet wadded up in the corner inside the closet. Beside the bed sat a rickety-looking nightstand that held a small clock and a broken lamp sitting precariously on the edge. Running parallel to the bed stood a long white dresser. It made it difficult to reach her closet without shimmying along the wall sideways. I offered to rearrange the room for her once so she could navigate around easier. She told me to mind my own business and get out.

I began my hunt, going quickly through her mostly empty dresser drawers and finding nothing. A small pile of clean clothes stacked in the corner held no surprises either, and the barren nightstand was a complete waste of time. No secret treasure under the bed either, except dust bunnies, lots of dust bunnies. Gross. About to give up, I thought to look under the mattress. On lifting it, the green tinge of money was not what caught my eye, but the soft beige of an eleven by fourteen inch manila envelope.

I withdrew it from beneath the mattress, reading the words written across the front aloud. "Last Will and Testament." Why she had a will was beyond me. We had nothing. I flipped the unsealed envelope open and dumped the contents out onto the bed. Four smaller white envelopes and a twenty-dollar bill tumbled out onto the mattress. I couldn't believe something good finally came my way. I tucked the money into my pocket and placed everything else carefully back under the mattress. I took off for the hardware store as fast as my legs could carry me.

I had enough money to buy a lock for each of the windows and one for the door, with two dollars and sixty-two cents left over. I stopped at the grocery store and bought a loaf of day-old bread and an off-off brand of peanut butter. I'd have to worry about finding food again now that *Secret Agent Man* was out of my life.

I went straight to work installing the window locks. Not owning any tools, I had to improvise. I found a kitchen knife to be a great screwdriver and a large rock from the front yard made a pretty decent hammer. Every time my heart began to mourn my loss, I'd twist a little harder with the knife.

The window locks took only forty-five minutes to install, not bad for a rookie. I put off the dead bolt for last. Even though the sun shined brightly, the breeze was quite cool. I didn't like having the front door open while working on the lock but it had to be done. We didn't have power yet, and no matter how hard it tried, our small gas stove just wasn't equipped to heat an entire trailer.

After struggling for over an hour trying to install the dumb lock, I took a break. I went over to the kitchen for a piece of bread, and to wiggle my cold fingers over the flames on the stove.

"You can't be serious?" I wheeled around to find Seth standing in the doorway, the dead bolt lying across his palm. "Can I come in so we can talk?"

"There're no drugs here. I searched the entire house, as did you and your cop friends. Did they find anything?" He shook his head. "I didn't think so. Now get out."

He cringed at my harsh words. I felt sickened and softened my tone. "I can't deal with this right now. Please, if you ever really cared, just a little, go away and leave me alone."

He looked as if I'd kicked him in the stomach. "I'm not giving up on us, Maggie. I'll give you time, but I'll be right here, waiting." He turned, picked up the makeshift tools, and finished installing the dead bolt lock in less than two minutes. Grrr.

"Do you actually believe this lock will keep out anyone who really wants to get inside?" He pulled back the left side of his jacket and flashed the gun strapped to his chest in a brown leather holster. I realized fifty dead bolts wouldn't have stopped anyone if they really wanted to get in and a wave of fear gripped me.

"I paid the electric bill. The power should be back on Monday around noon," he said, without looking back.

"Thank you," I whispered as he walked away.

This time I couldn't stop the tears. I sank to the floor and let them flow. I loved him. How was I supposed to live without him?

After my little pity-party, I locked up the house and went to the hospital. My mother was my focus now. I collapsed into the recliner next to her bed and stroked her hair, praying that she'd live. I felt somewhat safe next to her, though I had no idea why. She had never protected me in any way. Nevertheless, it was how I felt. A few hours later, the staff began serving up dinner to the other patients, and I decided I should leave since my stomach growled much too loudly.

"Don't die, mom, please don't leave me here all alone," I said, kissing her forehead tenderly. I brushed the tears off my face with the back of my hand and left.

The weather had warmed somewhat so I took the long way home, mostly to avoid the emptiness of my trailer. Many of the homes along the way had young flowers just starting to break through the soil, and the sky above was a royal blue instead of its usual hazy Upstate New York gray.

Walking past the library, I decided to stop and do a little research on heroin. With hundreds of books listed on the subject, I was quickly overwhelmed and sought out the librarian. A macabre looking girl, dressed completely in black, including her lipstick, sat behind the help desk. Her nametag read *Bambi*. I looked twice to make sure. I had a feeling if anyone knew anything about drugs, it'd probably be Bambi.

"I'm trying to find some books on heroin. Maybe something that has a few pictures and that lists the side effects of the drug."

"Sure thing," she said with a smile. She cracked a wad of pink bubble gum as she typed info into the computer.

"They're over this way," she pointed and walked a step ahead of me. "I don't know a whole lot about the drug world really," she said, spinning her nose ring. "It's not my thing, ya know?" I immediately felt guilty for assuming she was an expert. "I'm, like, totally into fantasy, you know, like elves and fairies." She pulled up her sleeve and showed me two fairy tattoos on her forearm. She twisted around, showing me a tramp stamp of an elf on her lower back. "And this one is for my boyfriend Alex," she said, lifting the leg of her black leather pants. "He's, like, totally into werewolves." A savage-looking werewolf sat tattooed above her ankle, and I hoped for her sake she and Alex never broke up.

Bambi led me to a large section of books that dealt with the different types of substances ranging from alcohol to a wide variety of drugs. "You look familiar. Do you go to Port Fare High?"

"Yes, I'm a senior."

"I graduated early, in December," she said, proudly. "You look good. Did you, like, gain some weight?"

"A little." I began thumbing through several of the books as she rambled on. She had a nice voice, deep and somewhat raspy, with a slight lisp when she got excited.

"I remember there was this really hot guy who moved in over the summer. What was his name?" She thumped her palm on her forehead, trying to remember. "I think it was Seth. Seth Preston or something like that."

"Seth Prescott," I said softly.

"Prescott, that's it. Man, was he ever hot. I was tempted to ask him to the Christmas dance, but he was only eighteen. I'm nineteen. October birthday," she said, pointing to herself. "Anyway, I have, like, a strict policy to never date younger guys. Alex is twenty." She let out a raspy breath and smiled. "Older men are, like, so much more mature. We've been together for four weeks. He is totally it for me."

She pulled up her pant leg and looked down longingly at her werewolf tattoo again. "Alex has the high score on Werewolf Island at the Burger Barn." I looked at her blankly. "Oh my gosh! Like, it's only the hottest video game on werewolves ever created. Okay, like, werewolves are the good guys for once, and if you make it to, like, level six, shape-shifters appear and help the wolves conquer the witch-demons so they can free the island. That's how Alex learned, like, everything there is to know about werewolves and shape-shifters." As she spoke, a tiny diamond embedded in the side of her canine tooth caught the light and twinkled.

Bambi was a wealth of information, showing me several books that would help in my quest. I thanked her, took my treasures to the checkout desk, and left for home with my booty.

To my delight, Fluffy sat on my doorsteps when I arrived. "Fluffy, where have you been?" He immediately jumped up, his entire back end wagging happily as I opened the door. I dropped the books on the couch and gathered up the fur ball, peppering the top of his head in kisses.

"I missed you. You're all I have left," I said, stroking his silky coat. "It's been a bad week, Fluffy. It turns out Seth is a lying dog . . . oops, sorry." I playfully ruffled up his fur. "I mean he's a lying weasel. Anyway, he's an undercover cop. If that isn't enough, my mom's in the hospital again." I held back my tears, burying my face in his fur.

Pulling myself together, I set him down on the couch next to me and began my research into the drug world, skipping dinner, mostly to ration the bread.

Fluffy stayed by my side the entire evening, more than once jumping up on my lap and sending the books flying onto the floor. I set him back down several times and even threatened to put him outside before he settled quietly down at my feet.

It didn't take long to discover why Seth thought my mom and I did drugs. Physically we had many of the signs: jutting bones, dark circles under our eyes, and pale skin. *Heroin Chic* is what one book called the look. *Starving to Death* is what I called it. I began to feel a little guilty for going off on Seth like I did.

After four hours, I set the books aside, let Fluffy out for the night, and went to bed. Not until three in the morning did sleep win out over my thoughts.

For the next several days Seth wasn't at school. I didn't see him, or ride with him to CaL class. My afternoons were spent at the hospital with my mom reading to her.

Dr. Colter informed me of her poor liver functions. They kept her sedated in hopes it would help her body to heal quicker. They were afraid if she were coherent she'd leave and start drinking again. He also said her drug screen came back negative, information I hoped he shared with Booker and Seth.

When I was home alone, the memories of Seth invaded my mind and heart. One particularly difficult evening while struggling to think of something to do to keep my mind occupied, I came dangerously close to taking out my Calculus book. Thankfully, I remembered the envelopes under my mother's mattress. I wanted to look at the will and check out what the other envelopes were. It was probably nothing, but I was desperate at this point.

I went straight to her room and pulled the large manila envelope out, dumping the contents onto her bed. The first letter read: Last Will and Testament. Self-explanatory, I set it aside. The other three had my name on them. One read: *Maggie, seven years old*, another read: *Maggie, eleven years old*, and the last one, dated this past November a month before my birthday, read: *Maggie, eighteen years old*.

24

The envelope titled *Maggie, seven years old*, was yellowed, and held several circular-shaped stains. If I were to hazard a guess, I'd say the bottom of a vodka glass had made them. Turning the letter over, I wondered if it contained photos of me or a past report card.

Remembering nothing significant about that year in my life, I held the envelope up to the light. It appeared to be a letter of some kind, but I couldn't quite make out the words. I looked at the sealed flap and noted numerous loose points. Feeling a rush of guilt, I thought of putting the letters away. After all, it was none of my business.

On the other hand, they did have my name on them. Curiosity won as my finger traced along the flap.

"Okay, if I can open it without damaging the envelope, I'll read it, if not, I'll put them away." Retrieving a knife from the kitchen, I sat on the couch and slid it carefully under the sealed edge. I got hardly any resistance as the envelope gladly opened itself up to me. I coaxed the letter out and straightaway recognized my mom's handwriting.

My sweet baby Maggie,

Happy seventh birthday. I decided to write you a letter each year on your birthday, beginning with this year. I'll give them to you when you turn ~~eighten~~ eighteen. My mom did this for me while I was growing up, and I always cherished those letters.

I wish we had money to buy you gifts today. As usual, we have none. I decided the best thing to give you would be my love. I've not been good at saying I love you, the last time being when you were a toddler, but I do love you.

You are such a happy, independent child. You never ~~complane~~ complain, not even when you're hungry, and you take good care of me, though I don't deserve it. I'm not a good mother, yes, I know, but things are about to change. Never again will you see me drunk.

Never again will I spend our last dollar on booze. This is my birthday gift to you. You mean so much to me. It's going to be better around here, baby girl. I was a nice person before I started drinking, and you'll see that now. It's going to be good for ~~me~~ us.

Love always, Mom

My mother wrote this? I was dumbfounded. She truly loved me, or at least she did at one point. I grabbed the second letter, opening it carefully and began devouring the words.

Happy 11th birthday, Maggie,

Well, I failed at writing you a letter each year on your birthday, and I failed at not drinking again. I'm an all-around failure. No matter how I try, I just can't seem to give it up.

This year will be ~~difer~~ different, Maggie. I'm entering a rehabilitation center for alcoholics. I found someone to take care of you while I'm at the center for a month. She's really nice, and I think you'll like her. I've known her for a while, her name is Mrs. Gianchi, and she's a mental health counselor. Her parents had a problem with alcohol too. She understands what we're going through, and I know she can be trusted with the most important thing in my life—you.

I've never told you this, but I was set to give you up for adoption when you were born. Surprised? But when the nurse placed you in my arms, I couldn't let you go. At the moment, I swore never to drink again, determined to be a good mom. I even managed to stay sober for five months, but obviously, I failed. I was selfish for not giving you up. You should have been placed into a good home with loving parents, plenty of food to eat, decent clothes to wear, and all the love you deserve.

I know I say cruel things to you at times. I'm so full of self-hate it just seems to spew out. I'm a despicable person, Maggie. Some days I want you to hurt as badly as I do. Whenever you bring your report cards home full of A's, I never acknowledge your achievements because I feel guilty knowing you had to study all by yourself, with no help from your drunk of a mother. I'm very sorry.

Yet despite my miserable example, you have a beautiful heart. I watch you play with the other kids in the ~~neiberh~~ neighborhood, and you're a little mother to them. You help them when they are hurt, and cheer them up when they're sad. You do for them what I should be doing for you.

Things are going to get better. By your next birthday, you won't even recognize me. We're going to have fun too. We may not have much money, but we'll have fun. You're the only good thing I ever did, sweetheart.

I love you, Mom

I re-read it four times, each time being filled with both love and anger toward her. Why had she never told me any of these things? For years I felt overwhelmed by the emptiness that engulfed me. As my body starved for food, my soul had a hunger of its own; it starved to be loved. So desperate for it, I wasted two months of my life on Zack, hoping he'd help fill the void, only he created a deeper chasm.

I'd felt loved once. I'd felt loved by Seth. Unfortunately that wasn't real either, just the desperate desires of a foolish girl. Why did I ever trust him?

My thoughts of Seth brought me back to the letters. I shouldn't have read them. They were my mom's private feelings. I was angry with Seth for the very thing I did with these letters, violating a trust.

I gathered up the two letters and put them away, promising myself I wouldn't read the last one. After carefully replacing them back between the mattresses, I took out my homework and began studying. I felt a peace inside knowing she had loved me once and an evil math assignment couldn't take that away. Sleep also came a little easier than it had the past few days as the thoughts of my mother's letters warmed my heart.

However, it didn't last.

"Miss Brown?" asked the unfamiliar voice on the phone.

"Yes." I was awakened from a peaceful sleep by the ringing of the cell phone. My heart pounded fiercely in my ears, making it difficult to hear.

"This is the receptionist at Port Fare General Hospital. Dr. Colter asked me to call you. He said it is urgent you get in touch with him."

"Can I speak to him?"

"You want me to try and find him now? I'm extremely busy. I have to answer these phones, take and deliver messages, and, well, many other things. You'll have to wait until tomorrow. If I happen to see Dr. Colter, I'll let him know. Good evening." She hung up. The woman was definitely in no danger of being named "Employee of the Month."

I was dressed and out the door three minutes later. Two blocks down the road, a police car came screeching up with its lights flashing. Was there a curfew I didn't know about? The door opened and out stepped Booker.

"Where exactly are you going? It's almost midnight. Don't you know we still haven't caught the men who tried to hurt your mother?"

"The hospital called, and Dr. Colter needs to talk to me. Something's wrong, I have to reach my mother," I said, not trying in the slightest to sound polite.

"I just talked to Cole, he didn't mention an emergency. I'll call him back."

"No, I want to see her, now." As I started to walk past him, he reached out for me. "Don't touch me!"

"Maggie." He looked as if I had slapped him across the face. "Stop acting like a child. It's not our fault this all happened. We have a job to do, and unfortunately, you're involved."

I didn't want to discuss Seth, or the drug case. "I just want to see my mother."

Despite my protests, Booker took out his cell phone, and while grumbling under his breath, punched the numbers on the keypad. "Hello, Cole, I have Maggie with me. She said—Yes, Seth's Maggie. No, I found her running down the street trying to get to the hospital. Yes, I pointed out the time, but someone from the hospital called her and said you wanted to talk to h—Yes." Booker handed me the phone.

"Maggie, the receptionist made a mistake," Dr. Colter said. "I asked her to call you in the *morning*. I wanted to speak with you about your mother. There's something important we need to go over."

"Okay," I said, taking a deep breath. His voice was calm and gentle, making it difficult to be upset.

"Thank you. How about tomorrow morning at ten? There's a café across the street from the hospital."

"Yes, ten is good."

"Have Booker give you my personal cell phone number, and feel free to call anytime. One more thing, please be careful, these drug dealers mean business. We were lucky with your mom. I doubt we'll be that lucky again." Booker handed me a piece of paper with a phone number written on it, evidently having heard our entire conversation.

"I'll take you home." I shook my head at Booker's request. "Sorry, you can't walk alone." He held out his hand in the direction of my house, and I started walking.

"Seth really does love you, you know." He continued, despite my silence. "I've known him his entire life, and I can honestly say I've never seen him as happy as he has been with you." Increasing my pace, he followed suit.

"Listen, Jailbait, he had a job to do. Put yourself in his place," he snapped.

Jailbait? What the heck! I was eighteen.

"We thought you were a drug addict. What was he supposed to do, ask you who you bought your stuff from?"

I reeled around so fast it startled him, and he stepped back. If it was possible to spontaneously combust, I would have done it right there on the spot. "How could you *possibly* think I was an addict? I've never been in any trouble."

"Maggie," he said softly, resting a hand on my shoulder. "You had many of the signs. We had no idea you were slowly starving to death. And for the record, I was the one that suspected you. Seth was adamant about your innocence, insisting that it didn't add up. He pointed to your high GPA, and how you tutored other kids in English during your lunch hour." He laughed. "He had it bad for you from the start. I'm sorry I didn't believe him."

Afraid I'd burst into tears, I pulled away and continued walking toward my house. I'd gone no more than three steps when Booker started up again.

"He's devastated about hurting you, and he blames himself. He wanted to tell you sooner, but when he finally got the okay, he was afraid of how you'd react. He was hoping by the time you did find out, your love would be strong enough that you'd forgive him. I guess he was wrong."

His statement cut through me. When we arrived at my place, I thanked him without looking back. "Maggie, whether you like it or not, it appears that somehow your mother's involved."

"Did Cole mention my mother's drug screen came up negative?"

"No, that is good news." He seemed genuinely pleased with the news.

"As did mine. So I guess you and Seth can leave us alone."

His smile vanished. "Please give him another chance."

I stared directly into his beautiful brown eyes. "My entire life I've never trusted anyone. I've never had *anyone* to trust. I've taught myself to believe in me, and no one else, and then the *one* time I do, I'm stabbed in the back."

"He's not perfect, Maggie, I'll give you that. However, if you think you'll find a perfect person to love and trust, you can stop looking, because one doesn't exist. Good night." He waited until I was safely inside before leaving. I went into my room, cranked up my clock radio as loud as it would go, and fell mindlessly onto my bed. No further thinking tonight.

Up early the next morning, I rushed to the hospital only to find a new device hooked up to my mother. "This can't be good." At quarter to ten, I made my way down the stairs and across the street to the café. Dr. Colter waited already with a plate of eggs and bacon in front of himself and one opposite him.

"I took the liberty of ordering you breakfast," he said warmly.

"I'm not hungry, thank you anyway," I said. The eggs looked delicious. After eating nothing but peanut butter sandwiches for several days, I starved for something different.

"You need to keep up your strength. It won't help your mother if you end up in the bed next to her." He smiled again, his deep blue eyes radiating kindness once more. I stood staidly. "Maggie, you're extremely pale, and I believe you've lost some weight. Please, sit down and eat some breakfast."

I caved. "Thanks." I sat and devoured the breakfast way too quickly. It felt good to have warm food in my belly again. When I finished, he summoned the server over and ordered more food. "No, I'm fine, I couldn't eat another bite." I could've eaten ten more platefuls only my pride reared its ugly head once more.

"You can take it home for later," he said casually. "Maggie, I'll get to the point. Your mother's condition has gotten worse, and she needs a liver transplant, the sooner the better. I'd like to place her on the donor list if I can stabilize her."

The server brought another plate of food as Cole informed me of the different tests they had run on her, and what they tried to do with medications. He said a liver transplant was her only option at this point. I immediately shoved the plate away, the smell made me sick. He had it taken away and boxed it up.

"Unfortunately, in her current condition she's not quite strong enough to endure a transplant. It's why we're keeping her sedated. If we didn't, she'd be suffering with nausea, vomiting, and extreme mental confusion because her condition. The strain on her already frail body wouldn't be good. I'm doing everything I can to help her, and I've called every expert I can think of for advice," he said frustrated.

I dropped back in my chair. "Can I donate part of my liver to her when she's strong enough? I remember reading somewhere you can be a live liver donor."

"You can, but honestly, Maggie, you're too thin. I don't think your small body would be up for the task. Even if you are a perfect match, I wouldn't give my approval for you to be a donor."

I nodded, knowing he was probably right.

"Does your mother have any other direct relatives?"

"No, just me." Swallowing hard, I asked the question I wasn't sure I wanted to hear the answer to. "Are any of her problems from drug abuse?" I kept my eyes on the table, unable to meet his gaze.

His warm hands covered mine gently, and I looked up. "No, Maggie, I don't believe for a minute that your mom has been doing illegal drugs. Her problem is alcohol, I'm sure of it. And yes, to answer your next question, I've told both Booker and Seth my opinion this morning."

"Thanks," I said softly.

"Is there anything I can do to help you?"

"Why do I need help?" I said, pulling my hands out from under his.

"Do you have a support system in place if things don't go well? Are you part of any support groups?"

"I'll be fine. I don't need anyone," I said, shooting out my chin in a stubborn stance.

He lowered his voice. "Maggie, I know Seth should have—"

"Is there anything else, Dr. Colter?" I stood and slid my chair under the table.

"No, that's everything for now." He exhaled loudly. "Would you be more comfortable if I handed her case over to my associate, Dr. Taylor?"

I looked at him, searching his gentle features. "No, I'd like you to stay on as her doctor," I said softly.

"As you wish." He gave a quick nod, handed me the boxed-up leftovers, and left without another word. I raced back to my mother's room, noting how peaceful she looked lying there.

"I love you, mom, don't give up." I stayed with her as long as I dared. With the sun hanging dangerously low in the sky, I left but didn't get far before a patrol car pulled up alongside me once again.

"You must have a death wish, Jailbait," Booker said, clearly exasperated. "Get in, I'll take you home."

"No, thank you. I'm in no mood to be lectured about . . . him." I also didn't care for his little nickname for me, but that'd be a battle for another day.

His mouth twisted into a wicked grin. "If I promise not to bring up *He-Who-Must-Not-Be-Named*, will you get in?"

Did he really think his stupid joke was funny? I shook my head defiantly. "Fine, I'll arrest you." He slammed the car into park, and was next to me before I could take another step. He took my arm, dragging me toward the car.

"What am I being charged with?" I pulled my arm out of his grip, proud of the fact that I didn't punch him because part of me sure wanted to.

"Hmm, let me think. How about loitering and resisting arrest?"

"Loitering? I'm walking home. How is that loitering?"

"I've been a cop for a long time, Maggie. I can come up with something."

"That would be lying, and no one will believe you."

"Are you serious? I have a stellar reputation on the force, and you're a teenager. Who do you think they'll believe?"

"Fine," I bit out. "You can take me home, except no lectures."

"Fine." He smiled politely and opened the door for me as if he were a gentleman. I put on my seatbelt, sitting as close to the door as possible. He chuckled low.

True to his word, he never mentioned Seth once. After dropping me off, he waited until I went inside again before leaving. I warmed up the leftovers from the cafe as my mind struggled with the stupid choices I'd made over the past week.

25

"*H*i, Maggie." It was Dwayne, my new cooking buddy. Seth had transferred out of all the classes we'd shared. At first I was relieved, now I wasn't so sure.

"Hey, Dwayne, what are we cooking today?" I had eaten the last of the peanut butter and bread for breakfast, and had no idea what I was going to do now that I had no money left. My mother's social security check wouldn't be here for another five days, and the dizziness and hunger headaches tortured me with a vengeance.

"I don't know, and by the way, you look awful."

I felt awful, not having slept well in I didn't know how long. If I didn't dream about my mother and the possible liver transplant, I dreamt about Seth.

When I'd first learned he was a cop, my dreams depicted him trying to hunt me down and shoot me. For the past two days, the dreams brought him back kissing me. The kisses seemed so real I'd wake up in the middle of the night with an ache in my heart. Booker's words haunted me also. I started to think I had overreacted to everything . . . big time.

Seth was an MET agent, and for some reason my mom was suspected of doing drugs. He really didn't have a choice. Still, knowing that, and not letting it hurt me, was two different matters.

Time to change the subject.

"I overheard Melody say you liked the new girl, Allison." I smiled.

"Allison? Leave it to Melody to get it wrong. I hope Karen didn't hear that." He looked worried.

"Karen, as in cheerleader Karen?'

He blushed. "Yeah."

"Does she know you like her?"

"No, but I said hi to her in the hallway yesterday." He actually seemed proud of his mediocre achievement.

"Dwayne, at this rate it will be the middle of summer 2018 before you ask her out." He dropped his head back and groaned. "Hey, did you know there's a Pep rally on Thursday? Karen will be cheering at it. You should go. Maybe you could ask her out while you're there."

"Oh, Maggie, you don't understand what I'm like when she's around. My palms get all sweaty, and my heart pounds so loudly in my ears I can barely hear. What if she says no?" He threw his arms across the desk and plopped his head down onto them. Poor guy.

Suddenly, he sprung back up. "Wait, I have an idea. You can go with me to the Pep rally, that way if she turns me down, I won't look like a total loser."

"I'm not following you."

"If we're there, you know, just a couple of friends hanging out together, I can act all casual when we see her, like, 'Hey, Karen, how's it going?' Then I could say something like, 'Do you want to go out for ice cream some time?' She'll think I'm just a friendly guy, no big deal. But if I'm there all alone, she'll think I'm a total loser that no one wants to date, and that I'm desperate, then she won't want to go out with me."

I couldn't follow his convoluted logic whatsoever. I also had no idea guys put so much thought into asking a girl out. Absolutely heartbreaking to watch.

"Sure, if you think it will work." I certainly didn't think it would.

"Thanks," he said, with a sigh of relief. "You're amazing, no wonder Seth's miserable without you." Dwayne turned to look up at the teacher as she gave instructions for today's cooking lesson, lasagna.

Walking home with the leftover food, my thoughts circled again to Seth. If he didn't really care, then why had he told me repeatedly that he loved me? He must have cared somewhat. He was a good guy, he wouldn't purposely hurt me. I suddenly got the feeling that maybe I'd just blown the best thing that ever happened to me. I was now as confused as when I listened to Dwayne and his crazy dating scenario.

A soft breeze ruffled the air as I walked to school the next morning. It felt warm and smelled of spring Hyacinths as it rolled around me and twisted through my hair. In my preoccupation with the breeze, I didn't hear Fluffy bounding up the street until he stopped in front of me, barking his soprano bark.

"Fluffy, where have you been?" I scooped him up, and he let out a small groan of excitement as he bounced around in my arms trying to lick my face.

"I've missed you. Have you been hanging out at Gertie's house irritating her possessed cat?" He barked once, clearly a yes. "I have to go to school. You'd better go back to Gertie's." I gave him a quick peck on the head and went to set him down when I spotted a hundred dollar bill clipped to his collar. I looked around fully expecting to see Seth, but instead saw a patrol car parked at the corner. I stomped over to the car with Fluffy still in my arms and handed Booker the money.

"Maggie, you know I could arrest you for bribery, right?" He had a smirk on his lips as he eyeballed Fluffy.

"I don't want this, and I know you put it there."

"No, you're quite wrong. I had nothing to do with it," he said, rather smugly. "Did you ever get this scruffy fur-ball neutered?" He reached out to stroke Fluffy on the head, who turned and snapped at him.

"Good boy, Fluffy." I gave him a squeeze.

"Fluffy?" he said, laughing loudly. "You named him Fluffy?"

I ignored him and turned back to the matter at hand. He may not have planted the money on the dog, but he knew who did. I knew who did.

"You can turn this money over to the lost and found at the police station." I grinned smartly.

"What a fine, upstanding citizen you are, Maggie. Get in." He jumped out of his car and held open the back door.

"What? I'm not trying to bribe you. I want you to turn this over to the lost and found." I didn't have time for this. I had to hurry for Mr. Googolo's calculus test, and he didn't allow make up tests.

"Yes, I know, except there's an enormous amount of paperwork involved when filing a lost and found report. It could take hours, all for a hundred dollars you and I both know will never be claimed," he purred sweetly.

"Argh!" Frustrated, I stuffed the money in my pocket and started for school, forgetting I still held Fluffy in my arms.

"Maggie, hand me the dog. You can't take him to school with you. I'll run him back over to your house." He reached out for Fluffy, and I pulled the dog protectively behind me.

"If I promise not to roast him over an open fire and eat him for lunch will you give him to me?" he said with a sincere expression on his face. "Though I may have him neutered. Do you know how many stray dogs and cats are running around? We could solve a huge portion of the problem with a simple snip snip of the scissors." Fluffy barked loudly at Booker, jumped out of my arms, and ran back toward my house. Booker chuckled.

"Smart little dog you have there, Maggie. Good luck with your calculus test," he yelled after me. How did he know about . . . ? Lousy cops.

The whole incident cost me precious minutes, and I now had to run to avoid being late for class. Mr. Googolo was closing the door as I arrived.

"Perfect timing, Miss Brown, you're lucky I forgot about shutting the door. Someone must be watching out for you. Hurry, take your seat." Still breathing hard, it took a few minutes before I could concentrate enough to begin the test. Overall, I thought I did fairly well. I wasn't the first one done, or the last.

I bought lunch from the cafeteria for the first time ever. Seth had always insisted cafeteria food wasn't real food. I couldn't believe the different choices they offered. I bought two slices of pizza. It tasted pretty good for not being real food. I wrapped the second slice in a napkin for later and slipped it in my book bag as Zack sank onto the chair next to me.

"Aw, let me guess. You're saving that for the stupid mutt hanging around your trailer."

"Go away. And he's not a stupid mutt. He's got more class in one paw than you have in your entire body." I pushed past him and darted into the hall, stuffing the last, *too big* bite of pizza into my mouth. Unfortunately, he followed me, and even more unfortunately, we ran into Seth and a pimply-faced tenth grader named Scott. My heart flipped over in my chest. I forced the oversized bite painfully down my throat, trying not to choke.

"Are you going to the Pep rally on Thursday?" Ignoring Zack's question, I tried swallowing some spit to force down the pizza wedged in my throat. "Maggie, do you want to go together?"

He must be on drugs.

I glared at him, and with my finally clear throat, announced, "I have a date." I turned to leave when he caught my arm, jerking me back. Seth turned around as I yanked my arm away from Zack.

"With whom?" Zack asked in a condescending tone.

"Dwayne Wrights."

"You're going to the Pep rally with Dwayne?" My stomach quivered at the sound of Seth's voice.

"He's a nice guy, what's wrong with that?"

Seth let out a short laugh. "Not a thing. I think Dwayne's a great guy." I turned and left before he could say anything else, though I did hear him mumble something about a frying pan and fire.

By the time Thursday came, my mom's condition didn't improve but rather had worsened, and sorrow dominated my heart. The idea of going to a pep rally pretending to be peppy didn't sit well with my overall mood. If Dwayne hadn't been so excited, I'd have canceled.

Thanks to the nice weather, they held the rally outdoors, a refreshing change from the smelly gym. Dwayne insisted we sit high up in the football bleachers, probably wanting as much space between him and Karen as possible. I could see the rest of the student body seated below us, including, to my surprise, Seth. He sat about ten rows up from the field. We'd never gone to a pep rally while we dated. He must have gotten a new assignment, and I wondered who the new target was.

Out on the field, I watched Hillary bouncing her pom-poms directly at him. It gave me some satisfaction to see he didn't pay much attention to her. She looked more than a little perturbed by it, and I couldn't help but smile.

Dwayne was adorable to watch. He never took his eyes off Karen. She appeared to have waved at us a couple of times, only I wasn't sure because of my preoccupation with watching Seth. Halfway through the rally, Hillary bounced up the stairs, seized Seth by the hand, and tried dragging him down onto the field. He escaped her grip and quickly crawled into a seat in the front row of the bleachers. Undaunted, she cheered directly in his face instead.

After the rally, I hauled Dwayne down to the field and straight over to Karen. "Hi, Karen, you looked great today."

"Thanks, Maggie. How are you? We haven't talked in forever."

"I'm fine," *aside from a broken heart.* "Do you know Dwayne?"

She tucked her pom-poms carefully into a bag and started changing her flashy, blue cheer shoes for tan sneakers. "Yes. Hi, Dwayne." Her face flushed, and she appeared nervous. *Did she like him*? "We have biology together. You probably haven't noticed me. I sit in the back."

"I've noticed," he said, smiling back shyly.

"I didn't know you and Maggie were dating." Her face registered disappointment. This was going better than I hoped.

"We aren't dating," I said. Dwayne froze in place until I nudged him.

"No," he said, "we're just friends."

"Really?" Karen smiled shyly.

"Dwayne, I have to use the rest room. Why don't I meet you at the car? Don't rush. I'm sure there'll be a line." He nodded. I turned to Karen. "Nice talking to you again."

Dwayne handed me the car keys, looking eager for me to leave. I took a shortcut through a couple of the buildings to reach the parking lot. Zack appeared out of nowhere, looking like he hadn't slept in a week. Probably overtraining for baseball again.

"Hey." He put his arm around me. I shoved it away. "I hope you're not still angry about lunch on Tuesday. I didn't mean to offend you. You know how warped my sense of humor is sometimes." I walked on in silence. "Maggie, it's not very nice to hold a grudge. Let me give you a ride home. We'll even stop at Burger Palace and get something for your dog to eat."

I dangled Dwayne's keys in his face. "Oh, well, I'll walk you to the car then." I continued to ignore him, and walked toward the student lounge, stopping only to gather some books from my locker.

"You look pretty today, Maggie. Real pretty." My mistrusting nature kicked into overdrive. He was up to something. He'd never complimented me before. "Wait, I need to get something from my locker."

I didn't wait, continuing instead as if he wasn't there. "Come on, give me a chance to prove I'm a good guy." He jumped in front of me with a ridiculous pout on his face. "Please." Fairly certain Dwayne would still be talking with Karen, I turned and silently followed Zack, although why I did I had no idea. I must be more desperate for human companionship than I thought—not that Zack was human.

He ran ahead a few feet and turned the corner to his locker. Rounding the corner after him, I looked down the hall and saw Seth, with Hillary wrapped around him, their faces mashed together in a kiss. I stepped back around the corner, falling against the wall, my breath catching in my chest.

"Sorry, I didn't realize they'd be here. They've been at it all day. It's really starting to get on my nerves." He draped his arm around my shoulder and led me away. Dazed, I paid no attention to where he took me. We went down several hallways before turning into a deserted classroom.

"All day?" I finally managed to speak. To think I had almost convinced myself I'd been wrong about him, and that he really did care for me.

"Yes. Rumor has it she spent the night at his house last night. Does that bother you? You two broke up, right?"

It took me a few seconds to realize he'd wrapped his arms around me and rubbed my back. "Stop it!" I shoved him away and turned to leave, not wanting Zack to witness my meltdown.

He had other plans. Grabbing the hand holding my book bag, he twisted my arm behind me, pulling me against him.

"Maggie, forget about him. He's out of your league. You and I are more logical."

"More logical? Based on what?"

He gripped my face, and I winced at the pain as his fingers dug into my cheeks. He dropped his slimy, foul-smelling mouth down onto mine.

"Stop it!" I twisted my head to the side and punched him in the chest. His grip stayed strong.

"No. I waited for you and your stupid ideas, then you started dating him and just gave-in. Melody told me all about it. You've been sleeping with him for weeks. You owe me, Maggie." Lust frothed his eyes.

"Melody's wrong. We didn't do anything." I swung my free arm at him. He caught it mid-swing and twisted it tight behind my back, next to the other. It felt as if he'd ripped them both off.

"Lies, Maggie. Everyone can see the way you look at him." His left hand grabbed my face once more as he tried to press his mushy lips to mine. This time I was ready. With my now freed hand, I swung my book bag around, smacking him hard on the side of his head, sending him toppling over a couple of desks. I rushed out the door and ran straight to Dwayne's car. Zack followed.

Before I could lock myself inside, he caught me from behind, slamming me violently onto the ground. I winced at the sharp pain in my knees while droplets of blood wept through my right pant leg. I glanced around looking for help, but the parking lot was deserted.

"I put up with your innocent virgin crap for months while I patiently waited for you." Patiently wouldn't be the word I would've chosen. It was more like a full court press on every date. "Then you go and sleep with that clown after how long, Maggie, three whole weeks?"

"I swear, Zack, we haven't—"

"Shut up." He dragged me up by my shirt and forced me against a nearby car. "Come on, Maggie. Kiss me like you kissed him."

I shook my head. "Please stop, Zack, please don't do this." Tears streamed uncontrollably down my face. He glowered at me for several moments, as if debating what to do next, and I didn't like what I saw in his eyes.

Slowly, very slowly, he let go of my shirt. "Vile piece of trailer trash. You're probably full of disease anyway." He brutally shoved me aside. I fell again, this time tearing the right knee of my jeans as I hit the asphalt. My book bag spilled open, spewing books everywhere. He gave me one last look before spitting on the ground next to me and walking away.

I sat on the ground, pulling my knees up against my chest and hugging them fiercely, refusing to let my mind replay what had just happened. I thought to lock myself in the car, only my body wouldn't move.

But I had to. I gathered up my belongings and forced myself up off the ground as Dwayne showed up. He wore a grin from ear to ear on his cherub face. Good, maybe he'd be too excited to notice my disheveled appearance. I quickly smoothed my hair back into place.

"I did it, I—what happened to you?"

"Nothing, I fell. I'm fine, really," I said, casually.

"That's not true, Maggie, what happened? Did someone hit you? Why are your cheeks red?"

"No, really, look at my knee. I fell and my jeans tore." I showed him the rip. There were several more blood droplets around the tear now. "Dwayne, I'm fine. Tell me about Karen. Did you ask her out?"

"Yes." Doubt filled his eyes as he answered. "She said she'd love to go out with me. She didn't just say yes, she said she'd *love to*." He relived the moment several more times while driving me home.

"Maggie, do you want to get a burger or something? It's still early, and I want to thank you for your help. If you hadn't gone with me today, I would have never asked her out. I owe you big time."

"You don't owe me anything, that's what friends do, they help each other," I said, stepping up onto my porch.

"If that's how you really feel, will you hear me out before you go inside?"

"Yes." *Now what?*

He looked around as if he wanted to make sure no one would hear him, not a good sign. "Seth wanted to tell you about his being an undercover agent for a while, but he was afraid you'd dump him when he did." He paused slightly. "And you did dump him, so apparently he was right." I had already heard this from Booker. I didn't want to hear it . . . Wait.

"You know?" Seth told Dwayne about himself, yet he didn't bother telling me until my mother was almost killed? It ignited the anger inside me all over again.

"Maggie, a couple of years ago, he arrested my dad for buying drugs. Instead of jail time, Seth convinced the judge to admit him into a rehab program. He's been clean for two years, and he has a job thanks to Booker. They've been good to my family," he said humbly. "My dad and I have been trying to help him find out who is supplying the area with heroin."

"Oh, Dwayne, I had no idea."

"He wasn't trying to betray you, Maggie."

"I'm starting to think you're right." I felt relief as I admitted it. I still felt betrayed, no matter how hard I tried not to, but under the circumstances I certainly could understand why things were the way they were.

I said good bye and went inside to try to figure out what to do about the mess I'd made, but only after showering a couple of times to get the feel of Zack off my skin.

26

Unable to sleep any longer, I got up at five and had a bowl of Cheerios, with milk. I decided to skip school and spend the day at the hospital. It'd be a wash anyway, all classes had been canceled, and the entire day was being dedicated to educating us on the dangers of drug and alcohol abuse, complete with guest speakers. I certainly didn't need to be made aware of the heartaches of substance abuse, I knew firsthand.

Washing my face, I noticed four dark spots on my cheeks. "What the heck?" Looking closer, I saw bruises where Zack had grabbed my face. "Who does he think he is?" He wouldn't get away with this, not if I could help it. Shoving my arms into my sweater, I left for the hospital, only I didn't get far before . . .

"Good morning, Maggie. I do believe you're heading in the wrong direction for school, not to mention it doesn't start for another hour and a half."

Booker. Good grief, the vulture must sit outside my door just waiting for me to leave. "How do I press charges for police harassment? Surely there's some law against this?"

"True, police harassment is against the law, but again, my stellar reputation on the force, against your word, a mere teenager, who appears to be skipping school I might add, no one would believe you." Booker grinned, obviously satisfied at his superior ability to outwit me. "I've also just completed law school, and I'm well-versed in loopholes. You'd never get the charges to stick." He climbed out of his car and held the door open with his Cheshire cat grin spread across his handsome face. Why I ever thought that grin of his was cute I'd never know.

I kept my face innocent and looked him straight in the eye. "Hmm, a liar and a lawyer. How redundant."

"Six in the morning and you still have a quick wit. Impressive." He sauntered around and got back into the car. "Alright, I'm guessing you are on your way to the hospital?"

"You should come with me; maybe there'll be an ambulance you can chase after."

"And," he ignored my jab, "since there's not enough time for you to get to the hospital, and then over to the school, I'm thinking I was correct about your skipping school today?"

"Hmm, sounds like circumstantial to me, Officer."

"You could be arrested for truancy, are you aware of that, little Miss Sarcastic?"

I shrugged.

"May I ask why you're skipping? Half the police force will be there today for an assembly on . . . ah, never mind."

"Yeah, never mind," I said quietly.

"Sometimes life gives us a raw deal, you know? We have to make the best of it." Okay, what was he up to? This was more than simple compassion.

"Agreed," I said cautiously.

"Take Seth, for instance." *That's what he's up to.* "He isn't perfect and he makes mistakes. Everybody does."

"I thought the rule was no lectures about Seth if I let you give me a ride."

"No, that was our deal the last time. Those conditions no longer apply. This is a different day and time."

I thought to protest, but decided against it. His lawyer-brain would just come up with some convoluted way to justify his actions.

"As I was saying, Seth makes mistakes. He should have told you about us sooner, without a doubt, and those of us who love him should overlook those mistakes and try to understand why he did what he did." He glanced over. "You have something smeared on your cheeks, by the way."

"This whole 'Seth made a mistake' theory is pointless, really." I softly brushed at the tender bruises, pretending to wipe my face off.

"Not if you'll forgive him."

"Yes, even if I do forgive him. He has a new girlfriend, Hillary Jeffers. They were kissing after the pep rally last night." My eyes welled up with tears, and I turned my head to the window to keep him from seeing. Booker pulled up in front of the hospital and took my face in his hand. I winced as his fingers brushed up against the bruises. He promptly let go.

"How did you get these bruises on your face?" He took my face gently in both of his hands, not allowing me to pull away, and turning it from side to side, he inspected the marks.

"I don't remember." I was too embarrassed to explain what had happened. Zack became a little overzealous, that's all. Besides, I'd already decided to talk to Mrs. Volkel about what had happened. Sharing this with a woman made me more comfortable anyway.

"Maggie, these bruises didn't just appear."

"Thanks for the ride." I pulled my head away and reached for the door when he caught my hand.

"Don't you think it's a bit high and mighty of you to be blabbering on about trust and keeping secrets, yet you won't explain something as simple as these bruises? And I might remind you that Seth wasn't *allowed* to tell you, not at first, anyway."

Insert knife and twist. Yup, he'd be a mad wicked lawyer.

"Maggie, I don't know why he was kissing Hillary." He shook his head in disgust. "I can assure you it wasn't his idea. He's hopelessly in love with you. In fact, I've never seen him as miserable as he has been these past two weeks without you. If you dyed your hair orange and stuck a bone through your nose he'd still be in with love you."

"What if I've hurt him so deeply he won't forgive me?"

"Not a chance," he said, leaning over and kissing the top of my head. "Talk to him. I know you can work this out. Look how comfortable you are around me now, Jailbait. A breathtakingly handsome MET agent just kissed you on the head and you didn't even flinch."

"I wish you'd stop calling me that, old man. I'm eighteen," I murmured getting out of the car.

"Barely," he grinned mischievously.

I went directly to my mom's room and ran into Cole. I decided there was no time like the present to start repairing some of the damage I'd done.

"Hi. I, um, owe you an apology. I've been a real idiot, for lack of a better word, since finding out about . . . everything." I looked around to see if any of the staff listened. "You've done a lot for us, Dr. Colter, and I'm grateful for everything."

"You don't have to thank me, and please, call me Cole," he said kindly. "I'd like to talk to you about your mom, if I may." I sat down in the chair, worried about what he'd say next. "She's stabilizing, although she's not quite strong enough for a liver transplant yet."

"Cole, do you think my mother will *ever* be strong enough for the transplant?"

He hesitated. "I don't want to lie and say I'm not gravely concerned. What's worrying me at the moment is her pancreas. It's starting to show signs of failure. Nevertheless, I have seen people in *worse* condition than her recover. I'm not ready to give up yet. I put in a call to a colleague of mine in Washington, D.C. who's a phenomenal doctor. If anyone can come up with a way to help your mother, it'll be her." I slumped back down in my chair. "Have you eaten anything today?"

"I'm not hungry, but don't worry. Yesterday on my way to school, I *happened* to find a hundred dollar bill. Imagine my surprise."

"He's not very subtle," Cole laughed, "but he does love you." His eyes settled on my cheek. "How did you get those bruises?"

"Ah, it's dirt." I raised my hand, pretending to wipe off my cheeks. An overhead page for him boomed through the speakers, calling him away before he could examine my face further.

I left the hospital later than usual and somehow was able to avoid Booker. Cole's words weighed heavy on my heart, and I didn't have it in me to banter with him tonight. My senses were at full alert as I rushed home in the dark. Every bark of an angry dog, every swish of an owl's wings caught my attention.

Once home, I hurried inside, immediately locking the door behind me. I made a sandwich and pulled out the last letter from my mom. I'd tried so hard to forget about it, but couldn't fight it anymore. I had to read it.

The envelope was dated January of this year, and for some reason this letter was the most difficult for me to open. I stared at it for a long time trying to talk myself out of it until I could wait no longer. Carefully removing it from the envelope, I discovered several small smudges on the letter. They looked to be watermarks from teardrops maybe, or maybe she'd accidently splashed her vodka on it. I crawled up onto her bed, took a deep breath and began.

Maggie,

If you are reading this letter, it means I've died. Don't grieve, it's better this way. I don't want you to feel any sorrow for me, just relief because I can no longer hurt you.

After you were first born, all my anger was directed inward. I was angry with myself for my poor choices, and the mess I'd made of things. What kind of mother gives her child to her parents to raise? It seemed easier to deal with the guilt if I was drunk. So drink I did. Lots and lots. Only it didn't help. I'd sober up, and the self-hate would still be there.

Over time, I turned my anger toward you. I'd see you cleaning the house when it should have been me, and the anger grew. You'd cook the meals and it would enrage me. You'd take care of me when I was too drunk to stand, and I became infuriated. I told myself you were judging me, even though you weren't. The anger grew until I couldn't drink it away, and I let it out. Cold, bitter, hateful words, all aimed at the most innocent one of all. You.

Even that you took it all in stride, never back talking, or rebelling. You just tried harder to please the truly unlovable one. ME. Anyone who's seen a small ~~fatu~~ fraction of your loving heart must know how truly despicable I am.

We had a ~~terib~~ terrible fight last night, and I called you some horrible names again. After you left, I tried to drink myself into a stupor so I wouldn't have to ~~pain~~ think about the pain I saw in your eyes as you walked out the door. It didn't work. Instead, I sat ~~worying~~ worried, praying you'd be kept safe.

I'll bet you didn't know I crawled into bed with you Christmas Eve and held you. It felt good to have my arms around you again, it also felt ~~hori~~ ~~hrib~~ horrible. I knew you were thin, still, I had no idea how thin you've become. I have no one to blame but myself for that. I drink all our money away, and yet I still won't give it up.

I'm writing ~~me~~ you this now because I'm afraid I won't make it to your ~~seven~~ eighteenth. I've been having a lot of stomach pain over the past month, and I've been throwing up blood, every day in fact. I've been able to keep it from you. I'm good at keeping the truth from you. I should be since I've done it your whole life. I have ~~dist~~ destroyed every chance with you, and I'm a failure on all levels. I reread the letter from your 11th birthday last night. I never made it

227

to rehab. I got completely drunk the night before and didn't wake up for two days. What a pathetic mess I am.

Lately, there are times when I am totally confused, sometimes it's a struggle to find the bathroom. Yesterday I went outside to mail the electric bill and somehow ended up at Gertie's house. Thankfully, she helped me get back home, and so you know, she lectured me the entire time about how lucky I was to have such a wonderful young lady for a daughter.

Okay, now I'm going to give you a little advice. I know, how arrogant of me to offer advice. Nevertheless, here it is: no matter what life throws at you, <u>never</u> give up. Life is tough, and there'll be times when things seem insurmountable. I can't tell you how many times I quit drinking. For the first few hours it was easy, then I'd cave in. I can't remember having endured anything. I gave up on love. I gave up on life. I gave up on me.

My parents weren't quitters. They tried hard to help me, never giving up hope that I'd overcome my trials. They were truly great parents, and I wished I could have told them that before they died.

I hope you take after them, Maggie, and I pray you can find the kind of love they had. I watched as my parents worked through ~~treh~~ their problems, never giving up on each other. I hope you won't settle for less.

My mother used to tell me, 'When you find that special someone, Barbara, love him as though your life depends on it.' I was so caught up in my ~~dringin~~ drinking, I could never see anyone except me and my instant ~~greta~~ gratification. It wouldn't be far off the mark to say I love booze as though my life depended on it. I lose. I'm going to die alone with no one to hold except my cold bottle of vodka.

You make me proud, very proud. I'm lucky to ~~be~~ have been your mother, your weak, reprehensible mother.

I have to go, I'm starting to feel sick again. I'll write more tomorrow, <u>I promise.</u>

I held the letter to my chest and cried deep mournful tears. It was as if every painful moment, every sorrowful thing that ever happened to me purged itself from my soul. I wept and couldn't stop.

I also felt robbed. If she didn't receive a liver transplant soon, we might never have any kind of relationship. I cried for a very long time, having no idea when the tears stopped. On waking in the morning, the letter lay crumpled in my hand, my pillow was still damp with tears, and my head pounded mercilessly. I dragged my weary body into the bathroom for some aspirin, forced down some breakfast, and went out to sit on the porch.

It was a beautiful morning. The sun shone brightly, the budding trees stood tall all around me, and the squirrels meandered precariously along the neighbor's fence. I sat and watched the wildlife, letting the sun bathe my face with its warmth until my head stopped throbbing.

I returned to the letter several more times, each time trying not to cry, and each time failing. I also spent time thinking about Seth. I quit on him. The first time a challenge came along for us, I tossed him aside. Now I regretted it with all my heart.

Time to move on, get over what had happened. Though it still hurt, I understood why he kept what he did from me. Whether or not I agreed with him, the police *thought* my mom and I were involved, and Seth had a job to do.

I realized I'd set him up to fail me, mostly because everyone in my life had. From my grandparents who died, though certainly not through any fault of their own, to a mother who neglected me in every way. I set the bar for perfection so high, no one could have reached it. In so doing, I forced him into Hillary's arms.

But not anymore. Hillary was in for the fight of her life.

I decided it was time to share my feelings more freely and stop holding back. Okay, that was probably a little overly optimistic. It would take time to change that part of me. I certainly wouldn't go hog wild and start crying on everyone's shoulders either, but I needed to start taking down the walls.

And there was no time like the present. I needed to call Seth, then decided this was best done in person. I pulled on my Lunch Swap jeans and Seth's favorite blue tee shirt of mine. I also put on the jacket he'd given me. Though not really cold enough for it, I wanted to feel him around me for added courage.

I arrived at his house in record time, but he wasn't there. I debated whether to wait for him, and decided if I left I might lose my nerve. I sat down on the porch swing and waited for two hours. He never showed up. Walking slowly back to my house, sorrow gripped my heart. He and Hillary were probably together.

I came back again on Saturday and once more on Sunday; still no Seth. By Monday, my new resolve had melted away. I pulled back into my self-made cocoon and threw up my walls, just like my mother.

Monday the walk to school felt more like a death march. Not only did I have to speak to Mrs. Volkel about Zack, but Seth and Hillary would be together, laughing, snuggling, and kissing in the halls.

I'd barely stuffed my extra books in my locker when Dwayne caught my arm and practically dragged me outside. He turned back and looked me square in the eyes.

"Dwayne, what's wrong? Did something happen with Karen?"

"You get up on your high horse about Seth and his secrets, what about your secrets?" He was furious. He looked funny. His face was usually so sweet and innocent.

"What are you talking about?"

"Come off it, Maggie." He threw his arms up in frustration. "Fine. How did you get those bruises on your cheeks?"

My voice stayed mute as I pulled deeper into my safety zone. Dwayne pressed harder. "It's all over the school what happened between you and Zack."

"Nothing happened between us," I said defensively.

"He and Hillary set you and Seth up. You were supposed to bump into Hillary *accidentally* as she jumped into Seth's arms to kiss him. She was positive once she planted her trashy lips on his, he'd forget all about you. Then you were supposed to fall into Zack's arms for comfort, and you can imagine what he planned on doing to comfort you."

"It didn't happen that way, not the last part anyway." Seth didn't kiss her, she kissed him. My heavy heart suddenly felt as if it could fly. Maybe I hadn't lost him after all.

"I know it didn't happen that way. Everyone knows that."

"How does everyone know what didn't happen? Surely Zack isn't bragging about failing to pull off his little plan."

"Melody, how else?"

"Who told her?"

"Zack did. Melody had a party Friday night and someone smuggled in some booze." *So much for the substance abuse assembly.* "Zack got completely plastered and could hardly stand. He threw up all over Melody's car."

We both laughed.

"He told Melody about grabbing your face so hard he was sure he bruised it." He glared once more at the marks on my face. "He said you knocked him in the head with your book bag and he went flying. Did you really?" A smile tugged at his lips. I smiled back. "He kept bragging about how hard he threw you down on the ground, and that there was blood on your jeans. He said he wouldn't be surprised if your knees were covered in bruises." I stayed silent. My knees were very bruised up, as were my wrists. I slowly slid my hands into my jacket pockets to hide the evidence. "Don't bother, Maggie, I've already seen those bruises. Why didn't you tell me?"

"Because nothing happened, Dwayne. After he got angry with me in the parking lot, he left. What's there to tell? He knocked me around a little?"

"Yes. He told Melody he debated about whether to . . ." He didn't finish his sentence. He didn't need to. I'd seen it in Zack's eyes. "You should have told me just like Seth should have told you sooner about himself. Zack's lucky Seth's been out of town this whole weekend. When he hears what happened, he's going to flip out. And I almost feel sorry for Zack when Booker gets a hold of him."

"Don't tell them, please."

"I sort of told Booker already, at least part of it. I called him yesterday and left a message on his answering machine. I didn't mention Zack's plan to . . . well, you know. I thought it would be better to tell him that part in person. You know how Booker can fly off the handle. He's with Seth, so he won't hear the message until they get back sometime this morning." Since no one escorted me to school this morning, my assumption was neither of them knew yet.

"Did you leave a message for Seth?"

"No, only Booker. He called me Friday and wanted to know why your face was bruised. I told him I'd try to find out, and you can be sure he'll tell Seth."

"The whole school knows?" A groan escaped my lips.

"Yes, Zack did tell Melody after all, and since when has she ever kept her big mouth shut?"

"How am I supposed to face everyone?" There had to be a rock somewhere to crawl under.

"Are you serious? Everyone's ostracized Hillary and Zack. The rumor is she's being dismissed from the cheerleading squad, and Zack is getting kicked off the baseball team."

Not good. This would all be turned against me. They'd take their revenge out on me.

"Don't worry. I'll protect you, Maggie." He wrapped his arm around my shoulders and gave me a side hug.

"Thanks." I hoped it would be enough.

A loud crack of thunder cut through the air, along with a flash of lightning. "Come on, we'd better get inside before it starts raining. If anyone says anything rude to you, I'll pop'em in the mouth."

Before I could ask if he was kidding, a shiny patrol car pulled up to the school. Booker. I certainly knew his car by now.

"Let's go see what Booker found out," Dwayne said.

"No, I don't want to." Dwayne seemed oblivious to that fact I'd planted my feet firmly on the ground as he dragged me across the small patch of grass separating us from the car.

I wasn't prepared for who got out of the car with Booker.

27

*S*eth. What was left of my bravado and determination from the weekend disappeared instantly. Seth stopped dead, his eyes flashed to me, then to Dwayne. I twisted around so only Dwayne could see my face and mouthed, "Don't tell them now, please."

"Seth's going to hear about it as soon as he walks into the school," he whispered back.

"Pleeease?" I begged silently.

"Fine," he growled aloud.

"Hey, guys, did you find out anything?" Dwayne asked as we approached.

"Yes." Booker looked to me. "Are you sure you want to hear this, Jailbait? It has to do with the undercover agents and lots of secrets," he taunted.

"I can handle it." Out of my peripheral vision, I saw Seth's head snap in my direction.

"As you know, those two men that were in your home were the Dreser brothers."

Finally Seth spoke. "I'm not so sure this is a good idea."

"She's been given clearance." Booker gave him a stern look. Seth didn't answer. Instead he folded his arms across his chest, and leaned against the hood of Booker's car, signaling for him to continue.

"As I was saying, the Dreser brothers are younger brothers to the dealer Seth and I killed several months ago. Dwayne, put your arm around Maggie before she faints."

"I'm not going to faint," I said, resting heavily against Dwayne. I already knew all this and had no idea why I let it affect me.

"Maggie, their older brother Jeffery was a murderer. His favorite MO, method of operation, was to hang out around the local elementary school and entice young children into buying his dope. He'd offer free samples of drug-laced goodies, pretending to be a friend to the friendless, you know, a fun, generous guy. He did whatever it took as long as they kept coming back to him until he had them hooked.

"In the end, he was responsible for the deaths of nine children. One was only ten years old," he said. "We had orders to find him and bring him in."

Seth began fidgeting. Plainly, this was the part of the story he didn't want me hearing.

"One evening we got a tip he was at a local pool hall. When we got there, it was clear he didn't intend on coming along peacefully. He drew out a sawed-off AK 47 from under one of the tables and began using my men as target practice.

"Jeffery ended up with three bullet holes, a couple of which were in his chest. If you ask me, we saved the taxpayers a hefty sum in court fees and housing costs," Booker said dryly. "We had no idea who Jeffery was at the time, not until his brothers broke into your house . . . for whatever reason," he added uncomfortably.

"You didn't find anything at my house. Seth told me so," I said bravely.

"No, you're right, and I'm holding off any assumptions until we have evidence. Innocent till proven guilty." He looked at me sincerely as he said it. "I picked Seth up from school Friday, and we flew out to Arizona on a lead. Harry Dreser was supposed to be there, and we hoped to arrest him for countless reasons, but our main goal was to try to flush out his son Alan. However, when we got to Harry's home he was gone. It appears he'd been tipped off right before we arrived. All he took with him were some clothes, the contents of a small safe, and his jeep.

"We found a large amount of heroin with a street value of over half a million. We were also able to retrieve a few emails from his computer, one of which was a confidential police report he'd somehow gotten his hands on about Jeffery's shootout. He had emailed a copy to Alan, with a note reiterating his desire to have Seth, myself, and our loved ones, murdered. Regrettably, Maggie, all this puts you in danger.

"And you may be able to lie to yourself about your feelings for the kid here," he tipped his head toward Seth, "but everyone else knows otherwise. I just hope you snap out of it before you push it too far and lose everything. Do you understand what I'm saying?"

The bell rang and saved me from having to answer. "I have to go," I said quickly. Booker let out a frustrated groan.

I'd only gone a few steps when Dwayne called out after me. "Maggie, how did you get the bruises on your face?"

I flinched. *Traitor.*

Seth was immediately at my side, timidly scooping my face into his hands, and tilting it to examine the bruises on my cheeks. His face darkened with outrage. Too busy noticing how soft his mouth looked, how beautiful his eyes were, and how incredible he smelled, I hardly noticed. When he looked directly into my eyes, I tossed aside self-control. I kissed him.

Somewhere in the distance Booker muttered, "It's about time." After that I heard nothing except Seth. His soft intake of air as he pulled me in close, his lips as they moved passionately against mine, and his sigh as I forced my mouth more fully onto his. His arms wrapped tightly around my waist and this time I sighed, not caring how loud it was. It felt wonderful to be back in his arms. It didn't matter who was after me, as long as Seth wanted me back.

The sweet urgency of his kiss told me that he loved me still, even after I'd hurt him. My heart pounded away violently as my mouth moved with determination against his. He responded in kind. Completely engrossed in his kiss, I didn't realized my hands had tangled themselves up in his hair, something I dearly missed doing the past two weeks. I didn't want there to be any doubts about my feelings. I forced my mouth a fraction from his. "I love you," I said breathlessly.

I actually said the words. It felt liberating. He pulled me back to his mouth, kissing me with even more abandonment. My head spun and my heart exploded inside me. Every cell in my body ached for his kiss. There couldn't possibly be anything in the entire world that felt this incredible.

All too soon he pulled away, taking deep breaths to steady himself. I looked around for Booker and Dwayne, but they were gone.

"I thought I ruined us." He ran his hands over my hair, resting his forehead on mine.

"I'm sorry for all the horrible things I said, and for the stupid way I acted. You've done nothing but help and protect me. And love me. I acted like a fool. I'm so sorry."

He caressed my jaw softly with his thumbs, slipping his hands around to the back of my neck. "I can't swear there'll be no more secrets, Maggie, it's the nature of the job. I do promise to tell you everything I can, but you need to be more open with me too, deal?"

"I promise." I leaned up and kissed him again.

With my lips still on his, he said, "Good. Tell me how you got these bruises."

"You set me up."

"Maggie, I just want to know who I have to . . . talk to about this, as if I don't already have a pretty good guess."

"Fine, except not here. I'll tell you later." I tried to kiss him again. Instead, he took my hand and led me toward the parking lot.

"Where are we going?" I ran to keep pace.

"To my car. We're going to my house."

"I can't afford to skip school again." Oh, shoot, TMI.

He stopped dead and turned. "Why did you skip school?"

I smiled. "I'll tell you when we get to your house." His lips pinched into a thin line. He took my hand and continued toward his car, murmuring the entire way.

He also drove way too fast. "You should slow down. It's beginning to rain. Besides, you're going to get a ticket if you keep driving this fast."

"I know a cop."

It poured by the time we arrived at his house. He lifted me out of his car and straight into his arms, carrying me inside, our lips never parting. He held me to him in the kitchen, still kissing me, neither of us wanting to move for a long time. He eventually set me down, keeping his arms around my waist.

"Do you have any idea how much I missed this?" I stroked the raindrops off his face.

He chuckled. "I have a pretty good idea."

I tried slipping my arms around his waist, instead bumping into a gun holster strapped to his shoulder. I instinctively stepped back.

"I'll put this away." He quickly removed the gun and walked toward the kitchen cabinet beside the stove. He opened the small drawer and pressed down on the bottom. A piece of the cabinet popped up.

"False bottom," he said, pointing to the drawer. "It's a great hiding place for my guns."

He had more than one? I didn't ask. Some things I'd rather I didn't know, at least not yet.

"Can I see it before you put it away?" In my mind, the thing looked ginormous. I wondered how much my fear had exaggerated the size.

"Sure," he said cautiously. He handed me a towel to dry my face and hair off with, setting the gun down on the counter next to me.

"Don't worry, I unloaded it," he pointed out. I carefully picked it up off the counter with my thumb and index finger. "Every night, well, every morning the past couple weeks, I come home, clean and empty it."

"What do you mean every morning these past couple weeks?" I said, gently setting it back down.

"I've been sleeping in my car," he shrugged. My mouth dropped open. "Did you think I was going to just walk away and let those goons come after you? When I said I loved you, I didn't mean for a week, or maybe a year, I meant always, in the good times and the bad, through thick and thin. I'm playing for keeps here, Mags. I hoped, given some time, you'd feel the same way and take me back."

Humbled, I wrapped myself up in his arms and laid my head on his chest. "Someone up there must truly love me to have sent you into my life. I guess you'd better tell me about your job," I said bravely. "If I'm going to love an MET agent, I should probably know more about it. As long as it doesn't involve math," I warned.

He laughed. "No promises. I'll start from the beginning to give you a total picture. My dad was a Chaplin in the military, and he was also an undercover agent."

"A spy?" I said, intrigued.

"Yes. He and Booker's dad, Clifford, were in the same unit. Clifford was my dad's commanding officer and his best friend. I guess you could say Booker and my friendship is a family tradition. He's like a brother to me."

"Do you have any other siblings?"

"No, my parents had a difficult time getting pregnant, so when I finally arrived they were ecstatic. My dad started training me as soon as I could walk."

"Training you?"

"He wanted me to be involved in espionage too, you know, sort of a father and son team. It used to drive my mother nuts," he laughed. "She'd come home from shopping and find her kitchen booby-trapped."

"I take it she didn't want you to be a spy."

"No, she thought a doctor was a safer profession. I, on the other hand, wanted to be a spy, like every little boy.

"My dad would spread out pots and pans around the kitchen floor, and I had to walk around them without touching them. As I got older and my skills improved, he'd push the pans closer together.

"When I turned twelve, he started placing bubble wrap on the floor. Do you have any idea how hard bubble wrap is to walk on and not make a sound?" He shook his head. "It took me two and a half years before I could cross it quickly and quietly, or *Poof*, as you put it, and not break any bubbles. We used to sneak up on my mom and scare the heck out of her."

I laughed. "Did you have to move around a lot being in the military?"

"Yes. It made schooling hard so I was homeschooled. My mom liked it because she could have her influence over me instead of my dad's all the time. She taught me to cook, and we took a cooking class together in France."

As he spoke, I noticed he had a tiny freckle on his left ear lobe. Why hadn't I seen that before? I stretched up to kiss it.

He shivered. "Are you listening?"

"You took a cooking class in France," I parroted back.

"I graduated from high school at sixteen, and went straight to college. I was able to get my bachelor's degree by the time I was nineteen."

I pulled back. "How old are you?"

"Twenty-one."

"You're twenty-one?"

"Does that bother you?"

"No. But why does Booker keep calling me Jailbait? I'm eighteen"

He laughed. "That's Booker. He must really like you if he gave you a nickname already."

"What's your degree in?"

"Mathematics," he said reluctantly.

"The way you love math is wrong on so many levels," I said, shaking my head.

"Come on. Let's go sit on the couch." He took my hand and led us into the living room.

"Good, my feet are killing me." Not to mention the fact that my knees hurt, still a little sore from being tossed around. We sat as he guided my feet into his lap.

"I'll massage them." He pulled off my shoes and began rubbing my feet.

"You and Booker must have spent a lot of time together growing up." I sighed when he rubbed an especially sweet spot on my foot.

"Yes, our families were tight. Booker's dad died of cancer when he was only ten, and his mom and sister were killed when he was sixteen."

"How?" I was mortified.

"Home invasion robbery. The robbers thought they'd killed Booker, too. My dad happened to stop by and discovered him barely alive. If he hadn't gone over when he did, Booker would've died."

"That's horrible."

"It was touch and go with him for a while. He eventually pulled through and moved in with us. I was only nine at the time. To me, he has always been my big brother.

"When he turned eighteen, my dad pulled some strings and Booker joined the military under my dad's command. He took to the spy world like a duck to water. My dad once told me he'd never seen anyone as talented as Book. He said the only thing that scared him was Booker's 'save the world' mentality, and the danger he put himself in trying to rescue someone.

"Booker was with me when I found out my parents died in the plane crash. I was nineteen, and had just graduated from college. He did for me what my parents had done for him.

"He'd finished his tour of duty a couple years earlier, and had gotten involved with the DEA, convincing me to join him, and we both ended up working with the local MET. We're still under the DEA, but we focus on drug enforcement in urban areas throughout western New York, like here in Port Fare.

"I didn't know there was a serious drug problem here. I mean, I know kids who do drugs, I just didn't realize it was enough to merit the MET." I remembered Zack trying to get me to smoke pot with him. As far as I knew, he never dipped into the hard stuff.

"When the three heroin deaths hit here last summer, we both wanted to work on the case."

"Do you still think my mom and I are involved?" I looked him straight in the eyes to watch his reaction.

"No, not you," he said carefully. "When Booker first asked me to get close to you and see what I could find out, I told him he was wrong about your involvement. He felt that physically you fit the profile, and he wanted me to find out for sure. Plus, there was strong evidence that your mom was involved."

"She's not. I searched the house from top to bottom. There are no drugs anywhere. Cole did a drug screen on her, and it came up negative."

"Maybe she and Hoffman are just friends then."

"He's a heroin dealer?" That made sense why they suspected my mom. The phone rang interrupting our makeup session.

"Hold on." He looked down at his cell phone. "It's Booker, I better answer. Hey, Book. No, not yet. Oh, really," he said. His expression grew dark. "I see. Anything else?" There was a long pause, and his eyes flared more than once. "Thanks for letting me know, I'll take care—No, Booker, I want to. Fine." Whatever happened, it wasn't good. "I see your point. Make sure you do it right. Thanks," he said, snapping the phone shut firmly.

"Is everything alright? Did he find out more about the Dreser brothers?"

"No, nothing new."

I decided to start being supportive and didn't press him for more information.

"So do you have a code name?" I teased, trying to lighten the mood.

"Kid. Booker's called me it my whole life. It doesn't help that I have a baby face, too."

"What about Booker?" Maybe I could get some ammunition for the next time he calls me Jailbait.

"He had several different names he used for missions. He liked to switch it up. His last name, Gatto, literally means *cat* in both Spanish and Italian, so he was partial to powerful cat names like panther or black tiger. The guys used to tease him about it. They'd call him things like Miss Kitty, or Garfield, pretending they had forgotten his real code name. He didn't think it was that funny."

"Hmmm, that's good to know," I said, already making a mental list of all the cat names I'd use on him.

"Don't push him too hard, Maggie," Seth said, reading my expression. "He can be one mean little kitty." I could hardly wait to see Booker again.

"I'm glad there are no more secrets between us, Maggie. Let's promise never again to keep anything important from each other, anything personal anyway."

"I promise." I held out my little finger and wiggled it. "Come on, pinky swear." He rolled his eyes as we intertwined our little fingers. "These are eternally binding, ya know." He nodded, kissing our little fingers as if to seal the deal.

"Alright, let's test this little pinky swear. How did you get those bruises?"

"You set me up again. You forgot to mention MET agents are devious." He threw his head back and laughed, and the sound filled my heart.

"It happened Thursday after the pep rally." He rubbed my calves, as I explained. It felt even more amazing than the foot rub, and I almost forgot what we talked about. "Focus, Maggie," I mumbled aloud. "Hillary and Zack planned it so I'd show up at his locker as she started kissing you. Hillary thought one kiss from her, and the two of you'd fall madly in love, forgetting I ever existed."

He let out a snort. "As if that could ever happen."

"Zack assumed I'd jump into his arms for comfort."

"Comfort? Nothing else?" He arched a brow.

"Okay, he was hoping for a little more. He grabbed my face and forced me to kiss him. That's what these bruises are from."

"And then?"

"He followed me out to the parking lot where we argued again. I was able to convince him to leave, and that's pretty much the whole story."

"How about your knees?" He slid the legs of my jeans up over my knees so fast I didn't have time to pull them away. He gasped when he saw the cuts and bruises. They looked worse today than the day it had happened.

"Dwayne," I hissed under my breath. I yanked my legs away and stomped over to the kitchen.

Seth followed. "Can I see your arms?" I thought of hiding them behind me except why bother. "I thought we weren't going to keep important things from each other, Maggie. I'd call this important."

"No, I told you what happened, he was a little out of control, but I handled it, *and* I'm planning on talking to Mrs. Volkel about it, so this is no longer an issue."

"No longer an . . . A little out of control?" he said incredulously as he lifted my arm. "I think this is more than just a little out of control." I backed away, lowering my sleeves. "He almost—" A loud crack of thunder cut him off in mid-sentence. The lights flickered and went out.

"Great, I can't see a thing." I moved forward, smacking my bruised knee into a barstool. "Ouch." Seth reached out and took my hand, wrapping his arms around my waist once I stood safely at his side.

"Let me guess, your dad taught you to see in the dark, too."

"I don't want to fight," he said, cinching me up against him.

"Seth, let me say something about the whole Zack thing. The reason I didn't go into greater detail about everything with you is because I don't want you to hurt him."

"You're worried about Zack?" he said incredulously.

"No." I shuddered at the idea. "I was worried you'd do something *to* him. I don't want to spend the rest of my life visiting you every other Wednesday in the state prison. Conjugal visits are not my idea of a good time."

"You'd visit me in prison?"

"I'd walk to the ends of the earth for you. Being without you the past couple of weeks has been horrible. I dreamt about you almost every night."

"Hmm, tell me about your dreams," he murmured against my skin.

"I'd rather show you."

28

"Thanks for taking me to see my mom this morning, she looks awful."

"I've seen Cole work miracles before, Maggie. Don't give up hope."

"I found some letters she'd written to me. You can read them if you like. She wrote that she loved me. She's never actually told me that, not ever."

"I know it's not the same thing, but I love you, very much."

"It may not be the same, but it's still wonderful to hear." I squeezed his hand. "So, Principal Nelson let you switch all your classes back? I hope you didn't have to use your gun." He flashed a cunning grin at my question as we walked into the cafeteria for lunch.

My eyes automatically gravitated to Hillary's usual table. She sat next to Zack, whose arm was in a sling. "What did Booker do to Zack?" I had to laugh. "Can't he get in trouble for police brutality?"

"Book didn't touch him," he said, disappointedly. "As I told you last night, Zack got pulled in for questioning over what he did to you after the pep rally. Then Booker took him aside and told him in no uncertain terms he was to never lay a hand, or anything else, on you ever again. Zack was also kicked off the baseball team. I don't think it was a very good day for poor old Zack." Not an ounce of pity in his voice. Seth had tried pressuring me into filing charges against Zack, but I'd refused, fearing retaliation. He insisted I worried needlessly. He obviously didn't know Zack as well as I did.

"There's nothing wrong with his arm, either. He's claiming he threw his elbow out during practice. He's telling anyone who'll listen that he quit the team to preserve his arm for college ball." Seth shook his head in disgust. "Lying weasel. I overheard the coaches talking last week. They were thinking of benching him anyway. His performance has dropped off lately.

"Of course Hillary was able to talk her way out of any real trouble, claiming she had no idea what Zack had planned to do to you, though she is suspended from cheering for the next three games," he said. "Here she comes, look at the stupid smile on her face."

I had never heard Seth speak with such anger about anyone before and it surprised me. I wrapped my arm around his and softly touched my lips to his cheek.

"I'm sorry. They've hurt you so deeply it's been difficult for me to overlook everything," he said, caressing my jaw.

"Kiss me," I whispered.

He looked at me surprised. "You do realize if I kiss you everyone else will see us?" He didn't care for my hang up over public displays of affection, but he never pressed the issue.

"Do it before I change my mind and leave you alone to deal with the evil cheerleader."

He encircled me in his arms, and while cradling my head in his palm, covered my mouth with his undeniable passion. Catcalls and hoots rang out throughout the cafeteria.

"Where exactly have you been hiding that kiss?" I blurted out when he pulled back. "When we get home, you need to bring him out again, maybe even invite a few of his friends over," I said, jouncing my eyebrows at him.

"Judging from your reaction, it's probably not a good idea."

"I'll worry about that. In fact, why don't we skip the rest of school and go home right now." My fingers began toying with his hair.

"I think you've skipped enough school, don't you?"

"Spoil sport." I had completely forgotten about Hillary. I quickly glanced around. She was nowhere to be seen.

After school, I reluctantly pulled out my math book for some heavy duty calculus tutoring. Seth and I worked on it until I took the book and chucked it across the table in tears.

"I. Hate. Math! I'm never going to use this tripe ever again in my life. Why do I have to know all of this?" He wiped the tears from my eyes and pulled me onto his lap. "I seem to remember a promise you made to me once about math." I nestled down into his arms.

"What promise?" He tucked the stray piece of hair I'd been twisting behind my ear.

"You said quote, 'You'll love calculus by the time I'm done helping you, if not, I'll kiss you so long and hard, you won't care about it anymore.'"

"I said that?" he bantered.

"Something like that, yes. I want you to kiss me so long and hard I won't care anymore. Kiss me like you did at school today."

"I think we've had a long day and we should go to bed."

"Seth!" I feigned horror at his suggestion.

"Aren't you just hilarious," he said, taking my hand and leading me upstairs.

"Does that mean you're not going to kiss me so long and hard I won't care about calculus anymore?"

"Not tonight."

"You should be a politician. Long on promises, short on follow through."

"Good night, Maggie."

The next morning, the air was alive with the unmistakable smell of waffles and burnt bacon, two of my favorites . . . minus the burnt part. I quickly brushed my teeth and got dressed. Peering over the staircase railing, I could see Seth in the kitchen in his gray basketball shorts and a blue DEA tee shirt removing a hot waffle from the waffle iron.

"Hot! Hot!" He tossed the waffle onto a plate, licking his singed fingers. I suppressed a giggle as he rushed over to the stove and fruitlessly tried to save the burnt bacon. He soon gave up, dumped it into the garbage disposal, and started over again with a few fresh slices.

I had never seen Seth so distracted before. He was all thumbs. I sat down to watch. I noticed his calculus book open on the counter. He worked on a math problem as he cooked, and if I wasn't mistaken, he struggled with it.

The bacon began spitting wildly on the stove and a splash of grease jumped from the pan, landing on his tee shirt. He jerked the shirt way from his skin and unplugged the waffle iron, setting it aside as he mumbled. I strained to hear.

"You have a degree in this, come on." He held up a slip of paper, and wrote a mathematical formula of some kind in the air with his finger. Still frustrated, he paused to set out a can of whipped cream and some fresh strawberries.

I fell in love with him all over again as he stood in the kitchen burning the bacon for a second time while complaining to his stupid calculus book that it had to be wrong. I climbed down the stairs as he dumped the second round of charred bacon into the sink.

"Now you know how I feel." He jumped at my words.

"Hey, you're not supposed to be up yet. I wanted to make you breakfast in bed. I have something for you. I was going to give it to you a couple of weeks ago, except . . ."

"I was too busy freaking out, maybe?" I suggested with a grimace.

He took my hand, leading me back up to the bedroom and pulled out a dark blue velvet box from the dresser. "I had this made for you."

Nestled inside the box was a silver heart shaped necklace with two stunning blue gemstones lying side-by-side that made up the heart. "This side is a tanzanite, your birthstone, and the other is a sapphire, my birthstone. It comes apart." He pressed firmly on the center of the heart, and the necklace split in two, each gemstone now half a heart. He snapped it back together. "It's us, apart we're incomplete, and together we're whole." He took it out of the box and put the necklace around my neck. The gemstones fell to the center of my chest and lay over my heart perfectly. "It's worked out really well that our stones are pretty much the same color, don't you think?"

I lifted the blue heart. "It's beautiful. Thank you." I pressed my mouth to his. When he pulled away, I ran my tongue over my lips to catch the last of his kiss.

"It drives me crazy when you do that," he groaned, crushing his mouth back over mine. I liked how this day was going so far.

"I made waffles with strawberries and whipped cream for breakfast. They're your favorite right?" he said, leading me back downstairs.

Everything was delicious, well, except for the burnt bacon. He showed me the math problem he couldn't figure out, insisting again that the book was wrong. When I pointed out that he had copied the problem down wrong onto the paper, he was so happy you'd think he'd won the lottery.

"Now that I've had my private tutor lesson for the day, I'm going to take a shower," he said.

I cleaned up the kitchen while he got ready, staring down at my necklace often. The lights in the kitchen made it sparkle even more.

"I promise it won't disappear." He descended the stairs looking delicious in a pair of worn jeans and a blue button down shirt.

"I love it. It's so beautiful."

"I'm glad you like it. Come here. Let me show you the security system Booker designed. It's pretty amazing."

The system was complicated, with its three backup alarms and two separate codes. I had no idea how I'd memorize all the numbers. He showed me how to program it, and how to bypass the windows so I could open them without triggering the alarm, which he then did so the burnt bacon smell could escape.

"No one has ever broken the code on one of his alarms," he bragged of his friend as he opened the last window. "Which brings me to my proposal," he said, fidgeting nervously with the buttons on his sleeve. "Ah, until they catch the Dresers, Booker and I . . . both of us . . . think it would be safer, if, um, for you to move in here. I know you probably feel uncomfortable with the idea, but Mags, your trailer's not safe."

He cleared his throat and continued, pacing while he spoke. "As you know, my dad was a Chaplin in the military, and he instilled in me strong core principles I value deeply. I've always planned on waiting until I was married to have sex, so if you're worried I'll try and pressure you into sleeping with me, I promise, I won't." His beautiful face turned bright pink.

When he had first told me about his dad being a Chaplin, I'd suspected that was why he never pushed our relationship physically, but it was good to know for sure. "Okay."

He looked at me carefully. "Okay? That's it?"

"I trust you." Completely. He'd more than proven he was trustworthy, and it was about time I showed him that.

He exhaled loudly. "Thank you. I guess we should go and pick up your things and bring them over here then."

I smiled. "I guess we'd better." It was nice to know even he got nervous sometimes.

It took all of five minutes to round up my clothes from the trailer. They fit nicely into two plastic grocery bags. I also gathered my mother's letters and stuffed them into my jacket pocket.

"This is it?" He looked with disbelief as he took the bags of clothes from me. "I guess we're doing some shopping this afternoon." I rolled my eyes. "Let's go. You can complain on the way to the mall."

We picked out several pairs of pants with coordinating tops. I was surprised to see how well he mixed and matched things. "Are you sure you're not gay?" I asked as he tried to find a shirt in *just the right shade* of green.

"That's stereotyping," he said, kissing me until I felt completely lost. "Tell me, would a gay man kiss you like that?"

"Definitely not." I leaned against a clothes rack for balance.

He also picked out a beautiful pink dress with black piping along the bottom and neckline, and a pair of black strappy pumps. The shoes looked almost identical to the ones I'd admired when he brought me to the mall last time, except these were better quality. "I wanted to buy you something special to wear," he said, putting his credit card back into his wallet.

I looked at the many packages in both our arms and felt a rush of guilt. "I need a job, Seth. I can't keep leeching off you."

"You're not leeching, Maggie." He shook his head.

"Can you understand how I feel, just a little? It doesn't matter anyway, I can't leave my mom alone for that long," I said, frustrated.

"If you're serious about getting a job, I think I have the perfect solution. We'll be needing some help with paper work at the Lunch Swap starting in June, and there's an extra laptop at the office. You can take it home and do the work there. You'll be with your mother, and you can earn some money."

"That'd be perfect." *A little too perfect.* "You're not making this whole job up just for me are you?" I eyed him suspiciously.

"No, our secretary is leaving to have a baby. You'd be doing me a big favor, although I do have an ulterior motive," he smiled sinisterly. "Since you'll be using a laptop, you'll be able to work at my house occasionally. And I promise to be a good boss and distract you from your work every chance I get."

"Hmm, sounds like sexual harassment."

"Darn straight. Maybe we should go back to my place, and I'll show you how I plan on distracting you," he said.

His cell phone interrupted a perfectly good kiss. I readjusted the packages in my arms while Seth took the call.

"Change of plans," he said, stuffing the phone into his pocket. The expression on his face could only be described as elation. "Booker invited us to have lunch with him and his grandfather, Sam. You'll love Sam. He's sarcastic, too."

***

We turned right on Country Cottage Lane and pulled up to number sixty-nine. It was a beautiful old colonial home, gray with black shutters and stately white pillars. Booker, and I presumed his grandfather Sam, stood out front to greet us. Time for all my cat jokes.

"Play nice, Maggie."

"I will." Maybe.

"Good afternoon, Jailbait." Booker walked over and gave me a hug. "Hear you're moving in with the kid?"

"Seth, you let the *cat* out of the bag and told Booker?" I said, scratching Booker behind his ears. Seth mumbled something about me not waiting even two seconds. I ignored him. This was going to be fun.

"You told her? You've betrayed your best friend to a girl?"

"You're still my best friend, but she's the love of my life. She would've found out sooner or later anyway."

"I would have preferred later."

"Don't be angry, Booker. I'll take you out for some catnip later if you promise not to be a sour*puss* all afternoon." That was a good one, even Seth laughed.

"I'd like you to meet my grandfather, Sam," Booker said, ignoring me. I stretched out my hand to the frail looking old man who took it in both of his.

"My, my. Booker wasn't kidding, you're a hottie."

"Grandfather!" Booker immediately turned to Seth. "I swear I never said that. I did say she's a beautiful girl."

Sam squeezed my hand. "Alright, maybe I'm embellishing a little. It still doesn't change the fact."

He guided me into a large dining room where an elaborate lunch of sliced meats and cheeses set out on glass platters. Condiments filled several small bowls and a black basket lined in red linen held oversized rolls. It was all spread out on an ornate Rosewood table.

"What a beautiful table." I ran my hand along the edge. It had the feel of silk.

"Booker built the table," Sam said with pride. "He built most of the wooden pieces of furniture throughout the house."

"You do good work, Book," I said, walking over to the equally beautiful china hutch in the corner with fantastic intricacies and details in the woodwork. It had to have taken months to carve.

"Thanks. Come on, let's eat," Booker said, embarrassed by the attention. Who knew it possible to embarrass Booker?

"I'm eighteen, you can't call me that," I said, sitting at the table.

"That's what you think," he smiled.

We ate and listened as Sam amused us with *'The Adventures of Booker and Seth,'* in which he chronicled the different assignments they'd been on over the past two years. A couple of the stories were hilarious, but way too many sounded dangerous. Seth reassured me Sam exaggerated. Somehow, I doubted it.

After lunch, Sam suggested Booker take me on a tour of the house. Booker's place was homey. It reminded me of Seth's home: beautiful, inviting, and nothing like my trailer. Each room housed magnificent wood furniture that Booker mostly built. Sam and his wife had traveled extensively before she died, and he had tokens from all over the world, such as an African tribal mask from Ethiopia, wooden shoes from Holland, and a jade Buddha from China. I found it fascinating.

Booker had an elaborate gun collection he kept locked up in a large wall safe, but the lock was broken so he couldn't show them off to me. I was way okay with that. He also had the most sophisticated security system that I'd ever seen.

"You can even set a code that will send electrical currents through all the doors and windows. If anyone tries to break in, *zap*. They get shocked with a thousand amps of electricity," Sam exaggerated. I think. *Was that even legal?*

Sam led us to an outside door and we walked down a small stone pathway to a separate garage behind the house. Sam opened the side door and we continued though a short hallway where two intimidating looking samurai swords hung on the wall.

"Are those things real?"

Seth nodded. "From Japan, and very sharp."

We stopped at the end of the hall and Sam announced, "Now for my most prized possession." He winked at Seth, who looked as if he was about to knock the door down. Sam slowly opened the door, and there sat the most gorgeous car I had ever seen, dark smoky blue color with a black convertible top. I knew at once what it was.

29

"This would be the celebrated Roadster, correct?" I asked needlessly.

"Mercedes-Benz SLR McLaren Roadster," Sam informed.

"What a lovely shade of blue," I said, stroking the front fender.

"Digenite Blue Metallic," Seth and Sam corrected me simultaneously, their eyes glazed over.

I coughed over my laugh. Booker didn't bother covering his snort. Evidently, he didn't share the same obsession with the car as Seth and his grandfather.

At the far end of the garage sat Booker's woodworking tools, along with large piles of wood neatly stacked against the wall. Between the tools and the false idol car sat a battered wreck of a car.

"What is that?" It was impossible not to sneer. Parked next to the Roadster, the poor old thing looked even worse.

"That's Booker's car, a 1983 POC, which means Piece of Crap, in case you couldn't tell." Sam scowled.

"I'm a simple man with simple tastes," Booker said heroically.

"More like a simple man with a simple piece of junk," Sam corrected.

"I don't need a silly car to define my manhood."

"It's a good thing because that car screams *wuss*," Seth said, giving Booker's car a look of revulsion. Sam nodded in agreement before holding out a small black rectangular box to Seth and pointing at the Roadster. "No, Sam, I never intended to drive it, I just wanted Maggie to see it."

"I haven't driven it since my stroke, and as you know, sitting for long periods of time isn't good on a car. Please, you'd be doing me a favor."

Seth stood staring silently at the strange little box, I wasn't sure but for a second I thought he was about to cry. Finally, Booker snatched it and walked over to the car. "Come on, I'll take you for a spin."

"No, I'll take her." Booker grinned at me as Seth promptly grabbed both the little box and my right hand, leading me to the car. He pushed a small rectangle on the side of the car and the door opened—vertically.

The inside of the car looked also stunning. The tan leather seats felt like silk against my skin as I climbed into the two-seater. Seth probably knew the exact name of the color; tan was good enough for me. A console nestled between the seats, with a myriad of intimidating buttons and a silver stick shift. The numbers on the speedometer read up to two-hundred-twenty. Hopefully it meant kilometers. I half expected James Bond to jump out and demand his car back for some secret mission.

Seth flipped open the top of the gear shift and pushed a button. The car roared to life. Whoa! The thing had some serious power behind it and we hadn't even moved yet.

"Usually you don't need a key," he explained, "you just type in a code and it starts. Sam had them replace the key pad with this button, claiming he was too old to try and remember another number after memorizing Booker's complicated security code."

"Don't you two be out late," Booker teased Seth as he slowly backed it out of the garage. "I've heard through the grapevine Donald's Pass was shut down for maintenance, which doesn't begin until tomorrow."

"What was the whole cryptic Donald's Pass message about?"

"It's where we can take this baby out, open her up, and see what she's got." Seth looked over at me and grinned. Oh boy.

Once we arrived at Donald's Pass, he climbed out to make sure no one else was on the road. After double-checking, he sat back down and pressed a button, opening the convertible top, before buckling his seatbelt and flooring the gas pedal. My head pressed back into the seat. I don't know how fast we drove, but it was definitely fast. The weeds and tall dead grass on the side of the road were mere blurs. Halfway down the road, he stopped the car and jumped out. Before I knew it, he opened my door. "Your turn."

"Oh, no! Except for Drivers Ed, and the time I used Zack's junkie car to take the road test last October, my driving experiences are nil."

"Maggie, this is a once in a life time opportunity. Besides, we're on a deserted road. You can't hurt anyone."

"Only us," I mumbled, reluctantly climbing out and going around to the driver's seat. A sense of power pulsed through my body as I slid into the buttery leather seat. I *felt* like James Bond. I revved the engine twice before engaging the stick shift. Out of the corner of my eye, I could see Seth struggling not to laugh. We took off fast and hit sixty miles an hour in less than five seconds. We were up over a hundred mph without me realizing it.

"Maggie." There was definite panic in Seth's voice. He wasn't laughing anymore. "Do you know how fast you're going?" I immediately removed my foot from the accelerator.

"This car is incredible. I want one." I drove for several more miles before Seth suggested we head back.

"We don't want Sam thinking we skipped town. Do you know the way back?"

"I think so. Don't you want to drive it again?"

"No, I want to watch you. You should see the look on your face."

I turned the car around and headed back, driving a little too fast. "I have to admit it's easy to understand your obsession with this car. It's so fun to drive. It feels like you're gliding along." Who knew I could channel Richard Petty?

"You're gliding along at sixty miles an hour. You probably should slow down."

"Don't worry, I know a cop." All too soon, we pulled back into Booker's garage. I guess I should have slowed down.

"He let you drive it? Must be love," Booker quipped. As I climbed out, Seth and Sam were already wiping the car down. Sam wiped off the fingerprints from where I touched the front fender earlier, and Seth began wiping the road dust from the rear wheel wells.

"How long will this take?" I asked Booker.

"It shouldn't be too long, Magpie. They have this little ritual down to a science."

Magpie? Hmm, I had a new nickname I could live with it. Anything sounded better than Jailbait. Besides, my grandfather used to call me Magpie.

I watched as Seth lovingly caressed the car with a yellow towel. "Do you always have a goofy smile on your face when you stare at him?" Booker reached over and messed up my hair.

"Bad kitty," I said, trying to fix the mess. "Are you always this annoying whenever you talk to people, or am I just the lucky one?" I taunted back, arching an eyebrow.

Seth appeared at my side before he could answer. "If you're done trying to steal my girl, I'd like to take her to the hospital to see her mother."

"I told you, my friend, I'm not into jailbait. Maybe if she were ten years older," he said, adding, "You'll have to let me go, Magpie."

I purred and rubbed behind his ears one last time before we left.

"What do you think about the car? Isn't it something?"

"It has no match."

"I wanted the Roadster, but the waiting list at the time was eight months so I bought the Lexus instead."

"Seth, this is a really nice car, too," I pointed out.

"It's a great car, don't get me wrong. I just wish I'd waited. Some things are worth the wait," he said, kissing my hand.

My mom was in bad shape. Her skin had yellowed dramatically, and three machines now pumped copious amounts of drugs into her thin body to try and build up her strength for the liver transplant. She looked frail, and we weren't allowed to stay very long.

"Are you okay?" Seth asked when we got back to his place.

"I guess." He handed me a hankie. I dried my face and tucked it into my pocket. The way my tears flowed lately, there was little doubt I'd need it again soon. "Would you like to read the letters she wrote to me?"

"I'd love to."

I busied myself preparing dinner while he sat at the bar and read the letters. He blinked back tears more than once as he went through them. Coming up next to me, he wrapped his arms around my shoulders from behind. I pressed my head back against him.

"I know she never said she loved me out loud, but at least she wrote it down. Although I do wish . . ."

"I wish you could've heard her say the words, too."

"I'm going to tell our children I love them all the time. I don't want them ever to doubt it."

"Our children? Does that mean you plan to spend the rest of your life with me?"

"Of course." As if I wanted to survive without him.

"I love you, Mags." He pressed a kiss to my head and held me tight as our dinner grew cold.

30

"*H*ow do you think you did on the test?" Seth asked, taking the books out of my arms as we walked toward my biology class.

"I don't know. I wish it all made more sense. It feels like I'm just writing down numbers and formulas without understanding why."

"Don't worry, sometime soon a little bell will go off in your head, and you'll see the big picture."

"You've been promising me that for a while. If it were true it would've happened by now. Besides, you've never shown me how all this intense math applies to my everyday life. It's totally useless."

"I could use it right this minute to figure out the slope of your very kissable neck if you'd like."

"I'd much rather you kiss the slope of my very kissable neck."

"It's a date. Today after school, you, me, and the slope." I watched him walk away as the last bell rang, not caring that I was late for class. It was a nice view indeed.

Out of nowhere, a hand slapped down roughly over my mouth, and suddenly someone dragged me down the hall. The sickening laugh in my ear made it all too clear who it was. Zack shoved me into a nearby janitor's closet and shut the door behind us. The overwhelming smell of ammonia and dust permeated the small space, gagging me.

"What are you doing? Let me out of here." Despite my fearless tone, my body trembled.

"You're not so brave without your cop boyfriend here to protect you."

"What are you talking about?" I lied, and I did it poorly.

"Save your breath, Maggot. I know all about him. I've made a couple of new friends of my own since being kicked off the ball team." His voice frothed with hate, all targeted at me. "Just so you know, your boyfriend is only after one thing from you, and it's not what I wanted either," he said with an evil grin. "He's bucking for some big promotion and busting up this drug ring is just the feather in his cap he needs to get it. You're being used Maggot. He's also on the take. How else do you suppose he can drive that expensive car of his on a cop's salary?"

"You're w–"

"But Alan and Bill have some plans of their own for your beloved." He ran a slimy finger over my cheek. I jerked my head away. "They also promised me I could have first dibs on you after it's over if I helped."

"Who are Alan and Bill?" I asked, swallowing down the bile in my throat.

"The Dreser brothers, stupid. Don't tell me Seth didn't tell you about them. Bill said your precious lover doubled-crossed their brother Jeffery, and then shot him in the back. You really know how to pick'em," he said, seizing my jacket and jerking me next to him. He wanted to kiss me. I did what any normal girl locked up in a closet with a nut job would do; I screamed at the top of my lungs. The door flew open and there stood Mrs. Gianchi.

"May I ask what is going on in here?" she said, glowering directly at Zack.

"Lover's spat, no big deal. I'm trying to break up with her, and she's coming unglued."

"I find that difficult to believe given the recent assault charges Miss Brown has filed against you, Mr. Finkle." She looked at me. "Is he telling the truth?"

"No, he and some of his friends are planning on killing Seth Prescott."

"Is that right, Mr. Finkle," she said. "Go to Mrs. Volkel's office immediately." He bolted out of the closet and ran down the hall. Mrs. Gianchi took out her cell phone.

"Seth, we have a problem." She quickly told him where we were, and he appeared within moments.

"Maggie." He grabbed my arm. I looked wide-eyed at Mrs. Gianchi.

"H-how did you know about . . .?"

"I'm helping MET with their assignment here at the high school," she said. My mouth dropped. "Never mind about that. Explain what happened with Zack." I quickly told them what Zack had said, although a small part of my mind tried to figure out who else at school might be MET.

"If he's hooked up with the dealers, this isn't good," Mrs. Gianchi said, rubbing her forehead. "You had better take her to your place. I'll give Booker a call to let him know." Seth nodded. "Be careful, something tells me Zack didn't go to Emily Volkel's office. He's probably out there somewhere, watching and waiting."

"Thanks, Holly."

Seth hustled me inside and set the alarm as soon as we got home. I hung up our coats as he began pacing around the living room. More than once, he stopped and turned toward me as if he wanted to say something, before changing his mind and resuming his pacing.

I knew what troubled Seth, and it wasn't just Zack's newly acquired knowledge about him either. Forcing him to sit on the couch, I cuddled up next to him. He looked apprehensive as I stretched up to kiss him. I could feel the tension easing from his body as he twisted his arms around my waist. "I love you, and yes, I know Zack's lying about you."

He sighed. "Thank you."

"Holly? So, Mrs. Gianchi's working for you, too. All those times in cooking class we were mysteriously teamed up together for an assignment weren't just coincidences, were they?"

"I called in a lot of favors to win you. I wasn't taking any chances." He grinned. "Holly does drug and rehab counseling in the evenings, and she volunteered to help out with this case. Her husband's a retired MET agent."

"No wonder we won the cooking contest back in January with *Maggie's Kiss*. The contest was rigged."

"Rigged? Are you implying I'm not a master chef?" He began tickling me, and we ended up on the floor with me in a hysterical laughing fit. The doorbell rang, and before we could get up to answer it, in walked Booker.

"Glad to see you two are taking this so well," he said frowning. "Would you like me to leave?"

"Yes," we both answered as Seth pulled me to my feet.

"We can't find the little weasel." Booker dropped heavily into the oversized green chair. "I've looked everywhere. His parents said he's out of town for the entire week attending a baseball tournament. Apparently they didn't know he's been kicked off the team.

"Seth, he's a fool if he thinks those dealers will show him any allegiance. They'll kill him as soon as he does whatever it is they need him to do." A foreboding look clouded Booker's face as he spoke.

"I have some bad news of my own. I've been subpoenaed to testify tomorrow in the Biden trial. I have a six a.m. flight to Albany." This was the first I heard of Seth's plan. Certainly, he didn't plan on going alone and leaving me here, did he?

"And no, you are not going. The safest place for you is here." He braced himself for my reaction. I was definitely in love with a very smart guy, because a reaction was exactly what he was going to get.

"I'm not staying here alone, so you can forget it." I pinned my arms tight across my chest. "Who's Biden anyway?"

"He was running a drug and prostitution ring in the Albany area. I was the arresting agent."

He sank down next to me. "Maggie, this is MET business. You can't come. I'm sorry. You know I'd take you if I could."

"Sam would like to see you again, Maggie. You're welcome to stay with us."

"Thanks, Booker," I said, less than enthusiastically, "but I'll stay here."

"I don't like the idea of you being here alone. I'd prefer you stay at Booker's."

"I thought your security system was top of the line."

"It is."

"And didn't you say no one could get through without the entire MET showing up on your doorstep?"

"Yes."

"I'll be fine," I said, defiantly.

"Okay," he said, too easily.

"So how many of your buddies are you going to assign to watch the house?" I might not understand calculus, but I certainly wasn't stupid.

He let out a heavy breath. "One, maybe two," he admitted.

"I guess Booker's security system is not as good as you both claim," I said casually.

Booker laughed. "She got you there, kid. Fort Knox has less security than this place. She'll be fine," he said, again too easily, which meant Booker would be volunteering to watch over me.

Seth ignored us both, changing the subject. "If we ask Booker nicely, he may take us to the shooting range tomorrow and you can practice shooting a gun."

I cringed. "Why in the world would I ever want to do that?"

"It sure beats being killed," Booker said. Seth glared at him.

"No guns," I said firmly.

"This is purely for self-defense. What if I'm incapacitated in some way, and you need to protect me?"

So unfair. It was a dirty trick. I'd do anything to protect him, and he knew it.

"Okay, but I bet I'm a lousy shot."

The next morning Booker picked us up at 9:00 a.m. and drove us to the range. Seth taught me how the gun functioned. I'd forgotten how heavy the thing was and after he placed it in my hands, they dipped several inches. "Wait until you shoot it," he said. "It has a fairly good kick." *Whatever that meant.* Too embarrassed to admit I was completely gun illiterate, I just nodded. Booker laughed. Nerd.

"Maggie, a few rules first. Never point a gun at anyone," Seth instructed.

"Doesn't that defeat the whole purpose?"

Booker laughed. He was really starting to get on my nerves. I stuck my tongue out at him, but he only laughed harder.

Seth ignored us. "Maggie, it's better to err on the side of caution is all I'm saying. You should always assume the gun is loaded. Even if you've removed the clip and have checked to see if the chamber is empty," he said, pointing to each part. "Always keep the gun pointed down at the ground until you are ready to use it." He aimed the tip of the gun straight down.

"Gun points down, got it."

Seth and Booker took turns shooting at the target first. The two of them and their macho egos battled it out to see who could get the highest score. Men.

The target was set to mimic random movement, making it harder to hit. After several loud rounds, Seth pushed a small yellow button, and two battered targets slid forward along separate wires.

Booker won by ten points. "You have to wait for the opportune moment, my friend."

"Yes, Captain Jack Sparrow, or be darn lucky," Seth said, begrudgingly. "Look, you missed the target entirely here," he said, pointing to a bullet hole an inch below the target.

"Even the best make a mistake now and then," Booker said, still gloating.

It was my turn next. "Face the target, Maggie, and slowly raise the gun out in front of you, cupping it in both hands." Seth reached his arms around me and positioned my hands properly on the gun. I stretched up, kissing his cheek.

"I doubt that will help, Magpie," Booker said.

"Doesn't hurt." Seth winked down at me. I refocused on the target, holding the gun as he instructed. "Good, now squeeze the trigger." I closed my eyes and pulled the trigger. The power of the shot threw me back into Seth's chest, and I completely missed the target. Booker laughed again.

"Can he leave?"

"Book, please stop. You're not helping."

Unfortunately, Booker's lack of teasing didn't help either. I shot the gun a couple dozen times, each time missing the dumb target.

"I can't do this. Remember the Winter Festival and the water gun game? I didn't get one drop of water in the cup." This whole thing quickly turned exasperating.

"Maggie, it may help if you keep your eyes open," Seth whispered in my ears. My eyes flashed to Booker, who had turned his back on us. His shoulders jounced in laughter. I looked fiercely at the target, and forcing my eyes to stay open, shot at the stupid thing one last time.

"I hit it. Look!" I punched the yellow button, and the target slid forward. There was a small nick out of the corner of the paper. I smiled. Seth smiled. Booker laughed.

"I've never heard of anyone dying from a flesh wound, but there's always a first time." The smile left Seth's face and was replaced by a look of nausea at Booker's words.

"I need more practice. I'll get better, promise." *I certainly can't get any worse,* I thought, setting the gun down and backing away from it cautiously.

"We're out of time, Seth. We'd better clean up." Booker patted him on the back. "Don't worry. We'll make sure she's with one of us at all times until these two are caught. We'll protect her with our lives, if need be." Seth nodded.

"What's wrong, Maggie?" Book draped his arm around my shoulders, giving me a nudge. "Don't let this shooting thing bother you, and I'm sorry for laughing."

"I'm never going to be able to do this," I bemoaned.

"Sure you will. Just remember two things. One, watch for the opportune moment." He stopped and smiled broadly.

I knew I'd regret asking, but I did it anyway. "And the second thing?"

"Keep your eyes open." He grinned devilishly before leaving to tell whoever was in charge we'd finished, taking the gun with him. Seth swept me into his arms and planted his delicious mouth on mine.

"I'd rather do this than shoot a gun any day."

"Yes, except kissing me won't save your life." I didn't tell him how very wrong he was. He took my hand, and we headed for the car. Booker stood outside waiting for us.

"I don't believe anyone's ever necked in the shooting range before."

"We need to find you a woman, Book," Seth said dryly.

"Just make sure she can handle a gun, please." I whacked him on the arm. "Hmm, did a butterfly just land on me?" He glanced around pretending to look for some nonexistent bug.

"One of these days, Book," Seth said. Booker threw back his head in laughter.

31

"*P*lease don't go." I cinched my arms around Seth as if I had enough strength to stop him.

"Maggie, I'll be back in a couple of days. You haven't touched any of the homework that Mrs. Gianchi sent over. Maybe without my distractions you'll be able to get it done."

"I like your distractions." I kissed him.

"You should go visit Sam. Booker has him under lock and key, too."

"No, thanks. I'm not in the mood to deal with Book's raillery." I smoothed out his brown tee shirt where I'd wrinkled it kissing him. "Please hurry back."

"I will. Remember, don't undo the code for anyone." I nodded. It was only the thousandth time he had said it today. After an all-too-speedy kiss goodbye, he left.

I reluctantly gathered my stack of homework and sat at the table. Seth was right. Without his distractions I completed my homework quickly, though it wasn't nearly as much fun. Later, Booker took me to visit my mother, which only depressed me more. After a bowl of chicken soup, I tried watching some old movies, except it didn't feel the same without Seth.

The next day passed by, just as monotonous, and to make matters worse it rained, which didn't help my gloomy mood any. I puttered around determined to find something to do. I cleaned out the refrigerator, dusted everything there was to dust, and vacuumed every room in the house. I even cleaned the bathrooms, proof positive the doldrums had taken possession of my soul.

I finally decided to take a bubble bath to kill time. Seth would be proud. Naturally, as I settled into the tub, my cell phone rang.

"Hi, I miss you," I said, surrounded by a sea of bubbles.

"I miss you, too. What have you been doing without me?"

I briefly narrated my boring morning to him. "I also finished all my homework, and currently I'm sitting in a tub of bubbles wishing you were here. How much longer before you come home?"

"Tomorrow. I'll try and catch the ten a.m. flight." I sighed. "Maggie, call Booker. Sam would love to see you again."

"Maybe I will." Wow, I was desperate enough to put up with Booker's teasing. Quite sad, really.

"I'll see you tomorrow. Love you." He hung up before I could say it back. I set the phone back down on the side of the tub and sank deep into the bubbles. Within seconds, it rang again.

"I love you."

"I love you, too, but sorry, Jailbait, you're much too young."

"Funny, Booker. How are you?" I scooped up a handful of bubbles, blowing them into the air.

"Actually, Sam's not doing so well today, and I have to go into work. I'm hoping you can spend the night here."

"Sure. What's wrong with him?"

"I don't know. For the past couple days he's been unusually tired and listless. I tried to get him to go see Cole, but he insists he's ninety-two, and ninety-two year-old people have been known to get tired. In any case, he shouldn't be here alone."

"I'll be right over."

"No, I'll pick you up."

"You don't want to leave Sam alone. Besides, I know there's an agent outside."

"Not for long. The storm's wreaking havoc, and he's being called away to help with the growing number of accidents. Maggie, do not leave the house until I get there, understand? I'll be over in ten minutes."

"Fine, good bye." I jumped out of the tub, quickly dressed, and shoved a few things into a bag, finishing as Booker's car pulled into the driveway.

I punched in the code and opened the front door while Booker shook off the rain droplets from his umbrella. He was in his full uniform, including a blue MET raincoat and large chunky rain boots.

"Why did you open the door?"

"Because it's rude to leave an MET agent standing on the doorstep in the rain. They shrink in water, you know."

"What?"

"I opened the door to let you in. You did want to come in, right?"

"You were told not to open the door for anyone. I know Seth's code. I can punch it in myself." He was *not* in a good mood.

"Sorry, I didn't think—"

"Exactly, you didn't think. Get your things."

"Wait a minute. Seth also told me not to leave the house. How do I know this isn't some kind of test, Puss 'n Boots?"

His jawed tightened. "Listen, funny girl, if you don't grab your stuff and get in the car, I'm going to arrest you for being a pain in the—" he cleared his throat, "neck." He stormed across the room, yanked my bag off the counter, and walked me out to the car.

I was glad to see the torrential rains had eased into a small thunderstorm. I sat soberly with my window cracked, smelling the rain. "What's wrong?" Booker asked.

"Nothing."

He let out a growl, a real live growl.

"Okay, fine, I miss Seth. Happy now?"

He rolled his eyes. "I'm sure it's been a rough twenty-four hours for you."

It's been thirty hours, actually.

He pulled into his driveway and turned toward me. "I shouldn't have lost my temper, Maggie. Sam's not doing well, and it's got me on edge. I just can't lose him." His eyes filled with pain as he spoke.

"Don't worry about it." I gave him a quick hug.

We walked in and found Sam stretched out on the recliner next to the couch. He didn't look well at all.

"Grandfather, are you alright?" Booker rushed over to him.

"You worry too much, I'm fine. Old men do have a tendency to sit down you know."

"9-1-1's backed up about an hour because of the weather, so if you need—"

"Have a nice day, sonny," Sam said with an edge in his voice. Booker rattled off the rules *again* to both of us, set the alarm, including the electric zapping one as he left.

"Thank heavens he's gone. It's time to party." Sam rubbed his hands together playfully. "Are you hungry?"

"I'll get it, Sam. What do you want?"

"Not you, too? I'm just tired. Now, what do you want to eat?" he demanded.

I tried to think of something easy. "How about a peanut butter and jelly sandwich?" He frowned, but said nothing as he struggled out of the recliner and waddled slowly to the kitchen, mumbling under his breath about my choice of lunch. He made the sandwich and set it on a plate when he'd finished.

"If you'll excuse me, I'm exhausted from making such a labor intensive meal. I need a nap." His sarcasm reminded me of Booker, and I almost laughed.

I attempted to draw him into some small talk, but he more or less grumbled his replies. After lunch I suggested we play a card game.

"Do you know how to play Phase Ten?"

"Are you sure my old heart can take the excitement?"

"I hoped you would fall asleep in the middle of the game so I'd win by default." Finally, a smile.

He won the first two rounds, but during the third, he became restless, and the game dragged on forever. When Booker called for the fourth time, Sam spent the phone conversation lecturing Booker about being over-protective until Book's cell phone finally died.

"Good. Maybe we'll finally have some peace." After the card game was over, Sam suggested we take a break before playing another. He slowly rose and walked over to the couch, collapsing onto the end.

"Do you feel like taking a little drive to the hospital? I do believe I'm having a heart attack." He said it calmly, as if he asked me to go on a simple drive through the country.

"No, we can't leave, Sam. I'm calling Booker."

His face was flushed, and he sweated profusely now. "His phone's dead. Besides, we both know he'd probably end up killing himself trying to get here in this weather. Please, Maggie, with 9-1-1 being backed up, it'll be faster if you drive," he said, clutching the front of his shirt. My eyes darted to the window. The small thunderstorm had blossomed into a full-blown monsoon. "The key's on the hook by the back door. Go get the Roadster and pull it around to the front. I don't think I can make it all the way to the back garage."

I grabbed the black, rectangular key and punched the complicated code into Booker's security system. I ran down the pathway to the back garage, darting through the narrow hallway. I passed by the samurai swords and entered the garage. Quickly tapping the garage door opener, I scurried over to the car. Before I could climb in, someone jumped out of the shadows. My breath caught in my throat.

"This was just too easy," spewed an oily voice. It was one of the Dreser brothers. He was the smaller, less evil looking of the two, not that there was much of a difference. The first thing I noticed was the blood red eyes embedded deeply beneath two bushy eyebrows. He was high. I also noticed the little silver gun he held tightly in his hand.

"Where's Booker's Granddaddy?"

"He's not here," I lied. "He wasn't feeling good so Booker took him to the hospital." I tried subtly to head back toward the hallway.

"Take another step, girlie, I'll kill you right this minute," he said, his voice as smooth as silk and deadly.

He leisurely skirted around me, licking his lips and smiling. I slipped my hand into my pocket and wrapped it around my cell phone. My only thoughts were of Sam. I had to get him some help. But who should I call?

"Get your hands where I can see them. Oh, and hand me your cell phone," Bill said.

"I don't have a cell phone."

"Yeah, right. Then what are you clutching in that pocket of yours?" he snapped. "Hand it over, *now*."

I pulled my hands out and slid the phone across the garage floor. It stopped at his feet, and he crushed it with his massive foot. "Car keys," Bill said, wiggling his fingers. I tossed the box to him and he dropped it to the ground, crushing it also into a wad of unrecognizable plastic and circuitry.

"Do you know why I'm here?" I didn't answer him. "My father wants us to avenge our brother's murder," he said, smoothing his ugly black shirt. "Me and Alan are also hoping to boost heroin sales for daddy dearest while we're at it. There is a lot of potential in Port Fare. Of course, if Alan doesn't stop killing those young girls just for the sport of it . . ." He shook his head in disgust.

"Just for the sport? He killed all those girls just because?"

"What can I say? The guy's ruthless with a knife, always has been," he shrugged. "He's amazing to watch once he gets started." Sickened, I leaned against the car, praying Sam would stay inside and not come looking for me. "Alan ordered me to kill the old guy, Sam. He's going to be real upset that I got to kill you instead of him. He thinks you are just about the prettiest little thing he's ever seen," he said, grinning. "You've made it hard for him to concentrate on our assignment. Maybe now with you out of the way, I'll have an easier time keeping him on task.

"Remember the night in the park? Alan swears you saw him. He watched you sitting there all by yourself, wanting you so badly. When we learned you were involved with the scum cop, it was like a bonus. He could kill you *and* cause the cop pain."

A chill ran through my body. I'd never see Seth again. The monster moved toward me. "Please, please don't do this," I pleaded.

"I wonder if my brother Jeffery begged your MET buddies before they killed him." The smile abruptly disappeared from Bill's face. He started circling around me once more, his withered tongue slithering across his lips.

My eyes traveled around the garage, searching for something, anything, I could use to defend myself with, yet in my heart, I knew the effort was fruitless. I saw a section of two by four, two feet in length, next to Booker's woodworking tools. Bill followed my gaze and walked over to pick up the board.

"Thanks, girlie. I was hoping to use something other than my gun." He slipped the gun into the pocket of his black slacks. "They're too easy, you know what I mean. Just aim and shoot, then the fun's over."

He preferred to beat me to death with a chunk of wood? My only hope now was to keep him talking. Maybe Booker would be his normal over-protective self and check on his grandfather again.

"Your brother Jeffery was killing children," I blurted out. Not the most brilliant thing to say to a savage killer, but my mind was a terrified blank.

His red eyes flared. "Do you have any idea how hard it is to be the son of an infamous drug smuggler? The pressure can drive you crazy. Jeffery had to build up the clientele or lose his ranking in the family business. He was tired of being dad's muscle, like Alan and me."

Bill mopped up the sweat that had gathered on his forehead with his jacket sleeve. "Jeffery was sick. He didn't have a choice. He . . . he had a nervous condition." He ran his fingers through his greasy hair. "He couldn't handle stress. Children are weak and easily manipulated," he said, shaking his head.

"Jeffery was a coward." I spun around to see Sam leaning against the door with one of the samurai swords in his hand. He looked horrible. He was pale, and his face shone with perspiration. "Your brother was the worst type of human. To prey on children is sick and depraved. He deserved to die."

"You deserve to die, old fool." Angry, Bill ran straight toward Sam. He hoisted the sword up, and the crazed killer stopped.

"You lied to me, girlie." He shook a stubby finger at me. "And you, old man, are too weak to kill me with that so put it down."

"Not happening. Put down the piece of wood and your gun, then we'll talk."

Bill laughed. "On second thought, pops, I like your spunk. It would be a shame to kill you off right away. I'll tell you what I'm going to do. I'm going to allow you a few more minutes of life by killing girlie here first. You get to experience the pain of seeing someone you care about die, and I get to beat the life out of a liar," he said, his face tight. "It's a win-win situation—for me, anyway. And out of respect for the elderly, I'll even kill you with my gun."

He started back toward me, but Sam stepped between us. "No deal." He still had the sword pointed at Bill, except his pencil-thin arms shook violently under the weight. Bill continued walking slowly toward us.

"You can't do it, old man," Bill reiterated. "You can barely lift the sword."

"If I'm incapable of killing you with this, why are you sweating so badly?" Sam asked defiantly.

"I'm ashamed to admit it, but I hate pain. You can't possibly kill me with that thing. Even so, you might get a lucky poke in." He took another step toward us.

Sam's arms finally gave out, and the tip of the sword clanked against the concrete garage floor. Booker's pain-filled eyes came to mind. His words *I just can't lose him* ran riot through my head. I had to do something. This evilness wouldn't kill Sam, not if I could help it.

"Wait. If you let him go back inside, you can have me. I won't put up a fight," I said, hoping he'd bargain.

"Maybe I like the fight," Bill said, adding a brutal grin.

"Okay, I'll fight you with my last dying breath. However you want it."

"However I want it?" I knew by the sickening grin on Bill's face we were no longer talking about my dying quickly. My soul cringed with thoughts of the sadistic torture he'd inflict on me.

I took a deep breath and whispered, "Yes."

"No!" shouted Sam.

"Alan's going to regret me coming here instead of him. Old man, leave."

"Not going to happen, freak." Sam stepped in front of me again and raised the sword.

"Sam, you're all Booker has left. Please go."

"I'm an old man, Maggie. My time is up."

"Please," I said weakly.

"I'll stab him with the sword, and you jump in the car and go.

"He crushed the key, I can't. Besides, I'm not leaving without you."

"Fine. Run into the house. I can keep him busy enough for you to get inside and turn the security code on, including the electrical current."

"No," I pleaded once more.

He ignored me. "I've already called the police. They should be here any minute." I listened, but couldn't hear any sirens. The weather must still be slowing everyone down.

"Hey, old man, I can hear you." Bill looked at Sam as if he were some stupid creature. "I can kill you and the girl," he said, patting the gun in the pocket, "in less than two seconds. Actually, this lovely creature has planted some rather exciting thoughts in my head. Slow torture is such a lovely way to die," he cooed. "Put the sword down, you old fool, and I swear you won't feel a thing."

"I don't think so. Why don't you come and get it, chicken? "

"Maybe I should just use my gun, you stubborn old fool." Bill stood there, fingering the gun, then slid it back in his pocket. "Nah, too easy. Two-by-four it is, pops."

Bill sauntered toward us, taking two steps forward, and one back, playing Sam like a cat with a mouse. Sam hoisted the sword back up. His arms immediately shook again under its weight, causing him to topple over onto one knee. I went to reach for the sword when Sam looked back and winked at me.

It was a trick.

Bill leapt at us, the two by four raised high above his head. Sam lifted the sword with all the strength of a twenty year-old man, and shoved it into Bill, impaling him through the chest. Clutching at the sword as blood gushed out of his wound, Bill fell over sideways with a loud guttural cry escaping his perverse lips. He twisted frantically on the ground before he finally stopped breathing.

Sam dropped to the ground at almost the exact same moment. "Maggie, call 9-1-1."

"I thought you already did."

"I lied."

I ran in and grabbed the phone, calling for help as I went back out to Sam. "Hold on, please don't die. Booker needs you." I cradled him in my arms while my tears soaked his shirt. I told him over again what Booker had said earlier, as if I could somehow guilt him into living. Booker arrived in less than two minutes.

I briefly explained what had happened while he lifted Sam up and placed him into the police car. He then ran over to his POC car and removed a small handgun from the trunk, handing it to me as he ordered me to get inside and stay there. He was beyond angry, and I didn't protest. I immediately set all the alarms and called Seth.

32

I sat on the floor of the living room with the gun at my side and my arms wrapped tightly around my knees, rocking back and forth. *Where's Seth? Why doesn't he answer his stupid cell phone?*

I'd called the hospital to find out what was happening with Sam and slammed the phone down in frustration when the receptionist wouldn't tell me anything. Only after I heard the back door open did I realize it'd gotten dark and so many hours passed already. Grabbing the gun, I darted behind a cabinet. A familiar shadow passed through the door and headed straight toward me, pinning me to the wall. Seth. I buried myself in his chest. A hand came down firmly over my mouth, squelching my voice.

"Is there someone else in the house?" Seth whispered in my ear. I shook my head and he released me.

"Why are you back already? Why didn't you call me?" I shouted my questions at him in a flurry.

"The trial ended sooner than I thought so I took an earlier flight home to surprise you. Booker called this afternoon to let me know you were staying with Sam. What exactly went on here?" His eyes focused on the gun in my hand as I gave him a quick rundown. He was on the phone before I finished. He must have gotten the same obnoxious receptionist because he slammed the phone down, muttering under his breath.

"Is the body still in the garage?" he asked, walking toward the door.

"No, the coroner came an hour ago."

Booker's car pulled up before Seth could ask any more questions. He walked in and sank down onto the couch. His face was stoic.

"How's Sam?" Seth asked cautiously.

"Dead," Booker answered coldly. I dropped to my knees in silent tears.

"I'm sorry, Book. Maggie told me what happened. It's not fair. He was a wonderful man. Was it his heart?" Booker didn't answer.

"Maggie said Dreser didn't touch either of them, thanks to Sam. He saved their lives." Seth sat down next to Booker, placing a hand on his shoulder. I tried drying my tears, but they kept coming.

"Did she tell you about the deal she tried to make with the foul scum?" Booker's voice was imbued with anger. "Tell me something, Maggie. What kind of a man do you think my grandfather is—was?" The bitterness in his voice was unmistakable. I had no idea what he was thinking. Why was he angry with me? "Do you honestly believe my grandfather would have gone calmly back into the house and allowed that loathsome pig to do whatever form of torture he wanted on you?" Booker asked harshly.

Seth's eyes turned to me. I was confused and had no response to Booker's anger. All I tried to do was keep Sam alive.

"He was a wonderful man, a good man, and he didn't deserve to die!" he shouted. "You don't make deals with drug dealers. They *never* keep their word. They are foul sick creatures who should be eliminated!"

"Book, this is not fair. She tried to help." Seth attempted to walk the delicate balance between comforting his friend and protecting me.

"Fair? I've had to bury my mother and my sister thanks to drugs. Now I have to bury my grandfather, courtesy of a drug dealer. That's not fair. When you have to bury her," he said, pointing angrily at me, "we'll talk again about what's fair."

Seth walked over and drew me up off the floor. "Perhaps we should go."

"Perhaps your girlfriend should learn to listen. What did I say, Maggie? Do you even remember, or where you too busy whimpering about not seeing Seth for a whole twenty-four hours?" His words ripped through my heart. "I said Don't. Leave. This. House. How do you expect me to protect you if you won't listen?"

"Enough." Seth's arm wrapped around me. Anger literally flew from his eyes. He practically dragged me out the door and into his car. Too distraught to speak, I remained silent the entire drive home.

I walked into his house feeling as if the world rested on my shoulders and I was about to break. "I'm really tired. I'm going to bed. See you in the morning." I barely kept the tears in while running upstairs and climbing into his too-high bed. Burying my head under a pillow, my tears fell freely again. Almost immediately, Seth's hands guided my shoulders gently onto his chest.

"I was trying to help Sam. He thought he was having a heart attack, and was afraid if we called 9-1-1, Booker would drive like a wild man to get home—"

"Which is exactly what would've happened," Seth interjected. "And with all the rain, he could easily have gotten into a wreck."

I nodded. "Sam wanted me to drive him to the hospital. It's the only reason I left the house, I swear."

"Book didn't mean it, Maggie. He's hurting. I can only imagine the pain he is going through. If I had lost you . . ." He didn't finish his sentence, instead he pulled me up tighter against him. "His past dealings with dealers and addicts have clouded his thinking. He's a passionate man, and doesn't always engage his head before he lets his heart scream out. His tongue can be brutal sometimes," he said with reproach. After several more bouts of tears, I fell asleep in his arms.

I awoke in the morning to Seth's soft sweet kisses on top of my head. "Good morning," I said, smiling weakly up at him, the happenings of yesterday still front and center in my mind.

He smiled and looked over at the clock, it was nearly eleven. "I have to go do Lunch Swap," he said, slowly pulling away. He'd already showered and dressed.

"I'm going, too."

"Maggie, I wish you wouldn't. Please, let me find out if there is any new information on the case. Hopefully, they've found the last Dreser."

My stomach knotted up as I thought of Sam again. "Okay, I'll cook up something wonderful for lunch while you're gone." I was in no mood to battle having to stay home. Truthfully, I didn't want to leave the security of his house. He brushed his teeth while I preoccupied myself in the kitchen. I noticed an agent sitting in his car out front. He yawned and stretched his arms, probably stiff from sitting out there all night.

Seth kissed me good-bye, never mentioning a word about staying inside, no doubt knowing Booker's words from yesterday still weighed heavy on my heart. The tears began again as thoughts of Sam played through my mind. I forced myself to stay busy. I couldn't think about him anymore, not for a while. It hurt too much.

Because of everything that happened yesterday, I didn't get a chance to visit my mom. I called the hospital, and the nurse said that she had developed a fever, and they ran some tests to try and learn what caused the change. More bad news.

I began defrosting some chicken, though I wasn't hungry in the least. I dug out Seth's favorite Spanish rice recipe. Maybe I'd want to eat something if I knew he'd enjoy it. As I browned the rice, the phone rang. To my frustration, it was a nettlesome telemarketer. I tried repeatedly to tell him no thank you, except the man was persistent, if not a little dense. I gave up on being polite and hung up on the guy, but not soon enough. The forgotten rice was now burnt and the entire kitchen was saturated in smoke.

The back door opened and the security system began beeping. Booker came in and punched in the code.

"I didn't know you were Jewish?" He smiled weakly as he opened the kitchen windows.

"What?"

He looked horrible, as if he hadn't slept at all. He walked over to the stove and stirred the blackened rice. "Burnt offerings, right?"

"Pretty weak joke, Booker," I answered cautiously.

"I'm sorry, and I'm not referring to my truly wonderful joke." He came over to me, gently taking me by the shoulders. "Maggie, I didn't mean any of those horrible things I said. I'm just tired of the heartache caused by drugs and these ruthless dealers." Anguish racked his face, and it took every ounce of my strength not to burst into tears.

"Cole said when they opened up Sam's chest in the operating room his heart was severely damaged. He didn't have a chance. He said Sam must have been having small heart attacks for a while." He wiped a tear from his cheek and continued.

"Knowing my grandfather, I'm betting he asked you to drive him to the hospital." I nodded. "He was probably worried I'd get in an accident trying to get to him." He squeezed his eyes shut and shook his head. "Like I said yesterday, he told me how you tried to save him, about the whole deal with Dreser." He stroked my cheek softly. "I can't believe you'd do that. Do you have any idea how badly he would've hurt you?" His eyes shut again, and he dropped his forehead to mine.

"You astound me, Maggie. When I said I wasn't strong enough to lose Sam, I didn't mean you should die for him."

"I know. I couldn't get your face out of my mind. I thought about your family all being gone, too. It's unfair."

"It wouldn't have been fair for Seth to lose you either. He loves you so much. I honestly think he would've gone insane if he did." He held me as we stood in the smoke filled kitchen sharing our sorrow.

"I don't suppose you've an older sister who's looking for an incredibly handsome man to fall in love with?" he asked, drying his face.

"You know an incredibly handsome man looking to fall in love?" I asked. He groaned playfully. "Sorry, I'm an only child."

"Drat."

"Drat? Do people still use that word? Man, you are old."

"You're real funny, Magpie. Come on. Let's see if we can fix this mess you are trying to pass off as food." I whacked him with the kitchen towel as he dumped the rice into the sink.

I was surprised to learn Booker was almost as good a cook as Seth. The lunch turned out pretty good despite the whole burnt offerings episode. Seth walked in as we finished setting the table. Book quickly crossed the room and the two men embraced, each saying nothing. They didn't have to. Booker eventually broke the silence as he tried to apologize. Needless to say, Seth wouldn't hear of it.

"We'll get through this together, like we always have."

Two days later we went to the funeral. It was heart wrenching. Sam was well known in the community, and it seemed like everyone in town came to say goodbye. Because of the size of the crowd, and since we had no idea of the whereabouts of the remaining Dreser, Seth and Cole never left my side. It was almost comical to observe me moving around with my "hot guy" shield. I was forbidden to go to the bathroom and therefore didn't dare eat or drink anything all morning, yet somehow I still had to go. Thank heavens Mrs. Gianchi showed up and saved me from an embarrassing moment.

I cried so many times during the service the skin around my eyes cracked and bled. Booker was a wreck. I wanted to wrap my arms around him, to hold and comfort him, but how do you comfort someone who's lost their entire family?

Booker decided to keep the burial part of his grandfather's service private. Only a few of us watched them lower Sam into the ground.

After the service, we invited Booker over to Seth's house. He declined, saying he wanted to spend a little more time at the graveside. My mind reeled by the time we arrived home. Seth and I sat silently on the couch in each other's arms for a very long time.

"How are you doing?" I asked, stroking his tight brow. For the past two days he had been so busy 'being there' for Booker, he hadn't taken any time to mourn his own loss. He'd known Sam his entire life, and his death had to be affecting him deeply.

"I'm okay. It's difficult to believe he's gone. He was such a driving force. He had more energy than most men did half his age. Part of me is happy for him. I know how much he missed his wife, and I'm trying to focus on how sweet their reunion must be. I do okay until I see Booker's face and the sorrow that owns it right now," he said, his eyes filling with tears.

I held him close and thought about how difficult it would be for both of us to be separated by death. I hoped we'd never have to experience it, though in his chosen profession the odds weren't in our favor. Why couldn't he just be a math teacher?

"You look tired, would you like to take a nap?" Seth asked. I hadn't slept much in the past two days, instead spending many hours at my mother's side. Her condition deteriorated rapidly. When I was able to sleep, my dreams were haunted by a dead drug dealer. I shook my head; no naps.

"How about a bubble bath?" he suggested. I was beginning to think *he* had a thing for bubble baths.

"You could kiss me. We've hardly kissed since you've come back. You didn't meet another woman while you were gone, did you?" I traced around the outline of his lips with my index finger.

"There are other women out there?" The look on his face was one of genuine surprise.

"Oh, you're good." I kissed his cheek. "Did you come up with that all by yourself, or is it a line from one of your old movies?"

"All by myself." Seth put his arms around my waist and drew me close. "You know, some serious kissing would be a wonderful distraction," he said. I continued to nuzzle his neck, working my way up to his mouth, kissing him softly before pulling back and looking into his eyes.

"Bubble bath." We both said it at the same time. He took my hand and led me upstairs.

After my long hot bath, I found Seth in the bedroom sitting on the bench seat below the bay window. His head leaned against the curtains with his eyes shut. I walked over and sat in his lap, wrapping my arms around his neck as he broke down in my arms.

His tears finally slowed as the phone rang. "Let the machine get it," he said as I wiped his cheeks. "No, wait, it might be Booker. You'd better answer it." I reluctantly moved to the phone.

"Hello, Maggie," Cole said, his voice heavy. "I know you planned on coming to see your mom around 7:00, but it might be a good idea if you came a little earlier today. I'm afraid she's not doing well." My head nodded at the phone and I hung up without saying a word. Seth already had the keys in his hand, and we immediately left for the hospital.

When we got there, we bypassed the elevator and ran straight up the stairs. Walking into her room, a feeling that could only be described as *death* wrapped around me. Machines beeped, and alarms screeched unceasingly. Several nurses and two doctors, one being Cole, scrambled around her. Some performed CPR, others injected her with drugs. I watched in horror as they gave her electric shock. After what felt like an eternity, the alarms finally ceased and the machines started chirping rhythmically again.

"I wish you hadn't witnessed that," Cole said, resetting the last monitor. "It's difficult enough having someone you love in the hospital, but seeing us working on them like that can be traumatic."

"She isn't going to live much longer, is she?" I dropped into a chair in the corner of the room.

"No, she's not. I'm sorry, Maggie, I doubt she'll last through the night. Virtually every one of her body's systems are failing now."

"Can you take her off the drugs? I'd like to try and talk to her one last time." My voice sounded detached. I was unsure of how much more I could take. The sleep I so desperately needed would not be happening for a while.

"We took her off them yesterday. Maggie, research suggests people in comas can often hear us. By all means, talk to her."

I did have things to say to her, but what I wanted most in the world was to hear her say she loved me. I wanted to *hear* her voice the words she had only written to me a few times. I didn't tell that to Cole. I didn't tell that to anyone.

Everyone left the room, even Seth. He seemed to sense my need to be alone with her. He knew me better than my own mother. I went to her bedside and took her delicate hand carefully into mine. The veins were visible through her almost translucent yellowed skin.

"Mom, can you hear me? I love you." I kissed her hand gently, but there was no response. I again pleaded with her to open her eyes. Still nothing. Numbness quickly took residence in my soul as I repeated my plea several more times before giving up and sitting back down.

The rhythmic sounds of the machines grew more and more irritating as the minutes past. Beeping and beeping and beeping. Over and over and over again. It didn't take long for it to get on my nerves.

I slapped my hands over my ears. "*Stop!*"

"Maggie, we should go home and get some sleep, you look awful," Seth said, taking my hand.

"Thanks for the compliment." I was more than a little embarrassed by my outburst. "I didn't see you come in."

"Secret Agent Man, remember? Poof." He winked, and for once, my heart didn't respond.

"I don't want to go. What if she wakes up? You can go. I'll be fine." He frowned and left, returning a few moments later with another recliner chair. He slid it up next to mine and took my hand.

"'*You can go.*' Sometimes you are just ridiculous," he said, kissing my palm. We sat for several hours making small talk, since sleeping was impossible with the alarms going off constantly.

Around 4:00 a.m., things began changing drastically. My mom started groaning and fidgeting around in her bed. I quickly jumped to her side, carefully taking her hand in mine again.

"Mom, can you open your eyes?" She groaned louder. After several minutes of coaxing, they finally opened. The whites were yellowed and lined with red blood vessels, and she seemed to be having trouble focusing.

"Hi, Mom, how are you feeling?" My eyes filled with tears. She was finally awake. She mumbled something incoherent and shut her eyes again.

I brushed some hair from her face. "Mom, it's me, Maggie. Can you open your eyes?"

"Gaa waaa," she whispered weakly.

"Did you understand her, Seth?" I looked at him hopefully. "What did she say?"

The look in his eyes told me he understood her only too well. He shook his head and replied, "No." A lie.

"Mom, I love you." The tears poured down my cheeks. I knew it would only make her angry, but I couldn't stop them.

"Go waaay!" she said louder, pulling her hand out of mine. This time I understood her. It felt as if the air had been sucked from my lungs, and I stumbled back a little.

"Remember, Cole said her liver is no longer functioning," Seth reminded me. "It's dumping poisons into her system. He said it could cause delusions, and don't forget about all the drugs they've had her on since she's been admitted." I knew he was trying to soften the harsh words she was heaving onto me.

"Mom, I love you," I pleaded this time. She wouldn't say it back. I knew it, and my heart broke into millions of shards.

"Drink!" she demanded. I put an ice chip into her mouth, and she promptly spat it back out at me.

"No, vodka! Stupid!" That she said clearly, too clearly. "Go 'way!"

Seth's lips pressed instantly to my ear once more. "Maggie, she's sick. We really should go." He pulled at me gently, only I couldn't leave.

"Mom, I love you. Please, mom, don't you love me?" I begged through my tears.

Her eyes looked into mine, and for an instant, I saw something there. Sorrow, or maybe even love.

It was love all right, only not for me. "I love vodka! Now get me a drink or go 'way!"

Those were her last words. The monitors screamed once more as her breathing turned shallow and labored. Cole, along with his staff, came rushing in and worked on her for over half an hour trying to bring her back. He pleaded with Seth to take me out of the room, but I begged him to let me stay, hoping she'd regain consciousness and say the words I needed to hear.

   She didn't.

33

"I'm sorry, Maggie. I did everything possible."

"I know, Cole. Thank you very much." I mindlessly patted his hand and walked out of the room, shedding no tears. My heart froze solid; no pain got in or out.

I couldn't believe the amount of paperwork there was to do after someone died. Several hours passed before we could leave the hospital.

Later that morning, Seth helped me make funeral arrangements. Since she didn't have any friends, I saw no need for the expense of a full-blown funeral. I planned a graveside service for late the following day, and of course, Seth paid for everything.

Throughout the day, my mind replayed her last few minutes repeatedly. I couldn't stop it, nor did I try. Seth walked around me as if I were a delicate piece of china.

By the end of the day, exhaustion owned me and sleep was my only escape, or so I thought. Regrettably, the two hours of sleep I did manage were beset with nightmares of my mom laughing and mocking me as she drank her vodka. Giving up, I sat and watched some of Seth's old movies the rest of the night, alone.

The service was at 4:30 in the afternoon. Aside from a preacher connected to the mortuary, Booker, Cole, Seth, and I were the only ones there. The preacher offered some kind words as we lowered her into the ground. My mind was empty, my heart was still frozen, and not one tear fell from my eyes throughout the service. In truth, my heart hadn't hurt since I pleaded for her love at the hospital. I also hadn't slept more than five hours over the past four days. I actually enjoyed the zombie like feeling it produced. I didn't want to think, or feel anymore. Emotions and feelings were overrated.

"Maggie, would you like me to give you something to help you sleep? You look exhausted." I yawned and shook my pounding head at Cole's offer.

"It was a nice service." Booker gave me a side hug and a quick peck on the head. "You look bad. Have this boyfriend of yours take you home and put you to bed. I've seen albinos with more color than you, and I won't even mention the dark circles around your eyes." He seemed repulsed by my face.

"Good. Don't mention them, Garfield."

Seth held my hand as we walked to the car. I giggled aloud several times.

"What's so funny?" Seth asked.

"I have no idea," I said with another giggle. His face was unreadable, or maybe it was just blurry. I really needed some sleep. "I want to sleep at my house tonight." He didn't argue and drove straight to my trailer.

I ambled around in the empty trailer, hoping to find . . . I don't know what. Closure? Peace, maybe? Only neither was to be found, just unhappy memories. No matter where I looked, I saw my mother drunk, which definitely didn't bring me any comfort. I wanted to crawl into a hole somewhere and never come out. Sleep. Sleep and never wake up.

"I'm going to bed." I could feel my defenses growing weak, and I wanted to be alone when I finally broke down. Besides, my head pounded, and I couldn't stop yawning to save my life.

"I can't leave you here alone, Maggie. We still have no idea where Alan is."

I nodded. "You can sleep in my room. It's only fitting since I sleep in yours all the time." I giggled again, his face remained emotionless.

I walked slowly into my mother's room and knew instantly I'd made a big mistake. As the door shut, my frozen heart began to crack, like a spring creek after winter, sending horrendous jolts of pain through me. I didn't bother changing into my pajamas, instead I fell onto the bed, crying and grasping at my broken heart. My mind replayed the last several months over again in my half-crazed head: the almost attack in the park, the Winter Festival Mirror Maze, Hillary trying to punch me, and Zack smacking me around at school. I saw Bill Dreser, his body pierced with the samurai sword, taking his last breath. I saw Sam collapsing, and Booker yelling at me.

I heard all the cruel bitter words my mother eructed at me daily. Haunting memories of her in a drunken stupor, every day, falling, and screaming at me repeatedly. I clapped my hands over my ears as if I could block out her words, but they still rang out crystal clear in my mind.

I could see her in the hospital with tubes running everywhere. I heard her shrieking for vodka and not for me as she died, sucking in her last haggard breath, leaving me alone, all alone, never telling me she loved me, only in some stupid letters.

Yet it wasn't enough. I wanted, no, I *needed* to hear her say it.

I jerked her pillow over my face in an attempt to smother out the pain, only to be greeted by the stench of alcohol instead. Then I realized how much the whole house reeked of it. Living here every day, I rarely noticed it, but now that I'd been away for a while, I realized the smell was all-encompassing. Her bedding was heavily saturated with the smell and it made me sick.

I remembered seeing some clean sheets on the closet floor, and through my pain, clawed my way across the bed to the pile of linen. I picked the spare sheets off the floor and a half-empty bottle of vodka slipped out from underneath, stopping at my feet. I picked it up and held it, mindlessly twisting it around in my hands. My fist wrapped tight around the neck of the bottle, and my eyes clamped shut. *No more pain*, I begged. *Please stop.*

A small flicker of joy entered my bleeding heart. Seth. I squeezed my eyes together tightly, and in my mind, I saw his smiling face, his kind eyes filled with love for me.

In the same beautiful vision, he exploded into a riot of blood. I screamed, smashing the bottle of booze against the wall. I didn't realize how close I stood to the wall until shattered glass and alcohol splattered all over me. My knees gave out, and I dropped to the floor. The door flew open and Seth, Booker, and Cole stood soberly at the door.

"Maggie, are you alright?" Seth asked. He stood frozen, not coming near me.

"Don't force her, Seth," Cole said.

Booker tossed his hands in the air. "Don't force her? What are we supposed to do, watch her die?"

"No, Booker. Force isn't the answer to everything, either. We need to let her work through this. Just talk to her. We'll stop her if it becomes dangerous," Cole said. I watched as Booker rolled his head back angrily.

What in the world were they talking about? Don't force me to do what? I shook my pounding head in confusion. My frozen heart was now completely thawed, flooding me with pain, too much pain, and I desperately wanted it to stop. I began rocking back and forth. It was somewhat comforting.

"Why didn't she love me? Why am I such an unlovable nothing? What's so wrong with me? Why did she love her booze more than me?" I pounded my fists on my knees, blurting my questions out in rapid succession. Not allowing anyone to answer my pleas, I continued.

"I was a good girl. I cooked for her and cleaned the house every day. I studied hard at school and got good grades, all in hopes of pleasing her. I never made trouble, ever. I didn't drink or do drugs. I didn't sleep with boys, either, in hopes of making her proud of me. Yet still I didn't matter to her. I *am* an unlove—"

"Maggie, please don't do this. I love you," Seth said.

Looking into his green eyes, I saw tears. I'd hurt him with my words, something I didn't want to do.

"You do love me, more than she loved her booze. You'd do anything for me. You'd . . . ."

"I'd give up my life for you." A single tear ran down his face, his beautiful face, but still he wouldn't come near me.

I looked down at my wet clothes. Maybe the smell of alcohol was more off-putting than I thought. That was when I noticed my bloodied hands. Each clinched firmly around several large shards of glass, fragments of the broken vodka bottle. I looked back up at Seth as he walked toward me in slow motion. I held my hands out to show him the blood. He stopped dead next to the bed.

"Maggie, put the glass down, please," Seth implored.

I looked at the handfuls of glass again, trying to figure out why it didn't hurt when I squeezed. Several large splatters of blood stained my clothes and the floor, yet I felt nothing but the pain in my chest.

"Why didn't my mom love me enough to give this up?" Pressing my bloodied hands to my chest, I squeezed my fists around the broken shards again. Confused, I lost my focus. *Stay on task, you stupid girl.*

"No more, I can't take anymore!" I told myself to calm down, except it was too late. Not only were the past several months of chaos drowning me, but a lifetime of stuffing my emotions deep inside and not dealing with things came back, consuming me. I couldn't catch my breath as the room began twisting wildly. My stomach threatened to regurgitate its content, and I fell sideways against the wall, all the while holding the shards tight in my fists.

"I'm here for you, Maggie. I'll always be here for you," Seth vowed. He looked incredibly sad and it broke my heart even more.

"Maggie, hand me the glass." Cole stepped closer to me. If he wanted the glass, he could have it. I certainly didn't want any souvenirs of life with my mother. He had such kind eyes. Why hadn't he found someone to marry? "Maggie, please."

Before I could hand the shards over, someone grabbed me from the rear, twisted my arms behind me, and pressed me to the floor.

Booker.

Seth flew over the bed, and he and Booker easily pried my hands open and retrieved the glass before I could do any more damage. Seth pulled me up into his arms, buried his face in my hair, and whispered my name repeatedly.

"I'm going to throw up," was my only response. A trash bin appeared under my mouth, and I followed through with my statement. I dropped back onto Seth's chest and lifted my head to look into his eyes, only the corner of a plastic bag protruding from the closet ceiling caught my eye instead.

Booker stepped toward us, following my stare. He reached up and knocked the ceiling tile up. Several plastic bags containing off-white powder showered down on us.

Drugs.

"*Noooo!*" I screamed. At the exact same moment, I felt a prick in my left hip. Cole injected me with something. The room really spun out of control then, and my head dropped against Seth's shoulder. Within moments, all the pain stopped.

34
Seth

"She's going to be asleep for some time, Seth. I'll take her back to your place and stay with her while you and Booker go talk to Hoffman." Nodding, I scooped her up in my arms and carried her to the car after watching Cole bandage her hands, thankful that the cuts were minor and would heal quickly. The damages on the inside wouldn't. She felt so small and fragile in my arms I didn't want to put her down.

However, I had a job to do, and interrogating Hoffman was something I looked forward to doing personally. Booker called in the team, even bringing in drug dogs, and the entire trailer was searched again, but nothing more was found. They were able to lift three very clear sets of fingerprints off the heroin bags, and Booker ran them through the computer immediately. One set belonged to Hoffman; he was arrested as soon as the results came in. Another set matched the ones we'd gotten off Bill Dreser during his autopsy, but not surprising, no criminal record turned up.

The last set came up blank in the database. Booker suspected Harry Dreser had used his powerful connections to have his two sons' prints eradicated from all records, not unlike what he had done for their older brother Jeffery. Even Alan's prints from his stint in jail had mysteriously vanished from the system.

Barbara Brown's fingerprints were not on the bags, or on any of the ceiling tiles. It gave me hope that just maybe she wasn't involved.

Maggie stirred as I lay her across the backseat. She was still restless, despite the heavy dose of narcotics Cole had given her. I kissed her head. "I love you, Mags," I said, squeezing my eyes tight.

"Once she gets a good night's sleep, maybe two, she'll be good as new. She's suffering from major sleep deprivation," Cole assured me. I said nothing, but stood in the middle of the road and watched as he drove away.

"Come on, Hoffman's waiting in the interrogation room. Let's go see what the weasel has to say," Booker said, patting my back. I didn't move. My eyes followed the taillights as they disappeared down the street.

"Cole's the best. She's in good hands," he said softly.

My anguish quickly turned to anger, setting my temper in full swing by the time we arrived at the precinct. I shoved the door of the interrogation room so hard, it flung open and hit the wall before it vibrated back at me. I grabbed it and slammed it shut. Hoffman jumped nervously.

The room was stark and bare, with the exception of three metal chairs and a small beat-up wooden table. Along one wall was a two-way mirror, with at least three agents on the other side watching.

"You're looking at twenty years," I barked at him. "I'm going to recommend to the DA that you get the maximum. I want your last dying breath to be from the stench of a six-by-eight foot jail cell. I'm going to hang you out to dry, you understand me?" I reached for him, fully intending to drag him to his feet and toss him against the wall. For starters.

"Whoa, Seth. Police brutality, however well justified, will only help get this guy off with a slap on the wrist. That's something we definitely don't want happening." Booker forced me down onto a chair, positioning the scarred table between Hoffman and us. Hoffman tipped his steel chair back and propped his dirty shoes up on the table's edge. He laced his fingers behind his head, a smug expression across his face.

Booker laughed. "Now, now Hoffman. I didn't mean for you to get comfortable either." He slapped Hoffman's feet to the floor. It pivoted him upright with the force.

"So, tell me, where did you get the drugs?" Booker asked, now propping his feet up onto the desk.

"What drugs?" he asked, stupidly.

"Your prints are all over the stuff," I said, leaning across the desk. "Yours and two others. One set matched a dead guy. Needless to say, he can't be prosecuted. The other set came up blank, which means you and you alone are going to hang for this. Are you willing to rot for your buddy?"

His eyes widened in fright. "I don't know any Dreser." The guy was a complete idiot. I wanted to arrest him for that alone.

"I don't believe we said his name was Dreser," Booker pointed out. "Okay, I'm tired, let's put all our cards on the table here. You tell us how Barbara Brown was involved with this, and tell us where Dreser is, and we'll talk to the DA about going easy on you. You'll serve seven years, maybe five with good behavior."

He sat soberly for a moment. "For a lousy deal like that, I'll only give you the scoop on Barbara. You'll have to do better if you want info on Dreser." He looked at Booker waiting for an answer.

"Let's hear what you got on Barbara first, and then I'll decide," Booker said, pulling out a notebook and pen from his left breast pocket.

"Barbara was a drunk," he laughed. "A worthless drunk, and she treated that kid of hers like dirt." He leaned forward. "Man alive, is her kid ever hot. With that sweet little face and those perky—"

I was across the desk and had the slimy fink-rat pinned against the wall before Booker could stop me. Two agents bust into the room and pulled me off him.

Booker hauled me out of the room. "I don't want you in there. Go home, be with Maggie. You're of no use to me like this."

"No, I'm okay, sorry. I have it in control now, I swear." I took a deep breath, forcing myself to calm down.

Booker shook his head and threw an arm around my shoulders. "Go home and that's an order." In his best Marlon Brando voice he added, *"I'm gonna make him an offer he can't refuse."* I smiled slightly, for the first time in days. "Trust me on this," he added.

He was right. I'd blow the whole case and needed to leave. We'd spent months trying to end this, and I didn't want to be the one to muck up the first big lead we had. I grabbed my jacket, jumped in my car, and headed home. Home to Maggie.

***

"How much longer is she going to sleep?" I slammed my mug of hot chocolate down on the slate counter, shattering the cup into pieces and spilling the steamy liquid everywhere.

Cole mopped up the mess while Booker fixed me a fresh cup.

"I just checked on her. She's stirring around some. I don't think it will be too much longer," Cole said calmly. He said everything calmly. I wondered if anything ever got to him.

"It's been almost thirty hours," I pointed out unnecessarily.

"She's exhausted and she needs sleep, lots of sleep," he reiterated again, in the same calm voice that was now getting on my nerves.

"She's going to need counseling," Cole said softly. "She was quite co-dependent on her mother." I shot up in my seat. "She'll be fine, she's one tough kid. Al-Anon has a great program that I think will help her. It will probably be best if you both go so you can watch for signs of her becoming co-dependent with you. That's what we need to be worried about at this point."

Booker set a green mug in front of me and plopped down on a stool to my right. "I'm glad we can finally clear her mother. I think it'll help."

In Booker's words, Hoffman sang like an American Idol hopeful. He'd been using Maggie's house as a storage unit. He'd bring over a bottle of vodka, which he made her pay for, get her mother plastered to the point where she'd pass out, then he'd hide the stuff up in the ceiling of her closet. When he needed to make a delivery, he'd repeat the process taking what he needed and leaving the rest neatly hidden. Because of his long police record, he didn't want the drugs at his house in case the cops caught on to the fact that he'd moved from marijuana to heroin. He had a slick little operation going, until now.

A scream coming from upstairs tore all thoughts of Hoffman and Dreser from my head. It was Maggie. I was up the stairs before I drew in my next breath. I shoved the door open and found her in the middle of the bed, staring down at her hands.

"I'm a complete loon, a total complete loon."

"You're not a loon, Maggie, you'd been functioning on overdrive, and it caught up with you." I stroked her hair in an effort to calm her.

"I wasn't trying to off myself, I swear. I didn't even feel the glass cutting me, because if I did, I can guarantee you I would've stopped." I could tell she tried keeping her voice from sounding frantic. "I'm sorry, Seth, you didn't deserve that on top of everything else." She hung her head, completely humiliated. "All of you didn't deserve this. I'm very sorry."

Cole sat down next to her. "Maggie, you were trying to function on only a few hours of sleep. The mind breaks down and doesn't perform properly. Add to it everything you've been through lately, I should have insisted you let me give you something for sleep." He rubbed her shoulders.

"How many stitches?" she asked softly, tugging on a loose string from the gauze.

"None. The cuts were superficial. You're quite the bleeder, though. I had to rewrap your hands several times," he assured her. "And, Maggie, I hope you realize that Seth isn't the only one who loves you. I daresay everyone in this house loves you." He kissed her forehead gently.

"Oh, and the headache I'm betting you have is my fault." His smile was plaited with guilt. "It's a side effect from the drug cocktail I gave you the other night to help you sleep. It's commonly referred to as a narcotic headache."

"The other night? Don't you mean earlier this evening?" she asked, unsure. "What time is it?"

"It's one-thirty, in the morning. You—you've been asleep for over thirty hours," Cole said carefully.

"You kept me sedated for thirty hours?"

"No, I only gave you two injections. One the first night, and one the next morning because you were still thrashing about and crying out in your sleep. Your body needed that much rest." She dropped her beet-red face back into her bandaged hands—even her ears were red. "Don't worry, the headache should be gone by tomorrow," Cole assured her.

"Thank you," she said through her fingers.

She still looked fragile. I wished we knew the whereabouts of Alan. I wanted this entire mess behind us. I wanted Maggie to be able to move on with her life.

Gathering my blue robe around her shoulders, I helped her off the bed. "Come, I'll make you something to eat and get you some aspirin, but first, I need to hold you." She sank readily into my arms.

35
Maggie

"So what exactly was in the plastic bags?" I tugged nervously at the sash on Seth's robe, not wanting to hear the answer.

"Heroin, mostly." I hung my head as Booker continued. "We dusted the bags for fingerprints and the closet ceiling as well. Your mother's prints weren't on any of it."

"Really?" The news seemed to soften the blow of her death somewhat.

"Really. We did find Hoffman's though, along with those we assume are the Dreser's. We arrested Hoffman, and he spilled his guts." Booker flashed me his signature grin. "He said he'd feed your mother vodka until she passed out, then stuff the drugs in her closet. She didn't know anything about it. He used your home to hide it so if he was ever busted, there were no drugs at his place to implicate him in the heroin ring."

"He claimed he had no idea where Dreser was," Seth said. "He offered to try and find out for us if we gave him complete immunity."

"Did you say yes?"

"Not complete immunity. Three to five years if he'll turn state's evidence against Dreser. Of course, once he's in prison, he'll be dead within six months for testifying against a smuggler's son. Thieves don't take well to rat-finks." Seth shrugged casually.

My mom wasn't involved. I felt as if a big weight had been lifted off my chest. In my excitement, I took the last steps rather quickly and sent pain rippling through my head. "Okay. Killer headache."

"I'll make you some toast," Seth said after I sat down at the table. Booker and Cole sat down next to me. They stared at me is if I were about to explode, and if they looked away they'd miss it.

Seth set the toast, milk and two aspirin down in front of me, along with a napkin. "Thanks." I took the aspirin and ate the toast while Seth cooked up some scrambled eggs.

"Ah, seen any good movies lately?" I asked, finishing the milk. Their stares were unnerving. Seth was the only one to laugh. He set a large plate of eggs on the table and pulled up a chair alongside me.

"How's the headache?"

"Still alive and kicking." I inhaled the entire plate of eggs within minutes. Seth poured a second glass of milk, which I drained too.

"Wow, guess I was pretty hungry. You'd think I hadn't eaten in a week, or thirty hours anyway." I and I alone laughed. With my slightly shaky hand, I wiped the milk moustache off my face with the napkin.

"I'm okay, guys, really I am. You can stop worrying," I said softly.

Cole scooted closer and took my hand. "I'm sorry for staring at you, professional habit." He squeezed gently. "I have to get going. I'm taking over for Dr. Taylor in an hour." I thanked him again as he and Seth walked out the door.

"Aren't you going to thank me, Magpie?" Booker asked, sitting down in the chair vacated by Cole. "After all, I was the one who *moused* up from behind and tackled you to the ground."

We both laughed at his little cat reference. "Thanks, Book." I thought to tell him I intended to give the glass shards to Cole right before he tackled me, but decided I didn't really want to talk about the embarrassing incident ever again.

I peered up into his eyes. They were still heavy with sorrow despite the smile on his mouth. I placed my hand on his. "How are you doing?"

"About as good as you are."

"I'll bet you didn't go mental on everyone."

"No, I didn't do that," he laughed again, "and I'll second what Cole said upstairs. Please don't doubt how much you're loved. I love your spirit, and I love your inner-strength. Notwithstanding the other night, you're one strong young woman. I'm also grateful for the way you love Seth. He's like a brother to me. I'm glad he has you." He ran a hand over my hair and flipped it everywhere, causing my head to throb again. "I guess that makes me your big brother."

"My very *annoying* big brother."

He took my hands carefully in his. "You and me, we're going to get through this. If you need anything, please call." He stood and pulled me into his arms, hugging me tight. "I love you, Magpie."

"I love you too, Book." I held his arm as he pulled away. "Will you promise me something?"

"Anything," he said without hesitation.

"Promise me you'll protect Seth. Promise me you'll do whatever it takes, short of dying yourself, to keep him alive. Please?"

"There's no need to make such a promise," he scoffed. "He's more than capable of taking care of himself. I do promise to do all I can to keep you alive, though."

"Promise me if you have to choose between saving his life over mine, you'll protect him first." He wouldn't answer my plea. "You of all people can understand why I'm asking this."

"You need protection, not Seth," he reiterated.

"Please," I begged once. He pulled me back into his arms and held me tight for several seconds. He dropped his mouth to my ear and said softly, "I promise." When he pulled away, I caught him wiping his cheek.

I held up my little finger. "Pinky swear?"

He rolled his eyes. "Don't you think I'm a little too old for a pinky swear?"

"You are never too old for a pinky swear." I wiggled my little finger, and he grudgingly wrapped his around mine. "Remember this is eternally binding. There's no backing out on a pinky swear."

"I never back out on a promise, or a pinky swear," he said, trying not to laugh. Seth walked in as we dropped our hands.

"I have to go also," Booker said, walking to the door. "Hoffman gave us an address for Dreser half an hour ago, and the chief issued a search warrant for the place. I'm thinking a three a.m. wakeup call's in order." He smiled. "Glad you're doing better, Magpie." He waved his little finger as he left.

"What's the little finger wave all about?" Seth asked, encircling me in his arms.

"I love you with all my heart and soul," I said, ignoring his question. He drew me up tight and kissed me. My pounding head pounded a bit harder. I didn't mind.

"I love you and always will," he vowed.

"I'm sorry about what I put you through the past few days, you deserve better." A yawn escaped my lips. How in the world could I possibly be tired after sleeping for thirty hours?

"Bedtime." He took my hand and led me up the stairs. I climbed into bed and, as he tucked the blankets around me, I pulled his mouth to mine for a long tender good night kiss.

I didn't wake until noon the next day, and just as Cole promised, my narcotic headache vanished. I took a quick shower and brushed my teeth. It felt good to be clean again. Seth sat finishing some homework at the kitchen table when I came down.

"Good morning," he said, pulling me onto his lap.

"Good afternoon," I corrected him.

"I have to head over to the police station to take care of some paperwork. I'll only be gone a few hours. Cole is on his way over to stay with you. How's your headache?"

"Fine, and I don't need a babysitter." I stood and folded my arms in front of me.

"I know you don't." A knock at the back door, was followed by a familiar, "Hello."

"Hey, Cole," Seth said, putting his books away.

"How are you, Maggie?"

"I don't need a babysitter." He laughed at my protest. I was glad he found it humorous.

"I'm not here to babysit you. I want to give you a quick check up and remove the bandages from your hands. I also need to talk to you about some things."

And it was the perfect excuse for Seth not to leave me alone in case I had another melt down.

Seth made his goodbyes as Cole pulled out a stethoscope from his little black bag. He gave me a quick once over, asked a few embarrassing questions aimed at my mental state, and removed the gauze bandages from my hands, replacing them with a few less-noticeable bandages, before giving me a clean bill of health. While tucking in my shirt, I noticed a bandage on his index finger that wasn't there last night.

"What did you do?" I asked, pointing to the bandage.

"I shut my finger in the car door this morning and lost part of the nail," he shrugged.

I winced.

"Doesn't hurt," he assured me. "Maggie, I'd like to talk to you about something. First, if I cross any lines here, I apologize. Some things you said the other night have haunted me these past few days, and I only want to help."

"I thought you said my breakdown was mostly from lack of sleep."

"I believe it was, but I also believe there are some other factors that played a part in it, such as the years of emotional abuse you've suffered." He put his ice-cold stethoscope back into the bag and pulled out some pamphlets, handing me one. "Maggie, living with an addict of any kind is seldom easy, and it's not uncommon for someone to become co-dependent."

Co-dependent. I was familiar with the term having learned about it once in my tenth grade health class. I browsed through the pamphlet, realizing that while I didn't have all the signs listed, I certainly had some, like: minimizing, or denying true feelings, perceiving yourself as unlovable, judging yourself too harshly, or as never good enough, and untrusting. Okay, so maybe I was a little co-dependent.

"I've seen people suffer their entire lives in silence," Cole said. "And I've seen others turn to the very addictions that caused the co-dependency in the first place to try and deal with their problems. Have you heard of Al-Anon?" I nodded. "Then you know that it's a support group for families, relatives, and friends of those whose lives have been affected by someone else's drinking problem. There's also a group called Ala-teen, which is basically the same thing, only it's geared toward teenagers. I'm not sure which you might be interested in so here are some brochures for both."

Okay, total humiliation.

"Maggie, I don't want you to go through life believing your mother didn't love you. She did, very much. Her addiction masked who she really was. There was nothing you could have done to change her. Only she could have done that. I feel these support groups will help you come to terms with your mother, and they'll help you wrap your mind around what happened to you while growing up. You're not to blame for her problem."

"So if I go to these meetings, I won't freak out again?" I asked, hoping he didn't think I was a complete nut.

"I don't think you're going to, *freak out again*, as you put it. You were exhausted and had just buried your mother, add to that everything else you've been through the past couple months," he said. "A lot happened in a very short period of time. I'm hoping you and Seth will talk about this right away. There are meetings almost every night at the hospital, and I think they'll be a tremendous help."

I studied him for a moment. "You're afraid I'm going to transfer my co-dependence onto Seth, aren't you?"

"It's a learned pattern. It wouldn't surprise me if you did."

He was probably right. I didn't want to be this way anymore. It was draining, unfulfilling, and clearly not healthy. I needed to heal, and this sounded like the best way for me to do it.

"Thanks, Cole."

"You're welcome. Now, Seth has a basketball standard just sitting in the driveway, begging to be knocked around. How about we shoot some hoops?"

"I stink at basketball."

"Good, so do I. Seth and Booker beat me every time. We'll be the perfect match up," he grinned.

"Sounds like a plan. I'll get my shoes on and meet you outside."

He didn't exaggerate about his lack of skill on the court. I won both games by a fairly decent margin. It felt good to be outside running around soaking in the warm spring sunshine. Winter had lasted entirely too long. Seth pulled up as I made my one and only three point shot.

"That's my girl." He scooped me up onto his shoulders, and we made a victory lap around the driveway. Cole's cell phone went off and he quickly excused himself, probably glad he didn't have to play against Seth.

"How badly did he lose?" Seth asked, lowering me to the ground.

"Ten points the first game, and twelve the second. He's really terrible."

"You'd never guess he's an incredible salsa dancer. He's even better than Booker."

"Salsa dancer? He has two left feet on the basketball court. He tripped over them at least a dozen times."

"I know, it's bizarre."

Finally all the bandages I'd seen on him over the past months made sense.

***

By Monday morning, apprehension was my constant companion. I was worried about what the rumor mill Melody had spread around about me, and tensions were still high as the manhunt for Alan continued. The search warrant was a bust. Alan had moved out of his apartment, and there were no leads as to where he'd gone.

Booker arranged for Wilbur, a humongous transfer student, aka *undercover MET agent roughly the size of a small town*, to escort me to all the classes Seth and I didn't share. Book thought it would be less conspicuous to have "Willy" hanging around me than to suddenly have Seth in all my classes. Any time anyone came near me, the *town of Willy* would close ranks. How that was less conspicuous was beyond me.

It felt good to have my life back in some type of order. Several kids offered their condolences on the death of my mother, and two invited me to go with them to their Ala-teen meetings. Knowing my mother wasn't the only parent in the world who had a drinking problem gave me comfort.

"Hello, beautiful, may I escort you to lunch?" Seth came to rescue me from my personal brute squad of one.

"Why, yes, I'd be delighted," I smiled. "Thanks, I'll see you later," I said to Willy. He grunted and left. "He's not very . . ."

"Verbose?" I giggled at Seth's choice of word. "It's good to see you laugh again, Maggie."

He bought cafeteria food for our lunch, a first for him, although he picked and grumbled at the entire meal.

"You should know Zack's parents reported him as a runaway. Booker's trying to convince the police department to treat it as a missing persons. Since he's nineteen, they won't do much if he is a runaway, whereas a missing persons report will generate a search. Did you know he flunked the second grade?" Seth took great pleasure in that little fact. "Booker is supposed to be here today to question some of Zack's friends." He took a bite of his pizza and groaned.

"Hey, Seth, I've missed you the past few weeks. How have you been?" Hillary strutted up to our table and flashed him a flirty smile.

"Maggie and I have been just fine. Thanks for asking, Hillary." He smiled back politely.

"Oh, hello, Maggie. I didn't notice you there." *Direct slam.*

"Seth Prescott, correct?" Booker appeared out of nowhere, in full uniform with a notepad in his hand. There was no mistaking it. Booker was an exceptionally good-looking man, but there was just something plain hot about him in his MET uniform.

"Captain Gatto, how are you?" The two men politely shook hands.

"And, of course, how can I forget this lovely beauty." He took my hand in his and kissed it. "Maggie, how are you? You get lovelier every time I see you." I threw him a smug grin. "Seth, you are a lucky man," he said, winking at me. Hillary eyes lit up like the fourth of July, just as Booker had intended. "I'd like to talk to you two about Zackary Finkle, if I may."

"Hello, Captain Gatto, do you remember me? I certainly remember you. I just love a man in a uniform, by the way." Hillary practically purred as she wrapped her arms around his and snuggled up to him. She flashed her perfect smile and batted her perfect blue eyes. I couldn't believe she'd flirt with such boldness.

"Ah, no, sorry young lady, have we met?" He made an unpleasant face and pulled his arm out of her grip. I made a mental note never to get on Booker's bad side; he was absolutely vicious. I loved it.

"Yes, that night at the Winter Festival, remember? Seth and his big, strong muscles smashed all those mirrors in the Funhouse." She kept feeding him details to try to trigger his memory, and he kept playing stupid. At last he threw her a bone.

"Wait, maybe I do remember you. You were with Zackary Finkle, correct?" She nodded, her face smug with an expression of, 'Naturally, he'd remember me.'

"Suzy, right?" Her mouth dropped. "Ah, no, huh? Is it Nancy?" She turned and stomped out of the cafeteria. All three of us exploded in laughter as soon as she cleared the door.

"A silly, high school girl, flirting with a twenty-eight-year-old, albeit undeniably handsome, man," he said, shaking his head in disgust. He murmured something to Seth about her being a stuck-up, snotty little thing that needed to be knocked down a few pegs. I giggled.

"You weren't supposed to hear that," he said with a crooked grin.

"Have you found any leads on Zack?" Seth asked.

"No, it's as if he's fallen off the face of the planet." Booker sat down at the table, grimacing after biting into Seth's pizza.

"Do you think he's still alive?" I asked the question I'd bet they both thought about but were afraid to voice in front of me. Seth looked at me cautiously. I glared back.

"He could be dead, I suppose," Seth admitted. "At the same time, Dreser's MO tends to be sloppy. If Zack were dead, we should have found the body by now."

"Probably carved up into a million little pieces," Booker said, taking a sip of Seth's Diet Pepsi. Now it was Seth's turn to glare.

"What?" Booker asked innocently.

"He's afraid I'm going to melt," I said wryly.

"Oh, sorry." Booker mindlessly began adjusting his shirt in an effort to avoid my eyes.

"I wish you both would forget about my little *episode*. I'm fine, stop shielding me."

"I better go and question a few of his ex-teammates. I'll drop by the house to let you know what I find out," Booker said as Hillary came back in.

"Hey, Mildred, can I speak to you for a minute?" Booker shouted across the room.

"Hillary. My name is Hillary," she yelled back, fuming.

"Oh, well, whatever." Booker turned and grinned at us.

"He must have a death wish," I whispered while heading to culinary class.

Mrs. Gianchi pulled me aside before class began and offered her condolences. "Maggie, did you know I taught your mother in Home Economics when she was in high school? You have her eyes," she said softly. "I remember she had thick brown hair that was never out of place, and she was incredibly fun to be around. She truly knew how to shine. She dropped out of school after becoming pregnant with you."

"She mentioned a Mrs. Gianchi once in a letter to me. Did you offer to take care of me while she went to Rehab when I was a child?"

"Yes, my parents were both alcoholics, but through a lot of hard work they were able to overcome it. I volunteer as an outpatient counselor for recovering addicts and their families. I really tried to help your mother, Maggie. Eventually she shut me out of her life completely. I was sad to hear she died." She gave me her cell phone number and told me to call her day or night if I ever needed to talk to someone.

Once we arrived home, I dumped out my small mountain of homework onto the table. There was several hours' worth, including my favorite, calculus. Booker and Seth sat at the table talking strategy the entire time. My nose was stuffed into my calculus book. My ears, however, were glued to their conversation.

After a couple of hours, Booker stood, stretched very cat-like, and poured himself a glass of milk. "Homework. I'm glad I don't have a baby face." He playfully pinched Seth's cheek. "I'd hate going to high school again. How's gym class, kid?"

"I like high school," he said defensively. "Did you get any new information from your new girlfriend?"

"Who?"

"Hillary."

Booker laughed. "She thinks you two are destined for each other."

"Still delusional."

"She saw Zack near the mall talking to a badly dressed man the day before he confronted Maggie at school."

"Do you think they were trying to recruit him into selling drugs?" Seth questioned. I pulled my head up, no longer interested in my calculus homework, not that it'd ever held any interest to me.

"I don't know, maybe he's picked up a little drug habit," Booker offered.

"Could be. If he has, I pity the little fool."

Booker nodded and set his glass in the sink before grabbing an Oreo from the cookie jar. "Well, kids, I have to go. Have fun doing your homework." He reached over and messed up my hair.

"You're annoying."

"And you're fun to tease, Magpie." He hooked my pinky around his and gave it a slight squeeze before he left. Seth walked him to the car while I cleared away my books, my brain sizzled for the night.

"Are you going to tell me what all this pinky business is between you and Book?" Seth asked as he came back inside.

"Seth, there's no pinky business going on."

"That's what Book said, except he's a much better liar than you. I could kiss it out of you," he threatened, as if that were really a threat.

"You could," I said, wrapping myself around him, "if there was something going on with our pinkies." I quickly turned my head away and sneezed, twice.

"I think you're getting a cold. No kissing, you need sleep."

"Hey, I want a kiss. Don't tell me the big ol' undercover agent is afraid of a little cold." I taunted while he led me upstairs.

"This undercover agent never gets sick." He swept me up into his arms.

"Never?"

"Well, seldom," he said.

Seth gave me a kiss, on the top of my head while I tucked the blanket up under my chin. "Good night. I will always love you, cold or no cold," he assured me needlessly.

"Good night, chicken."

36

By Saturday, my body had lost the battle, and I was in the thick of a nasty head cold, which progressed rapidly into my chest. Outside, the rain, originally forecast as a spring shower, poured relentlessly. Spring shower my eye. It was more like a rabid hurricane. I drew the quilt over my head and curled down into the mattress.

"Stay in bed, Mags. I'll try and hurry my Lunch Swap deliveries." I peeked out from under the quilt to watch Seth set a glass of orange juice on the bedside table next to my Nyquil.

"How can it be warm and sunny one day, then freezing cold and rainy the next?" I sniffled.

"Welcome to spring in Upstate New York." He touched my forehead. "I've coerced Booker into going with me after he finishes some paperwork. We're meeting up at Miss Ethel's place." We both laughed. A healthy dose of Miss Ethel would be good for Booker.

"I don't think he will be nearly as fun to cuddle with." He nodded at me in agreement. "You're leaving me here alone without a babysitter?"

"Keep it up, beautiful, and you'll be wearing this orange juice," he said before sneezing.

"Hmm, I thought you didn't get sick."

"I'm fine." He reached into his jacket pocket and pulled out a small red cell phone. "I bought you a new phone. Keep it on you at all times, even if you decide to take a bubble bath," he said, toying with me.

"Ah, the cell phone is my new babysitter." I placed my hand on his forehead to check for a fever.

"Stop worrying, Maggie."

"I'm not worried, I'm concerned."

"Do you remember where I hid my gun?" he questioned, adjusting his Lunch Swap shirt.

I thought to ask him if I looked thick before deciding sarcasm probably wasn't the politest way to handle this since he was trying to protect me. "In the kitchen cabinet next to the stove," I said, smiling angelically. Okay, maybe I was a little sarcastic. He ruffled my hair in response. Why did these guys insist on doing that?

"I wish we could've practiced shooting a bit more."

The few times we had gone didn't seem to help my aim much. Yesterday, I only managed to hit the target three out of twenty-four times. My stomach tightened at the thought.

"Hurry back and please, *be careful*," I said as he left.

Still freezing cold, I slumped back down under the blankets, tightening them around me, but my efforts were in vain. My body wouldn't warm up. "Brrr, I'll bet he forgot to turn the heat up again." I slipped on some socks and hunted down one of Seth's sweatshirts. I wanted to feel him around me even if it was only his scent.

It sat conveniently waiting for me on his bedpost, and since he had worn it only yesterday, it would still be rich with his incredible smell. I inhaled deeply, or tried to, and ended up coughing instead. Stupid cold.

Slipping the oversized shirt on and dropping the cell phone into the front pocket, I imagined him *in* the shirt since I could barely smell him *on* it thanks to my stuffy nose.

A clash of thunder cut through the air interrupting my daydream. The rain came down in vertical sheets, with bolts of lightning rending across the sky. Now I was grateful for my cold because I certainly didn't want to be out in the craziness.

I went downstairs as another loud crack of thunder shook the house, taking me by surprise. "Calm down, Mags, you're overreacting. It's just thunder," I counseled myself out loud, afraid of having another freak out. A twinge of pain gripped me as I remembered my mom, and I pushed it away. I tried not to do so much pushing away of my emotions per advice given at the two Alateen meetings Seth and I had gone to, but it was still second nature to me. I promised myself a good cry after I warmed up.

"The security system is on, and there is someone watching the house." I peeked outside at the patrol car to make sure. After making up some toast, I found one of Seth's cooking magazines and curled up into a chair to read. Thanks to the Nyquil, I nodded off almost immediately.

I awoke to a terrible howling that sounded so much like Fluffy. I ran over to the window to check. Horrified, I saw him lying on the ground, the storm pounding on him mercilessly. My heart sank into my stomach. My first instinct was to run and grab him, but Seth and Booker's warnings screamed out in my head.

The cell phone. Seth answered on the first ring.

"Is everything okay?" His voice was tight.

"Yes, Fluffy's outside on the sidewalk, and I think he's hurt. I need to go out and get him."

"I don't know, Maggie. How did he get clear over to my house? Check and make sure the agent is out front still."

"He is. I looked already. Please, Seth, Fluffy's in pain."

"Give me a couple minutes to call dispatch. They'll give the agent the heads-up that you're coming out. Be careful. Look around before you go out there."

I double-checked to make sure the agent was still there. I couldn't tell who it was with the rain coming down so hard, but there was definitely someone sitting in the car. I slipped on my ugly shoes, punched in the complicated security code and ran outside toward my furry little friend.

"Fluffy!" I squatted down next to him and stroked his fur. He didn't move, nor did his eyes open. I could see his chest rising and falling in short pants as he laid there whimpering. I slipped my hand underneath him and found blood. His underside had a huge gash down the middle. I clutched him to my breast. "No, please, don't die." My tears mixed with the rain as the agent climbed out of the car and walked toward me. "He's hurt, we have to get him to—" The words dried up in my throat as I looked not into an undercover agent's eyes, but into Alan's.

"Hello, girlie, sorry 'bout the mutt. I had to do something drastic to get you to turn off that intense security system." Alan was dressed in camouflage cargo pants with a matching raincoat. He had a large duffle bag strapped to his back, and his fingers wrapped tightly around his bloodied pearl-handled knife.

Staring at the knife, I thought of all the horrible slasher movies Zack had dragged me to last Halloween. In every movie, without fail, some stupid girl put herself into a dangerous situation, a situation the entire audience knew would lead to her demise, and it always did. I was that stupid girl. I should've smelled this coming a mile away.

The agent, what happened to him? My eyes shifted to the car, and to my horror, I saw him slumped across the passenger seat.

Despite the rain, I could see the blood shrouding his twisted body and smeared on the window.

"As you can tell, he can't help you," Alan said, following my gaze. "My guess is he regrets falling asleep on the job right about now." He casually wiped blood from the blade onto his jacket and threw his head back in laughter. All color drained from my face. "Oh, and remind me to thank dispatch for the heads up that you'd be coming out to get the mutt. It certainly made my life a little easier." He casually seized Fluffy by the head, ripped him from my arms and eye-balled the dog's barely moving frame. "He's got ten minutes left at most." He turned and tossed him carelessly across the yard. Fluffy's poor body flopped around like a lifeless ragdoll. "I like dogs, too. Oh, well," he shrugged.

I sprang up to run, only Alan seized a handful of my hair and yanked me back. "I don't think so, girlie, we're going inside." His face contorted into a brutal grin, and he slapped his hand over my mouth as I tried to scream. "Save your energy for later," he moaned in my ear.

I clawed at his hand, twisting around, frantically trying to break free, but my efforts were fruitless. He kicked the door shut and slammed me into the black granite counter in the kitchen. The blow cut into my ribs and I doubled over, unable to catch my breath.

He sneered as he took in the room. "Nice digs your pig MET agent's got here. He must be on the take." Using the kitchen towel to wipe the rain from off his face, he tossed the duffle bag onto the counter next to the fridge. It landed with a thud. "Too bad I got to kill him right away. It'd be kinda sweet to have him live here with the memories of your hacked up body scattered everywhere, you know what I mean? An arm in the cupboard, a toe in his morning glass of juice." He barked out a laugh, then his face went dark. "But since I'm the only Dreser brother left, time is no longer a luxury I have."

Slipping lifelessly to the floor, I pressed my wet face to the cool tile and tried desperately to come up with a plan. Somehow, I had to warn Seth.

He jerked me to my feet by my arm. "Get up. You don't honestly think I'm going to kill you without a fight, do you? I want to hear you scream and beg. And believe me, *you will beg.*"

I remained liquid, sinking back to the floor. If he planned on killing me, I wouldn't help him in the least. He took his foot and embedded it into my back. Tightening my body, I braced for the blow, but it didn't come.

"No, I think I'll wait until your boyfriend gets back." He released me and reached into his front pocket, pulling out five yellow cable ties.

"Cable ties, don't leave home without 'em," he paraphrased with a hard laugh. "I'm going to tie him up, so he can watch me kill you, inch by screaming inch, then I'll take him apart. Neither of you will die until I'm through. And it's gonna be a long time till I'm through.

"Now, since we have some time to *kill*, go fix me some food. I haven't eaten all day, and don't try putting anything deadly into it, you'll be tasting everything first." He plopped down on a bar stool to watch me.

I walked mechanically over to the fridge and took out the leftover stroganoff I'd made two weeks ago. With any luck, he'd get food poisoning. I heated it in the microwave before setting the plate down in front of him.

"You first," he said, pointing to the stroganoff. I took only a small bite, afraid I'd choke on anything bigger. Satisfied, he picked up the fork and shoveled half of it into his mouth in one swoop.

I added some stale cookies to the meal in an effort to stretch out the time a little longer. When I returned to the table with a glass of milk, the stroganoff was gone. My hand shook as I placed the glass on the table.

"What's this?" he asked, wrinkling his nose.

"Milk."

"I know that, smart mouth. Don't ya got any beer?"

I shook my head. He picked up the glass and inhaled half its contents in one gulp.

"Get over here." He seized my wrist and pulled me onto his lap. "Man alive, you're hot." He fondled my neck with his slimy mouth. "Your lips are driving me insane," he said before pulling my head in for a kiss.

I don't think so.

Before his mouth touched mine, I reached out and *accidentally* knocked the rest of the milk on his lap. "You freakin' moron!"

Shoving me out of the way, he wiped the milk off his pants with his hands.

"Sorry, I'll get a wet towel, otherwise it will smell sour when it dries." I ran over to the sink and pretended to search for a towel while carefully opening the drawer with the gun instead. It was the only option I could think of.

You can do this, Mags. In theory, the idea sounded great, only with my poor aim the gun ought to be my last resort. The idea of knocking him out with one of Seth's cast iron pans crossed my mind, but with him watching me, no way I could grab it without being seen. Besides, what if I didn't hit him hard enough?

Which brought me back to the gun. I was fairly close. I couldn't possibly miss at this range, could I?

As Alan came around the bar, I quickly shut the gun drawer and handed him a clean towel. He dribbled some water on one end and rubbed at the spill on his pants. Before I could try for the gun again, someone pounded on the back door.

Glaring at me through the glass in the door stood Zack. Alan groaned. It was clear he didn't care much for Zack either. The gun was definitely not an option now. No way would I be lucky enough to shoot them both.

This was just getting better and better.

Maybe I could convince Zack to help me. Yeah, right. I knew Zack well enough to know that wouldn't happen . . . unless there was something in it for him. He wanted me. I could promise him me. Of course, I'd definitely renege later. I prayed Zack had a speck of humanity left in him as I went for the door.

"I'll let him in," I said a little too eagerly.

"Think he'll go away if we ignore him?" Alan shoved me back into the kitchen on his way to the door.

I had to stay in control. If Zack would distract Alan, I could do this. I'd run to the mall where there'd be too many people for him to grab me. Maybe Zack would even let me borrow his car.

Okay, now this was turning into a full-fledged fantasy.

I had to let Seth know what happened. Pretending to sneeze, I turned around, slipped my hands into the pocket of the hoodie, and grabbed my cell. Since I didn't have much time, I decided to text the numbers 9-1-1 to him, though my hands shook so badly I had to do it twice before sending it.

What if he decided to *call* and see what was wrong? I immediately shut the phone off. If that didn't send up a red flag, nothing would. All this raced through my mind before Alan reached the back door.

Why couldn't I think this fast in math class?

"Hello, Maggot, long time no see," Zack sneered. Alan loped across the room and searched out the front windows.

"Please, please help me," I whispered. "He's going to kill me. If you could distract him long enough for me to get outside and down the road, I'll do anything in return. Anything." I briefly toyed with the idea of giving him a short kiss to help sway him, but decided throwing up wouldn't help my cause.

"Sure thing, Maggot, I'll even let you borrow my car." He smiled widely, dangling the keys in the air just out of my reach. "After all, you've done so much for me. She wants me to help her escape, Alan. What do you think, should I?" My heart leapt into my throat at Zack's betrayal. My hopes of surviving were rapidly depleting.

Alan cut the space between us, grabbed my shirt, and pitched me across the room. "No one's going to help you." My body landed heavily, sliding across the kitchen floor, and stopping only when my rib cage collided with the island cabinet. I felt a sharp stabbing pain in my already tender side.

"Why are you here, Zack? You're supposed to be keeping an eye on Seth." Alan resumed his pacing from window to window.

"Relax, big guy, he's not even halfway through delivering his little lunches. We got a good hour before he's done." Zack spoke calmly, meanwhile his hands shook. I noticed how pale he was, and how much weight he had lost since I'd last seen him.

Zack was on heroin, and I was as good as dead.

He walked over and yanked me upright by my hair. With my ribs hurting too badly to stand erect, I hunched over to one side to relieve the pain. He ran his perpetually sweaty hands over my face and smiled a twisted sick grin.

"Why are you helping him? He's a killer," I said, buckling over in pain. Alan's head snapped in my direction.

"I. Have. A Right. To. Defend. *My*. Family!" Spittle flew from his mouth as he darted toward me. I cringed back.

"Hold on there, Alan," Zack said boldly. "You said if I helped you to get in here, I could have first dibs on her before you killed her." He wiped his nose on his sleeve and continued.

"I'm the one who told you about the stupid little dog she loves so much, and I tracked it down for you. I'm the one who's been watching the house for the past week, like you asked, learning Seth's routine. Didn't I warn you there'd be an agent that you'd have to take care of before you could get inside? And who called to let you know she was here alone?"

Alan didn't answer, instead he stomped back over to a window, all the while his eyes stayed fixed on me. Zack beamed proudly, as if his actions were a real accomplishment.

"Get a move on, her cop boyfriend will be back soon, and I need to catch him unprepared. Make sure you don't kill her when you're done either. I have a few of my own plans for her," Alan said with a leer.

"I can help you. I'll have her after we kill Seth," Zack said hopefully. "If you can just give me a little stuff to keep me tied over until we're done." He began clawing at his arms.

"Zack, please don't do this," I whispered. "This guy's going to kill you when he's done using you. Seth can help get you into a treatment cen—"

"*Shut up!*" Zack's hand ripped across my face, sending me to the floor again. A warm trickle of blood ran down my lip. I wiped it away. He dropped down on his knees and shoved his face into mine, glaring at me as if I were some foul creature. But despite all his bravado, he failed to hide the trepidation in his eyes. He was worried that I was right.

"Tell her, Alan, tell her she's a liar." When Alan didn't answer, Zack continued his demand. "Tell her you're not going to kill me!" The crack in his disposition widened. He grabbed my hair and pulled me back up onto my feet, shoving me hard against the counter. This time I heard my ribs snap. A sharp pain cut through me, and it grew harder to breathe without sending agonizing pain throughout my insides. Alan walked over and put his hand on Zack's upper back.

"My dear boy, you are way too much work." He slid his thumb around to the front of Zack's neck, and with one swift motion, crushed his airway. Zack reached out to me, gasping for air.

"Stop it!" I begged.

"Have it your way, girlie," Alan said casually. He reached into his pocket, pulled out his knife, and shoved it into Zack's chest right over his heart, then callously dropped Zack's dead body to the floor.

"Zack!" Before I could reach his lifeless form, Alan grabbed my face and lifted me onto my tiptoes. My battered lungs begged for air. Dragging his slimy mouth along my neck he muttered, "I've waited so long to have you, I'm afraid I'm not going to be able to control myself as long as I'd hoped."

He then stopped and pinched his eyes shut before dropping me back to the ground. "No, Alan, you can wait a bit longer for your revenge," he counseled himself while stroking my hair. "But maybe a little taste wouldn't hurt." He jerked my face to his, dropping his foul lips to mine.

Something inside me snapped. If I was going to die, I was going to go out fighting, so fight I did. I raked my fingers over his face, digging up flesh, while forcing my thumbs into his eyes. I brought my leg up between his, hard, crushing his groin.

He stumbled and fell on top of me, pinning my battered body to the ground. His weight added unwanted pressure to my already tender ribs, and I screamed out.

However, Alan's screams overshadowed mine. He was in serious pain. I scratched, bit, and punched every inch of him I could make purchase with, holding nothing back. Still reeling from my well-placed knee, he spewed out a list of profanities a mile long as I broke free and forced my broken body across the kitchen floor toward the gun. I was almost to the drawer, when, from his prostate position, he hooked my foot, dragging me back several feet.

I looked back at his sweaty face, now scarred and bleeding thanks to my fingernails as he leered at me. "You. Will. Pay. For. That." Reaching into a pocket by his left knee, he pulled out a syringe. "Let's see how well you do with a little Eightball coursing through your veins." He bit the cap off the needle with his teeth.

I remembered Seth telling me about Eightball a few days ago. It was a mixture of heroin and crack, as if one wasn't enough. "Over my dead body," I said.

"Oh, not yet, girlie, but it *will* take some of the fight out of ya."

With every bit of strength I had left in me, I jerked my left foot free and sent it crashing into his face. He rolled away moaning as blood splattered everywhere.

Panting to keep my pain down to a minimum, I inched back over to the cupboard and reached into the secret compartment. Grabbing the cold steel gun, I contorted my battered body sideways to find Alan leaning against the bar, mopping up the blood from his face with his sleeve.

"It's a good thing I love a fight, otherwise you'd be dead by now." He took a step toward me, and I held up the gun. It shook violently in my hand. "Forget it, girlie, Zack's already told me you can't hit the broadside of a barn with a cow." His head rolled back in laughter.

"I guess Zack made two mistakes today." Before I could pull the trigger, a figure passed the window, drawing my attention away from Alan long enough for him to kick the gun from my hand. It went sliding across the kitchen floor.

"It seems your boyfriend's back, so I guess I'll be changing my plans a little. Too bad, this was just getting interesting." Dropping the syringe onto the counter, he quickly tugged open his canvas bag and pulled out what looked to be an extra-large handgun. He backed up to the door, swiping at the blood still teeming down from his nose as he waited for Seth to come inside.

Oh, no! It is not going down like this.

"Seth!" I screamed as the door opened. "He has a gun!"

The force of the door had Alan flying back to the wall. Regrettably, he maintained his balance, all the while holding onto the gun.

"You move, and I kill your little girlfriend," Alan said, pointing the gun at me. Seth stood motionless in the doorway.

"Let her go, and you'll be allowed to live."

Alan laughed. "I believe I'm holding all the cards at the moment, pig." He glared hard at Seth. "And judging by the way your girlfriend's panting over there, she either has it for me really bad, or her lungs are filling up with blood. I've watched it happen time and time again at the hog farm. I'd guess she has fifteen, maybe twenty minutes before she's dead." Alan's eyes never left Seth as he spoke. It was obvious whom he saw as the threat.

I used the opportunity to edge slowly over and picked up the gun he'd kicked out of my hands. Seth seemed to know what I intended to do and he kept Alan talking as I tucked it into my sweatshirt pocket. I hurried back to my original position before Alan noticed.

Seth took a step toward Alan. "You had better stop," Alan said, pulling the hammer back on the gun. Seth stopped again. "It seems we're at an impasse here, my friend. Put the gun down. *Now!*" Alan aimed his gun directly at my head, and Seth dropped the gun, kicking it away.

"On your knees." Seth dropped to his knees at Alan's command. "You got your cuffs on you?" Seth nodded. "Okay, cuff yourself to the refrigerator door. I'll save the cable ties for your girlfriend here."

I had to shoot Alan now. Even if I missed, it might be enough of a distraction for Seth to save himself. I palmed the gun, placing my finger on the trigger. As I flipped the safety off, Booker flew into the house with his handgun pointed directly at Alan, who merely laughed.

"Thanks for coming, you've made this so much easier for me," Alan said. "Nice little gun ya got there. Mine's bigger, and you know what they say about size mattering."

"Yes, but if you know how to use it, size don't mean a thing. And I know how to use it," Booker added with a truly wicked grin. "Now, put the Lupara down."

"Ah, you know your guns. I suppose you also know that I can kill all three of you with only one well-placed shot using this bad boy." He reached into his bag, keeping his eyes on Booker now that Seth was cuffed to the fridge door. He pulled out a second Lupara and slithered closer to Seth. "Imagine what I can do with two," Alan said calmly. Booker bit out a curse as he stepped toward Alan.

"No, Booker. He'll kill Seth before you can stop him. Please do as he says." Booker ignored me and continued advancing toward Alan. "Remember your promise, Booker."

"I can do this, Maggie. It's what I'm trained for," he said, his jaw tight.

"Please," I begged, forcing myself up off the floor. "Please."

"Oh, how sweet, she's begging for her boyfriend's life," Alan said sarcastically. "Drop the gun and kick it over here," he instructed Booker. I looked at Booker and could almost see his mind working as he tried to come up with a way out of this scenario. Slowly, he set his gun down and kicked it away. Alan stepped to the left of Seth as it came sliding toward him.

It was my *opportune moment*. I drew the gun out, quickly took aim, and forcing my eyes to stay open, I pulled the trigger. Alan looked at me, wide-eyed. With blood now streaming down his face and out his mouth, he dropped to the floor, dead.

The force of the shot hammered me back against the cupboards, and my world faded away as Seth's name escaped my lips.

37

"She's going to make a full recovery, I promise." I heard what sounded like Cole's voice, speaking. He added, "But it won't happen overnight. She was a mess."

"Thank you for the compliment, Cole." I slowly pried my eyes open. It took almost more energy than I had. I lay in a hospital bed with an IV running into my arm. My ribs ached, too. I reached up and felt a tube nearly as big around as a garden hose coming out of my side, and it hurt big time.

"Maggie, how are you feeling?" Seth's hands caressed my forehead.

"I've had better days."

"You did it, you shot him right between the eyes. He's dead." I didn't have the heart to tell him I aimed for Alan's stomach. "You saved our lives."

I shut my eyes, dearly wanting more sleep.

"Not bad, Magpie." It was Booker's voice now. "Who would've thought you could make a shot like that?" I slowly stuck out my tongue at him. He chuckled.

"Are you in pain?" Seth asked.

"I felt a lot worse back at the house. I'm mostly tired now." I pried my eyes open again.

"That's because you're heavily medicated," Cole explained as he injected something into the IV tubing leading to my arm.

"Is this going to give me one of those headaches again?" I asked, grimacing.

"No," he laughed. "Maybe," he teased. I hoped.

"Is Fluffy . . ."

"Yes, I'm sorry, Mags," Seth said squeezing my hand.

My poor sweet Fluffy was dead.

"You have three broken ribs, one which perforated your lung, collapsing it. That tube you felt coming out of your side is draining off the excess fluid. You also have a small head fracture and multiple bruises. You took a real beating," Cole said gently.

"You should've seen the other guy," I smiled.

"What exactly happened to his face?" Booker asked.

"He attacked me so I fought back. I scratched his face, and kicked him in the . . . ah."

"I think I get the picture. You did good," Booker grinned, giving me a gentle high-five. Seth looked as if he wanted to throw up. I took his hand and pressed it to my lips.

Booker's smile turned mischievous. "So, Magpie, I'm curious, what were you aiming for when you shot him?"

"His stomach," I grudgingly confessed. "And remember, Booker, curiosity killed the cat." *Obnoxious goofball.* "And let me guess, the only reason you so easily handed over your gun was because you had another one hidden somewhere on you."

Booker laughed. "I carry a small, but powerful little gun, strapped to my calf, just in case. I was waiting for the opportune moment, but it seems you beat me to it."

"And I knew Booker was right outside, or I wouldn't have given up mine," Seth added. It'd dawned on me as I fell into the cabinets that neither he nor Seth would've given up their guns so easily without some sort of backup plan.

After a series of yawns, Cole kicked everyone out. "You should get some sleep, Maggie, we'll come back later." I wanted to argue, but I fell asleep.

One month later

"Please, *please* don't do this to me. Haven't I already been through enough? I thought you loved me?"

"Mags, you're overreacting," Seth said, pulling the rest of my belongings from his car and setting them on the lawn in front of Booker's house.

"Overreacting? Okay, fine. You move in with Booker. I'll stay at your house." I dropped onto the hood of the car in defiance.

"Mags, you know why it has to be this way." He pulled me up into his arms. "You're just too appetizing." He began playfully nibbling on my neck. "It's hard enough keeping my hands off you, but having you with me, alone, night after night, it's killing me."

"It's hard for me too, but moving in with Booker seems a little drastic. Can't I sleep in the garage?" He rolled his eyes. "Okay, how about Cole's? He has a big house. I'll bet he wouldn't mind if I stayed there."

"Cole's never home, he spends most nights sleeping in the resident quarters at the hospital, which means you'll be alone. It has to be this way until we can find Harry Dreser."

That could be forever. All leads, and ninety percent of the heroin sales, died when Alan did. The MET operation at the high school would end at the end of the month, allowing them time to tie up a few loose ends.

I decided to pick up some hours volunteering at the Lunch Swap. I needed to work. It helped me feel stronger. Seth readily agreed, probably because he could keep an eye on me easier. He didn't like knowing Harry Dreser was out there still, probably plotting his revenge, and no one knew where.

I buried my face into his chest. "I'll go crazy living here." My head bounced against his chest as he chuckled.

"I could move back into my trailer. I've proven I can take care of myself. Booker can hook up an electric zapper alarm thingy." I knew the trailer meant a losing argument, but still, I tried. We'd had it several times already, but I was desperate. It wasn't that I didn't love Booker, I did, very much, but his constant teasing drove me up the wall. Seth assured me it wouldn't be that bad, and he promised Booker would stop after a few days.

"Maggie," he said solemnly. "If anything were to happen to you, I'd go crazy."

Okay, falling in love with this beautiful guy yet again. How could I fight him now? I resigned to my fate. "Fine, I'll stay."

"Did you ever ask him how he got the name Booker?" he asked with a sinister grin.

"No, I forgot."

"Hey ya, Magpie, or should I say *roomie*. I have your room all set up. Pink's your favorite color right?" Booker knew it wasn't, we'd already discussed it. "I bought a lacy pink bedspread and matching eyelet curtains." I doubted Booker even knew what eyelet was, still I decided to play the game.

"Oh, goodie. Maybe we can pop some popcorn later and paint each other's toenails?"

"Sure, I only have black polish though," he warned, gathering up the last of my belongings off the lawn. He twisted back toward the house, whistling.

Across the yard, a black furry object raced toward us. It tripped and tumbled, head over heels, before bouncing back up on all fours, oblivious to the fact that it had just fallen.

"Is that your puppy?" I stepped toward the little black lab and dropped to the ground. The puppy jumped into my lap and bathed my face in puppy kisses.

"Mine? No way, I hate dogs," Booker said with disdain. "She's yours. Daisy May, meet your new owner, Magpie. Magpie, Daisy May."

"Booker . . ."

"She's no Fluffy, but she is pretty cute for a dog," he said casually. "And you're cleaning up all the puddles," he added.

"Thank you, Booker." I held her tight to my chest. "I take back every mean thing I ever said about you."

"Yeah, right, until tomorrow," he laughed. "I'll bring your stuff in the house before it gets dark. Come on, flea bag, let's leave these two love birds alone." Booker turned and stepped into a fresh pile of puppy poo.

"And this is why I prefer cats." He scraped his shoe along the grass, grumbling at the "flea-bitten mutt" as he made his way inside.

"Great, now I feel bad." I slipped into Seth's arms.

"He's a pretty great guy. I'd better get going. We've got a math final tomorrow, and I want to get some studying in," he teased.

I laughed and kissed him. "Are you sure you don't want to come in and watch one of those goofy old movies you like?"

"My movies are not goofy," he said.

"Enough talk. We can debate this later." I pulled him to my lips and wrapped my arms around him. All too soon, he pulled back.

"I desperately need a hobby." He gathered up my face in his hands and lifted my mouth to his again. I could almost feel the blood racing though my veins. After several minutes, he pulled away. "A very involved, time consuming, physically exhausting hobby."

Looking up in Seth's green eyes, happiness, real happiness, filled my heart for the first time ever in my life. I was coming to grips with my mother and my co-dependent ways, thanks to the intense counseling sessions with Mrs. Gianchi. Some days were better than others, but I was continuing to heal. I felt stronger, more alive, and in charge of my life for the first time ever. I decided to put off college for a year and focus on getting my feet under me.

I had people in my life that truly loved and supported me. My future looked bright, and I was in the arms of the most wonderful guy in the world. Life doesn't get much better than that!

Other novels in the Port Fare Series

Unbelievable Book two in the Port Fare Series ~ Cole story: It's been two years since the Dreser brothers tried to take over Port Fare. Rumor has it their father, Harry Dreser, was killed in a drug deal gone badly; but rumors are not always true. The Dreser brother's half-sister, Delilah Lopez Dreser, has come to town to finish what her brothers started, and now Cole is brought into the mix.

Unbearable- Book 3 of the Port Fares series ~ Booker's story: Booker left the police force to pursue a career as a lawyer. True to his *Save the World* ideas, he's hired a nervous, timid woman named Tess to work for him as a secretary. As Tess and Booker grow closer, Booker learns of her secret and is determined to free her of the past while convincing her to take a chance on love again. But is *he* ready to take the chance again?

Other novel by Sherry
Not So Easy
Pete & Tink A Novella
Loving Marigold
Angel in a Black Fedora

Find me at WordpaintingsUnlimited.com
Twitter.com/sherrygammon
Facebook.com/sherrygammonauthor